"You can put down that rifle,"

the stranger said in the commanding tone of a man used to giving orders. Then, as though he had just become aware of the creature who balanced his life in her hands, his voice softened. "I'm not going to hurt you."

His cool demeanor was irritating and insulting. "Keep going, and I promise I won't hurt you, either," Lindy's curt reply bounced back, his slight chuckle shaking her confidence.

"After coming out of the war with my hide intact, it would be the fulfillment of a Confederate curse to finally be set in my grave by a woman as fragile looking as yourself. Most would think you wouldn't have the strength in those spindly arms to hold one of those things for more than five minutes."

A slow smile melted over his lips, sending a wave of heat up Lindy's spine. "Then I suggest you keep riding," she snapped back. "Because before my arms give out, I'm likely to pull the trigger."

Dear Reader,

Although summer is drawing to a close, Harlequin Historical continues to provide the best historical romance has to offer.

This month, reacquaint yourself with bestselling author Willo Davis Roberts in the reissue of her epic saga, *To Share a Dream*. Three sisters flee England to find a new life in the colonies, but Massachusetts is not at all what they expect.

Healer Damaris Fleetwood battles for possession of her home in *Thornbeck*, a medieval romance by Lynda Trent. But when the Queen sends aid in the form of Sir Gavin Rutledge, can love yet win the day?

Author Susan Amarillas premiered in March Madness 1993 with *Snow Angel*. Her latest release, *Silver and Steel*, centers on Mary Clancy, who is convinced that the railroad is the answer to Rainbow Gulch's prayers, though attorney Alexandre Moreau is prepared to fight her every step of the way.

Popular historical author Ann Lynn makes her Harlequin Historical debut with *Beautiful Dreamer*. In this heartwarming tale, ex-Confederate soldier Connor O'Malley finds new purpose in life at Lindy Falen's dilapidated ranch, as well as a secret the beautiful Lindy is determined to hide.

We hope you enjoy these selections. Look for Harlequin Historicals next month when Claire Delacroix takes us once again to the pageantry of the Middle Ages and Merline Lovelace pens her third book in the *Destiny's Women* trilogy. Join us for all four exciting titles!

Sincerely,

Tracy Farrell
Senior Editor
Harlequin Historicals

Please address questions and book requests to:
Harlequin Reader Service
U.S.: 3010 Walden Ave., P.O. Box 1325, Buffalo, NY 14269
Canadian: P.O. Box 609, Fort Erie, Ont. L2A 5X3

Ann Lynn

Beautiful Dreamer

Harlequin Books

TORONTO • NEW YORK • LONDON
AMSTERDAM • PARIS • SYDNEY • HAMBURG
STOCKHOLM • ATHENS • TOKYO • MILAN
MADRID • WARSAW • BUDAPEST • AUCKLAND

ISBN 0-373-28834-4

BEAUTIFUL DREAMER

Copyright © 1994 by Ann Lynn.

ANN LYNN

lives in New Jersey with her husband and two sons. She holds degrees in fine arts and education. When she is not writing, her favorite pastime is to visit museums and historical sites, where a new story idea is sometimes born.

This one's for you, Bob

Chapter One

Texas, 1875

Lindy didn't have all day to dig a deep grave. There was only enough time to get the body covered before coyotes and vultures were attracted to it. She knew the ninety-degree heat would hurry the decomposition soon enough. Even dead, Hank was going to mean trouble for her.

With the back of her hand, Lindy pushed back a damp lock of tawny hair and wiped the beads of sweat from her forehead. She looked over to Luke. For all his fourteen years, her brother understood the urgency to get the man buried. Since wild animals were not their only worry, his shovel also continued to grate without pause against the hard-baked earth.

Six months in the southwest triangle of Texas had yet to fade nineteen-year-old Lindy Falen's natural beauty. The sunny climate seemed to nourish it. Her long hair was burnished to a rich gold and her skin glowed with the same colors that painted the Southwest landscape in shades of salmon, brown, and amber. Lindy didn't consider the light dusting of freckles across the bridge of her nose and the high ridges of her cheekbones to be a flaw any more than she lamented her eye color—a muddy green with curious flecks of gold running through the depths. In her young life, there had been little time to gaze into mirrors. If she had, she would have understood why the men of Dry Bed paused to admire her and why she found it necessary to wear her mother's wedding band and assume the fictitious name of Mrs. Rigby.

Now Lindy's rich coloring looked drained, her skin pale, her eyes dark and troubled. The stifling heat and humidity inside the henhouse hung around them like a wet wool blanket. Regardless of the discomfort and the awkwardness of the cramped space, Lindy couldn't think of a better location to hide a freshly dug grave or a fitter resting place for the likes of Hank Cobb than under a pile of bird droppings. She bit her bottom lip and forced all of her hundred pounds on the shovel. Awkwardly, she piled some more dirt to the side under the hutch of nests. Three stoic hens eyed the movement of the shovels, refusing to budge even when Lindy and Luke began to violate their domain.

"They're the bravest chooks I've seen," Lindy told Luke in the Australian accent that set her far apart from Mexican and Texan. "Remind me not to put them in the stew pot."

"You probably wouldn't catch them," Luke replied, grunting as he heaved aside another shovelful of dirt.

Brother and sister vainly attempted to make light of their work, but each knew the other too well to be fooled. Burying the dead was no pleasure, even if it was a no-good like Hank Cobb.

Lindy supported herself on the handle of her shovel. Suddenly the air seemed heavier and the walls of the coop closer. Her skin felt hot and then cold. She broke out in a sweat and shivered. Her stomach knotted, and for the second time that day, threatened to heave her insides up. Her hands sliding along the wood handle, Lindy knelt beside the grave. The dark hole reminded her of the fatal wound she had put in Hank's chest.

Luke was worried about his sister's pallor. "Get some fresh air, Lin. We've almost got it deep enough to set that ol' bitzer in."

Lindy looked down into the hole. The smell of fresh earth and chicken dung put the final touch on her queasy stomach. She gripped her middle and hurried from the henhouse. Leaning against the coop, she closed her eyes and felt herself spinning in the dark. *I am not going to be so weak as to faint now. Not when Luke needs me to be strong. Not when our very lives are at stake.* Lindy forced herself to breathe deeply. If only they hadn't gone into town that week. Hank would be alive and she wouldn't be a murderer.

The sound of Luke's shovel persisted; it would haunt her forever—the scraping, scratching sound of grave digging. She cursed Hank Cobb's soul to hell for putting her and Luke through such misery. Not a prayer would she say over his body. She lifted the hem of her apron and wiped the dirt and cold sweat from her face. When she was done with this awful business she'd take a bath. Then she'd feel better.

Her dog, Buddy, sensing her upset, bounced up on his hind legs and placed a pair of dusty paws on her skirt. His head tilted to the side and his brow knitted together, lending his expression an almost human look of concern. Lindy squatted and cradled his furry head in her arms. Buddy's tongue flicked out and licked her cheek. "You're a good boy," she praised, remembering how the Shetland sheepdog had valiantly tried to protect Luke.

Luke joined her outside the coop. He straightened his stiff back and sucked in warm, fresh air. At his full height, Luke was nearly as tall as his sister. Lindy looked up from where she squatted with Buddy. In another two years Luke's lean, sometimes awkward body would be bound with the muscles of a man. He had inherited their father's golden eyes and his mother's sandy hair. A dimple creased his left cheek when he smiled at Lindy, adding charm to an already handsome face that would one day melt many a heart. She fretted that, lately, smiles came slowly to Luke's face. He wiped his sweaty hands on the coarse fabric of his pants and spoke in the serious voice of someone much older. "That's done. Ready?"

Lindy stood up and nodded. She placed her palm lightly under her brother's chin. "What's he done to you?" Her eyes swept gently over Luke's swollen and bruised face. The tears caught in her eyes. She held them back for Luke's sake. "I'm sorry, luv."

"You've nothing to be sorry for, Lin," Luke said, leveling his shoulders and taking her hand in his. "Stop fussing like I'm gonna kark. All he did was—"

"He was going to kill you!" Lindy reminded him. "I'm sorry it's not better. It will be better," she promised. She turned away from Luke and wiped her eyes with the back of her hand, smudging dirt across her cheek. Her father had been such a dreamer—writing to them about a paradise that had never existed in this part of Texas. Whether it had been his guilt for leaving them all to find a better life for them that had made him pen such lies, or his hope of someday turning the near-barren land into green meadows, she couldn't hate him for falsely building their hopes. She should have been better prepared for disappointment. She had know her father well—always the optimist. A rainbow chaser, her mother had called him, and she supposed she had inherited that trait herself.

After her mother had succumbed to consumption and her brother Matt had been murdered, she and Luke had closed the door on their life in Australia and had journeyed to Texas, hoping to surprise their father. Little had they known that they would be the ones to get the biggest surprise, finding their father's grave to greet them, dry land instead of lush, rolling hills, and a house in ill repair. At least two facts had been accurate—the town, Dry Bed, and the ranch,

Broken Gate, had been aptly named. It had been her own fault that she had refused to see the obvious clues. She really had wanted to believe that her father had found paradise.

Luke tried to boost his sister's spirits. "We'll show everyone. We'll turn father's dreams into reality. Broken Gate will be the best sheep ranch in Texas."

Lindy managed a weak smile. "We will, Luke, won't we." She sighed, looking over to where Hank's body was hidden. "I suppose we need to finish this daggy business first."

They each grabbed Hank by a boot and dragged him from the brush behind the henhouse. Getting the man into a grave inside the narrow confines of a chicken coop demanded the agility of a contortionist. Once Hank was settled, Lindy threw his gun on top of him. Luke stared covetously at the pearl-handled Colt resting on the dead man's chest. "You want to check his pockets?"

Lindy's voice strained from her dry, dust-lined throat. "We're not thieves, Luke." Luke shrugged his shoulders and picked up his shovel. Lindy felt her muscles tighten as the first shovelful of dirt landed with a thud on Hank's bloodstained stomach. It was such a final sound. "God Almighty," she said in sudden realization, "we're more than thieves, aren't we? Check his bloody pockets, then. And hurry." Leaving the rest of the burying to Luke, Lindy fled the henhouse.

Lugging enough pails of water to half fill the oversize galvanized washtub was as much a tonic for Lindy's nerves as soaking in the tepid water. She stripped away all her clothes and tossed them in a pile. Her green gingham dress was bloodstained, torn and dulled with dirt from the henhouse floor; it didn't matter, for she was going to burn it anyway.

She sank down into the water and closed her eyes. A vision of Hank came through the back of her eyelids. No matter how hard she tried to clear the past few days from her thoughts, the events that led to Hank's murder played out before her.

Hank and his brother, Jeb, worked for neighboring rancher Clay Claxton. But, from what Lindy could see, they spent as much time in the saloon as they did working cattle on Claxton's ranch.

Lindy blamed herself for making the mistake of walking past Minerva's Saloon rather than crossing the street, but she had been in a hurry to get her business done and get back to Broken Gate before dark. Unfortunately, Hank and Jeb Cobb had stumbled out of the saloon and knocked her off her feet. All three of them tumbled into the street. One of the men landed on top of her. The stench of whiskey, stale cheroot and filth made her hold her breath until she crawled from under Hank's weight.

"Get off me you pie-eyed scunge," she said, choking on the dust their struggle made. She pushed with all her might against the heavy body that flattened her to the ground.

Their senses, dulled by too much whiskey at an hour early enough for breakfast, slowed the brothers' reactions.

The tall, lanky one spoke first. "Sorry, ma'am, for knocking you down. This here's my brother, Hank. The one who was lying on top of you. I'm Jeb. Jeb Cobb," he added with a smile and a gallant tip of his hat. Limp slices of greasy hair were pasted to his forehead. When he spoke, his nose and the ragged ends of his mustache twitched like rodent's whiskers.

"I'd appreciate you moving out of my way."

Hank broke his silence and moved to completely block her passage. "Look at those eyes." He reached out and grabbed a loose strand of tawny hair between his dirty fingers. "Green as Kentucky clover."

"Naw," disagreed Jeb. "They look kinda like cat's eyes to me."

"Ain't you gonna introduce yourself—bein' as we was so close?" Hank tormented her with a lusty chuckle, never losing the cheroot that hung limply from a corner of his mouth.

"She ain't the friendly type," Jeb said with such sarcastic hurt she almost choked.

Hoping she could make the memory of Hank and Jeb disappear, Lindy opened her eyes and stared at the familiar sight of her kitchen. But as much as she wanted to bury them both, she needed to reassure herself that Hank's death wasn't completely her fault. They had pushed her to come to her own defense. Even after Luke had returned from the blacksmith, the two brothers continued to harass them.

Lindy didn't doubt they hoped she or Luke would provoke, in even the slightest way, Jeb's temper.

She twisted the ring around her soapy finger while she thought of how intently their eyes had stared at the gold band. She had taken to wearing her mother's ring and, since then, unwelcome suitors in the cow town were soundly discouraged by the piece of jewelry. She had hoped the Cobb brothers would be deterred, but Hank had grinned as though the game was merely made more challenging.

"I'd think a husband would've come to town with a charmer like you," he had said, making it clear to her that a woman without a man at her side was prey for men like Jeb and Hank.

It didn't matter at the time that she failed to finish her business in Dry Bed. All she wanted to do was get away from the two men. She had a bad feeling about Hank and Jeb Cobb. All through the day's ride back to Broken Gate, she kept looking behind, expecting to see Hank and Jeb break through the dust.

They hadn't disappointed her. She'd stepped out on the porch and greeted them with the business end of her rifle.

Hank leaned forward. A grin split the stubble that shadowed his face. "Ain't you the hospitable type. We just come lookin' for one of Clay's cows. Mighta wandered out this way.'' His beady black eyes roved around the ranch in search of a telling movement. By habit, his hand brushed against the leather holster at his hip. "You ain't seen any strays, have you?'' Hank grinned confidently from atop his horse.

"You won't find any of Mr. Claxton's cattle here. So I suggest you leave right now.''

Jeb's grin faded when Lindy raised her rifle. She aimed high. The air cracked and Jeb's hat flew off his head, landing in the dirt. Their horses threw up their heads in alarm and started to bolt. Before Hank and Jeb could recover from the shock that she could and did fire at them, Lindy had already snapped a new cartridge in place. "Get off my land,'' she ordered, her aim now level at Hank's chest.

Jeb drew rein. "Come on, Hank.'' Hank followed his brother, but not before giving her a chilling look. "Lady, as sure as there's fire in hell, you'll regret pointin' a gun at me.''

Lindy rubbed her hair vigorously with a cake of soap. Her soapy hand slipped over her breast and she winced at the feel of broken skin. Her eyes lowered to the purple and red bruise just below her collarbone. It would no doubt scar, leaving her with the memory of Hank's attack.

She heaved the cake of soap. It careened across the floor and spun around into a corner. Her regret wasn't going to change the fact that she had killed a man and would have to live with that memory buried in her soul for the rest of her days. If Hank hadn't returned, he wouldn't be lying under the dirt floor of the chicken coop.

It was less than eight hours ago when Hank rode back to Broken Gate alone. She had come out of the henhouse, a basket of eggs on her arm, when she saw him slide out of his saddle and tether his horse in front of her house. There was no doubt in her mind that some sort of revenge was his intent.

Foolishly she had left her rifle inside. It might as well have been back in Dry Bed for all the good it would do her. Straightening her spine, she fought the urge to run and hide. With her chin held high, she summoned her courage. As though sensing her presence, Hank slowly turned from the house and faced her. Lindy felt all the strength she had gathered dissipate with Hank's first step toward her. Her eyes lowered to the gun at his hip. He was going to kill her. Lindy's fear not only paralyzed her legs, but her thinking as well, rendering her helpless to imagine a way out of her predicament.

Hank stopped, leaving a man's length between them. "Well, well, now. How'd you know I was comin' for breakfast? I do believe you were expectin' me. Where's that young brother of yours?"

"I don't think you came here to see my brother."

Hank's smile showed a row of corn-yellow teeth. "You're right about that. My interest's in you alone. I couldn't help layin' awake last night thinkin' about how you'd want to apologize for your ill manners. I kept thinkin' about all the ways you could do it, too." Flint-black eyes moved over her obscenely, lingering at her breasts until she felt her face heat with anger and her fingers squeeze tightly around the handle of her egg basket.

"Get off my land," Lindy ordered, still holding her ground.

"Now see, that's jist the point. You've got no manners." Hank took a step toward her. "You need someone to learn you the right way to treat a man who comes callin'."

Lindy positioned the basket of eggs between them and stepped back.

"Let's get back to how you're gonna fry me up some of those nice eggs." Hank's hand shot out and grabbed her arm. He held her so tight, she winced. "Ask me nice," he demanded through clenched teeth, and in case she thought he wasn't serious, he buried his fingertips into her skin.

"Let me go. You're not welcome here."

Hank shook her, and the basket of eggs fell between them. The breakfast Hank had said he wanted was now dripping all over his boots. His lips curled into a hideous snarl, reminding Lindy of a rabid dingo. She tore away from his hold and ran toward the house. If she could only reach her rifle.

Hank's long reach quickly closed the distance between them. His hand grabbed her hair and pulled her off her feet. She stumbled to her knees, but before she could scramble away, Hank flattened her to the ground with his body and hissed in her ear. "Bitch! You'll tell me you're sorry before I'm finished with you, but it won't make a difference."

Pinned by his weight, her mouth clamped shut on his hand. Lindy could do little else than thrash him with her arms. She heard fabric tear as Hank's free hand pulled aside her skirt. Fumbling through her petticoat, his callused hand roughly grazed her thigh. Her senses were assailed by the smell of his body, a nauseating mixture of sweat, stale whiskey and tobacco. Her breakfast began to rise in her throat.

"I'm gonna teach you to be real nice," Hank whispered in her ear.

Lindy clutched a handful of his greasy hair and ripped out a good amount of it. That did nothing more than provoke a string of expletives, the like of which she had never heard before, while Hank shackled her wrists with his hand.

"Scream all you want, but don't you think of bitin' me," he warned. "'Cause I'll loose every one of them pretty teeth with my fist. Now you jist stay still 'cause Hank's gonna have every little bit of you."

Lindy's heart pounded in her chest as Hank pawed at her breasts. "Yes, sirree, every little bit of you," he repeated while grasping at the buttons of her dress. Eagerly, he tore away the fabric and pulled at the laces of her chemise. An emotion akin to the frenzied feeding of a pack of wild dogs descended upon him. His hand cupped her bared breast and squeezed until he forced a whimper from her lips. His teeth bit her tender flesh until she satisfied him with an agonized scream.

A bitter taste of terror came to Lindy's mouth as she realized how much Hank enjoyed hurting her. Her helplessness, her cries of pain from his clawing, pinching and biting of every inch of her exposed skin, only heightened his excitement, making his eyes glow with a demonic light.

It must have been her screams that alerted Luke and called him back from the farmyard, for all of a sudden Hank's weight was lifted off her chest. Her starved lungs filled with air. After a moment, she recovered enough strength to raise herself off the ground, only to see Hank hanging Luke from his shirt collar and throwing a punch nearly hard enough to snap the boy's neck. Lindy heard her scream fill the air as the sounds of Hank's fist hitting Luke tore into her heart. She ran at Hank and threw herself at his back, trying vainly to end his pummeling of her brother. With a swift backward swipe of his arm, Hank threw Lindy to the ground. Half crawling, she scrambled to the house and retrieved her rifle. Her ragged breath heaving her chest, her arms shaking and her legs ready to give way beneath her, Lindy leaned against the porch. Tears rolled down her cheeks at the sight of Luke's blood-covered face.

"Stop! You'll kill him! Stop it, or I'll shoot," she screamed. But Hank ignored her warning, so intent was he on beating Luke.

Lindy's rage and fright wiped out any arguments her conscience could conjure when she saw the hulk of a man beat Luke to the ground.

Even her dog, Buddy, couldn't stop the man's fury. The dog's attack only made him more vicious. Buddy hung from Hank's shirtsleeve, but the man ignored the dog's sharp teeth. Straddling Luke, he aimed his gun at the boy's chest. It wasn't enough that he had battered Luke to near unconsciousness, he was going to shoot him. A loud explosion roared in Lindy's ears, and through a blur of tears, she watched Hank stumble back and fall next to Luke.

Lindy's stomach turned when she remembered the fountain of blood that soaked Hank's shirt. She ran to his side. Luke waited and watched with her as the last breath tore convulsively from Hank's throat. Hank slumped to his knees, his eyes frozen in disbelief.

Lindy supposed she'd go to hell for killing Hank.

She poured water over her head from a white enameled pitcher. Soap bubbled down water-darkened strands of hair, slid over her shoulders and into the tub. Rinsed and completely waterlogged, she rose and wrapped a towel around herself. Once dressed in a brown ankle-length skirt and coarse yellow blouse, she searched for Luke.

Lindy found her brother leveling the mound of dirt over Hank's grave. Without looking up to her, he mumbled, "Can't have a hill of dirt in a henhouse. Someone may figure—"

Lindy rushed to finish Luke's worry. "No one is going to figure anything. Hank was a bushranger, an outlaw. Anything can happen to his sort."

"What about Jeb? What about the sheriff? They were kin."

Lindy saw her own worry reflected in Luke's eyes. There was nothing thicker than blood and she had killed the sheriff's nephew. It was bad enough that she had killed a man, but that man had happened to be the sheriff's kin; a complication that made her worry about the murder even more.

She sighed with the weight that settled heavily on her shoulders. "Who would want to admit to kin like that? But you're right, they are all kin. That's why we must never, ever, let on what happened here today. Not to anyone, and especially not to Sheriff Hayes. It doesn't matter that Hank meant to harm us, he'd hang me for sure. There's just no justice to be counted on, Luke, unless it's in heaven. That's what Father always said."

Luke pulled his bottom lip between his teeth to stop its quivering. Lindy put her arm around his shoulder. "Oh, don't worry about them," she assured her brother, taking the shovel from his hand. "No one will suspect any ill could have come to Hank here."

Chapter Two

Hammer in hand, Lindy stood on her tiptoes and stretched to reach the top hinge of the front door. Holding a nail steady between her fingers and the hinge with the palm of her hand, she brought the hammer down onto the head of the nail in short firm taps until it was driven into the wood. She moved her hand aside and hit the nail with all the force she could muster. Disappointingly the nail bent over and soon joined the four like it at her feet. Not easily deterred, Lindy stretched up on her toes and began again. Another expensive nail fell through the wood slats of the porch. The adobe brick wedged under the door just wasn't working, and she wasn't tall enough to hit the nail straight on. She needed someone's help, and Luke was busy out back.

"Someone tall," Lindy thought out loud. She lowered her aching arms, rested her forehead against the door and sighed heavily. "And someone strong."

Buddy pricked up his ears. His whole body came to attention. The Shetland sheepdog's black, button eyes were trained on something in the distance. He yipped, turning Lindy's attention away from her problem.

The high whinny of a horse caused her heart to bolt. Since Hank's death a week ago, she had been on edge. Expecting a surprise visit from Sheriff Hayes or Jeb, Lindy found herself looking over her shoulder at every sound. She had purposely avoided riding into town for fear Jeb was still there, or that the sheriff would ask her if she'd seen Hank.

She tried to convince herself that Jeb wouldn't think of looking for his brother on their farm. After all, it was reasonable that he would start looking for Hank somewhere else. Restless men like Hank and Jeb usually did not hold sentimental feelings for one place. It wouldn't be that surprising for either one to pull up stakes and move on. She hoped the sheriff thought the same way, even if they were his kin.

The strange horse called again, a high-pitched warbling that lingered on in rolling echoes. It sent another spine-chilling wave up her back and tightened the skin across her scalp. She squinted over the distance and saw the shadow of a rider perched atop a high ridge. Buddy ran out beyond the farmyard. The fur on his neck stiffened with anticipation, his little nose quivered, and his lips curled back to show sharp canines.

Lindy uttered a quick prayer. She put down the hammer and picked up the rifle that leaned against the house.

The still figure of a horse and rider quivered in waves of heat. Lindy waited for the stranger to leave the safety of distance behind him, but the man wasn't in a hurry. He stayed on the ridge and surveyed the expanse of dry, flat land that stretched on all sides of the small wood and adobe house. Lindy looked around and saw what he saw: the hen yard, clothes of white muslin and dark woolen breeches hanging on a line, the barn with its swaybacked roof, the outhouse and, finally, the modest cross at the head of her father's grave.

Lindy felt panic grip her. As meager an existence as it was, she wasn't going to let a single bushranger take any of it— even if she had to kill him. She surely hoped she didn't have to do that. Hank appeared every time she closed her eyes. She didn't need the specters of two men giving her nightmares.

Although Lindy told herself Hank deserved to die, she couldn't pretend to feel good about killing him. While the shadows of bruises on Luke's skin and the glaring red mark on her breast, plus the emotional scars of Hank's assault left little doubt of his evil intentions when he rode out to Broken Gate, maybe a warning shot would have been enough to send him on his way; maybe she could have spared his wretched life. But Matt's murder was still fresh in her mind. Something had warned her that Hank was like the bushrangers in Australia who had terrorized her neighbors and had gunned down her brother, and that her strong instinct for survival was what had saved her life and Luke's.

When the stranger eased his horse down the ridge, Lindy lifted her rifle and pointed it directly at him. His unhurried pace as he came nearer played havoc with her nerves, tightening her stomach, sending waves of nausea and a cold sweat over her body.

A slight breeze, like a sudden gust of warm air escaping from behind an opened door, lifted the ends of Lindy's tawny hair and curled the bottom of her apron. No other movement betrayed the fearful anticipation that quaked inside her. She eyed the man through the sight of her rifle. Her eyes braved the punishing sunshine to stay on him. She drew a bead on his face and challenged the blue-gray eyes that watched her with equal intensity. The tan skin around his eyes crinkled seriously. A mustache twitched once over the straight line of his mouth.

"That's a fine good-morning, ma'am. Name's Connor O'Malley," he said, while seriously contemplating the muzzle of her rifle. He calmly regarded the slender fingers wrapped around the gun, in particular the one that rested against the trigger.

Lindy's concentration didn't falter at the head-to-toe assessment he gave her, or at the calm resonance of his voice. She met the stranger's bold approach straight on and tried to ignore the panic that throbbed at every pulse point.

"You can put down that rifle," he said in the commanding tone of a man used to giving orders. Then, as though he had just become aware that his life was balanced in her hands, his voice softened. "I'm not going to hurt you."

His cool demeanor was irritating and insulting. "Keep going, and I promise I won't hurt you either," her curt reply bounced back.

A slight chuckle shook her confidence. "After coming out of the war with my hide intact, it would be the fulfillment of a Confederate curse for me to finally be set in my grave by a woman as fragile looking as a teacup. Most would think you wouldn't have the strength in those spindly arms to hold one of those things for more than five minutes." A slow smile melted over his lips. "I prefer the lighter Winchester, myself."

The truth was, Lindy's arms were screaming for her to lower the heavy rifle, but she didn't care. His reference to her arms as "spindly" only made her more determined to hold her ground. Even though realizing he meant to distract her with conversation while her rifle held him at bay, Lindy snapped back. "Then I suggest you just keep riding, because before my arms give out, I'm likely to pull the trigger."

Lindy summed up the man's options. He could keep riding as she had suggested or challenge the dark barrel of her rifle further by dismounting. She didn't think he would take the chance if he placed any value on his life.

"For some water I'd gladly help you with that door you've been struggling with." His chips were on the table. With the assurance of a poker player, the stranger left his saddle before receiving her reply. Although Lindy reluctantly agreed by her silence, her finger tightened on the trigger.

If her mother looked down on her from heaven, she thought, she would have been appalled by her bad manners. When she followed Lindy's father to Australia, Lucy

Falen had left behind a genteel way of life in England, never forgetting her own upbringing in a family considerably more privileged than Lawrence Falen's had been. Scandal was what Lucy had caused when she had married a man below her station, ruining her parents' plot to separate her from him by accusing him of thievery and using their influence with the court to have him exiled. Lindy realized as she got older that her father had felt badly that he could not provide his wife with the kind of life she had been used to, never realizing that material worth had never mattered to Lucy. Lindy supposed that she had inherited her mother's strength and conviction to do what she wanted, and her father's starry-eyed optimism.

Lindy lowered her rifle but kept it by her side. That the man had offered to fix her door didn't mean he wasn't just as dangerous as Hank had been.

Moving slowly, Connor squatted to the ground, his hands on his thighs. A low whistle passed over his lips. Lindy watched as he coaxed Buddy to come closer. The dog was cautious at first, approaching him slowly, his belly nearly scraping the ground. Connor let Buddy stretch toward him and sniff the scant space between them. The dog put his black nose to Connor's boots, then to the cuff of his pants. A sixth sense that only animals possess seemed to tell the dog that the stranger was not a threat. Submissively Buddy rolled over and exposed the white bib of fur on his chest and stomach. Connor scratched the dog's belly. To Lindy's surprise, he had made a friend of Buddy in less than a minute.

Connor stood and carefully approached the jack pump, all the while keeping his eyes half on Lindy. The rusty lever made a grating sound when he moved it up and down. Brown, sulfur-smelling water trickled from the spout and into his hand. A barrel beneath the pump caught the overflow. "A little greasing in the right places will save your pump," Connor suggested casually, splashing some water on his face.

"I'll be sure to relay your suggestion to my husband," Lindy said, glad for the opportunity to let him know that she wasn't alone. In fact, she had no husband, only an imagined man who would come and love and protect her.

Lindy watched Connor sip water from his hand. The precious liquid wet his dry lips. It trickled over his full bottom lip and rounded the curve of his chin. His throat moved slightly with each slow swallow. Like a connoisseur of fine wine, he tasted each drop. His eyes were shaded by the brim of his hat and his dark lashes. Revealing a long day in the saddle, the crests of his cheekbones were tinged with sunburn. His face was smooth except for a slight stubble of beard. From under the wide-brimmed, pinch-creased Stetson he wore, Lindy could see wild locks of sun-streaked hair reach down his neck. A neckerchief that had once been red hung loosely at his throat, its pointed end resting on his chest. His clothes were yellowed by trail dust. He was the handsomest man Lindy had seen since arriving in Texas.

"Do you mind if I fill my canteen?" he asked, startling Lindy from her perusal of his face.

"No. Please help yourself."

While Connor held the mouth of his canteen under the spigot, Buddy nudged his leg. Connor stooped and offered the dog some water from his cupped hand.

A shuffle of feet came up behind Lindy, and without looking, she knew it was Luke.

"What's he want?" asked Luke, surprised to see Buddy lapping water from a stranger's hand.

"Just some water," Lindy answered, also impressed with how Buddy and the man were getting along. She watched Buddy's pink tongue lick water from Connor's fingers. Lindy noticed they were long, strong fingers. Like the rest of him, she thought, glancing at the way his pants stretched across his thighs and the way his shirt pulled slightly at each button. Connor O'Malley was definitely a strong man, and from the way he handled Buddy, a man who was also gentle.

"Thank you for the water, ma'am." Connor straightened and looked up at the door balanced on the adobe brick. One slight touch and it would fall off its hinges.

Lindy looked down at Connor. "I'm Mrs. Rigby and this is my brother, Luke. I'm sorry for the rude welcome but—"

"It's better to be cautious of strangers, especially when your husband's not home," Connor agreed as he stepped up to where she stood. Lindy detected a sad tone in his voice as though he spoke from personal experience, but she quickly forgot about the reason for his warning when it dawned on her how quickly he had assessed she was alone.

Worry clouded Lindy's face. The man knew no one else was around. He knew she and Luke were alone. It wouldn't take much for Jeb or anyone else to figure the same thing. Maybe Jeb already had. She rushed to explain, "My husband's not far. In fact, we're expecting him any time now."

"That's good," Connor said as he inspected the top hinge. "It's not safe for a woman to be alone." He shed his gun belt and tossed it aside, then picked up the hammer from where it rested at the tip of his boot. Lindy and Luke exchanged glances. A smile bloomed on Lindy's lips. She looked up at the blue sky. He was not only strong and gentle, he was tall, too. It would be a definite advantage to have him around, she thought.

Ready to help, Lindy stood next to Connor. Satisfied that his sister had matters well in hand, Luke returned to his chores with Buddy loping behind him.

Connor kicked aside the brick and leveled the door. "Here, hold it like this."

Lindy grabbed the door with two hands and held it steady while Connor adjusted the hinge.

"Do you have a few nails?"

"Yes. In my..." Lindy's gaze lowered to where her apron fit snugly over her chest. "In my pocket," she said faintly.

After some uncomfortable deliberation Connor asked, "Which pocket?"

Letting go of the door would cause it to fall, so Lindy continued to clutch it firmly. The thought of Connor's hand so close to her heart caused an unwelcome blush to deepen the tan on her face. "In the top pocket," she said in barely a whisper.

Two of Connor's large fingers fumbled inside the pocket. However lightly, Lindy felt his unintentional touch graze her breast through the fabric of her dress. Prickles danced all over the surface of her skin, followed by a warm sensation and quickness of breath. Truly, she was letting the fact that the man was as handsome as he was generous rule her good sense.

After what seemed like forever, Connor finally fished out the two nails. He held one between his lips while he hammered the other into the wood frame.

While Connor worked, Lindy studied his face. There was not a hint of emotion in his blue eyes other than intense concentration. Getting the door repaired was all that seemed to concern him. Lindy felt ashamed that she'd let something so innocent affect her when Connor obviously did not have an indecent thought in his head.

However, such close proximity seemed to have an effect on Connor, too, though she couldn't determine what kind. He fumbled with the nail and lost it between the cracks in the porch floor. Shortly after, another nail slipped through his fingers. "Damn!"

A small gasp came from Lindy and their eyes met for a long, silent moment before Connor spoke. "Sorry, ma'am." Sweat beaded his brow as though he had just finished plowing a field. Lindy watched his gaze follow the gentle slope of her nose and trace the lines of her lips. She felt the touch of his eyes brush over her face, and warmed from the inside out. It was a curious heat, so different from the fire dealt by the persistent southern sun. His look drew her in to him. She leaned closer, then, catching herself when she felt the hard length of him pressed against her, put back the distance between them and dismissed his frustrated exclamation. "I'm not offended."

Connor's attention returned to the job at hand. "I hope that wasn't your last nail."

"I think there might be some in my dad's toolbox. I'll get it for you if you'll..." Lindy glanced at the door between her hands.

Connor quickly took it from her. His face was flushed with embarrassment.

Lindy riffled through the toolbox, her thoughts on Connor. She could tell he was a decent man. Back in Australia, Matt had never been so concerned with offending her with his language, nor had their stockmen. She looked over to Connor from under the curtain of hair that had fallen over her shoulder. He probably attended church twice a year. Lindy thought he was the type to be married. He didn't seem like the usual drifter to her. She was sure he had a wife and family. A pang of disappointment warned her to be careful. He was probably a homesteader, and his family would surely be arriving after he was settled.

"Find them yet?" Connor asked, his voice touched with impatience.

"No. I'm sure there're more in here. Oh, here they are. The last four."

While Connor hammered, Lindy watched. She watched his hands, strong and tanned; his face, so serious and handsome; his eyes, intense; and his shoulders, wide and powerful. There was much Connor could do with ease, where she had to struggle just to get her saddle up and over the back of her horse.

"Keep the door steady," Connor reminded her.

Lindy adjusted her grip. Her eyes strayed to what was in front of her, Connor's belt. Fine tooled leather wrapped around his waist. His hips moved slightly as he hammered a nail into the wood. Lindy diverted her eyes to his boots. It wasn't proper to admire a man's build so boldly. Only a bawdy woman would so directly appraise a man. Then again, she thought, if he didn't know the difference...

Connor adjusted the door. "Hold it level like this."

Lindy placed her hands on both sides of the door.

"Can you raise it a little more? A little lower. That's it. Now stay...no, you moved." Connor put his hands around Lindy's waist and moved her in front of him.

Lindy felt her muscles tense and her heart beat wildly, not with fear, but with an emotion that was new to her.

"That's it. Keep it steady and level."

Lindy could have done a much better job of assisting Connor if it hadn't proved so torturous an ordeal. She couldn't concentrate on anything with his muscled legs astride her and his arms raised over her. Each time he moved she felt his body brush against hers. She could feel his muscles strain as he hammered, his hips lean into her back, and his thigh brace against her leg. Every move he made brought his body closer to hers. When the back of her head touched his chest, she felt his muscles tighten in response. The warmth from his body wrapped around her. She inhaled the heady scent of man and leather and was at once intoxicated. She began to tremble and was besieged with a feeling of panic strong enough to make her want to run. Never had she felt so overcome by feelings that surfaced of their own volition. All the strength drained from her arms. Lindy felt weak from the struggle to keep calm. Her palms became sweaty. The door slipped from her hands and ripped away from the frame.

Lindy didn't see the door fall, but she felt it crash into her head and then heard it clatter down the steps. She tried to blindly catch it. So did Connor. In their efforts to prevent the door from crashing down on them, they merely got in each other's way. When Lindy's senses returned, she was down on the porch floor with her skirt tangled around her legs, her long, blond hair hanging loosely around her shoulders and Connor sitting next to her. She winced at the pain in her temple. Automatically, she touched her forehead and felt a warm stickiness.

Connor pulled off his neckerchief and grabbed her wrist in his hand. "Let me," he said, frowning intensely at the cut on her head as he dabbed at the blood. "It's not as bad as it looks."

Lindy noticed Connor had lost his hat in the scuffle for the door. His hair was thick and, like his mustache, streaked with sunshine. It fell over his forehead and turned up at his neck. She was struck with an urge to brush it away from his eyes just to feel it softly curl around her fingers.

"I suppose I wasn't much help," Lindy admitted, pulling her face away from him each time he touched the cut.

Connor held her chin in his hands and met her eyes with his. "No, you weren't. Keep still. Is your brother any better at holding doors?"

"I suppose he would be. I...I am sorry," Lindy said, watching Connor suddenly walk away from her and over to the jack pump.

Connor pumped more water. It was a move to waste time, to get away from the woman who turned him into a clumsy fool without barely trying. The feeling completely shattered his resolve never to care about another woman in that way. It was something more than desire that the lady stirred in him, it reminded him of what he had felt when he had first met his wife. Mrs. Rigby possessed a certain quality that endeared her to him before he even knew very much about her.

Connor rinsed the neckerchief under a trickle of water. Like his wife, Mrs. Rigby was left on her own until her husband returned from wherever it was he had to go. Like his wife, she was left in danger, but with luck, Mrs. Rigby's husband would return soon. His own wife had not been so lucky.

Connor felt the sharp pang of guilt and sorrow cut away at the fibers of his heart. He couldn't let himself care again, or love again; he couldn't bear the pain of losing again. Connor retreated within himself, and newly composed, returned to where Lindy sat.

He handed her the cool, wet neckerchief, ignoring her bewildered expression when her eyes looked up to him. They were trusting eyes, eyes the color of an autumn meadow, cool and warm at the same time. There was no question about it, he could see the danger in her eyes. Her lips parted as if she was going to speak and he found himself thinking about how soft they would feel, how sweet they would taste. There was danger there, too, he could almost taste it.

A trickle of blood slowly made its way down her forehead. Connor groaned and took her hand in his. It was small, too delicate for a woman who had to do the heavy work required of farm life. She would not last very long. Connor pushed aside the returning concern, and when he spoke his voice was short and gruff. "Here, just dab like this, don't rub. Where's your brother?"

Lindy stood, and he balanced her with a hand on her elbow. "Thank you, Mr. O'Malley. I'm fine, not a bit dizzy. I've had worse bumps in my life," she said as she struck the angle iron to call Luke. Its sound pealed across the farmyard in long clear notes. Connor had already picked up the door and was assessing the damage caused by its fall.

After sprinting across the farmyard, Luke stopped short of the porch steps gasping for breath. Lindy knew he expected to see the door swinging nicely on its new hinges. Instead, it was completely off the frame and in Connor's hands. She didn't think of what the whole scene looked like until she saw the concern on Luke's face.

"What happened?" he asked, his eyes on Lindy's forehead.

Lindy touched the spot where Connor had so gently dabbed his neckerchief. The memory of his touch made her smile. "Oh, this. I'll be apples. Just a little nick from the door. Mr. O'Malley would appreciate the help of someone with steadier arms than my own 'spindly' ones."

Connor glanced up at Lindy's teasing smile.

"Surely," Luke said with noticeable pride in his voice. He gripped the door with his hands and braced his legs against it. Lindy had no doubt that with Luke's help the job would go more smoothly the second time.

"I'll put the billy on," Lindy said and stepped inside the house.

Connor pulled his attention from Lindy and looked down at Luke. "I suppose you've got a lot to handle around here when your sister's husband's not home."

"I'm used to work. We had our own station—I mean ranch—in Australia before the bushrangers came."

"That explains it."

"What?"

"Your accent," Connor said.

Luke frowned. "What do you mean, my accent?"

Connor reacted to the defensive tone in Luke's voice. "You don't sound like a Texan, that's all. Neither do I, if that makes you feel any better."

Lindy had heard the end of Connor's apology. She leaned against the house with her arms crossed over her chest. She understood how Luke felt. There wasn't anything he wanted to be more than a Texan. Luke tried to lose his Aussie ways, starting with the words she found so hard to discard. He'd never say "chook" or "billy." It was American to say chicken and kettle. Sometimes she remembered; most times Luke corrected her. But still, sometimes when they were alone Luke forgot, too. He'd drop his r's or say "g'day" instead of "howdy." He was trying hard to become a cowboy. She worried that he tried too hard.

"When you two are finished, come in for a cuppa." Lindy caught Luke's explanation before she was out of earshot.

"She means a cup of tea."

Connor finished with the last nail and closed the door. "Now if you don't let the wind catch it, it'll last." He dropped the hammer into the toolbox.

"Mr. O'Malley, will you join us?" Lindy asked when she saw Connor step off the porch.

"I thank you for your invitation, ma'am, but I've got to be going. As it is, I'm afraid I've already worn out my welcome."

Lindy stepped down and twined her arm through his, intending to pull him into the house if she had to. "Indeed you haven't. I insist you stay for..." She looked over her shoulder at Luke. "Tea."

"Mrs. Rigby, I really should—have to be going. I've stayed longer than I planned to."

"And it's my fault for agreeing to let you fix my door when I knew what a difficult job it would be. For that I apologize and insist you stay for tea."

"It wasn't difficult."

Lindy persisted. "The least you can do is let me repay your kindness with a cuppa and some biscuits."

"Thank you kindly, but the water from your well was payment enough."

"After all you've done," Lindy pressed, "it will certainly not do. Now come inside. I've already put up the table."

Connor reluctantly took off his hat and followed Lindy inside. Lindy pointed to a chair at the table.

"I hope your husband won't mind a stranger sitting at his table," Connor said as he lowered himself into the chair.

"He'd probably shoot you," Luke said flatly while stuffing a cookie in his mouth.

Connor raised a brow.

Lindy swiftly grabbed the cookie from her brother's hand. "Mind your manners...and stop telling tales."

Luke looked perplexed by the reprimand. "It was you who said—"

"Luke!" Lindy sharply cut off Luke's words. "Never mind," she said more gently and picked up the china teapot. Until that day she had wanted everyone traveling through to think her husband was the terror of Texas. Since her husband's absence was obvious to Sheriff Hayes, she had had to fabricate the story that Billy Rigby, her beloved husband, was still in Australia.

"So," Lindy continued, "where do you come from, Mr. O'Malley?"

"Maryland."

"That's where we heard some cowboys were planning to drive some cows."

"I think that was Montana," Connor corrected, while he contemplated the fragile cup in front of him.

Connor quietly watched Lindy pour tea. The greenish liquid tumbled over the chip in the teapot's spout and gently fell into each cup.

Lindy fanned out her skirt and sat down. Noticing Connor's interest in his cup, she said, "This was my mum's set. All that's left of it," she explained. After Lindy had filled her own cup she carefully placed the teapot on a crocheted doily. "It's not often we get to use more than two cups."

Connor looked up. "You don't usually have tea with your husband?"

Lindy's face blanched. "He doesn't like tea," she quickly explained.

Connor finally picked up the cup, nesting it in his palms. "Maybe it's the cup your husband has an aversion to."

Lindy looked at the teacup in his hands and had to admit, it did look out of place. He held it as if it would crumble from even the slightest pressure. All ten fingers wrapped around it. Lindy checked each one. There was nothing on his fingers to tell her he was married, not even a telltale mark of untanned skin. Perhaps he didn't have a wife or a family or any place to call home. Perhaps he needed a place to stay and was too polite to suggest it. She certainly could use his help. With Connor's strength and skill, Broken Gate would become the station she dreamed of that much sooner. As independent as she was, she was smart enough to admit a little help wouldn't hurt, and a lot of help would be even better.

Lindy smiled at Connor over the rim of her teacup. "Would you like another cuppa?"

Connor's eyes met Lindy's. At that moment something intangible passed between them and moved him to get up from his seat. "No. No thank you, Mrs. Rigby. I really must be going now. Thank you for the tea."

"I've made a whole pot and it will just go to waste. Please stay a little while longer."

"Mrs. Rigby, I—"

Lindy stood and faced Connor. Luke stared up from his third cookie, his eyes as wide as saucers and his mouth gaping.

"All right. But in a tin cup this time. You do have a tin cup?"

"Oh yes. You can use my husband's cup. He likes to have his morning coffee in this one." Lindy wiped the dust from the inside of the cup and poured tea up to its brim.

"I don't have any more sugar. I'm afraid I used it all up in the biscuits. Do have another biscuit, Mr. O'Malley. I imagine you must be hungry after riding all day." Lindy rested her chin in her hands and gazed up at Connor. "You've come a long way, then?"

Connor's eyes met hers a long moment before he answered. "A long way." He gulped down half his tea.

Before he could object, Lindy refilled his cup. "What's Maryland like?" she asked.

"Green in summer and cool in winter."

"Then it's nothing like we've ever known. I think I'd like Maryland. It's a pretty name for a place," Lindy said, tipping the teapot.

"Why did you leave it if it was such a nice place?" Luke asked pointedly.

Lindy would have admonished her brother for his surly tone if she hadn't been so curious herself to know what had made a man exchange a green place for one that could be dry as a chip one day and then turn into a sea of mud with the next sudden thunderstorm.

Just as pointedly, Connor replied, "I needed a change of scenery, one that wouldn't remind me of Maryland."

Lindy spoke before her brother had a chance to reply. "Then there seems to be a lot of people like you, Mr. O'Malley. We've seen some come this way homesteading. Most just pass through. The ground isn't good around here for crops. The men come first. Some with their wives and nippers. Do you have a family, Mr. O'Malley?" Lindy watched Connor's face. His eyes seemed more gray than blue now. A very sad gray.

He finished the tea in his cup before he answered. "Nope. I'm traveling alone."

"It must be a lonely journey," Lindy said.

"I prefer it that way."

"Are you homesteading?"

"No. I'm not a homesteader. Settling in one place is not for me."

Lindy was disappointed and encouraged at the same time. He didn't have a place to put down roots, but he didn't want one, either. It was beyond her comprehension why anyone would not want to settle in one place. No one could be happy just drifting. No wonder he looked so sad. Except for his saddle, he didn't have a place to call home.

"How do you live, then?"

"I pick up odd jobs when I need them. Sometimes I'm lucky at cards. I do fine, Mrs. Rigby."

"Oh," Lindy said, disappointment flattening her voice. She couldn't possibly pay the man enough to keep him there. "Mr. O'Malley, I know you said you had to leave, but unless someone is expecting you, it really can't matter if you stay the night or not."

"Lin!" Luke nearly choked on his tea. "What about Billy?"

"Billy?"

"Your husband!" he reminded her, kicking her under the table.

Connor looked from Luke to Lindy.

"Oh, William!" she exclaimed. Lindy faced Connor and smiled. "Every time Luke calls him Billy I have to stop and wonder. Don't I, Luke?"

Despite getting the sharp point of Lindy's boot in his shin, Luke continued, "Billy wouldn't like the idea of a stranger staying the night. You remember how he nearly killed that cowboy who came looking for strays."

"Luke, how you exaggerate. Mr. O'Malley's been riding all day. William would insist he join us for supper and rest for the night. Especially after seeing to our door."

Connor grasped the opportunity for escape. "Luke's right, Mrs. Rigby. Your husband may not like coming home to find a strange man in his house, and I sure don't want to wake up looking down the barrel of a gun."

"Luke, would you leave Mr. O'Malley and me?"

"But Lin—" Luke began to object, but was turned out of the house by his sleeve.

"Go see to the goat's milking."

When Luke was out of earshot Lindy crossed her arms behind her back and looked to the floor. "My husband's in Australia, Mr. O'Malley. I'm telling you this because I believe you are a good man and I can trust you. So you see, you don't have to worry about his gun."

Connor shook his head. "You and your brother are living out here all alone?"

Lindy recognized the disapproval in his voice. "We're not alone, Mr. O'Malley. We have each other."

"You can't manage a farm by yourself."

Lindy's spine stiffened with pride. "It's not a farm. It's a station. And I am managing."

"I could see that when I first rode in."

Considering she hadn't made a good first impression with her struggle to repair the door, Lindy decided not to dwell on how self-sufficient she was. If there was a chance of convincing him to stay, it would be in letting him think she needed help. She could fend for herself. If she hadn't been in such a hurry to build up her station she would have ignored Connor's prejudice and wished him well. Instead Lindy swallowed the snappy retort she had in mind.

"Then you'll stay?"

Connor jumped up from his seat. "No." He grabbed his hat and strode out of the house with Lindy at his heels, talking all the while.

"But Mr. O'Malley, you don't have anywhere to go. No one's expecting you. You said so yourself. You need money and I need a few things done that I could manage on my own, but I have to admit it would take me some time, and— look, the sun is setting already."

Connor stopped short. Lindy plowed into his back before he could turn around.

Reacting quickly, Connor grabbed her shoulders so she wouldn't fall. "Ma'am, don't you ever take a breath long enough to listen? I never said I needed money. I said—"

"Wouldn't it be wiser to wait till morning? You don't have to give me an answer now. Sleep on it."

Connor turned away from Lindy's hopeful eyes and glanced at the fireball of a sun. It was low in the sky and ablaze with the last burst of daylight before the encroaching night would snuff it out completely.

"All right, ma'am, a soft bed of hay in the barn can do for one night."

A wide smile brightened Lindy's face.

"You did what?" Luke's loud whisper was a screech.

"You heard me."

"Do you have kangaroos in your top paddock?"

Lindy glared up at Luke from the stove. "I suppose I might. I didn't see any harm in admitting Mr. Rigby was not with us. Mr. O'Malley's promised to keep our secret, and I trust him. I didn't tell him I'm not really married, just that my husband is delayed is all. He wouldn't have stayed otherwise."

"We don't need him. I'm almost fifteen. There's cowboys younger than me. You treat me like you're my mum." Luke glared at the chicken Lindy planned to roast. "And you're treating him like the president. You don't know anything about him. He could be a rustler, a murderer—I'm sorry, Lin, I—"

"I know you didn't mean it like that."

Lindy saw the hurt in Luke's eyes. Luke must have thought she didn't have faith in him, that he couldn't manage the station alone. "Luke..." She reached out to him but he pulled away. "Luke, please. You know I couldn't do without you. It's only that more can get done with three pairs of hands than two. If Father were here he'd offer him a job."

"He'll want to get paid," Luke reminded her smugly. "He won't want to stay here for long once you tell him all he'll be getting is two meals a day and that it won't be chicken every night."

"Stop your grizzling, Luke," she said sharply, annoyed now that he persisted in questioning her decision. "Tonight, Mr. O'Malley's staying the night and he's sharing your room. We'll talk about pay in the morning."

"You're not thinking of using the money in the bank? That's all we have to live on until our own stock start producing, and they're not even here yet. It's the money Father put aside for the ranch, for us—not for some drifter we hardly know."

Lindy would not be swayed by her brother's argument. "I'm the oldest, Luke. I'll make that decision. And believe me, any decision I make will be for the ranch and for us. I'm not about to spend our savings frivolously."

"You're a woman," Luke said in anger. "Matt should have left me in charge. At least I'm thinking with a clear head."

"Luke!" Lindy was shocked and hurt that Luke would blaspheme their brother's dying words. "My head's as clear as water."

"Well, the water here is darn muddy."

That night, Lindy lay in bed thinking about Connor. She thought of how much had been accomplished at Broken Gate in only a few hours. And how it was her good fortune that Connor was not only skilled but also nice to look at. Her thoughts kept sliding back to Connor's face, Connor's hands, Connor's shoulders and arms. Every wonderful part of him was memorized right down to his boots. She told herself he would speed the building of Broken Gate into the fine station she envisioned, and with her father's sheep arriving soon, she'd need the extra hand. In addition, having a man around would ease her worries about Jeb. Even if Luke didn't agree, the more she thought about Connor, the more she was sure she didn't want him to leave.

Chapter Three

Lindy was wrong about Jeb. Only a week after they had buried Hank, Jeb rode out to Broken Gate with Sheriff Hayes.

Clouds of dust rising from the flat ground at first blurred the two riders, but as they came closer, they separated and Lindy recognized Sheriff Hayes's big bay gelding and Jeb's gray mare. She found herself wishing that Connor hadn't left with the first light of day, but then, it would have been a complicated matter to explain his presence. Hayes was not going to be in the best of moods if he had been dragged away from one of his poker games by Jeb. There wasn't anything he liked better than poker. If Hayes had a weakness that could be relied upon it was his afternoon card games with the boys.

Since Lindy had ignored Hayes's good advice to move in with Widow Lawtey until her husband arrived, Hayes was going to be even more upset that he had to ride out to Broken Gate. Lindy felt agitation tighten around her middle like a rope. Jeb was giving the sheriff another reason to suggest she move in with Hallie Lawtey. The sheriff could make the suggestion if he wanted to, but he couldn't force her to move off her land.

Jeb reached the house before the sheriff and swung down from his mount a moment before the gray came to a halt.

When he regarded Lindy, his eyes flickered dangerously, much like two sticks of dynamite spitting sparks. Brown, leathery skin wrinkled over his nose and around his eyes. Like a snarling bulldog's, his teeth threatened through curled-back lips. Not about to show the fear that made her tight as a wire, Lindy stood against the strong urge to back away. She returned Jeb's hard glare. A frightening understanding passed between them. Lindy knew the reason for Jeb's visit even before he spoke.

"What'd you do to my brother?"

Lindy wondered if Jeb knew Hank had ridden out to Broken Gate. Regardless, she couldn't risk a hint of fear in her face or in the tone of her voice. Jeb would smell her fear and pounce on her like a mountain cat.

"What are you jabbering about?" Lindy returned.

Sheriff Hayes stepped between Jeb and Lindy. His mouth was the same thin, straight line that hardly ever turned a smile. The only thing warm about Hayes was his brown eyes and even they could frost one's nerves on an August night when he felt perturbed. His only visible eccentricity was that he liked to wear his sideburns long so they bushed out at his jawline like fuzzy caterpillars. Attired in a white shirt, black trousers and vest, and a string tie, he would have looked like a banker, Lindy thought, if it had not been for the weapons he wore.

After a while, Hayes pulled at the ends of his mustache. "I'll do the questioning, Jeb. You keep your mouth shut."

Sheriff Hayes's voice hummed in the deep monotone Lindy had become familiar with. There was no telling how the man felt from the pitch of his voice. It was always the same steady tone that could soothe, infuriate or put a person on edge. Goober Hayes was a master of disguise when it came to hiding emotion. Never knowing how he really felt from one minute to the next kept a person cautious until impatience proved too strong to resist, then matters fell neatly into the sheriff's hands.

Since the sheriff became a widower, the unwed ladies of Dry Bed had considered him fair game for a husband. They would cast him flirtatious smiles from under the protection of their bonnets whenever their paths crossed. Almost shyly, Hayes would acknowledge them with a nod or a casual touch to the brim of his black Stetson.

Despite his tough exterior, Hayes was said to be kind, honest and fair. If Lindy could just convince herself that a man of the law could be all three she would admit to killing Hank. However, too much in her past had proved otherwise, and that Hank and Jeb were his nephews made her even more reluctant to tell Hayes what Hank had done and the result of his violence. It would be a stranger's word against kin, and no matter how bad an apple Hank had been, kin stuck together.

"I'm sorry, Mrs. Rigby," the sheriff said once he tethered his horse to the hitching bar in front of the house, "but Jeb here's been yellin' about his brother ridin' out this way. It seems Hank's missin' and..." He turned to study Jeb and then brought his attention back to Lindy. "I couldn't reach down deep enough for a guess as to why, but ... have you seen Hank around here? His horse's tracks were found out this way."

Lindy stiffened and glared at Jeb. "No."

Jeb stared hard at Lindy. "I don't believe she's tellin' the truth. Frank said Hank told him he was comin' out here to look for a missin' cow." Jeb's sun-cracked lips turned down. His sharp eyes squinted and converged on Lindy.

Despite the heat, Lindy felt goose bumps rush over her skin. "You're welcome to look around—with the sheriff."

"I don't need no invitation, lady," Jeb rejoined, his height magnifying the threat in his voice. "I intend to do just that."

"Jeb! Mind you're talkin' to a lady."

Jeb snarled and strutted away toward the barn.

Keeping one eye on Jeb and the other on Lindy, Sheriff Hayes pieced together what he knew. More to himself than to Lindy, he said, somewhat puzzled, "We found his horse. A boy don't abandon his horse like that. You can understand why Jeb's upset."

Lindy wasn't certain she noticed it, but the sheriff's expression seemed to soften slightly. Before she could be sure, his face returned to its stern set. The moment was so brief Lindy concluded it was only her hope for understanding that was cast in the man's face. The harshness that took over his usually calm voice verified that and made it clear to her that he had come ready to defend his family.

"It ain't safe out here for a woman and a boy all alone. You've no right bein' out here tryin' to do a man's job. Widow Lawtey wouldn't mind the company, and sure as there's Mexican bandits runnin' through here, I wouldn't mind knowin' you were safe. They'd like a sweet blonde like yourself. When your pa—"

"You told me that six months ago, Sheriff, and I'm still here."

"By God's will," he countered.

"By my own will," Lindy snapped. "My father would want me to continue what he began. Broken Gate is going to be the station he imagined."

"Yeah. He's six feet under. Pardon the reminder, but maybe it'll make you see reason. All I see here is a small farm, some chickens, goats and three horses. Where're the sheep?" His face grim, the sheriff surveyed a farmhouse and barn badly in need of repair and the dusty surrounding earth that begrudged the toughest grass.

"I'll have them, Sheriff." Lindy couldn't help but smile a bit smugly. The Falens were of good stock. It was up to her now to rebuild the family name and she would. Along with the wealth she had garnered from the station in Australia, the money her father had left her and the calling-up of favors from friends, sheep at Broken Gate would soon be a sight for all to see.

"Exactly how will you have them?" the sheriff pressed.

"Before leaving Australia, I made arrangements for the transport of my father's band, just as he had been planning to do before his death. Their safe arrival is entrusted with a fellow Aussie who is coming to Texas with a band of his own."

Lindy forced the irritation from her voice. "Thank you for your concern, but as you can see, everything has been well arranged. Broken Gate will have its sheep."

"Don't mistake my advice for concern, Mrs. Rigby. I just don't want trouble is all, 'specially from folks not of these parts." Hayes moved to join Jeb, who was inspecting every inch of ground for clues. As an afterthought he turned and glanced at Lindy from under the brim of his hat. "You'd tell me if there was trouble, wouldn't you, Mrs. Rigby?"

Silence walled up between them until Lindy was finally able to speak in a steady voice. "Of course. As I said, I haven't seen him."

"You understand I still have to look around," he said without pausing for her reply. Lindy watched the sheriff walk away and winced at the sharp flashes of light shooting off the spurs of his boots.

As far as Lindy was concerned, Sheriff Hayes represented an easily manipulated system—the same one that had unjustly condemned her father as a thief. Lawrence Falen's pleas of innocence had been ignored by the court, so he had been forced to leave his native England, sent into exile in Australia. Her mother had rebelled against her parents' ploy to separate them, secretly marrying Lawrence and sailing with him. Lindy supposed that her mother's parents had been dealt justice by the loss of their daughter, and later their grandchildren.

Lawrence Falen dreamed of making a better life for them all. His dream eventually called him to America. For two years, Lindy, her mother and Luke had listened to Matt read their father's letters and had waited anxiously for him to send for them. He never did. Looking out over the landscape of mesquite and chaparral, Lindy now knew why—it was not the dream he had wanted for them. Her father must have felt like a failure. It was up to her to prove that he wasn't, and she would, if Hank's ghost didn't pop up and ruin everything.

Lindy didn't think self-defense would matter much to Sheriff Hayes, since Hank was his nephew; her father's experiences had already instilled in her a deep distrust of men like Hayes. The sheriff had made it clear on more than one occasion that he thought she was asking for trouble by staying on at Broken Gate, so he wouldn't be very sympathetic to her problem.

Lindy felt her heart slam against her chest when she saw Hayes and Jeb around the henhouse. If she didn't do something, the fear inside her was going to bolt like a spooked horse. To keep from losing her fragile calm, Lindy grabbed the broom leaning against the house and began to whip up a storm of dust as she swept the porch clean. When Luke got in the way of her broom, she snapped, "Don't you have chores to do?" Luke nodded and left for the barn, where he had been replacing some rotted boards earlier.

The minutes dragged while Jeb and the sheriff inspected the farm. To Lindy's relief, they made only one circle around the henhouse before riding to the barn. Luke's hammer paused when Jeb walked past him. After giving Luke a friendly slap on the shoulder, Sheriff Hayes followed Jeb into the barn. From the scowl on Jeb's face, Lindy was sure they hadn't found a clue to Hank's disappearance.

When they came back to the house, Jeb was quiet, apparently warned to silence by Hayes. Sheriff Hayes cleared his throat, a sound he often made before saying something he knew might meet opposition. "I told Jeb he could take a quick look through the house." Lindy felt the fire in her eyes. "Now, Mrs. Rigby, I'll be right by the boy's side. Try to understand—he's just worried about his brother," Hayes explained in a vain effort to smooth her ruffled feathers.

The boy. Lindy's thoughts simmered. He talked about Jeb as though he were still an innocent child, when, in fact, he had grown to become a dangerous man. It became strikingly clear to her that Hayes did not suspect the evil that lurked inside his nephew.

Lindy noted the triumphant look on Jeb's face and grew livid. She backed to the doorway and blocked it with the broom still clutched in her hands. "You'd allow this roof rabbit to go through my house!" she shrieked, suddenly regretting her outcry when she realized that she had just insulted the sheriff's nephew.

Jeb started forward but was held back by an arm swung quickly across his path.

"Mrs. Rigby," Hayes said tersely, "there's no call for insults."

Lindy's hands spanned her hips. "Are you accusing me of some ill doing? Because if you are, I want to know right now."

"You don't have to act like a hen caught in a rainstorm. I didn't say any such thing."

"Then you've got no reason to come through my station or my house." Lindy's voice was strained. "You don't think I'd be entertaining a man in my house do you?" Her eyes pointed accusingly at Jeb.

The sheriff's face was patient, but hard set. "My nephew's missin', Mrs. Rigby, and it's my job to find him. His horse's tracks are all around here."

"How do you know it was his horse?" Lindy challenged.

"I told you, we found the horse," the sheriff said calmly, then elaborated to end all further argument. "The mare's got a cracked shoe. Ain't no way of mistakin' that horse's tracks. Now, sooner you move aside, the quicker we'll be out of your hair."

Jeb pushed beside the sheriff and scowled. When he spoke, the empty spaces once occupied by teeth caused a sound like that of a hissing snake. "I believe you know where my brother is, you—"

"You'll be keepin' your mouth shut," the sheriff warned. "Nothin' comes of a gate swingin' in the wind 'cept a loose hinge." Hayes turned to Lindy. "I'm truly sorry but—"

Lindy stepped aside, not wanting to hear again how he was driven by his dedication to the law. Knowing Hayes, she'd be debating the issue on her front porch until supper, and she didn't want to feel obliged to invite him even if there was a chance of it softening his current opinion of her. "Go ahead. But I'll be behind you both."

Lindy followed Jeb and the sheriff through the house and watched closely as Jeb eyed every corner for something that would indicate his brother had been there. Her smug satisfaction cooled when she saw Jeb casually pick up the porcelain doll from her bed. Its white lace apron fell over his dirty hand. The fragile doll lay helpless in his hands. It was in his power to let it fall and shatter on the floor. Lindy felt weak with dread at the cruel twist of his smile. The sheriff was intent on his own search for evidence, and so he failed to notice Jeb's subtle threat.

"You were right, Uncle," Jeb said slowly, throwing the doll back on the bed. "My brother ain't been here." His eyes bored into Lindy, promising she hadn't seen the last of him.

Jeb pushed past her and left the house. Once she heard the galloping hooves of his horse, Lindy breathed again.

Sheriff Hayes shifted his weight from one leg to the other and cleared his throat. "Sorry for the inconvenience."

"You said that already, Sheriff. I know you're doing your job. No sense in apologizing for it. Just make sure your nephew understands he's not welcome to come riding out here with more unfounded accusations."

"I don't think Jeb meant anything by it. He was always close with his brother. They'd die for one another if they had to. It's like you and Luke."

Lindy could only nod in agreement. If the sheriff had any inkling that Hank had met his end at her hand, no doubt she would be tried and hanged for the man's murder. The sheriff wouldn't want to believe she had killed his kin in self-defense. It already seemed like he was taking Jeb's side. Lindy wrapped her arms around her middle and shivered, a strange move when the temperature was rising past ninety degrees.

Sheriff Hayes looked at the white, almost colorless sky. "It's a hot one. You be careful now," he warned, mounting his horse. "I can't be expected to protect a lone woman so far from town."

When the departing sheriff was nothing but a black speck in the center of a yellow dust cloud, Lindy's relief escaped her in a long sigh. She went back into the house. The first place she looked for comfort was in the letter she had tucked away in the bureau drawer. She lifted it from the now ragged envelope, opened the folded paper and felt its reassurance between her fingers. She sat down on her bed and pulled the porcelain doll onto her lap. Besides the farm, the letter and the doll were the most important things her parents had left her. They were a part of them, as much as the gold wedding band, the testimony of their love, that she wore on her finger. The illegible scrawl over the yellow paper meant as much to her as a portrait. The doll had made its way from England, surviving without a chip in its fragile face or hands. It often renewed her strength to carry on despite the overwhelming odds she faced.

Lindy stared at the lines of ink sprawled over the brittle paper in her hand. How she wished she knew how to read the words. She tried to remember what Matt had read all those years ago. Matt had not lived to read this letter, but she was certain it was like the others before it, so not much of what the letter told would be true.

Before he died, Lawrence Falen had gilded Dry Bed with flowery words, but like a picture frame, beneath the gold lay nothing but wood. The land was dry and mostly barren, but she knew sheep would fatten on the coarse grass scattered in gray patches over the dry ground. Their wool would bring income to support her and Luke. With a large enough band, she'd have enough wool to send north and enough money to replenish her dwindling bank account and expand her station. Then, there'd be stockmen to hire, pens to build—there was so much to be done. How could two people manage it all?

Lindy folded the letter back into its envelope and hid it away. She'd spent enough time dallying over her dreams when reality was outside the door crying for attention.

The sound of pounding hooves sprang Lindy from her bed. Drawing back the curtain, she was once again set into a panic by the sight of Sheriff Hayes, returning. What could he want now?

Luke had also spotted the sheriff and was running across the wagon yard from the barn to meet him.

Lindy stepped outside, gripping her skirt in her fists to keep her hands steady. "Sheriff, have you forgotten something?"

"Yes. This came for you." Sensitive to her illiteracy, Hayes read the telegram aloud. "Your jumbucks will be arriving the third day of June. They're comin' up from Galveston." He looked up from the yellow paper. "What's jumbucks anyway?"

Luke was quick to explain. "Sheep, Sheriff."

Hayes's brow wrinkled with concern. "This is from the fellow you were tellin' me about? The one who was bringin' your father's sheep from Australia?"

Lindy nodded.

Hayes cleared the dust from his throat. "Is he plannin' on settlin' in Dry Bed, too?"

"No."

"Well, thank God for that. I don't think Dry Bed would stand for more than one of you. Mrs. Rigby, you know that Clay Claxton will likely have a fit if he sees sheep trottin' out of cattle cars, especially after he's gone through the expense of layin' those miles of track for his cattle." With a sigh of defeat, Hayes added, "I can't stop you from raising them critters on your own land but—"

"Sheriff, it's a small band of jumbucks. Hardly anyone will notice. Luke, Buddy and I will have them out of town before anyone is the wiser."

Hayes's mouth was set in a firm line. "See that you do," he said flatly and put the telegram in Lindy's hand.

How she wished Mr. O'Malley had not been in such a hurry to leave.

Hayes gripped the saddle horn and put his foot in the stirrup. Effortlessly he swung himself onto the back of his horse, stretched and panned Broken Gate with discriminating eyes. "Let me know if you hear anything about Hank."

His comment caught Lindy off guard. "Don't worry, Sheriff," she said. "I'm sure he'll turn up."

"Nah. Doubt that he will," he answered without looking directly at Lindy. His eyes still seemed to be searching for something. "They're my sister's boys, but—" Hayes stopped short, catching whatever it was that had caused his troubled reflection, casting more shadow than insight on his feelings for Hank and Jeb.

Lindy didn't dare ask, but she certainly did wonder why the sheriff was so sure Hank had disappeared for good. She swallowed her question and thanked Hayes again for bringing the telegram.

The next morning, Lindy sat in the buckboard waiting for Luke. She wore her split riding skirt and an oversize, flat-crowned black hat. It was hardly the type ladies wore, lacking in ribbons and secured under her chin by only a leather thong. She had found the hat hanging on a peg in the kitchen the day they arrived and liked to think it had belonged to her father.

Lindy was growing impatient. Her toes tapped against the floor, she wrapped and unwrapped the reins around her gloved hand and glanced back at the barn. Luke finally emerged with the bay dun. He mounted his horse and trotted up to the buckboard. Lindy snapped the reins over the backs of her horses and the wagon jerked ahead. Buddy yipped and wagged his tail.

"Do you think he knows?" Luke asked with a smile as broad as the brim of Lindy's hat.

"Sheriff Hayes?"

"No. Buddy."

She looked behind her. Buddy's nose quivered like a rabbit's. She was sure the dog sensed their excitement. She turned away her worries. It wasn't every day sheep arrived from Australia. It had been a long wait but Hal had come through as he promised. The small band she had left in his trust was arriving on the two o'clock train. All her wealth and dreams had been invested in the delivery of her father's sheep. When Lindy thought about it, she could feel her insides dance with happiness. Broken Gate was on its way to becoming a station that would one day be as magnificent as Clay Claxton's place. Yet disappointment tempered her elation; she and Luke would have to manage alone until she could afford to hire help.

When Luke and Lindy arrived in Dry Bed, people were already seeking shelter from the midday sun. The shaded boardwalks were crowded, horses were tethered to hitching rails, a few children shot marbles in the dirt, and some Mexicans brightened the scene with colorfully striped serapes thrown over their shoulders. Farther down the street, a traveling man was beginning to draw a small crowd. His voice was deep and projected like that of a great orator or an actor playing Shakespeare upon a stage. From a distance, Lindy admired his elaborately painted wagon. Roses, leaves and vines curled around sprawling gold letters that read: Dr. Richfield's Tonic for Men, Women and Children, and in smaller letters below: Livestock, Too. Red velvet curtains were drawn over the back opening of the wagon, giving the appearance of a stage show. The gray-haired vendor, distinguished looking in a black suit and shoestring tie, stood on the platform that extended from the back of the wagon. He held a cobalt-blue bottle toward the assembling crowd.

Luke's eyes widened at the theatrical presentation of Dr. Richfield's tonic's miraculous results. "Can I go see, Lin?"

"All right," Lindy agreed reluctantly. "I've got some items to purchase from Mrs. Quinn anyway." Luke was off before she could change her mind. "Don't forget the time," she called after him.

Lindy patted Buddy on the head. "You stay."

She stopped short of entering the mercantile. There in the window was the most beautiful bonnet she'd ever seen. It was a frivolous show of pink ribbon and lace the color of eggshells. Certainly not the kind of bonnet she needed or her frugality would allow. It was the kind worn by a lady, not by someone who tilled soil and scattered grain to chickens. She looked up, and through her reflection in the glass saw Hester Quinn peering at her from behind the counter. Lindy grimaced. Hester no doubt had seen her admiring something she thought was beyond her means. Holding her chin high, Lindy pushed the door open and stepped inside. A bell hanging over the door announced her entrance.

Hester Quinn was snugly positioned between the counter and shelves of apothecary jars. She wore her gray hair in a tight knot at the top of her head. With a sausage-link finger, she pushed up her Ben Franklin spectacles. It was an endless battle to keep them from sliding down to the round tip of her nose.

"Afternoon, Lindy. Haven't seen you in a while," Hester said, her pink cheeks plumped with her smile.

Lindy placed her basket of eggs on the counter. "Can you use these today?"

Hester's smile disappeared and her eyes sharpened as she inspected each egg for the slightest crack. "I suppose. But it won't give you enough for that bonnet."

Lindy knew Hester couldn't wait to mention the bonnet and point out that it was beyond her means. "I wasn't thinking of trading my eggs for a bonnet like that. I need sugar and flour."

While Hester filled her order, Lindy flipped through the pages of the latest fashion catalog. The scent of lavender soap tickled her nose.

"Anything else, Lindy?"

"How much is a bar of this soap?" Lindy lifted the paper-wrapped bar from a basket.

"Five cents."

Five cents! She'd have to withdraw money from the bank for such luxury and she wasn't about to submit to that kind of weakness—at least not today. "I suppose another time. Some molasses and that'll be all for now."

Hester's arms crossed over the front of her white apron. Lindy often thought there was enough muslin in the woman's apron for the sail of a ship. The mere breadth of her alone was intimidating. "You got your jar? You know it's two cents more for a jar."

Lindy sighed, the smell of lavender still on her fingers. "I know. I forgot the jar." She reached into her reticule and rolled her last bit of change onto the counter.

Hester spooned the gooey brown liquid into a mason jar. "You still alone on your pa's farm?"

"You know I am, Hester."

"When's that husband of yours comin'? I'd be lookin' for another man by now. After so long a woman's got a right to start thinkin' of herself. Time don't stand still. Your age, I had myself three babes."

Lindy's interest wandered to the bolts of calico and gingham as Hester rambled on. She caught bits and pieces of what she said while she pretended to listen but was actually thinking of a new dress to replace the one she had burned. Then Hester said something that brought her back.

"Now there was a gentleman in here the other day. Never seen him before. From the East by the way he spoke. Eyes as soft as Confederate gray. Charming, too... for a Yankee," Hester pointed out as if it were some grand mark against his eligibility. To Lindy they were all Yankees. She didn't yet understand the difference or the feelings of hatred she sensed between the Americans. She supposed it was something akin to how the English felt toward the Australians.

"You'd fancy him though," Hester continued, slipping her finger along the outside of the jar to catch a stream of syrup. "Got young Carrie mighty flustered when he insisted on carryin' her supplies. Weren't nothin' too heavy. I know she could have managed, like she always does, but she must have been struck dumb by the looks of him. Her pa would take a switch to her if he knew she was flutterin' those long lashes of hers right in his face."

Lindy's eyes narrowed. Hester had ears for gossip, and as she liked to hear it, she loved to tell it. "Did you ask him his name?" Lindy tried to sound as though she was obliging Hester with conversation, but her heart thumped wildly.

Hester's mouth dropped open. "Of course not! I'm not a busybody."

"Oh, I'd never think that. You can't help what people tell you." Lindy had to leave the mercantile before her smile gave her away, but before she did she asked one more question. "Do you know if he's still in town?"

"He took a room at Tilly's. Far as I know he's still there, but he came in this mornin' for some coffee. My guess would be he's—you're awfully interested. Like you already know the man."

Lindy couldn't stop the telltale blush from rising to her cheeks. "Now how can that be? I've just arrived in Dry Bed." She gathered up her bags and hustled out of the mercantile, very aware that Hester Quinn's sharp eyes followed her.

Lindy had tried not to give Connor O'Malley much thought, but she had been unsuccessful. She was disappointed and annoyed that he had left without giving her a chance to thank him again for his help. At least that was what she tried to tell herself. Actually she just wanted to try once more to convince him to stay. For someone who had nowhere to go and no one to meet he certainly set himself on a schedule.

Lindy put the sacks of flour and sugar into her wagon and nestled the jar of molasses between them. Hester was probably describing someone else who just happened to have gray eyes. When she looked across the street and saw Connor's horse hitched in front of Minerva's Saloon, her doubts ended. There was no mistaking the horse with its long white stockings. At once her mind began to work. She leaned against the buckboard and watched the front of the saloon.

His hands behind his back, Luke came up behind her. He turned his head around to see what had caught Lindy's attention. "Something interesting over there?"

Lindy smiled. It was the kind of smile that warned she wanted something and nothing was going to get in the way of her having it. There would be no argument that could be used to deter her resolve.

"It's one-thirty. Don't you think we should be going over to the depot?" Luke asked, still staring at the front of Minerva's Saloon.

Lindy seemed not to hear him. "Do you see that horse in front of Minerva's? The one with the long stockings and the blaze on its muzzle? That's Mr. O'Malley's horse."

"Lots of horses look like that," Luke said, trying to discourage her anyway.

"No. It's his."

"Well, even if it is, he doesn't want anything to do with us. If we don't hurry—"

"Why do you say that?"

"You know he was in a hurry to get going."

"How can he be in a hurry when he has nowhere to go? I want you to go in there and find him. Just tell him that I need to talk to him and that it's important. And don't let those fancy women distract you. Best thing to do is not even look at them. If one tries to talk to you, remind her you're still a nipper."

Luke's color deepened, and his eyes flared with the anger and hurt Lindy heard in his voice. "I'm not a boy any longer. If you're so worried, why don't you go yourself?"

"I would if I could. You don't find decent ladies in a place like that. Luke, I—"

Luke didn't linger to hear any more of what Lindy had to say. His legs reached out over the ground in long, stiff strides. "And I'll bloody well give them all a second look," he said loudly, turning the heads of several passersby.

"Luke! Don't dare dally in there!" Lindy warned. She just didn't understand why Luke was so argumentative lately.

Luke turned around in the middle of the street and stomped back to her, raising a cloud of dust beneath his feet. He came right up to her. Lindy looked up at him, and for the first time noticed how tall he'd gotten since they had arrived in Texas.

Luke shoved a small blue bottle in her hand. "Here, the gent said it was good for covering bad smells. I thought we could sprinkle it in the henhouse."

"Luke, you didn't tell—"

"Of course not! Do you take me for a mozzle?"

Lindy asked, "How much, Luke?"

"One dollar."

"One dollar! Where did you get—"

"It was in Hank's pocket."

Lindy saw she hurt him for a second time and felt annoyed with herself. He did notice how she worried, he did think of Hank, and all she could think of was lavender soap and impractical bonnets, and a man she hardly knew. When she looked up from the bottle, Luke had already started to cross the street.

Lindy paced the edge of the boardwalk. Luke was right, she behaved like his mom. Still, as time passed, she began to think it had been a mistake to send someone as young as Luke into a bawdy place. Buddy also waited for Luke to appear from behind the swinging doors. He sat alert on the seat with his nose pointed in the direction of the saloon.

Lindy imagined ruffians and buxom women getting hold of Luke before he could find Connor. And she worried about his remark. What did he mean, he'd take a long look? Could it be that her dear little brother had grown in more ways than height and she hadn't noticed? She had noted the beginning of whiskers and the change in his voice, and how his eyes shined whenever he looked at young Clara, but the arrogance—that was new. Judging from his mood of late, it would be just like him to linger in the saloon to spite her. What was taking him so long?

"Well now, look who's here."

Lindy spun around to face Jeb. He wasn't alone, but with some other men. The smell of whiskey hovered like a cloud around them. It had to be payday—all were dressed in their finest. They wore their best boots and hats. The rowels on their spurs rolled over the wood planks, making a jangling sound when they walked. Most distressing to Lindy were the flashy six-shooters at their hips. Her admiration fell short of what the men expected. She backed up against the wagon. All she could think of was that she was alone and her rifle was lying in the back of the buckboard.

"This a friend of yours, Jeb?" one of the men asked through a leering smile.

"Naw, she ain't the friendly type. She's the fightin' kind."

"That's the best kind." All the men chuckled at her expense except Jeb. The murderous look on his face still remained from the day she shot a hole through his hat.

Lindy turned her back on the men and prayed they'd leave. A low, vibrating warning came from Buddy's stomach and shook from his throat. It was an ugly sound but failed to discourage Jeb from grabbing Lindy's arm and spinning her around. Buddy got up on his legs. His snarl was enough to make the other three men back away a little. But Jeb was either too brave or too stupid to be deterred by the dog's bared teeth. Lindy surmised the latter. From Buddy's perch on the buckboard, his teeth were level with Jeb's face.

"I wasn't done talkin' to you," Jeb said in a low voice that resembled the dog's growl. "I'm not done with you at all."

"What's bothering you? That a woman put a bullet through your hat when it could well have been your head if she fancied?" When she heard one of his friends chuckle, she knew she'd made a dangerous mistake by embarrassing him.

"You never told us that story, Jeb."

"Shut up, Frank. It was a lucky shot, but a stupid move."

Jeb's squeeze on Lindy's arm tightened. "Call off your dog before I shoot him."

"You go for your gun and he'll be at your throat before you can clear leather."

"Come on, Jeb. Clay's gonna be missin' us if we don't get back."

Jeb summed up Buddy and decided to let go of Lindy. Lindy let her forearm throb rather than rub it in front of him. She watched the men leave. Buddy still vibrated with his growls. Lindy stroked his trembling body. "It's all right now. There's Luke, thank God."

From the alarm on his face and his hurried pace Lindy knew Luke had seen Jeb. She noticed Connor was behind him but not in much of a hurry.

"What'd he want?" Luke asked with more than a trace of protectiveness in his voice.

Lindy didn't want Connor to think she associated with such riffraff as Jeb Cobb. What would it look like, an unescorted woman conversing with cowboys on the street? No, she certainly didn't want Connor to come to any conclusions about that. "Shh, it's nothing," she whispered to Luke, and smiling at Connor, said, "Mr. O'Malley, what a nice surprise to see you again. I noticed your horse and—"

Connor spoke quickly and to the point, "Luke said you needed to talk to me."

"Yes, I...we are in dire straits. We're expecting some supplies from Australia. A friend of mine put them on the train." Lindy ignored Luke's astonished look. Well, they were sort of like supplies. "It's too much for just the two of us to handle, and seeing you were in Dry Bed we thought to ask once more for your help. If there was someone else we could turn to we—"

By the tight look on his face, Lindy knew Luke didn't care for the way he was included in her request.

Connor leaned one hand against the buckboard. Buddy stretched out and quickly licked his cheek. Connor petted the dog, setting his tail to wagging furiously. "I wasn't staying in Dry Bed. In fact, I was just getting on my way."

"Why, then that's perfect," Lindy exclaimed. "Since you were leaving anyway, you could just come along with us. Isn't it grand how things can work out? Here I was worried about how on earth we'd manage." While Lindy talked, Luke hammered the tip of his boot into the ground.

Lindy was already afraid Connor wasn't going to be convinced and she hadn't even mentioned sheep yet. She watched him for some encouragement. There wasn't any in the serious slant of his eyebrows while he contemplated his answer. Her eyes followed his hand as it moved methodically over Buddy's fur, beginning at the top of the animal's head, then moving unhurried, in one long motion, down his neck and over his shoulders and back again. She became aware of the sudden change in her breathing, the slight quickening of her pulse, and the warm rush of blood that made her languish for the same gentle touch. Nearly gasping for breath, she quickly looked away, hoping Connor did not notice the agony she wrestled with as she wondered how it would feel to be caressed in such a way.

By his own admission Connor wasn't on a time schedule and Lindy knew there wasn't an honorable way for him to refuse her. Unsuspectingly Connor had backed himself into a corner. "I suppose it won't hurt to help you load your wagon," he finally said. "There isn't much that can fit in the back of a buckboard anyway. What exactly are you expecting?"

"Exactly?" Lindy glanced obliquely at Luke, who tenaciously awaited her reply. "Well . . . jumbucks, exactly."

"Clothing?" Connor guessed aloud.

Lindy smiled weakly back at him. A sound like a hiccup popped from Luke's throat and his eyes rolled skyward.

Chapter Four

"What the hell is that?" Connor shouted above the melee that rumbled out of the stock cars.

"You're looking at my jumbucks," Lindy announced, her voice filled with pride.

In their rush for freedom, a flock of driving sheep nearly knocked Connor over. It was all he could do to hold on to his mare's reins as the white tide parted and flowed around them. Luke and Buddy drove the band down Main Street, stirring up a dust storm that sent the less curious searching for shelter.

The tanned skin around Connor's blue-gray eyes crinkled when he looked down from his horse. "You said you needed help with your clothes."

"*You* assumed clothing, Mr. O'Malley. *I* said I needed help with my jumbucks."

Connor fought with the reins to keep his horse calm. "I expected trunks and hatboxes—not sheep. You deliberately made me believe—"

"It's not my fault you don't know what a jumbuck is."

"Well, now I guess I do. And in case you haven't noticed, this is Texas, not Australia. They're called sheep here and there are a few other names the cattlemen call them, and none of them is jumbuck. If you'd said sheep in the first place, I'd have known what you meant."

Lindy felt her irritation rise and shouted above the rumble of hooves, "Does it really matter?"

Connor looked down the street at Clay Claxton and some of his men. "To some, it does."

Lindy also noticed the group of men. They had all lined up to watch her sheep ramble down the street, and by looking at their faces, anyone would have thought the circus had come to town. Even Dr. Richfield had stopped hawking his tonic to stare at the procession. They all looked as though they'd never seen sheep in their lives.

Lindy recognized one man in particular—Jeb. He stood next to Clay Claxton, the rancher whose property abutted hers. Success had generously padded him, but Claxton hadn't softened in any other way. He was the most powerful man in Dry Bed. No one dared cross him. Everyone, except the sheriff, followed his advice.

Lindy wasn't in the least intimidated by Claxton. "This is a free country," she said to Connor. "There aren't any laws that say I can't bring my jumbucks to Texas."

"You're going to find there are a lot of unwritten laws in Texas. Now may I suggest we get your sheep out of town before those men recover from their shock and start shooting?"

"Shooting! They wouldn't dare shoot at my stock."

"Believe me, ma'am, they will. And they'll aim to kill."

After that sobering statement, Connor joined Luke on the other side of the band of about a hundred sheep and watched in fascination as Luke whistled and voiced commands from atop his horse. Immediately the little sheepdog became a whiz of gold and white. He raced back to the far end of the band, around the edge, then crisscrossed behind them, all the time keeping the band moving and confined to the center of the street.

Despite her determination, Lindy looked wary as she approached Claxton and his men. She forced a smile when her wagon jostled by them. What else could she do? They were standing in a line, their mouths nearly agape while they watched Luke and Buddy handle the band. Claxton, who had never before given her much notice, acknowledged her with a tip of his hat. Her confidence returned. Connor had been wrong. Already she had gained some of the respect reserved for men like Claxton. She was not just raising chickens anymore. The mills would soon be buying her wool.

Sheriff Hayes was among those who watched Lindy and her sheep move down the center of town, and he wasn't happy. He hadn't expected more than a half dozen of the critters and had hoped they would be able to leave town without anyone's notice. But as it always seemed to be with Mrs. Rigby since she had arrived, there had been plenty of surprises. Of everyone, Claxton seemed to be the most surprised. He had nearly bitten off the end of his cigar when he saw the sheep. And not long after that he had begun to look for Hayes.

"Hayes, what in bloody hell do you call this?" Claxton's round face was as red as the mercury in a thermometer.

The sheriff suppressed a smile. "I think she said jumbucks."

"What?"

"Jumbucks. That's what they call them down under."

"Down under or up above, you know as well as I do woollies and cattle don't mix."

"No one's askin' you to take any on."

"You know what I mean, Hayes. Those animals will turn this land to dust. There's nothing more destructive than those beasts."

"What do you want me to do? I can't tell her what she can and can't do on her own land."

Claxton grimaced. "Maybe you can't or just won't, but I don't plan to wait until it's too late. I'm not tolerating sheep."

"You're gonna have to, Clay. There ain't nothin' you can do unless they come onto your land. Then I'd hope you'd at least give her a warnin' before you did anything drastic."

"I'll give her a warning all right. Only I'm not going to wait until I start seeing woollies on my land."

The star pinned on Hayes's chest flashed when he moved to directly face Claxton. The spark of light caught Claxton's eye, reminding him that Hayes was the official law in Dry Bed.

Hayes knew Claxton too well to be fooled by his smile. "Clay, I'm gonna keep an eye on you and your men. I'll not take lightly to anyone harmin' a woman."

Claxton took another cigar from the inside pocket of his fine jacket. A gold and black brocade vest with shiny brass buttons showed that the man was dressed just as richly underneath his topcoat. He offered a cigar to Hayes, who politely declined. "I wasn't thinking of harming her, Hayes. Just a little gentle persuasion is all," Claxton said matter-of-factly as he lit the end of his cigar.

"Make sure it's gentle."

"It'll be gentle all right." Claxton puffed on his cigar, took it from his mouth and regarded it thoughtfully. Its bright end glowed in his eyes. "I never noticed just how attractive she is."

"She's married," Hayes reminded him.

"Maybe I should be talking to her husband, then."

"Can't. He's still in Australia."

"A man sending his wife on ahead of him. Doesn't that strike you as peculiar, Hayes?"

The sheriff shrugged. "I never gave it much thought, bein' as though it ain't any of my business how people conduct their married lives."

Claxton squinted thoughtfully at the buckboard that bounced along in the middle of the wave of sheep.

Once they were outside the boundaries of town, the pace slowed. Luke took the point and Buddy kept his eyes trained on the outer edge of the band while Lindy stayed to the rear.

It wasn't long before Connor turned his horse around and rode back to Lindy's wagon. The grim look on his face told her he was still peeved over her trickery.

"Mrs. Rigby, had I known what you intended—"

"I know. You wouldn't have agreed to help me."

"Then you admit deceiving me?"

Lindy hadn't actually planned to fool him, it just had happened that way. "No," she said, a little indignantly. "I never intended to trick you into helping me. Must we have this conversation all over again?"

Connor looked into her face. "Your brother and your dog look like they can manage without help."

"Now, yes. But what if we are attacked by coyotes? These animals have come a long way, and I don't want anything to happen to them. Just about all my savings have been put into getting them here. If it hadn't been for a good friend transporting my father's band with his own, I'd only be dreaming of a fine station. They are my future, Mr. O'Malley."

"You're chasing rainbows, Mrs. Rigby."

Lindy's pride was wounded. "I'll find my rainbow's end without any help from you. Luke and I will manage just fine." She slapped the reins over the horse's rump and the buckboard bumped on ahead of Connor.

Lindy found that one disadvantage of riding in a wagon was that she couldn't outrun a man on horseback. In no time Connor was riding next to her again, an irritating grin curving his lips.

"I said you're free to go to wherever it is you're in a hurry to be," she shouted over the rattle of the buckboard. When Connor didn't answer right away she looked up at him. "Did you understand what I said this time?"

"I said I'd see you back to your farm and I will."

"It's not a bloody farm! It's a station."

"We just came from a station. Trains stop at stations. *You* live on a farm."

Lindy opened her mouth to continue the argument, but closed it again when she saw him smiling. So, he was teasing her for fooling him.

"All right the—farm if you will, a big sheep farm."

"We call it a ranch."

She gritted her teeth and repeated, "Ranch!"

Connor laughed. Then suddenly the smile faded from his lips. He spurred his horse and loped off to the front of the band, and then fell back to an easy trot.

Now that the band steadily followed the lead ewe, Luke rode back to his sister. "Did you ever think there'd be so many?"

"No. And they're a sturdy bunch to survive such a journey, aren't they?" she said wistfully.

Watching Connor's back, Luke asked, "Are you still insisting he come all the way to Broken Gate?"

"No, *he's* insisting. Is something wrong, Luke?"

Luke shrugged. "Nothing's wrong."

Thinking of how Luke had protested against asking Connor for help reminded Lindy of the tonic he had put in her hands just before he had run into the saloon. With all that had happened that day, she had forgotten to thank him. "I appreciate the tonic, Luke."

Luke grunted. "Maybe it'll make the henhouse not smell so bad."

"Luke, he's buried!"

"None too deep. What if one day the sheriff looks up and sees vultures circling the henhouse?"

"He'd think a chook had died."

"Just the same, I don't think it'll harm sprinkling some of Dr. Richfield's tonic over his grave."

Lindy hadn't given the possibility of animals discovering Hank's grave much thought. What Luke said frightened her. What if he was right? Hank had been hastily buried in a shallow grave. Now she not only had the sheriff and Jeb to think about, she had to worry about animals discovering Hank's body too.

At dusk, under a satiny sky laced with ribbons of orange and pink, Luke and Connor set up camp. They listened to coyotes yipping at the moonrise and watched the fleeting shadows of bats pass over the pale backs of the sheep. A beacon of light from a quarter moon cut across the camp, and stars peppered the sky. The sweet smell of flowers that had simmered during the day seemed more pungent in the cool evening air.

Connor volunteered for the first watch, leaving Lindy and Luke to sleep. Lindy couldn't sleep. She didn't want to take her eyes off of her fine merino sheep, for fear that they would somehow disappear if she did. Their angular bodies were covered with a thick woolly fleece that would make the finest wool cloth. She thought of how nice it would be if Connor stayed to help with the shearing, but that was not likely. She really had to forget about him. For some reason, Connor seemed driven to wander. Lindy wondered what could make a man so restless. She could see him silhouetted against the sky and tried to imagine what was in his thoughts. She was planning her future. What kind of future did he plan?

Connor had turned his back to Lindy long ago, deciding that admiring the beautiful sunset was much safer than appraising the attractive and intriguing woman. He had met many women in his journey from the East, but none of them was as fascinating as the Aussie.

He wanted to know more about her, but did not want to burden himself with the responsibility of a woman and a boy who were left alone. The less he knew about Lindy and her brother, the easier it would be for him to leave them once they reached her ranch. From what he did know about her, he realized it would be a big mistake to get entangled in her life—already he was more involved with her than he cared to be. Everything pointed to a brewing disaster: the sheep she had trotted past the citizens of Dry Bed with her own style of graceful arrogance, her peculiarities, coupled with living alone except for the young Luke. All spelled trouble. Trouble he did not want.

Connor's thoughts were far off when Lindy came up behind him. A slight sound alerted trained reflexes. He spun around. The grip of his gun nested in his palm, its muzzle pointed at Lindy.

"Lord!" Lindy gasped, flattening her hand on her chest and staring down at the barrel.

"What are you sneaking up on someone for?" Connor's voice broke the quiet night.

"Who were you expecting?"

Connor slid his gun back in its holster and warned her softly, "That's a dangerous thing to do, Mrs. Rigby."

"Why don't you first make sure who it is behind you? You could kill someone."

"By then I could be dead," he answered automatically. Connor grimaced at the fright that still paled her face. "I'm sorry if I frightened you. What are you doing out here? You should be asleep."

"I'm too excited to sleep. I wanted to look over the band. Aren't they beautiful?" Her eyes melted over the sheep. "And Buddy's happy as a lark in spring with jumbucks to nose around rather than chooks. Those poor birds didn't know what to think when he started at them—pushing them all to one corner of the hen yard."

Connor watched the light in her eyes sparkle while she chatted away. He found her voice very satisfying to listen to, her excitement almost contagious. She was beautiful, charming and so full of life that she reminded him of happier days, bringing on a sudden melancholy.

"Did you have a farm in Maryland?" Lindy asked, chipping into his indulgence of self-pity.

"I had everything back East, and buried it there," he answered curtly, and then to divert her interest in him, he responded with a question of his own. "How'd an Aussie end up in Texas?"

"It was my father who had wanted to come here. He was looking for a better life for us. What made a Yankee come out West?"

Connor's lips curved slightly. "Wild country, wild horses and wild women."

"You're not serious. There must be another reason." Lindy moved closer. Her face was darkly shadowed in the faint light of the moon. Connor dared to look right into her eyes, a luminous green in the faint light.

"Ghosts," he whispered. The dark, sensuous tone of his voice made Lindy step back. But he drew nearer, placing his hands on her shoulders to stop her retreat and pulling her close enough to feel the rapid rhythm of her heart. A warm feeling washed over him, and even though the night was cool, he felt like a candle melting under a hot flame. It had been so long since such feelings had spilled through his veins. Though he knew he should push her away, he held her close. Night became a dark cloak of secrecy wrapped around them. Under its cover his lips came near to touching hers until he heard the hard click of a Colt's hammer being cocked. In the silence it sounded as loud as cannon fire. Connor's grip tightened painfully on Lindy's arms.

Connor heard Lindy suck in her breath. It wasn't until she revealed Luke as the one who had given them both a fright that he turned slowly around. Connor's eyes drifted down to the pearl-handled Colt in Luke's hand.

Lindy was the first to speak. "Luke! What in God's name? Put that away before someone gets hurt."

Luke lowered the gun and Connor released Lindy. "I thought he was—"

"We were having a conversation."

"It looked like—it sure as blazes didn't look like you were talking...or watching the band!" Luke shouted before leaving them.

Lindy avoided looking Connor in the eye. "I'm sorry. Luke's never been so...I don't know what's the matter with him."

Connor placed his hand under Lindy's chin and tilted her face up to his. Starlight dusted over her skin and seemed to get caught in her hair, setting it to glitter like gold. Lindy didn't oppose his touch; her innocent trust encouraged it, tempting him to return to the moment they had had before Luke's interruption.

"Your brother means well. He's protecting his sister." Connor let her go and walked away.

Lindy felt the warm sun on her face and knew she had slept much longer than she should have. She propped herself up on her elbows and smiled at the grazing sheep dotting the terrain. It hadn't been a dream—she had her jumbucks at last. And what had happened the night before hadn't been a dream either—Connor's embrace started an ember of desire glowing inside her and...and Luke...Luke had Hank's gun. He couldn't go flashing that piece of evidence about. She promised herself to speak to him the first chance she got.

She kneeled up and stretched, groaning at the stiffness in her back. Her body would never get used to sleeping on rock-hard ground. She felt as though every stone had made its mark in her flesh.

Usually Lindy was awake by dawn, but usually she didn't have trouble falling asleep nights. Thoughts of Connor had kept her mind working with questions she wanted to ask him but knew he wouldn't answer. He had been intensely private during the drive. Maybe the challenge of finding out who he was was what intrigued her most.

She watched Connor dig into his saddlebag. He squatted, stretching his pants over his thick thighs and as he leaned over, his shirt pulled taut over his shoulders. Connor's clothes seemed to mold to his body, showing the powerful form that lay under them.

Conscious that her hair most likely looked as tangled as tumbleweed, Lindy ran her fingers through the knots. She searched her bedroll for her hair ribbon, then tied her hair back. After straightening the vest she wore over her blouse, Lindy brushed her skirt smooth, something she wouldn't normally have given a second thought to. Suddenly she stopped. Things that hadn't been so important before now seemed to matter. She had never wanted to set a gleam in a man's eye before, but that was before Connor had ridden into her life.

When Connor turned around, Lindy was caught staring at him. Her face quickly flushed with embarrassment. She grabbed her hat from the ground and plopped it on her head, pulling it down to shade as much of her face as she could.

"Found it," Connor exclaimed. He held up a small burlap sack. "Coffee. Can't start my day without at least two cups."

Lindy looked around. "Where's Luke?"

"I sent him for water."

"I'm surprised he—"

"Left you? He didn't want to, but I tempted him with this." Connor shook the sack. "It was either get the water or wait for tea, and Luke sorely wanted coffee."

"Luke could have waited. It won't take much longer to get to Broken Gate."

"But he wanted coffee and so do I," Connor said firmly, so firmly it made Lindy take notice. Had he expected her to come back with an argument? She didn't like getting the impression that he was in charge, even if it was just from the tone of his voice.

By the time Luke had returned with water, the buck-board had been packed and Connor had started a small fire. Lindy watched as he poured water and ground coffee into a small pot. She hadn't minded the smell when the steam from the simmering brown liquid permeated the air, but when the taste of it was in her mouth she couldn't help wrinkling her face. Connor watched her reaction and smiled into his cup.

Lindy knew Luke didn't like the drink any better, so she was more than a little surprised when he accepted a second cup.

"What do you think?" Connor asked Luke while he poured the steaming liquid.

"Good."

Lindy looked up from her tin cup. Her eyes dashed from Luke to Connor.

"I can tell you've got a man's taste, Luke." Connor winked at Lindy's gracefully arched brow. "Tea's more for the delicate palate."

Lindy witnessed Luke's animosity toward Connor mi-raculously soften over a mere cup of coffee. It appeared Connor's talent for taming didn't only apply to Shetland sheepdogs. She sent Luke a promising smile. "I'll have to make sure I offer you coffee in the morning from now on. Since you have *a man's taste* you'll probably be wanting coffee at teatime also."

"Perhaps not twice a day," Luke said carefully, not wanting to give Connor the impression he had a weak stomach.

"Honestly." Lindy emphasized the word for Luke's ben-efit. "I doubt I could get used to the drink." She handed her full cup back to Connor. "Thanks for the taste."

Connor kicked apart the small burning sticks and poured what coffee remained over the fire. The embers sizzled and died under a cloud of smoke.

Luke took his turn driving the buckboard while Lindy rode the rest of the way to Broken Gate on horseback. It felt good not to have her bones nearly rattled loose and her bottom pounded by the rough ride over ruts, stones and badger holes. The best part was that she got to ride alongside Connor.

For a while Lindy kept silent, her eyes lingering on the woolly backs of her sheep. She thought of her ranch and was reminded of all the work ahead of her and Luke. Only two pairs of hands for all that work. A stock pen needed to be built, and so did a bunkhouse for the hands she would later need, and corrals for horses, another barn and perhaps a windmill.

Her eyes drifted to Connor. "Mr. O'Malley, do you believe in divine providence?"

Lindy's question interrupted Connor's peaceful ride. "I'm not a religious man, Mrs. Rigby."

"Just when I thought none of my plans were ever going to work out, the knots in my life started to unravel. You came and fixed my door, my jumbucks arrived, and here you are helping us back to Broken Gate. Divine providence."

Connor chuckled. "I was passing through. Pure luck."

"Maybe." Lindy lifted her chin and cocked her head to one side. "Maybe I'll keep getting lucky."

Lindy pressed her heels into her horse's side and trotted off. Her hat bounced down off her head to her shoulders. A mane of tawny hair flew out behind her and the split skirt she wore flapped around her legs. To Connor, she had the spirit of a wild horse and was as exciting to look at as the untamed country they traveled.

He watched her backside bounce in the saddle and admired her legs wrapped around the sides of her horse. The thought of making love with her came to him. Her bare thighs wrapped around him, the soft, most intimate part of her on his stomach; all of her set before his appreciative gaze and touch. Connor knew that getting involved with Mrs. Rigby would be like playing with a scorpion. But she was everything a man would find hard to resist, especially a lonely man; one who had been on the trail for a long time trying desperately to forget his past; one who would be easily tempted to forget that past tangled in the arms and legs of a beautiful and alive woman such as Mrs. Rigby. She was wholesome, intelligent, sweet—a challenge to communicate with.

Despite himself, Connor grinned, but the half smile faded when the face of his dead wife returned to haunt him. He remembered the charred remains of his Maryland home. There hadn't been anything left of her or their son to bury, so he carried them in his heart: two souls he could not put to rest. With their deaths, it was as though he had been turned to ash and scattered to the wind, to drift wherever fate would carry him in a frantic attempt to forget that he had not been there when they needed him the most. When he caught himself caring just a little about someone, he began his retreat. And he was beginning to care about Lindy—thinking about how she would run a small ranch with only her brother to help, the dangers she would face from animals, the sometimes violent weather, the cattlemen who would soon be riding out to her ranch with their petitions. She needed someone she could depend upon to protect her, someone who was not afraid to gamble with his heart. But he had already given up his heart once and had lost it.

Connor recognized the lone cottonwood and the sudden growth of tall grass around it and knew they were close to Broken Gate. Close enough that Lindy and Luke could make the rest of the way by themselves. There wouldn't be any danger of coyotes now, and his recent thoughts had made him anxious to get on his way, so he was not prepared for the sudden rearing of his horse.

"Ho!" Connor gripped the horse with his knees and fought to calm her before he was unseated. Luke stood up in the buckboard, and Lindy turned her mount toward the commotion.

By the time Connor had settled his horse, Lindy had ridden back to him. "What is it?" she asked breathlessly.

Connor patted his mare's neck and murmured soothing words to the nervous animal. "A rattler. I think I heard it, but my—I wasn't paying attention," he snapped at Lindy.

Connor dismounted and ran his hands over each of the mare's legs.

"You should pay more attention, then," Lindy said sharply, piqued from the accusation in his tone.

Connor patted Jester's side. "She's fine. If we looked around in the grass we'd probably find a headless rattler." Connor mounted again and cast his eyes down on Lindy. "It's not far now. Good luck with your...station." He tossed up the flap of his saddlebag, reached in and pulled out the burlap sack of coffee. Reaching down to Luke, Connor placed it in the boy's hands. "Make sure your sister makes you two cups every morning."

Luke beamed at Connor's friendly wink. "Thanks, Mr. O'Malley."

The crisis over, Connor offered a bare trace of a smile and a tip of his hat to Lindy. "Ma'am, I hope your luck continues."

Connor turned his horse away but he did not get far before he sensed Jester's irregular gait. For some odd reason, his next thought came like the peal of a church bell—divine providence she had said. "Luck," he mumbled to himself. Luck was with someone and it wasn't with him. He swung from his saddle again and led his horse back to Lindy and Luke.

"The rattler?" Lindy worried aloud.

"Indirectly. Jester's weight must have come down on one leg. I hope she stomped the damn snake to bits, because it's going to hold me up a few days. It looks as though your luck is still holding out. Have you ever considered playing poker?"

Very matter-of-factly, as though she wasn't thrilled with the prospect of having him trail along with them, Lindy answered, "I'd accept help in exchange for room and board. There's a stock pen waiting to be built."

In the bright sparkle of her eyes, Connor saw the elation he was certain she tried to conceal. "I'm sure you would, Mrs. Rigby."

Connor kept an eye on Lindy while he tied his horse to the back of the buckboard. As he suspected, it didn't take long for her smile to finally show. She wasn't smiling at anything in particular, so he knew it had to be her thoughts that made her happy.

"Does your sister always get what she wants?" he asked Luke.

Luke thought for a minute before answering. "I know she said she'd like some of that smelly soap from France, but she's never bought any. So I guess I'd have to say, no."

Luke's answer wasn't exactly what Connor had expected, but then, he had already formed his own conclusions about Lindy—she seemed to have better luck than a cardsharper, or did everything neatly fall into her hands according to her plan? Like a fool, he had agreed to help her with her jumbucks without even thinking to ask what they were. He suspected she had known he had no idea what a jumbuck was and had used his ignorance of her jargon to engage his help. Then the rattler. He had to concede that hadn't been her fault, but the incident had certainly played well into her hands. Now he was on his way back to her farm with the agreement that he'd build her a stock pen. Connor felt the small annoyance snowball inside him. Divine providence! The next request she made of him was going to be met with a resounding no.

It wasn't long after they had arrived at Broken Gate that Connor got his chance.

"Do you mean to tell me that you don't have another pair of strides?" Lindy asked in horror and disbelief.

When he said he had left everything back East he had been serious. His wardrobe of gentleman's clothes had been reduced to cinders by the time he returned to Holly Hill. There had been no reason to replace them once he made his decision to leave his home behind. Apparently Lindy felt it hard to believe that he could make do with one pair of pants.

"Mrs. Rigby, till this moment, I haven't had anyone question me about the size of my wardrobe. I don't see a need for more than one pair of pants."

"But how do you wash them?"

"In a stream, or, if need be, on my back."

Lindy returned to her original question. "I'm going to wash tomorrow. Will I see your clothes out here or not?"

Now Connor was growing annoyed. "I'm beginning your stock pen tomorrow. Are you suggesting I do it in the nude? Because if you are, I'm bound to get a devil of a sunburn."

Lindy's face turned the color of brick. Connor didn't care if it was anger or embarrassment tinting Lindy's face with such a shade of red—his point had been made. Luke, who had been listening, exploded with laughter.

Lindy cast her brother a scalding look. It wasn't enough to calm her brother, but he wisely left their presence.

"Have it your way, Mr. O'Malley." Defeated, Lindy spun around on her heel and sought shelter in the house.

Connor likewise turned on his heel, but slowly. He checked on Jester again, happy for the dark solitude of the barn. Thinking about the shock on Lindy's face made him grin. He thought it must have been a long time since she had heard anyone refuse one of her demands. It made him think about the kind of man she had married. Had her husband kowtowed to all of her wishes, or was she just enjoying a sudden freedom from a man who had made all of the decisions? Regardless, there were certain things a woman was not going to tell him, especially one he wasn't married to.

* * *

After leaving Connor, Lindy pulled Luke into the house. There was an important matter to be settled that could not wait.

"I'm sorry, Lin," Luke said before his sister had a chance to speak. "I know it was rude. I shouldn't have laughed like I did, but Connor—"

Lindy crossed her arms over her chest and narrowed her eyes on Luke. "You mean Mr. O'Malley. Forget about his clothes. If he wants to wear dusty strides till they're stiff as barn boards, then I suppose that's his business. I wanted to talk to you about something much more important. Where is it?"

"What?"

"Hank's gun. What have you done with it?"

"I—"

"Do you realize what a jolt it gave my heart to see you pointing that thing at Mr. O'Malley? It should have been buried with Hank."

"A gun like that?" Luke's voice rose. "Burying such a fine weapon would have been close to sacrilege."

"What if the sheriff or Jeb came by and saw it? Jeb would be bound to recognize it. Having that thing in our possession could get me hung."

Luke's eyes were downcast. "I didn't think of that." He looked up hopefully. "What if we hide it until Hank's forgotten, until Jeb's gone?"

Lindy paused with indecision. She turned around and walked to the stove, and then back to the table. She sat down and sighed. "I don't know why you'd want it. There are places I could hide the gun. But you're first going to promise never to touch it again unless absolutely necessary."

"I swear. Lin, I won't touch it again."

"All right, get the gun. I don't want to see it in your hands after today."

Lindy took the pearl handle in her hand. It had a smooth, silky feel to it. As her fingers curled around the butt she wondered how many men Hank had killed with it or whom he had killed to own it.

"You're never to touch this without my permission," Lindy reminded Luke, then rolled the weapon inside the serape at the foot of her bed. She wouldn't need that blanket until winter. And if she was lucky, they'd never need Hank's gun.

Chapter Five

Connor woke up to the smell of coffee. At first he forgot where he was. Then he remembered.

Propping himself up on his elbows, he looked around Luke's room. The night before, Luke had graciously given him his bed, stating that the band needed watching. After Connor lost the battle over where he would sleep, in the barn or in the house, he had reluctantly agreed to spend the night in Luke's bed. It was either that or get no sleep by debating the issue with Lindy. Still, a nice soft pile of hay near his horse would have been preferable to the strain of being alone in the house with a pretty woman only a step away.

Daylight revealed a room that was simply furnished and bright with color. A serape of orange, red, black and yellow stripes was folded over the foot of Luke's bed. A pair of breeches hung over a ladder-back chair. Long underwear and a shirt descended from pegs along a whitewashed wall. Connor's shirt and pants hung next to Luke's. When he looked upon Luke's extra clothes, Connor was reminded of Lindy's insistence on washing his. It made him self-conscious enough to sniff at his shirt.

"I don't see why she's made such a fuss," he grumbled. It had been less than a week since he gave them a good rinse in a riverbed. Granted it wasn't the same as when his clothes had been laundered and pressed for him, but those were bygone days, a time in his past a part of him wanted to forget.

Thinking of Lindy laundering his clothes was all too reminiscent of the family life-style he had had and lost. The whole reason he kept moving on was to avoid the blind trust women tended to put in him. On the surface, Lindy seemed safe enough. She was married and at least tried to be independent, despite the odds her sex threw against her. Still, where was her husband? Had he deserted her? Did Lindy view himself as her savior? The thought put a knot in his stomach. He was only responsible for Connor O'Malley; he was not going to fall into the trap of caring for the woman and her brother. Broken Gate was not the end of his journey. He had not left Maryland in search of a woman to take his wife's place in his heart, or a boy to make him forget his son.

Connor shoved his arm through one sleeve and then the other. Buttoning up the shirt, he grumbled to himself, "Females think you need to smell like a flower."

After tucking in his shirt, Connor sat on the edge of Luke's bed and pulled on his boots. The beckoning aroma of coffee and biscuits put him in a better mood. He stopped short in the doorway of Luke's room where he had a view of the combination kitchen and sitting room. His eyes swept by the long table set with graniteware. A wildflower bobbed its head from a used tonic bottle placed in the center of the table. A sense of culture peeked through the ruggedness of the house. Bone china and flowers shared space with iron pans and tin plates, and crocheted lace-edged doilies were draped over hand-hewn shelves; an elegant past exchanged for life on the frontier. What had taken Lindy away from a world of china cups and silver spoons? Certainly her husband hadn't dragged her away. Her father perhaps? These were ridiculous questions. He couldn't imagine anyone dragging Lindy away from something she wanted.

In the empty house, Connor's curiosity became as persistent and as nagging as his hunger. Trying to ignore it was impossible when his senses were touched by every aspect of Lindy's life.

Her room was a scant two steps to the right of Luke's. Connor was drawn to it. At first, he just stood in the doorway, visually collecting all the clues he could about Lindy Rigby. Here were her treasures, small windows to who she was. The bed she slept alone in was small but wide enough for two. Other than the size of the bed Connor didn't see anything that would indicate she had a husband. Under the window a small doily-covered table supported a double-globe oil lamp. Light shot through the ruby glass globes, scattering shards of yellow, orange and red gems of light over a white quilt. Next to the lamp a photo in hues of warm brown caught his attention. Entering the room, Connor walked over to it. The tapping of his boots against the floor was the only sound in the house. Connor picked up the oval brass frame and studied the picture of a mustached man who stared out from a moment frozen in time. It wasn't Mr. Rigby, that Connor was sure of—the resemblance to Luke was too obvious in the nose and eyes. The photo had to be that of Luke and Lindy's father. Again, questions came to him. What happened to Lawrence Falen and why was Lindy left alone, seemingly abandoned by her father and husband?

After putting down the frame carefully, Connor walked over to the bed. Unlike Luke's functional bed of pine with its straw-filled tick to rest on, Lindy's was of dark walnut. Though nicked and deeply scratched from its travels, it richly cradled a thick mattress. Connor suspected both had been passed down through generations. A doll rested at its head and a serape was rolled at its foot. A beloved father and a childhood treasure. Strangest of all, of the mementos that had been brought from Australia, none was of Lindy's husband. His curiosity stoked even more, Connor left the room. He was standing just outside it when Lindy entered the house.

Her arm was looped through a wire basket of eggs. She greeted Connor with a warm smile that set the gold flecks in her eyes to glitter. At that early hour, light streamed through every window, filling the house with sunshine, turning her hair to a light honey color. "Good morning. The chooks have delivered your breakfast," she announced, proudly hailing him with the basket.

"After yesterday I dare not assume you mean hens," Connor teased.

Lindy laughed. "I promise you they are what you think they are. Fresh eggs from my *hens*. How would you like them?"

"I'll leave that to you while I check on my horse."

"I already did," Lindy said quickly and immediately began cracking eggs into a bowl, keeping her back to Connor.

"Did what?"

"Checked on your horse. I gave it a bucket of oats. It's foreleg is still a bit swollen. I didn't think you'd mind."

Lindy furiously whipped the eggs into a frothy mixture.

Connor sat down reluctantly. He didn't know whether to rebuke his hostess for taking it upon herself to tend his horse or to keep his mouth firmly closed, lest he say something to set the day off on an uneven keel.

While he watched Lindy's back, he drummed his fingers on the table. No, he didn't suppose anyone could have sent her out here against her will. She was the most willful woman he had ever met. She was certainly nothing like his wife. Christa had been delicate in appearance like Lindy, but there the resemblance ended. Christa would never have touched a rifle. Perhaps, if she had, she would be alive and he would be living at Holly Hill instead of sitting at Lindy's table contemplating the differences between the two women.

Lindy leaned over the oven, clearly avoiding eye contact with him. One hand held the door open, the other wrapped a folded towel over the edge of a pan. A long braid of straw-colored hair snaked down her back, nearly touching the bow of her apron. When she turned around, her face was rosy from the heat the oven had thrown into the room. Short pieces of hair curled at her damp forehead. Her dress clung to her skin and hung in limp folds over her hips like petals of a wilted flower. There wasn't a hint in her expression that suggested she had noticed Connor was unhappy.

"Aren't you and Luke joining me?" Connor asked when he noticed his was the only plate set on the table.

"We ate already. I like to get as much done as I can in the cooler part of the day."

While Connor sat, thoughtfully silent, Lindy bustled about him, spooning scrambled eggs onto his plate, setting biscuits on the side, and next to that a jar of honey. Then she returned to the stove for the coffeepot. Steam wafted from its stained spout as she filled Connor's cup. "All the lumber is behind the barn where my father left it. Luke can help you find whatever else you'll need," she said.

Connor thought it odd that Lindy spoke more of her father than of her husband. He was gaining the impression that the elusive Mr. Rigby was hardly missed, and even toyed with the possibility that Lindy might have fled from the man.

"You live here long with your father?"

Connor's eyes met hers. She seemed to search his face for a sign of trust. Connor slid his fork under his eggs, aware he had touched on a sensitive subject. "You don't have to tell me if you don't want to. It really is none of my business."

"I don't mind—in fact, I'd like to tell you. It all seems like a mystery to me, lacking so much in details. My father had already been buried when Luke and I arrived. Sheriff Hayes told us Indians had killed him. That's all we know."

Connor immediately doubted the story Lindy had been told. He knew if Indians had killed her father, Broken Gate would have been nothing more than a pile of ashes. "You say the sheriff found your father?"

"No. One of Claxton's stockmen buried him, and then when the man reached Dry Bed, he told the sheriff. Sheriff Hayes then came out with the preacher and marked the grave. That was three months before Luke and I arrived."

"Your father had been expecting you, then."

"At some time he was. How's your breakfast?" Lindy asked, after setting down the coffeepot.

Connor's fork paused over his plate. "Very nice, but unnecessary."

When Connor looked as if he was about to ask another question about her father or her imaginary husband, Lindy turned the course of their conversation to the day ahead. "I wouldn't think of sending you out of the house to do a full day's work on an empty stomach."

"This certainly will keep me going until tonight."

"You mean until noon. Lunch is at noon. Tea and biscuits at three." Lindy smiled at Connor's astonished face.

"I won't be getting much done with all those breaks."

"You can't work while the sun is directly overhead," Lindy stated as though she had just settled the matter.

Connor lifted his eyes from his plate. "I can and I will if the stock pen is to get done by the week's end." His tone was just as firm. He was going to set his own schedule and that was that. The sooner he got the stock pen built, the sooner he would be able to leave Broken Gate. He had an unsettling feeling that the longer he stayed, the more Lindy was going to find for him to do. Of all the women he had met in his travels, he knew Lindy was not one he wanted to become indebted to.

Connor gulped his coffee. Instead of the taste he was accustomed to, a very bland flavor, hardly resembling coffee at all, washed over his tongue. Surprised, Connor asked, "What do you call this?"

Lindy's eyes were wide and seemed to swirl with color. She was obviously perplexed. "It's coffee."

"This isn't coffee, it's—" Connor became silent when he saw the hurt look on Lindy's face. Here she had tried to please him and he had acted unappreciatively. Annoyed with himself, Connor pushed back his chair and stepped over to her. With one finger, he brushed a loose strand of hair back from her face. His eyes poised on her lips. He felt suddenly drawn to her. Break away before you sink into the mire of caring, his conscience warned.

"I'll show you how to make coffee," Connor said. Taking the pot from the stove, he added, "I thought you said your husband drank coffee."

"Yes," Lindy said quickly. "He often made it himself, but I never paid much attention."

"Well, pay attention this time," Connor said good-naturedly. "We'll start from the beginning." He held the door open for her.

Lindy followed Connor out to the jack pump, where he cranked the handle up and down until the well delivered close-to-clear water. Back in the house, he measured rounded spoonfuls of coffee into the pot, and then set it on the flame.

"Now listen for it to boil and then time it for ten minutes. I like my coffee dark and near thick as molasses, not like water in a trough."

"Thick as molasses," Lindy repeated.

Connor's lips turned up into a tease of a smile. "Now don't take your eyes off my coffee."

Lindy lifted the lid to the coffeepot at least four times to check the color of the brew. When it was a deep, steaming brown, she poured it into two cups and took them out to where Connor and Luke stood at the corner of the barn. On the way she paused to watch them together, her attention focused on Connor. She was already plotting how she could keep him at Broken Gate. He made it clear that he didn't want to stay for very long, that he was not the kind to put down roots. He also didn't seem the type to put much store in dreams. What did he call it? Chasing rainbows. Like her father, she was definitely a rainbow chaser, always hoping for something better, knowing that if she could just hold on and follow her rainbow to its end, she would find a pot filled with more than gold. At the end of her rainbow waited the culmination of all her hopes and dreams: a life blessed with love and family. Her gaze admired Connor's physical strength. A man who looked like that and carried such an air of confidence about him was just what she needed to help her find her rainbow's end.

With her mind set on convincing Connor to stay indefinitely at Broken Gate, Lindy walked over to him. He had been discussing with Luke where he thought the stock pen should be. With Luke's help, Connor had found a shovel, a saw and a posthole digger. They had also dragged out a good supply of rails and were ready to begin work.

"What do you think, Lin?" Luke asked, pointing out a location to the far side of the barn.

Lindy handed her brother and Connor hot cups of coffee. "I think it's just where Father would have built it."

Luke and Connor simultaneously took their first sips. Lindy waited anxiously for Connor's praises. Instead, both he and Luke spit out a brown spray of the brew.

"Lord, Lin, what are you trying to do? Poison us?" Luke gasped, and choked dramatically. Lindy felt her face flush warmly. Connor wiped the back of his hand across his mouth in an unsuccessful attempt to hide his smile.

Lindy was frantic. She looked to Connor. "What's wrong? It's the right color. It looks thick as mud."

"Right color, wrong texture. You forgot to let the grounds settle."

Lindy flattened her palms on the curves of her hips. "You didn't tell me that. All you said was—"

A sudden pounding of hooves, high-pitched whoops and a frantic sheepdog darting around panicking sheep ended Connor's fun. All three watched as two riders cut through the band with obvious intent to disperse the animals. They quirted their horses and shouted war cries while they systematically destroyed the calm that had existed at Broken Gate.

When Luke made a move, Connor grabbed his shirtsleeve. "Leave them. They can be gathered up later."

Lindy's urge to stop the men was difficult to keep under control. She knew Connor was right—it wouldn't do much good to try and recoup order when two lunatics on horseback were chasing her sheep. Her breath caught in her throat when she realized one of the riders was Jeb Cobb. Lindy's heart immediately began to thump and her stomach lurched. She closed her eyes and gripped Luke's hand in hers. It wasn't until the thunder stopped that Lindy dared to search the yellow cloud of dust for Jeb and his partner.

Lindy quickly measured Connor's reaction, fearing she'd soon be asked to explain more than she could or wanted to.

"Those sure are skittish critters," Jeb said, exchanging a pleased smile with his friend.

Connor's resolve to keep out of Lindy's trouble began to dissipate. "No more skittish than cattle."

Jeb's eyes searched Connor from the crown of his hat to the tip of his dusty boots.

"What is it you want?" Lindy asked, choking back a mouthful of dust. She hoped to get rid of Jeb as quickly as she could.

The leather of Jeb's saddle creaked when he moved. He looked at Connor when he spoke, etching the newcomer's face in his memory. "Nothin' I want. It's Claxton who wants you." Jeb looked down on Lindy, sending shivers up her back. "Wants to talk to you soon. He'll be in town tomorrow."

"Tell Mr. Claxton that I'll be needing the day to round up the band you so effectively scattered."

Jeb's color deepened. "He'll be expectin' you anyway."

"Then he'll be disappointed, won't he? And it will be up to you or your friend to tell Mr. Claxton why I won't be able to take him up on his invitation."

"Maybe if you help the lady gather up her sheep she might change her mind," Connor added dryly.

"I ain't no shepherd," Jeb said. He spat on the ground at their feet. "You best be there, lady, or..." He looked to Connor and warned, "If I were you, I'd be careful of that lady." Jeb yanked the reins across his horse's neck and gave the animal a sharp jab with his spur. The horse instantly turned and galloped away. Jeb's companion followed, sending dirt and pebbles flying into their already dust-covered faces.

Lindy sensed Connor was looking at her. She glanced at him quickly, then turned away, hoping to discourage any questions about the incident. Connor didn't have a question—only a statement. "I tried to tell you most cattlemen don't like sheep. And it sure seems Mr. Claxton is like most cattlemen."

"Well, they're just going to have to get used to seeing my jumbucks, because no one is going to frighten me into changing my mind about building a station here, especially that Englishman and his rowdy bunch of bushrangers."

"They can make life awfully miserable for you, knowing you're alone without a man to protect you."

"I'm not alone now," she said, charming him with a smile before setting off to join Luke and Buddy in the search for her sheep.

Connor stepped quickly to keep up with Lindy's determined strides. What did she think she was up to, assuming that he was here to stay? "Now hold on, Mrs. Rigby. I never said I'd take up your fight with these cattlemen."

"But you did defend me. I liked the way you suggested to that awful man that he help gather up my band. Did you see his face?"

"I saw his face. It had murder written all over it—yours and mine. Stop thanking me for nothing and quit smiling at me like that."

"Like what?"

"Like you're sure I'm going to take up your cause, which, by the way, is a crazy one and one that's likely to get you hurt. I know about men like them—they like to prey on the helpless."

"I'm not helpless."

"How could I forget what I'm dealing with here? A pig-headed, mulish woman in iron breeches."

"I beg your pardon?"

"You understand exactly what I mean and don't pretend otherwise. These men are going to play with you and then—" Connor detected a glassy look in her eyes. He suddenly felt oafish at upsetting her with his blunt talk. No matter what she said, she was still a woman with soft insides. "I'm sorry. I just don't want you to misunderstand me. I can't stay long." He looked over to where the lumber lay. "I'd best get back to your corral."

"Are you going, Lin?" Luke asked as he and Lindy watched Buddy move one ewe back into the band. The sheepdog ran off to another ewe hiding in a twisted crop of chaparral and nipped at the air behind its legs until it bolted into the quickly assembling band.

"Of course not." Lindy whistled another command for Buddy.

"Aren't you wondering what Mr. Claxton wants?"

"He sent Jeb. Any blind Freddy can see that Mr. Claxton isn't just being a friendly neighbor. We've been here six months. If he was such a good neighbor he'd have made a gesture of welcome long ago."

Lindy guessed at the reason Clay Claxton wanted to see her. Whatever it was, she was going to be cautious. She didn't agree with Connor that all the fuss was over little more than a hundred sheep when Claxton had thousands of heads of cattle. There had to be another reason. Perhaps Jeb was setting a trap, hoping to catch her alone. These thoughts were still troubling Lindy when she rode back to the farmyard.

With her head down and her mind distracted, she dismounted and walked her horse over to Connor. Looking up from the ground, she gasped. Connor's shirt hung over a post instead of his back. All of his skin, right down to the waistband of his pants, was exposed. In that shocked instant she saw the form that had only been suggested under his shirt. He was tan, muscled everywhere and glistening with the sweat of his labor. The sight of him nearly took her breath away. Except for a pale scar running down his side, Connor was as perfect as she could imagine.

He looked up from the hole he was digging. "Find them all?"

Lindy hardly heard Connor. She was still gaping at him when he stopped digging and stared at her.

Connor rested on his shovel while he waited for Lindy's answer; a lazy grin crossed his face, making her even more uncomfortable. "Your jumbucks? Find them all?"

Lindy suddenly came out of her stupor. "They're all accounted for."

"Good."

Looking to the sky, Lindy wished she were anywhere but beside him. Anything so as not to have to look at his naked torso. Her eyes were turned skyward for so long, Connor finally asked, "See anything?"

Lindy didn't have to see herself to know her face had turned a shade deeper than its usual color.

"Surely I'm not the first man you've seen without a shirt. Luke must have had his shirt off once or twice."

"Luke's my brother." And he certainly doesn't look anything like you, Lindy thought, swiping Connor's shirt from the post. "As long as you're not wearing it, I may as well wash it," she said, gathering up some of her lost dignity.

"Suit yourself." Connor hammered another nail. The muscles in his arms seemed to explode with strength. Beyond helping herself, Lindy sucked in her breath and admired the flexing muscles that bound his arms and chest.

Connor stopped his hammer in midair and regarded her interest with twinkling blue eyes. "Is there something else you want?" He looked down to his pants, and her eyes automatically followed his.

Lindy gasped at his insinuation that she was waiting for him to remove his pants, too. "Heavens, no! I—I—" she stuttered and reached for some sensible thing to say. But there was no graceful way around it—she had been caught staring at him in a very unladylike manner. Finally she pointed to the fence in progress and said, "I think, for a little more support, you might try putting a nail here."

Connor wiped the back of his hand over his sweaty forehead and grinned. "I certainly thank you for pointing that out."

Lindy nodded and quickly made her retreat.

Clay Claxton had been working over a leather-bound ledger when Jeb and Frank entered his office. From the looks on their faces, he knew something had gone wrong. Claxton calmly listened to Jeb's account of their visit with Lindy. Since settling in Texas, Claxton had become accustomed to having things go his way, so it was annoying to him that Lindy had refused his invitation. Yet it almost amused him that a woman promised to be a burr in his side, and ironically, the daughter of Lawrence Falen at that. Claxton picked up the twelve-inch bowie knife that lay next to his hand. Jeb and Frank immediately tensed. Aware of their discomfort, Claxton considered the blade a while before scooping up an orange from the bowl on his desk. He made a thin slice in the skin, then looked up at Jeb.

"It must have been your methods," Claxton decided. "A woman takes more patient persuasion than either one of you could muster up in your whole life. It's not Lawrence Falen we're dealing with anymore. We have to be very careful with this one. Jeb, you know your uncle has a soft spot about the way women are treated. I'd think you would have been more careful, instead of charging in there like a bull."

Jeb unconsciously took a step back to the door while still keeping a nervous eye on Clay's hands.

Claxton pulled apart the orange. "I don't want you to go near Broken Gate. I'll ride out there myself tomorrow. If the lady won't come to me, then I'll go to her."

Chapter Six

From over the top of a basket of wet clothes, Lindy watched the approach of a black circuit rider. The usual red flag of caution that had always accompanied an unexpected visit had failed to raise an alarm until she saw Clay Claxton rein in the silky black steed. At the sight of the stocky man she was immediately put on her guard. Once his thickset legs were planted on her land, she felt a familiar wave of possessiveness race up her spine. Lindy dropped the basket of laundry under three rows of clothesline.

Before acknowledging Lindy, Claxton measured Connor with sharp, black eyes, then his gaze found her again. A smile emerged from the tight line of his lips; however, it failed to soften the granite-hard look in his eyes. Claxton removed his hat respectfully and stepped towards Lindy.

Lindy didn't feel compelled to reach for her rifle because she didn't believe Claxton intended her any harm, at least not while Connor watched from the distance with his rifle within easy reach.

Dressed in black from his boots to the thin tie at his neck, Claxton was a stark figure set against the bright blue sky. Before he left his ranch, Claxton's clothes had gleamed like the feathers of a raven. However, Texas defied spit and polish and eventually covered everything with a film of dust. Lindy knew Claxton's boots must have been rubbed to a shine and that his black hair had been carefully combed back from his forehead. But now his coat and boots were dulled with dust and his thin, straight hair hung in disarray over his forehead. Lindy wasn't impressed with Claxton's efforts; she sensed he was just as ruthless as Jeb, only dressed better for the occasion.

When Claxton's jacket flew open with his quick walk, Lindy didn't only notice the blue threads shimmering from the paisley-print vest underneath or the glittering gold chain of his pocket watch. All too obvious, the butt of a gun stuck out from the finery. It was intimidating, but then it wouldn't be unusual for Clay Claxton to carry a gun.

"Good afternoon," he said. He held the tight smile on his lips and extended his hand to Lindy. Lindy automatically put her hand in his and introduced herself. She couldn't help but stare at the red scar running from his ear down the side of his neck in a long jagged curve. As if admiring it, Claxton ran his thick fingers along its length. "A gift from a friend," he explained before touching the back of her hand with his lips.

Lindy's mouth came unhinged. "A friend!" A red wave of embarrassment followed her shock. "I am sorry."

Unexpectedly Claxton laughed. "Don't be. I think it gives me a roguish look."

Lindy smiled weakly, wondering how Claxton had survived someone's attempt to slit his throat from ear to ear, yet she was glad when he changed the subject, and spared her the gruesome details.

"I've come to beg your pardon for being so delinquent in welcoming you to Dry Bed," Claxton said smoothly, turning the felt brim of his hat in his hands. "And to apologize for the recklessness of my men. I hope they didn't cause you too much trouble."

"They caused me a lot of trouble, Mr. Claxton."

"Then I hope you'll let me make amends for their stupidity. Friends call me Clay. Since we're neighbors, I don't see a reason for being so formal."

Lindy glanced at Claxton's outstretched hand, then gripped the basket of laundry in both her hands, putting it between them. "I do, Mr. Claxton."

Lindy noted that Claxton was a man of contrasts: charming and threatening, all at the same time. Full, dimpled cheeks seemed a mismatch to his sharp eyes and tightly controlled smile. The formal attire he sported was more suited for city life than life on the range, and his speech was definitely more cultured than she would have expected.

Needing a diversion from the uncomfortable moment, Lindy ducked under the clothesline, dropped her basket and pulled out a shirt. She shook out the wrinkles and pinned it neatly to the line stretched between them, a trick Lindy used whenever she wanted to avoid something was to do something else. In this case, she wanted to avoid looking Claxton in the eye. He had an unsettling way of staring right through a person, giving the impression he could read every unspoken thought.

Claxton turned and looked over his shoulder at Connor. "Your husband wouldn't like that much, I suppose."

It was at that moment Lindy realized the scandal Connor's presence at Broken Gate could stir. In an attempt to hide her concern, she continued to pin up clothes, effectively building a wall between herself and Claxton. She prodded Claxton to get to the point of his visit. "Did you come to borrow a cup of sugar? Or is it eggs you need?" Lindy bent down for another piece of clothing, whipped out the wrinkles and pinned it to the clothesline.

Undaunted, Claxton smiled and tugged on the line between them. "Neither. I thought to ask you to lunch. Tomorrow is your usual day to come into town, and it would be considerably easier talking to you without a clothesline in the way."

Lindy shuddered at the thought of lunching with Claxton. She couldn't help but think of Connor's pessimistic remark that her notion of raising sheep so close to Claxton's land was going to be as popular as picnicking in a patch of prickly pear. "My husband wouldn't like that." She bent down again and, leaving her petticoat at the bottom of the basket, she fished out a bed sheet instead, and added it to the growing line of clothes.

"Your husband's not here to object, is he, Mrs. Rigby?" Claxton asked, too discerning for comfort.

Dread swept through her. She had hoped he thought Connor was her husband. Peering over the line, Lindy asked, "What is it you want?"

"Dear lady, do I detect a note of suspicion?"

Lindy was vexed at having to answer Claxton's question without getting an answer to her own. Instead of accommodating him, she sallied back, "Should I be suspicious, Mr. Claxton?"

The Englishman's smile became more natural. "You strike me as one who would expect nothing less than an honest answer, so I'll be honest." Claxton put his hat on his head and adjusted it to fit. "Meet me for lunch and you can judge for yourself."

Lindy watched him walk back to the circuit rider. Claxton didn't take a step without being sure where it would land, she thought. She was sure he had something else in mind besides a get-to-know-you lunch.

They were nearly out of nails, so Connor accompanied Lindy to Dry Bed while Luke opted to stay at Broken Gate.

Her walking with Connor drew more than one curious look from those who knew Lindy, and when Hester Quinn noticed Connor loading the wagon with supplies, she didn't attempt to hide her interest.

"Well?" she asked Lindy as she watched Connor leave the mercantile with a ten-pound sack of salt pork.

"Well, what?" Lindy tried to sound indifferent to Hester's prying, in fact, she was quite annoyed.

"Are you gonna tell me who that handsome man is and what you're doin' with him?"

"I thought you'd remember him. He's Connor O'Malley...the Yankee. And anyone can see that he's helping me."

Hester started at Lindy's sharp response. "Yes. Now I remember. The one with the gray eyes."

"They look more blue to me."

Hester studied Lindy's face over the top of her glasses. Just as her mouth dropped open to speak, the door slammed behind Connor.

"Thank you, Hester," Lindy said as she hurried out of the mercantile, taking Connor with her. "That sticky beak," she said under her breath.

"Sticky beak? Is that anything like a jumbuck?"

Lindy's heels tapped angrily against the planked walk. "Hester Quinn cannot mind her own business."

"You mean she's a busybody."

"Busier than anybody in Dry Bed."

"And what did she say to get your ire up?"

"Nothing. It's nothing important."

"I think I've gotten to know you better than that. Old Hester Sticky Beak has noticed that you've come to town with an escort other than Luke and had just been wondering who this man might be. Perhaps she even offered advice as to how a married woman should conduct herself. Did she ask if I was sleeping in the barn or in the house?"

"Neither. I didn't let her get that far. And she can just wonder where you're sleeping."

Lindy heard Connor draw a breath. "I don't like the idea that tongues are wagging already. Your husband is bound to hear of me and then draw his own conclusions based on Hester's and everyone else's exaggerations."

Lindy noticed one of Claxton's men leaving Tilly's. Connor was right. She was certainly going to give Hester a wealth of gossip: suddenly showing up in town with him, lunching with Claxton, then leaving again with Connor. She sucked in her breath. It would have been better for her not to have been seen with Connor. Hester was probably making all kinds of assumptions as to what was going on between them. Too late now.

Connor continued, "It won't do your reputation much good if I stay any longer."

Lindy rejoined quickly, "But the stock pen's not finished—you can't leave."

"Luke can manage the rest."

"You said you'd stay—"

"My horse has been ready. I only agreed to stay that long," he reminded her.

"I assumed you'd finish the job." Disappointment weighted Lindy's words.

Connor growled with frustration. "What about your husband? What's he going to think when . . . Hell, I can't help thinking what kind of a husband you have. What sort of a man would send his wife alone to a strange country to wait for him?"

Lindy was beginning to become uncomfortable with her lie. No matter that her story had been contrived for protection, it was growing bigger by the day. "I have no doubt my husband will come to Broken Gate. There are important matters he has to settle first."

Connor stepped in front of Lindy, blocking her way. She tried to walk around him but he held her still. "What can possibly be more important than the love of his wife? If I was your husband I wouldn't—" Connor's voice broke off. Looking down into Lindy's eyes, he struggled with what he wanted to say. "I wouldn't let you out of my sight for a minute," he admitted in a gruff whisper. "I wouldn't risk anyone else touching you like this." Connor placed his hands on her arms and, forgetting they were in view for the whole town to see, pulled her closer.

Lindy lost herself in the depths of Connor's dusky-blue eyes. She rested her palm against his cheek. Connor covered her hand with his and then brought it to his lips. She felt the warm touch of his kiss glide over her fingertips. Her legs wobbled under her skirt like jelly, and she felt as though she would soon melt into a puddle at his feet. For an instant, Lindy imagined Connor was her husband, her lover, her protector, and would always be with her. Even though she hardly knew him, the fantasy warmed her to her toes.

Suddenly realizing they were standing in the middle of the boardwalk with a half dozen pairs of eyes watching them, Lindy backed away and said, "I'm going to be late for lunch."

During the short walk to Tilly's Restaurant Lindy thought about what had transpired between her and Connor. She was sure he was running away from someone—someone or something that drove him on. For now she had stopped him. Lindy placed her fingertips on her lips. They still tingled from Connor's kiss. In that kiss she had felt an admission of desire flow from his lips to hers, and the prospect that Connor O'Malley desired her made her tremble. She thought of his wide hands pulling her up against his chest, the tilt of his head as he bent down to cautiously touch her lips with his, his warm breath against her neck. Her appetite for food suddenly diminished and another sort of hunger began to build in her stomach.

The realization that she desired Connor in such a way came as a shock. Lindy clamped her hand over her mouth. What was she going to do? She was supposed to already be married. A problem of this dimension demanded much thought. When she was finished with lunch, she would give it some more attention, but for now, a more unpleasant problem loomed behind Tilly's front door.

The brass doorknob warmed in Lindy's hand before she gathered enough courage to finally turn it and push the door open. When she did, a shaft of light rushed into the dimly lit room, cutting a bright path across the thick Oriental carpet. Lindy closed the door, chasing away the intruding daylight and returning the dining room to a hushed dimness. Several oil lamps hugged the dark corners with their soft light. Four round tables were covered in crisp, white linen cloths and set with polished silver. The dusty street, which would have reminded Tilly's guests of their otherwise rugged existence, was hidden from view by heavy curtains drawn across the windows.

Once Lindy's eyes had adjusted, finding Claxton was not difficult. Since he was the only patron in the room, she couldn't help wondering if he had insisted upon privacy for their meeting. Lindy swallowed even though her mouth was dry. She navigated around the dining tables to where Claxton stood to greet her.

"I'm glad you decided to join me. Tilly's prepared a wonderful meal, and it would have been disappointing not to share her talents with someone. Besides, I hate eating alone."

"As you suggested, neighbors should get to know each other," Lindy returned pleasantly. Muffled footsteps came up behind her. Lindy smiled at Tilly while the lanky woman set a pitcher of water and a pair of glasses on the table. Lindy reached for her water glass as soon as it was filled and wet her dry throat.

"I feel lucky to have a woman sitting across from me today instead of her husband," Claxton said.

"I'm sure my husband will want to meet you also, but he's—"

"I know."

"You do?"

Claxton nodded and returned to what really concerned him. "You have about a hundred woollies grazing on your land."

"One hundred fifty if you want an exact count."

"There isn't much future for that kind of ranching in Texas," Claxton said, taking a sip of his water.

"Why not? My jumbucks can survive on less water than cattle and will eat what your longhorns won't touch. I think there's a better future for them in Texas than cattle." While casually buttering a piece of bread, Lindy failed to notice Claxton's mask of pleasantness quickly turn sour.

Anyone who knew Claxton would not have believed the measure of control he managed to sustain through their conversation. Though somewhat strained, his smile returned. "You're a pretty woman. Why would someone like you want to ranch? You're stuck out there all by yourself. You shouldn't be scratching in the dirt like a hen. You're wasting your life. You'll be old and haggard in a year."

"I'm not wasting my life. I'm building one, just like you are."

"But you're a woman. What do you know about ranching?"

"I grew up on a station. In fact, I ran it when my father left. I know the perils and pitfalls. We had our share of wild dogs, drought, and bushrangers."

"Your creatures will eat everything but the dirt, leaving nothing for the cattle . . . my cattle."

"My animals will graze on what your cattle leave behind."

"What if they get to the good grazing land first?"

Lindy sampled her soup. "This is rather good," she commented, noticing Claxton had not tried his. "I've done some research, Mr. Claxton. Your animals pull the grass up by its roots, destroying the plant; mine simply cut the grass and leave the roots unharmed. The pasture my animals graze will return—yours will not. I should worry about *your* animals."

"Forget sheep. Cattle makes much more sense in dollars. In the north they're selling for forty dollars a head. If you insist on this silly notion of ranching I can set you up with a few head from my own stock."

Lindy had no intention of considering Claxton's offer, but she was curious as to just how far he'd go to change her mind. "That's all very generous, but how'd I get them north to sell them?"

Claxton wove his fingers together and smiled. "Why, I'd drive them up with my own herd. You wouldn't even have to come along. It would be too dangerous for—"

"A silly woman," Lindy said, spinning her spoon between her fingers.

Claxton leaned back in his seat. "There's nothing for you to worry about."

"I don't know anything about cattle, Mr. Claxton."

Claxton reached for her hand. Lindy looked down at the large brown hand twice the size of her own and resisted pulling away. "I'll help you all I can. And that's an offer I wouldn't have made to anyone," he said.

"I'm sure. But there's one problem." Claxton waited, ready to ease any worry she had. "I'm not raising cattle."

Claxton squeezed Lindy's hand hard before he let her pull away, then he turned to sour-faced Tilly and motioned for her to take away their unfinished bowls of soup. "We're ready for the next course now." The woman quickly did as she was bidden.

After Tilly returned to the kitchen, Claxton devoted his attention to Lindy. "Mrs. Rigby, I'm going to be honest, and forgive my straightforwardness. Remember, I've tried to offer you a more acceptable solution to your problem. If you insist on breeding sheep, then I'm letting my men know they're fair game. Had your husband been here instead of yourself, it would have been my first offer, not my last one."

Lindy couldn't hide the indignation that showed on her face or in her voice. "*My* problem! *Game?* Are you telling me you intend to shoot my jumbucks?"

After a moment of hesitation Claxton asked, "Your *sheep?*" He leaned back so Tilly could place a platter of meat in front of him.

Lindy stared down at the plate Tilly placed before her. The dish looked familiar and smelled even more familiar—lamb!

Claxton glanced at his plate. "I suppose that's the meat of my message. Now that that's understood, we can continue with lunch and enjoy more pleasant conversation. You're right, Tilly runs an excellent kitchen for being so far away from civilization. The food *is* truly excellent," he said, holding up a chunk of lamb on the sharp tines of his fork.

Lindy bolted out of her seat and slapped her napkin on the table. Claxton stood up simultaneously. Each challenged the other with a hard look.

"Mr. Claxton, I'm not here for a walkabout. I've come to raise my jumbucks in a free country and I well intend to make a go of it. Now that we've both said what we had intended to say from the start, and we understand each other, I bid you g'day."

Not one to let the last word spout off anyone else's lips, Claxton pointed his fork at her. "Your father also thought he'd raise sheep and look where that got him."

Connor watched the smithy's hammer rebound off the anvil as another nail took shape and was tossed onto the pile that had grown on the dirt floor of the blacksmith's shop. To keep his mind off Lindy and Claxton, he counted each ring of the hammer, but he found that it only reminded him of how long Lindy had been gone. More than once Connor had walked out into the street and had looked down to Tilly's. How long could it take to eat lunch? He felt his muscles tense with worry.

He stepped back into the heat and listened to the clinking of the smithy's hammer, but it failed to drown out the memory of failing someone he had loved. He told himself that Lindy could take care of herself. Even though she didn't have her handy Henry packed in her purse, she'd probably beat Claxton to death with the bag if he tried to harm her. An emerging smile tugged at the corner of his mouth.

"Whatcha doin' with all them nails?" the smithy asked while pumping the bellows. Coal heated to an orange color under their laborious panting.

"Building a corral."

"Mind if I ask where?" Toby checked the glow of the tip of a long, black piece of iron that he had laid in the coals.

"Broken Gate."

Toby smiled, plumping up his shiny cheeks. He wiped his sweaty forehead with the back of his hand, which only smeared more soot across his face. "Nice woman. A little strange, though. It's too bad about her pa. Comin' all this way only to be killed by Comanches." He raised his hammer and pounded another nail. "She hire you?"

"No. Just letting my horse rest a lame leg. Did her father ever mention that he intended raising sheep?"

The smithy's music missed a beat. "He did. And was proud of his plans. Talked about his family too. He couldn't wait until they were all together again. Poor Mrs. Rigby and her brother had to come find him in his grave."

"Had anyone given him trouble?"

"Not that I know of. But there's a lot of folks who don't like woollies, if you know what I mean. I'd sure hate to see anything happen to Mrs. Rigby or Luke." He tossed the last nail on the pile. "There, that should do it."

Propelled by her anger, Lindy nearly sailed into Connor.

"How was lunch?" Connor didn't have to wait long before Lindy started to spill out the details in a jumble of angry Australian.

"He's as flash as a rat with a gold tooth," she said, hoisting herself up onto the seat of the buckboard. "And a common bushranger—despite his fancy clothes."

"I take it lunch didn't go well." Connor sat next to her and took the reins in his hands.

"Tilly makes a beaut of a soup. I wouldn't know about anythin' else. What a mozzie I was. Do you know what the main course was? Lamb! And likely my own. Quite a subtle warning, don't you think?"

Connor found himself smiling as Lindy's accent got thicker. A sudden urge to hold her came over him. Instead, his hands gripped the reins tighter. "I could have told you what to expect, but you wouldn't have listened." Connor dodged her glare and tried to divert the topic to something else. "Toby filled a sack with nails. You'll have some extra."

"Good. Has *he* ever got starch in his strides! He actually thought he could change my mind by giving me cows. And when that didn't work, he served up one of my own jumbucks."

Connor was surprised. "Claxton tried to bargain with you?"

"Tried. I'm not the total mozzie he took me for."

Until they were outside of town, Connor listened to Lindy's account of her conversation with Claxton. Her quick speech was peppered with her native jargon. In context, Connor understood the gist of it. Lindy was angry. Claxton had played her for a fool and she was now more determined than ever to show him otherwise. Connor couldn't help but admire her sand, but, at the same time, couldn't deny the urge to warn her of the dangerous struggle ahead. He stopped the wagon and turned to Lindy.

Lindy wore the same wide-brimmed Mexican hat. It was pushed back but still shaded her face. Her eyes were darker in the shadow, and some light freckles bloomed across her cheeks. Her face was as perfect as a cameo, defined by strong bones, a rich cream and peach complexion and eyes that changed color with her mood as often as a chameleon changed his hue. She had secured her hair at the nape of her neck, and it swept over her shoulder now in a long pony-tail.

"What is it?" Lindy asked, interrupting his admiration of her.

"We should rest the horses," Connor said, though he didn't immediately make a move to leave the wagon.

"Yes, we should do that," Lindy replied, but she also did not move.

Connor placed the palm of his hand against her soft cheek, then moved it down under her chin. Lifting her face, he bent his head and kissed her.

Their lips barely touched at first, timidly exploring, teasing, then melting into a long, lingering kiss. Connor's senses filled with Lindy. Her scent reminded him she was a woman, and that thought in itself sent a warm trail blazing through him. His arms wrapped around her and pulled her close. His kiss was on the edge of becoming more than sweet—of releasing the desire that had been building inside of him. Then as suddenly as it had happened, it ended when his hand touched the gold band on Lindy's finger. Control returned and Connor broke away, looking as perplexed about the incident as Lindy did.

"I think the horses have rested long enough," Connor suddenly announced, knowing that horses had nothing to do with why he had to release her.

Chapter Seven

Connor put his toolbox down and searched the ground for his saw. He thought he had put it in the barn the night before. Another delay. Bracing his hands on his hips, he looked east where the sunrise had begun to paint wide ribbons of orange and gold across the ground. In the distance, a primitive cross marked Lawrence Falen's grave. A feathery green mesquite shadowed the resting place with long, protective arms. Once a day Lindy visited the rocky mound as though it were the well she drew her strength from. While Connor watched with guarded interest, she'd stand on top of the small rise that overlooked the farm. Southwest colors resonant and vibrant as stained glass surrounded her, casting their rich tones over her hair and skin.

Something troubled Connor, and for the moment distracted him from his search. Apaches and Comanches did not generally enter the south Texas triangle. They preferred to stay on the plains where they could follow the bison. For this reason, he suspected Lindy's father had not met his end at the hands of Indians. Mexicans, perhaps, but not Indians. Who had told the sheriff it was Indians, and why? His first suspicion was that Claxton had had a hand in Lawrence Falen's ill fortune. If his guess was correct, then Lindy was living on the edge of disaster. No matter how strong-willed the woman was, she was no match for a man like Claxton.

Connor swore at himself for letting his emotions pull him into a situation he wanted to avoid. Involving himself in a range war was not why he had come out west. He scanned the ground again for the missing saw. Building a stock pen was also not one of his reasons for heading west. All he had wanted to do was find himself a little peace. Instead, he had ridden right into a tangle of wills.

Connor returned to the task of getting his day started. Luke hadn't seen the saw, and Lindy had sworn she didn't know where it was. He remembered he had put it in the barn the night before, but after he checked everywhere the saw was still nowhere to be found. Work on the stock pen could not continue until he had something to cut wood with. One more look in the barn, then if need be, he would resort to using an ax.

As Connor's eyes began to adjust to the dim interior of the barn, he scanned the straw-covered floor once again. It wasn't until he began displacing straw with his boot that he uncovered the missing tool. His first thought was that Lindy had hidden it. Then he laughed at himself. She wanted the stock pen finished as much as he did. The idea of her hiding the saw was absurd—or was it? He was beginning to feel she'd do almost anything to keep him there, and during fleeting moments, when he was bereft of reason, he would imagine staying on just a little while longer. A number of times a day he had to remind himself that she was a married woman and that the way he found himself looking at her was an insult to his wife's memory and to Lindy's innocent trust of him.

Feeling pressed for time, he did not welcome another setback, but teatime was one delay Lindy insisted upon, even though he declined the diversion. When he refused to join her in the house, she had brought a packed basket out to him.

"Your sister's late today," Connor said to Luke, who was presently struggling with the posthole digger.

Luke laughed. "Why don't you humor her today? It would make her happy."

Connor slammed a nail into the wood. "One of us taking a break is enough. Besides, it took me half the morning to find the blasted saw."

"She's much easier to live with if she gets her way."

"So am I," Connor said flatly, making Luke grin.

Lindy walked over with a covered basket and serape hung over her arm. As on the other days, she spread the blanket on the ground near them and unpacked the hamper, and as on the day before, Connor's body tensed.

"Would you care for a cuppa today, Mr. O'Malley?" Lindy's voice was sunny compared to Connor's gruff reply.

"No." Connor stomped off, mumbling something about tea parties and getting more wood.

"Mr. O'Malley is quite short with his temper when he's working," Lindy remarked to her brother, her gaze remaining on Connor until he disappeared behind the barn. "Why do you think that is?"

"I wouldn't care to express my opinion on that," Luke said, grinning at what he refused to tell. "Lin, did you do anything with the saw?"

"I haven't used it if that's what you're asking. Why?"

"Mr. O'Malley said it took half the morning to find it."

"Oh, is that it? I think a little break is what he needs. Then maybe he'd be more chipper." Lindy sipped her tea. "Perhaps he's afraid of not finishing the stock pen. I could help."

"I don't know, Lin…" Luke glanced at Connor, who was rounding the side of the barn, his arms wrapped around a heavy bundle of fencing. "This isn't work for women."

"Luke! I've never heard you say a thing like that before." Lindy looked accusingly at Connor. "Of course I can help," she said, getting up and brushing off her skirt. She gathered up a handful of nails. "I can hand him these."

"As long as you're going to help, you wouldn't mind then if I check on the band, because I don't care to be standing here when you present your offer to Mr. O'Malley."

"Go ahead, coward. Mr. O'Malley and I will be just fine," she said while he hurried away.

Connor dropped the lumber nearly at Lindy's feet. The crashing sound made her jump.

"Where's Luke off to?"

"Back to the band."

Connor settled his eyes on her. "I hope you're not planning on getting underfoot," he commented grimly. "I thought you'd be done with your tea."

"Oh, I am. I'm going to help you." Lindy held out a nail to him and returned his grin.

"You're going to help me?"

Lindy nodded.

Connor's dubious look melted into a wry smile. "All right. It's too hot to argue. I'm not ready for that yet. Do you think you can steady a board over here while I trim it up?"

"Of course."

Connor peeled off his gloves and tossed them to her. "Put these on or you'll get splinters."

Even though her hands swam in Connor's buckskin gloves, making it difficult to get a good handle on the board, Lindy wore them without protest. Following his directions, she braced herself at the opposite end of the board and balanced it on the sawhorses. At his end, Connor moved the saw back and forth. The smell of Texas pine escaped from the plank as the saw's teeth bit deeper into it with each stroke. After a while, the sawed-off piece of board fell to the ground. Holding on to her end, Lindy followed Connor to the fence posts. She kept the board steady while he nailed his end to the post. Once it had been secured, Connor moved down to where Lindy stood. Unintentionally his arm brushed against hers when he took the board from her. He did not expect to feel the shock waves that rolled over his insides.

"I'll have that nail now," Connor said abruptly, holding out his hand.

Lindy pulled off her gloves and handed him the nail. Connor held the nail in his hand a long time before finally setting it into the wood. In silence, Lindy handed him another nail and then another.

Connor put all the strength in his arms and shoulders into his labor while he struggled with the warm feelings she ignited in him. He tried to stay distant; he tried to keep cool and unaffected by the pretty woman standing so close to him. Yet he was unsuccessful in battling the feelings of desire that betrayed his vow to keep Lindy out of his thoughts. For nearly a week he had denied that he wanted to touch her and taste her lips again. Now silently, while driving yet another nail into the fence, he admitted he wanted her in every way. Slowly the ghost of his wife was fading from his memory, and replacing the pale visage were the muddy green eyes, sun-kissed cheeks and full ripe lips of Lindy. Lindy Rigby was so full of life, so real and vulnerable, he couldn't help but want to take her in his arms. He had lain awake nights just imagining what it would be like to bed down with her. Connor had never considered a married woman before. The idea of taking another man's wife had always been unthinkable, but he had thought of doing just that with Lindy.

When the hammer came down on Connor's thumb, the disturbing thought of coveting another man's woman flew out of his head. He considered it a painful delivery of divine justice. A slew of expletives rushed from his mouth as he doubled over and braced his hand between his thighs. Spots of blood spattered the fence and then seeped onto his pants.

"What can I do?" Lindy asked in a strained voice.

"Do you have any spirits?" Connor slid down against the fence post and closed his eyes. He felt the blood drain from his face, his ears ring, and his head spin. Through blurry vision he saw Lindy fairly fly to the house and back again.

"Mr. O'Malley! Oh, my!" Lindy fretted and fussed over him. "Mr. O'Malley?"

When he looked up, Connor saw Lindy kneeling beside him, pouring whiskey into a cup. He took the cup and gulped all of it down. It burned a warm, soothing trail to his stomach. A few more cups and he'd soon feel no pain. With a shaky hand, Lindy filled the cup again. Her eyes widened in surprise when he poured the rest over his finger and then took the bottle.

"What are you doing?" she gasped, staring down at Connor's battered thumb.

"It stings like hell at first, but dulls the pain." Connor guzzled the comforting liquid.

Along with the bottle of whiskey, Lindy had brought a knife and an old petticoat. While Connor drank his "medicine," she systematically ripped a length of fabric and began to tightly wrap his finger.

"I'm glad you're not one to faint at the sight of blood."

"What good would that do? You'd probably bleed to death."

Connor winced as Lindy bandaged his thumb. The white cloth turned pink, then red, as the blood soaked through the first layer of cloth. "I'm surprised your thumb didn't go through the board," Lindy commented, while tying off the bandage.

"I tried," Connor joked. The whiskey he had poured into his empty stomach had begun to take effect. He watched Lindy tear another strip of fabric and forced a smile. "I hope you haven't ruined a good petticoat for me."

Lindy blushed. Avoiding his warm gaze, she concentrated on his hand. While she worked, her plaited hair fell over her shoulder. Connor reached out with his uninjured hand and ran the braid through his fingers. As he did so, the back of his hand brushed against her chest. The soft feel of her breast warmed him even more.

Lindy wrapped another bandage around his finger and the back of his hand. "There, that'll do," she said, then stretched across Connor to take the whiskey bottle from his side.

He grabbed her wrist and pulled her off balance. Even though he was weakened by pain and whiskey, he was able to pull her into his lap. She fell into him, landing hard against his chest.

Lindy's eyes met Connor's. His other arm came around her waist, bracing her against him so closely that he could feel the beat of her heart against his chest. He held her with his arms and his eyes. They were drawn like magnets, each unable to resist the other. In that moment, Connor forgot Lindy had already been claimed and that he wanted nothing to do with her. His wife's memory faded even more with her in his arms. He wanted Lindy, and not for the moment. He wanted her until she quenched the thirst inside him.

Connor closed the gap between them and their lips touched cautiously. He moved his lips over hers in a tender kiss. She waited, absorbed as much as he was in the warm contact of their skin. Connor kissed the corners of her mouth, coaxing her to part her lips, then he claimed them fully with his until Lindy ventured to respond. Connor's head spun. He wondered if it was Lindy's kiss that made him dizzy or the whiskey he had drunk.

Connor no longer had to hold Lindy. She shifted to a more comfortable position. Facing him, she wrapped her arms around his neck and her legs around his thighs. She leaned back and gazed at his face.

"This almost makes pounding my thumb worth it," Connor said. He closed his arms around her waist and pulled her closer.

"Does it hurt much?" Lindy asked, threading her fingers through his hair.

Connor smiled faintly. The pain at the moment was not in his thumb. "I hardly notice it." As if to prove that, Connor covered her mouth again with his. His kiss slowly left her lips. His unshaven face grazed her smooth skin as his mouth traveled across her cheek. He grabbed her earlobe with his teeth, then lightly traced the curves of her ear with the tip of his tongue. Connor felt his body react all at once. It felt as though his blood boiled in his veins. He wanted to know if the same feelings raged in Lindy. He set a burning path of kisses down her neck in search of the pulse point that divulged her secret desire. Satisfied, his lips wandered farther down her neck until his mouth was cradled in the hollow of her throat. Lindy pressed closer, her breasts crushing against his chest as he methodically devoured the sweet taste of her skin.

Lindy brushed her palms against his cheeks. Holding his face in her hands, she kissed him.

The whiskey Connor had downed so quickly and the excitement he felt at Lindy's positive response made him bolder. His hands moved uninhibited from where they rested at Lindy's waist to the curve of her hips. He answered her tender kiss with carnal desire, probing deeply into the dark and wet recesses of her mouth, teasing her tongue with his.

Connor took measure of what lay underneath the yards of gingham and was not disappointed. When his hand moved up her thigh, she pushed away from him, suddenly sitting back on his legs and accidentally catching his injured thumb between her buttocks and his thigh. The pain that shot through Connor was sobering, his howl shattering. Realizing she had hurt him, Lindy flew off Connor's lap.

"I'm sorry. Are you all right?"

Connor winced. "Mrs. Rigby, I . . . I had no right to take such liberty. Right now your husband would be within his rights to shoot me. And it would certainly put me out of my present misery if he did. Dammit, you're a danger to get close to," Connor said as he struggled to stand on unsure legs.

That night, an awkward silence prevailed through supper. Several times Connor opened his mouth to speak and then didn't. Lindy was afraid the incident that afternoon had been disturbing enough to send Connor away before the end of the week. After all, in his eyes she was a married woman and he had seduced another man's wife. Any man with morals would remove himself from further temptation, and a faithful wife would do the same—only she wasn't married.

Lindy didn't want a weak moment shared by both of them to spoil her hopes of convincing Connor to stay. There was so much to be done at Broken Gate. If she admitted to him that she wasn't really married and that she had only meant to protect herself by lying, he wouldn't feel so guilty. No, he'd feel deceived instead, and that wouldn't do, either. Distraught, Lindy hoped a better solution to her problem would come to her in the morning.

Luke looked to his sister and then to Connor. "You two are certainly dangerous together," he finally said, trying to release some of the tension in the room. "I think you ought to stay miles apart."

When Lindy exchanged looks with Connor, she was afraid that was exactly what he was thinking.

Throughout the next day Lindy blamed herself for having weakened under Connor's kiss. Assuring Connor that she had not felt an attraction to him was going to be difficult when every time she looked at him she became tongue-tied and dim-witted.

In pensive solitude, Lindy followed the trail of fleece dotting the sharp branches of chaparral like ripe cotton.

While she tried to work out her newest dilemma, she plucked the fleece balls free and stuffed them into a sack slung over her shoulder. The bits of fluff would be used to fill in the drafty cracks of her house, stuff pillows and perhaps replace the straw in Luke's mattress. In the distance, varied tones of clanging bells softly hailed Lindy's trained ear. From each sound, she knew where the belled sheep were and what they were doing. For now they were safe and contently grazing under the watchful eyes of Luke and Buddy.

Every now and then Lindy looked over to Connor. She had watched him from a distance for most of the day, but hadn't approached him for fear he would tell her what plainly showed on his grim face. He was leaving her. Lindy knew he would not stay, out of respect for her husband.

Once every bush and stick had been cleaned of fleece and there was no longer an excuse to avoid Connor, Lindy straightened and marched off to face him. Her only ammunition was an apology for her behavior.

When Lindy returned to the farmyard, Connor was nowhere to be found. The area around the house was deserted except for a few scratching hens and a goat. Panic swept over her when she remembered that once before Connor had left without a farewell. Hoping he might be in the barn, Lindy decided to search there for him. The dry smell of hay and ripe manure assaulted her at the entrance. Jester turned her head and snorted a greeting. Lindy leaned against a supporting post. All the worry and tension receded, leaving her weak at the knees.

"Thank heavens it's not too late," she said to herself.

"Too late for what?"

Lindy spun around and faced Connor. He stood in the entrance to the barn, his familiar form a silhouette against the bright light shining behind him. It wasn't until he stepped into the barn that Lindy could see the details of his face: nebulous blue eyes glowed against his tanned skin, the shadow of a beard emphasized the natural planes of his face, and burnished hair fell softly over his forehead and around his ears. His shirtsleeves were rolled up to his elbows, calling attention to the muscles in his arms and the wide plane of his shoulders. The handle of her father's toolbox was gripped in his hand.

Lindy composed herself while Connor's eyes adjusted to the dim light. To her consternation his gaze settled quite comfortably on her.

"Too late for what?" Connor repeated, walking past her and setting the toolbox against the wall of the stall.

Lindy realized there was no use trying to come back with some witty answer. The opportunity to broach the subject of Connor's eventual departure was now upon her. She inhaled deeply, and began what she had rehearsed all afternoon, finding it certainly had been easier to talk when she had only pretended Connor was listening.

"It's too early to quit work." Her voice quivered with dread. "I'm sorry about yesterday," she hurried on, unable to look Connor in the face, her downcast eyes settling on his bandaged thumb. The white scrap of petticoat was now dingy from a day's work.

Misinterpreting the meaning of her words, Connor held up his hand. "It'll heal."

There was an uncomfortable pause before Lindy could answer him. "I was not referring to your hand alone, Mr. O'Malley."

"Oh?" Despite being aware of what Lindy meant, Connor let her struggle over her words.

"I don't want you to think that I...that it would happen again." Lindy searched Connor's face, hoping to see that he understood her meaning. "I was overcome with concern for your finger, nothing more. I only meant to comfort you in your pain. You had a lot of whiskey and...I know it wouldn't have happened otherwise." She looked for some sign in his face that he knew she didn't blame him.

Connor moved close to Lindy, close enough for her to feel the heat from his body. And just as when he held her in his arms, she felt the now familiar rush of tingles quickly sweep over her. "You mean to say that it wasn't your lovely face or full, tempting mouth that beckoned my own?" Connor's finger softly traced her lips.

"I—"

"Or your eyes. You don't think I notice how they glow as though a fire burns behind them or that my fingers might ache to comb through your hair, like this." His fingers loosened the braid that bound her hair, releasing it into a waterfall of gold that fell over his hands. He lifted her hair and pulled his hands through it.

"Mr. O'Malley—" Lindy felt her breath suddenly go shallow.

"Perhaps you never gave it a thought that I longed to kiss the soft rise of your bosom or feel your silky legs wrap around me. No, it wasn't the whiskey that made me want you. A man can't put blame on whiskey for his actions, and I can't deny I'm attracted to you, or promise that I won't want to hold you in my arms again."

Lindy was finding it very difficult to breathe or look at Connor until he tilted her chin up, forcing her eyes up to his.

"I've given my presence here a lot of thought," he said. "I'll be leaving in the morning before my welcome wears thin or…once more, my need arises to seek comfort in your arms."

Connor's last words were strained, imploring her to understand their meaning. Despite the warning, Lindy was willing to take the chance that Connor would want her again and that she would be helpless to stop him or herself. "But the stock pen?"

"I've just told you how you befuddle my good judgment, and all you're concerned about is your stock pen? If I were you I'd worry more about keeping my drawers on because, in case I haven't been clear enough, next time I'm going to forget you're a married woman.''

Shocked at his blunt words and stung by his intention to leave, Lindy responded harshly. "There are no responsibilities that call you to attention, are there? No home, no family, no ambition except one—to run away from all of those things. Do you know what I think, Connor O'Malley? I don't think you're afraid of cheating my husband or saving my reputation. You're afraid of letting loose your feelings." Lindy ran out of the barn, not caring if Connor left without a farewell.

Connor followed her, closing the ground between them with long, determined strides. He reached out, grabbed her arm firmly and turned her around. "Damn if I'll let you saddle me with guilt. You're not my responsibility, Mrs. Rigby. I never promised I'd stay."

Lindy shrugged off Connor's hold. Not until he walked away did she wipe the tear from her cheek. She wasn't going to fall apart over his leaving. She was made of stronger stuff than that.

"I think you should go after him like you want to."

Lindy whipped around to see Luke standing at the corner of the barn. "Luke, you sticky beak! You'd best keep to tending the livestock."

"They're apples. It's you I'm worried about. I've never known you to let go of something you wanted."

"And what makes you think it's Mr. O'Malley I want?"

Luke smiled. "I've seen the way you look at him when his back's to you, and I've heard how the teacups rattle in their saucers when he's at the supper table. It's more than a stock pen you want. I think you should tell him you're not really married. He would stay then."

Lindy knew the high color in her cheeks would contradict any denial she made. It was true she wanted more than a stock pen from Connor. She liked him a lot, so much that at times she wondered if she was beginning to fall in love with him. Her eyes bored into Luke. How much did he really notice and what *did* he think she wanted?

"What makes you so sure he'd stay?"

Luke shrugged his shoulders. "Just a feeling, I guess."

"I can't tell him that I've never been married, and neither will you. Connor wouldn't like feeling he's been fooled, no matter the reason. Now you better get the band together before dark. I don't want to hear of any more of our lambs finding their way to Mr. Claxton's dinner plate."

After Lindy left Luke she had intended to return to the house, but she had been attracted to a piece of clothing caught in the bushes. On her way to investigate, Lindy realized Connor was sunk deep in her wooden washtub. He was barely visible behind a screen of clothing, but now and then she caught flashes of tan skin moving behind the intersecting branches. A slow, mischievous smile teased at the corners of her lips. With quiet, deliberate steps she moved closer to where Connor bathed. She closed her eyes a minute and whispered, "Forgive me, Mum and Dad, but my intentions are good."

Lindy came to an abrupt halt in front of Connor. There he was in all his naked glory from the waist up. The rest of him—she thanked her stars for that—was hidden below the rim of the washtub. A cake of soap clenched in one hand, he was in the midst of sudsing up a broad expanse of shoulder. With a wide hand, he slathered suds down his biceps, over the muscles that crisscrossed his chest, down his torso and into the tub. Lindy's eyes locked on Connor's masculine form; each part of him gleamed from under a slippery film of soap and water.

Lindy admitted that watching a man bathe without his knowledge was certainly sinful and would shock Dry Bed's citizens at least half as much as her sheep had, but she was still rooted to the spot. Connor was just too interesting to watch.

* * *

Connor thought he had found a secluded spot where he could luxuriate in a tub of cool water. He had carted the tub a distance from the house, set it behind a crop of chaparral and then filled it. He'd hung his clothes over the branches, providing a curtain of privacy. He had secretly bathed behind the screen of brush before and no one had been the wiser.

At least, that was what he had thought until he heard the crack of a twig under someone's foot. He had sensed he was not alone. Without showing alarm, he nonchalantly sank down into the tub. His arm already hung over its edge to keep his bandaged thumb dry. Unnoticed by Lindy, Connor reached for the rifle that rested against the blind side of the tub. Only when his fingers touched the reassuring metal did he chance to look through the hedge. Recognizing Lindy, he quickly sat up, sending water over the sides of the tub.

"What are you doing?" His voice boomed, making Lindy flinch. "If you don't quit sneaking up on me, you're going to find yourself dead," Connor said tersely, leaning his rifle back against the tub.

"I . . . I . . ." Stammering, Lindy stepped from behind the hedge. "I wanted to talk to you."

"Can it wait? As you can see, I'm detained at the moment."

Despite Connor's agitation, Lindy still came closer. "No. It can't wait. I may not have the same opportunity." Connor's eyebrow arched. "I mean, later you might be gone," Lindy clarified, flushing with embarrassment.

It was different when the man being secretly appraised knew it. Lindy fought to keep her composure and tried to concentrate only on what she had to say. While she averted her eyes and stared over Connor's head, Connor continued with his bath. As though unaffected by her close presence, he raised his leg out of the water, exposing his calf and foot, then began to vigorously scrub the cake of soap down his leg. Lindy stared at Connor's bare leg and then, realizing what she was doing, quickly looked away, but not before Connor had caught her eyes with his.

"What is so important that you have to interrupt a man's bath?" Connor asked. An amused smile told her that he thoroughly enjoyed her discomfort.

The sound of sloshing water failed to cool Lindy's hot face. "I need to know exactly why you're leaving. You seemed to be comfortable here. If it's my husband you're worried about—"

"I thought you already knew," he said, referring to her speech about responsibility. Failing to get a rise from her, Connor continued, "Dry Bed's already buzzing with gossip. Your reputation doesn't deserve to be tarnished by my presence here."

"It doesn't matter to me," Lindy said with questionable conviction. "Luke wants you to stay. He needs a man to talk to now and then."

"Luke hasn't asked me to stay. Regardless, working on a sheep ranch is not one of my goals. Now, if you don't mind, may I have some privacy so I can dress?"

Lindy wasn't satisfied. Goals were not something she thought Connor had. She forced herself to look straight at him. She had seen him shirtless before, now she just had to forget he was naked below the waterline as well.

Glancing at the string of clothes decorating the scrubby Texas brush like a Christmas tree, Lindy realized she had Connor at her mercy. Despite his cool composure, she gambled that he didn't want her to see all of him naked. Confidence bolstered her nerve and she was able to get closer to the tub. She even walked around it, circling like a hawk.

"You haven't stayed long enough to know ranching is not what you're looking for. Broken Gate is going to be a fine, profitable station, and I'm offering you a part of that if you'll be my foreman. It's an opportunity no man in his right mind would turn down. At least give it a go for a month, then decide. I need you."

Lindy casually began to pick Connor's clothes from the bushes and fold them over her arm.

Connor sat straight up. "What are you doing?"

"You weren't going to put on dirty clothes, were you?" Lindy rejoined innocently. "Meanwhile, you can think some more about giving Broken Gate a fair chance. If you don't like it here after a month, I promise I'll saddle your horse myself."

Connor's eyes narrowed. "This sounds suspiciously like blackmail, Mrs. Rigby."

"Certainly not. You can have your clothes back after—" Lindy couldn't help but smile playfully "—after I've washed them."

"Come back here with my clothes," Connor called to no avail. "Don't think I'm going to sit here waiting for you," he threatened.

Grinning, Connor sank back into the tub. He had relinquished all hope of finding anything worthwhile after the tragedies life had dealt him, then he had encountered Lindy—the one person who had uncovered something of his old self. He had to admire Lindy's nerve. She'd be back, that he was sure of. If not, he was going to find her. And wouldn't she be surprised? Connor's smile broke into a private chuckle.

Connor was just about waterlogged and nearly glowing with a bad temper by the time Lindy returned. Afraid to get too close, she kept her distance.

"It's good you're standing out my reach, Mrs. Rigby," Connor said seriously, noting with some dread that she had come empty-handed. "Where are my clothes?"

"Did you think about giving us a fair chance?"

Connor almost laughed. "There are any number of men in Dry Bed you can hire. In fact, they'd shoot each other for the honor."

Lindy was persistent. "I don't want anyone else. I want you."

"What is it going to take to convince you? No!"

Lindy had not prepared herself for disappointment. Like a spoiled child she flew into a tantrum. "I've washed your clothes, Mr. O'Malley, but until you agree to stay one month you're not getting them back," she said and stomped off.

Connor began to lift himself out of the tub. "I swear, woman," he shouted at Lindy's quick retreat, "if you don't get back here in five minutes with my clothes, I'm coming after you. Decent or not!" Deciding five minutes was too long to wait, Connor reached for the only remaining article of clothing left at his disposal—his boots. At least he wouldn't have to get spines in his feet.

Lindy shuddered at Connor's threat. Indeed, she hoped it was just that. She passed his clothes drying on the line. Once back in the safe haven of her house, she tied on an apron and began to prepare supper. Before long, she heard the door fly open and then slam shut. She hoped it was Luke—it had to be Luke, it couldn't be Connor—he wouldn't dare. She turned from the stove. Even expecting the possibility, she started at seeing Connor. The frying pan she held crashed to the floor.

There Connor stood, naked as a jay except for his boots and a branch of chaparral held over his vital parts. Lindy stood stone-still and speechless. For his part, Connor had a lot to say.

"Surprised?" Connor smiled at Lindy's shock. "If you call a man's bluff, ma'am, you'd better be ready to show your hand." Lindy gulped when Connor stepped nearer. "It seems you've lost your bet."

"So it seems." Lindy's voice was deflated with regret. "I'll get your clothes," she offered quickly. Anything to get out of his bare presence.

But Connor blocked her way. "They're wet as washrags. So... I suppose I'll just have to wait till they dry. You don't mind, do you?"

"You can't! You can't stay like that in...in boots and...twigs." Staring at his appearance, Lindy couldn't keep the bud of a smile from blooming into giggles. It was likely to infuriate Connor even more, but once she had recovered from the shock, she couldn't help it—Connor made such a comical sight standing in his knee-high boots with a branch held over his lower body. Lindy covered her mouth with her hand.

Looking down at himself, Connor frowned. "May I remind you that this natural attire is not by choice. How are you going to explain this to Luke?"

The smile returned to Lindy's mouth. "You have nothing to worry about. He'll be coming in long after your clothes are dry."

Now Connor smiled, and stepped toward Lindy. "Good."

Lindy didn't like the satisfied tone of Connor's voice and became apprehensive. "Sometimes he finishes early," she reminded Connor.

With each consecutive step closer, Connor forced her to step back. Soon her back met the wall. Her voice cracked with worry. "Mr. O'Malley, my brother—"

"Luke won't be back until much later," Connor said. He dropped the branch at her feet.

Lindy's gaze followed the branch to the floor. Her eyes slammed shut after that. For all she saw of him, Connor might as well have been fully clothed.

"Mr. O'Malley, please. There's a blanket on my bed. It should do until—" From the sound of his boots Lindy knew he drew nearer still. She felt her skin grow scarlet with the mix of emotions that heated in her veins. And, as much as she wanted to run, the fear of colliding with a naked man rooted her to the spot. Lindy merely hoped Connor would do as she had suggested. But when his hand slipped around her waist and she felt herself being drawn to him, she knew better. An unexpected gasp escaped her.

"Open your eyes, Mrs. Rigby." She heard the husky whisper near her ear and felt the warm breath of his words against her neck.

"I can't."

"You had no trouble looking at me in my bath, or leaving me stranded without my breeches or accusing me of being afraid of getting close to someone."

"I hadn't meant it like this."

"No?"

"No! I . . . I meant as in needing—"

"Oh, I do have needs, Mrs. Rigby."

"Not those kinds of needs, Mr. O'Malley, you're naked!"

"I thought that's how you wanted me."

"No!"

"Then you want me dressed?"

"Yes. Right away."

"Then I wish you'd make up your mind. My clothes are wet."

"The air's dry as a chip, they can't still be . . . I see you have revenge in mind," Lindy responded stiffly, her eyes still tight as clamshells, her chin steady and proud. "You have completely mortified me. Now that you've accomplished your purpose I beseech you to—" She felt Connor's hold tighten and pull her against his bare chest. His other hand moved up her back, stopping only to brace the back of her neck. Anticipating what he planned to do next, Lindy swallowed hard.

"Open your eyes," Connor ordered harshly. This time, Lindy's eyes opened. Connor smiled. "If you still think you want me for your foreman, knowing the risks at hand, then I will stay the month."

Lindy was surprised and suspicious; it seemed to be Connor's intent to scare her into sending him off. If so, his plan was not going to work. Despite how she felt about him at the present moment, he was just the man Broken Gate needed and she was ready to do almost anything to keep him there. She bit her bottom lip. "Then it's settled. Is Luke's room still to your liking?"

"For now," Connor replied suggestively.

To Lindy's surprise, Connor lowered his mouth to hers and covered her quivering lips with his. He leaned into her, crushing her between his solid body and the wall. Lindy tried not to think of Connor as naked, but her memory kept her acutely aware of every bare inch of him pressed against her. Whatever part of her Connor touched, trembled. Lindy tensed from the unexpected and intense reaction of her body. She could neither name nor understand these new feelings that increased each time she came close to Connor.

As Connor's kiss became more demanding, a whistle came from the farmyard, a light ditty that might as well have been a pail of cold water poured over their heads.

"Luke!" Lindy whispered in alarm.

Connor immediately ducked into Lindy's room.

Seeing Connor streak for cover brought tears of hard laughter down Lindy's cheeks.

"I'm not finished with you, Mrs. Rigby," Connor playfully called from her room.

"Hush!" Lindy said outside the bedroom door. "There's a blanket on my bed."

When Luke strolled into the house, Lindy became serious. As was Luke's habit at a day's end, he walked straight to the stove. "No supper yet?"

Lindy quickly turned away from Luke. "I . . . I got a late start. Would you mind putting out the plates?"

A dull thud came from Lindy's room. Luke and Lindy turned their heads to the sound.

"What was that?" Luke asked, already starting for the bedroom. Lindy blocked the path to the door.

"Something must have fallen. I'll go see. You go ahead with what you were doing."

Luke eyed her suspiciously before reluctantly returning to the table, making sure to keep one eye on his sister while she peeked into her room. Lindy's breath left her when she saw Hank's gun on the floor and the serape missing. She felt a nervous rash creep over her body, and hoped that Connor had not thought anything unusual about a gun hidden in a blanket.

"Lin?"

Closing the door, Lindy tried to keep her voice calm. "Nothing to worry about. Just as I said, something must have fallen." She saw that Luke was still perplexed. "You can look if you like."

Saving an uncomfortable moment, a fully clothed Connor stepped into the kitchen and, imitating Luke, sauntered over to the stove. "No supper yet?"

"Is that all you men think of, is your stomachs?" Lindy said, noticeably distressed.

"Well . . ." Connor paused to pass Lindy a devastating smile. "It's one of the things we think of."

Chapter Eight

Lindy glanced up at the white-hot sky. Any more days like this one and her sheep would start to drop from the heat. Already they had stopped eating. From their self-inflicted starvation, their fleece would begin to break off in worthless clumps. If she was to save her crop and the lives of her sheep, shearing couldn't be delayed a day longer. With the three of them working from dawn to nightfall, they could save some of the wool.

She and Luke were adept at shearing sheep. It took her only fifteen minutes to neatly peel fifteen pounds of fleece from a ewe—Luke was even faster. She looked over the band and groaned after calculating how long it would take them to shear more than one hundred sheep. There was no use procrastinating, the sooner they began the odious job, the sooner it would be done.

Once Luke and Connor had penned thirty sheep, enough work to start, they erected a tentlike shelter at the end of a chute leading from the stock pen. Not long after the oil-cloth tent had been raised, Lindy pulled the first ewe between her legs, soothing it with a calm voice. Luke grabbed another ewe and was halfway through shearing off its fleece before Lindy began.

Lindy looked up at Connor and was encouraged. He was interested, at least, and appeared amazed at how the fleece had peeled off in one piece, leaving the ewe looking perplexed and almost embarrassingly naked.

Lindy helped the shorn ewe back on its feet. Buddy, who had been watching in the same controlled silence as Connor, pointed his nose and directed the ewe down the narrow chute to the holding pen. Once Lindy had tied the fleece with paper twine, Connor volunteered his help, stuffing the bundle into a burlap sack.

"I can show you how, if you'd like," Lindy offered.

Connor looked doubtful as the next ewe came down the chute. "That's quite all right. I'd rather leave clipping woollies to the experts."

"It really isn't difficult—just backbreaking."

"If Lin can do it, you can," offered Luke, grinning at the look his sister returned.

Lindy's head tilted endearingly. "And I'd say, if a nipper can learn to shear a sheep, certainly a man can be taught."

Luke chuckled good-naturedly as he slid his shears through the thick fleece. "Go ahead, Connor, show her up. I'd bet you beat her time before we're done with the band."

Already pushing up his sleeves, Connor grinned. "I'm always up for a good bet, and this one seems…" He looked down at the ewe already between Lindy's knees. The animal's trusting eyes looked up at him, and his smile faded into a straight line of determination. "It looks challenging enough."

Lindy began the lesson with a tight smile. "Now. You need to keep her still, like so." Connor watched as Lindy demonstrated, trying to keep his eyes on her hands rather than her nicely curved backside. The helpless ewe was on its back with its head braced between Lindy's legs as she bent over it.

"She can't get away from you if you keep her head pinned. With her head back like this, you draw her skin tight, so you won't accidentally nick her with the shears.

Clip toward her ear, starting at the brisket, opening up the neck like so."

Lindy pushed the shears into the fleece, clipping down the ewe's neck, creating a path free of wool. She parted the fleece with her hand. "See?"

"Looks easy enough," Connor commented. He stole a glance at Luke. The boy had already sheared three sheep in less than a half hour.

Lindy beamed with pride. "He *is* good. I'll give him that much." Luke smiled at his sister's compliment. "Now, back to your lesson." Connor frowned slightly at the authority in Lindy's voice. "Keep the blades flat and the skin always taut. Would you like to try now?" Her eyes flashed impishly.

"How difficult can it be?" Connor said. He traded places with Lindy, straddling the animal with his legs.

"Put your left foot here under her rump," Lindy said as she and Connor struggled to position the squirming ewe. "Wait till she calms. There. Your left hand goes here. Now, keep the shears flat, skin tight—push and clip, push and clip... that's it."

"There's nothing to it, Connor," Luke encouraged as he stretched his back between sheep.

Connor pushed the shears through the thick fleece and clipped down the ewe's stomach. The wool peeled away like an overcoat slowly being shed. Lanolin coated his hands.

Lindy pressed Connor's hand flat against the ewe's side. "You need to tighten up the skin once the wool starts to pull away. Now, push in the shears and clip toward the backbone. Be careful, she may kick if she tries to stand up and that could—"

Lindy's warning had hardly been said when the ewe struggled to right herself. The sheep squirmed, kicked and turned between Connor's legs, throwing him off balance before bolting away. Connor landed on his backside as Lindy tackled the runaway sheep. Luke howled at the sight before him—Connor on the ground and Lindy lying on top of a hundred-thirty-pound ewe.

"You've got to keep her head down—" Lindy looked over her shoulder "—or she can throw you off balance and knock you down."

Connor laughed so hard his sides began to hurt.

Lindy interrupted his glee. "Once you've collected yourself, I could use some help getting up."

Connor stood, found the shears and came over to Lindy. He pulled her to her feet and caught the ewe before it hurried away.

"I think she knows a novice is working on her," he said lightly.

"I'm certain she does," Lindy agreed with a smile that slightly parted her lips, striking Connor with a sudden urge to kiss them.

Reining in his emotions, he positioned the fretful-looking sheep once more and began where he had left off.

Working so close to Lindy made it difficult for Connor to concentrate on what he was doing. Every time their hands touched, sparks shot up his arms; when her hair brushed his cheek, he wanted to bury his face in its soft, fragrant mass; when she moved, her hip nudged his and a fire flared in his loins; when she smiled at him and her face came close to his, he fought not to plant a kiss on her rosy lips. He was sweating and gasping for breath; he was delirious with desire.

"It's not so easy, is it?" Lindy commented when they were halfway through shearing the ewe. At that Connor almost popped his buttons laughing. He turned his head and looked up at her. There was a slight pucker to her lips. If she knew how much energy he had to expend to keep his mind on the job at hand, she'd be shocked. He dragged his arm across his forehead and was quite tempted to tell her.

"If you need a rest—" she began.

"I don't need a rest, Mrs. Rigby," Connor said in a low voice, thinking how he was working up a sweat just trying to decide which was softer, Lindy's body or the ewe's fleece. By comparison, shearing was easy.

Lindy misinterpreted his symptoms. "Perhaps you should rest. I can—"

Connor quickly clipped at the fleece.

"Be careful."

"I am being careful. Can you give me some room?" he asked rather tersely.

"Why do you have a problem being close to me? If it's my hus—"

"I don't have a problem with it."

"Really? It seems that's when you snap at me the most."

"With you hovering over me, I'm bound to cut off something with these shears," Connor replied, resting the long blades across his knee.

Lindy folded her arms over her chest to put more distance between them. Satisfied, Connor slipped the shears through the fleece and clipped around the ewe's back leg. Luke exasperated Lindy with his grin. If she hadn't been so afraid of his answer she would have asked him what he found so humorous.

After forty minutes, Connor had successfully sheared one sheep, then stepped back, shears in his hand, to admire his work.

"Well, she certainly does look daggy," Lindy said flatly, as the unevenly shorn ewe trotted off. "But with practice you'll get better at it."

Luke laughed. "That's as close to a compliment as you're gonna get from her," he called out.

With a tease of a smile, Lindy challenged Connor to try to match her skill.

"There's a first time for everything…and practice makes perfect," Connor said to Luke, though his attention was centered on Lindy. He smiled with satisfaction at the bright color that rose to her cheeks.

"Well, you've certainly got a lot to practice on," she said, drawing his attention to the rest of the sheep in the stock pen.

Before the day's end, Connor had reached closer to Lindy's shearing time of fifteen minutes. When he had six ewes to his credit, a blister on every part of his hands and an excruciating backache, he looked over to Luke. "How long?"

Luke grinned from ear to ear, showing the dimples he and his sister had inherited from their mother. He pushed aside the shock of tawny hair hanging over his eyes and looked around for Lindy. "You have a ways to go yet, but you're getting there. Here comes another one."

Connor positioned the ewe and Luke checked his father's pocket watch. In twenty-eight minutes yet another fleece was bundled, tied and stuffed into a sack. Looking at his watch, Luke announced, "Thirteen minutes too slow." Connor groaned and rubbed his back. "Well, it's only the first day."

With only two shears between the three of them, one could stretch and rest from the grueling job while the other two worked. It was while she was on her break that Lindy noticed the ominous-looking sky and felt a cooler touch of air on her arms. A storm now couldn't have been more unwelcome. Until their lanolin formed a shield against the elements, the sheared sheep would be unprotected and susceptible to pneumonia. While Lindy fretted over that possibility, the rising wind picked up a tumbleweed and lazily rolled it across the farmyard. Immediately she raced across the yard to where Luke and Connor huddled over their sheep.

"Luke! There's a storm coming," she called in alarm.

Luke and Connor looked up. The oilcloth tent that provided their shade blocked a clear view of the sky, but was already quivering, as if anticipating the stronger wind that would rip it away.

"It hasn't rained since I arrived here," Connor said.

"Of course not. We don't want rain now, so it will rain."

Lindy didn't think the wind and dark clouds were merely fooling. And neither did the sheep. They stood still as statues, all pointing their snouts in the same direction, watching and waiting.

"We'll finish up here and get the shorn sheep in with the woolly ones," Luke said, as he hurried to finish the ewe gripped between his knees.

"I'll take Buddy and get as many in the stock pen as I can," Lindy said. She lifted her skirt above the top of her boots and dashed off to find her horse, with the dog ahead of her.

Lindy hadn't seen a whole lot of rain in Dry Bed since they arrived six months ago, but from the stories she'd heard and the increasing darkness, she expected the sky to suddenly open and pour down everything it had saved over the long dry months.

A roll of thunder sounded, and lightning flashed blue and white over rocks and sparsely spaced trees, illuminating the backs of the huddled sheep that cowered against the ground. Lindy called to Buddy; her whistles and commands drove him around the band, but he was one dog and she was alone; it would take more than the two of them to control a band of frightened sheep. As if the lightning and thunder weren't enough, a strong gust of wind tossed tumbleweeds at the band. There was nothing more disturbing to a band of sheep than to be the object of a tumbleweed attack. Immediate panic took hold and the band splintered into small groups. Lindy despaired at the sight of her sheep stampeding every which way; it was a drover's nightmare. Buddy barked his frustration while frantically chasing the frightened ewes.

By the time Connor and Luke had reached Lindy, the stampede and wind had whipped up a thick dust cloud, making it nearly impossible to distinguish ground from sky. Lindy's skirt flapped around her legs, and her hair whipped at her face. She had pulled her bandanna over her nose and mouth, but even with that precaution, dust choked her and forced her eyes closed. Lindy prayed for the rain to come; at least, it would wash the dust from the air. However, instead of rain, she was pelted with what felt like sharp pebbles. Her skin stung from the biting hail that preceded the rain. Lost in the sudden deluge of ice and rain, Lindy strained to hear Luke's voice and Buddy's barks, and called out to whoever was near enough to hear her. In answer to her cries, she felt a hand close around her arm. At first, it was a relief to feel the presence of another person.

"Mrs. Rigby." Even though Connor was only a foot away, he had to shout above the rushing noise of wind and rain. "Come with me."

"I can't." Lindy pulled her arm away, but Connor found her reins and tore them from her hands. "My jumbucks—"

"You can't do anything now but get yourself killed." Connor insisted on leading Lindy out of a storm that had yet to show its full force. He listened and heard doors banging. Following the sound, they came to the barn.

Lindy didn't wait for Connor to help her down from her horse—she nearly fell from the slippery saddle in her haste to escape. But Connor didn't intend to let her run back into the storm. He latched the door, locking them in darkness until the storm subsided.

Connor caught Lindy in his arms as she charged the door. "Where are you going?"

"Let me out of here. Luke and—"

"From what I've seen so far, Luke can take care of himself, and so will your sheep. Animals have an instinct for survival. You'll find the strong ones when the storm subsides."

Lindy wiggled from his hold. "What do you know of sheep? Or my brother?" She tried to shove aside the heavy beam that locked them in.

Connor leaned against the opposite end of the beam. "Certainly more today than I did yesterday," he said with a touch of amusement.

"Knowing how to shear a jumbuck doesn't make you an expert on the animal, Mr. O'Malley." Lindy waited for Connor's reply and was sorry that she couldn't see his face well enough to decide if he was ready to let her go or not.

Connor continued to defeat her efforts, but damn if she wasn't going to be stubborn about it, he thought. "Mrs. Rigby, you may be the expert on sheep, but I'm smart enough to know that sitting atop a horse on flat land with lightning flashing around my head is asking for an early grave."

"I'll worry about my own grave—you worry about yours," Lindy retorted. "Now, if you'd please help me with this door—"

"Since I'm the one who'd most likely have to dig your grave in the hard-baked earth, I'll have my own say in the matter. If you'd ever had to dig more than a foot deep in this ground, you'd understand why we're staying put until this storm blows over. I just hope Luke doesn't disappoint my faith in his good sense and try to round up those woolly-backs himself."

Lindy didn't make so much as a sound of protest. Instead, she sulked, listening to the howling storm and thinking how much like a monster it sounded—a monster after her sheep and her life. Connor was right, of course—there wasn't much she could do now, but it had never been her nature to quit, even if the odds were stacked against her. She sat down on the floor and leaned back against the door. If it wasn't for Connor O'Malley, she'd be out looking after her sheep with Luke.

Connor struck a match and lit the kerosene lamp that hung from the wall, casting the interior of the barn in orange light and oily smoke shadows. Lindy wrapped her arms around her knees and pulled them up against her chest. She tried not to glare at Connor, but wasn't very successful at hiding her unhappiness over the way he had taken control out of her hands and forced his opinion on her. She had always been in control; having it taken away from her, even if she had been wrong, was unsettling. Who did Connor think he was?

"You can glare at me if you like, or you can just accept the situation," Connor said bluntly.

Lindy forgot her determination to suffer her indignation in silence. "And which situation are you referring to?"

"Why, the storm, of course. There isn't anything you can do about it, so why sulk over it?"

"I'm not sulking."

"Excuse me if I beg to differ on that point."

"I don't sulk! That's a childish trait, which I've long outgrown. And I don't excuse you, in the least, for locking me up in this barn. I don't like feeling helpless—and that's all there is to it."

Connor walked over to Lindy and sat next to her. Picking up a piece of hay, he twirled it in his fingers. "Not for a moment had I considered *you* helpless. I just thought you liked living more."

Lindy wasn't sure whether to take that as a compliment, so didn't make a comment, only stared over the top of her knees. She tried not to think about how close Connor was next to her, or about what had transpired the last time they were alone. But it seemed the more she tried not to remember the feeling of Connor's arms around her and his lips warm against hers, the more the memory nagged at her. And then her heart began to race again; her body warmed and her pulse pounded at her temples, making her head ache. Lindy was annoyed at the emotion she had no control over, so when she talked to Connor, her voice had a sharp edge to it. "I've had to be self-sufficient for a long time. I'm not accustomed to people telling me what to do."

"Your husband must have a time of it, then."

Lindy dodged the subject. "We have one thing in common, Mr. O'Malley—we've both traveled long distances to get here. Only I have a clear reason—as you know—for settling at Broken Gate. But you—what's driven you out here?"

To her surprise, Connor's answer was direct. "A woman. I suppose what always drives a man ... is a woman."

Lindy felt disappointment swamp her. Suddenly she didn't want to hear any more of Connor's explanation. She regretted asking him, for now all hope of his staying at Broken Gate for good vanished. But Connor continued as though she weren't there, as if he just needed to finally tell his story, no matter who listened.

Lindy pictured Connor as he described himself in his dark blue captain's uniform—only more handsome than he would admit. She imagined the military attire must have deepened the color of his eyes, and the gold braid and shiny brass buttons with their raised eagles surely would have made any young girl weep to marry him. Lindy resisted the urge to ask Connor if he had loved his wife before he married her, or if it had been the urgency of the war or the rashness of youth that had made him grasp at marriage. However, it was clear from his pained voice that he still blamed himself for his wife's death, and, whether he had loved her or not, he suffered over never having found the men who had been responsible for taking her from him. It tugged at Lindy's heart to hear that an infant son had also been victim to the cruelties of war. Connor had spent five years searching for the men who had murdered his family and burned his home, only to be brought to graveyards and deserted farms.

It occurred to Lindy that she and Connor had more in common than she had thought: they had each lost loved ones and had been driven in their own way by their ghosts. But the paths they followed were so different, and had only brought them together for the moment—eventually they would go their separate ways.

"You see," Connor concluded, "I've had everything you desire—family, acres of lush farmland, and none of it brought me happiness, only pain. The more you have, the more you stand to lose. I don't want another home and a family. I don't want anyone depending on me. I don't want to lose that much of life again."

Lindy kneeled up and faced Connor, her eyes wet with tears. "Mr. O'Malley, I—" She wanted to tell him she was sorry and give him the comfort he needed. She understood Connor's pain but not his defeat; she wanted him to fight for the love and happiness he deserved. But before she could say a word, Connor wrapped his arms around her and pulled her into his lap. His strength made her feel safe and secure; it made her want to depend on him—the very thing Connor was afraid of. Lindy straightened in his hold. "Mr. O'Malley, this is not what you want."

"I do want you, Mrs. Rigby," Connor confessed. His eyes traced every part of Lindy's face; his hand smoothed over her hair and down the side of her neck. "I want you in every way a man could want a woman. I can't live here day after day without wanting to touch you . . . like this." Connor held Lindy's face in his hands and lightly kissed her lips, then trailed his warm mouth over her chin and down the length of her neck.

Lindy admitted to herself that she wanted Connor, too. When his mouth returned to her lips, his kiss was as sweet as any honey she'd ever tasted. Connor's kiss had the power to make her forget the storm and all her worries.

"Mrs. Rigby," Connor said in a husky voice, "your husband is a foolish man to leave you out here alone."

At that reminder, all of Lindy's worries, and then some, returned. She pushed away from Connor. He only wanted her because she was safe. What woman could be less of a threat than a married one whose husband was far away? She was perfect: married and independent. Connor couldn't lose someone he thought he couldn't really have. He could ride out of her life just as suddenly as he had appeared. It was she who had to protect her heart from Connor. Trying not to look at him, Lindy stood up and brushed off her skirt.

"Mrs. Rigby, I—"

"Please, no apologies." She wiped her cheek with the back of her hand. When Connor got up from the floor, she turned away from him.

Connor grabbed Lindy's shoulders and turned her around. "As long as I stay, I promise you there will be moments like this. The next time we kiss and I feel the same longing on your lips, I swear it won't matter to me if you're married. So think hard on it, Mrs. Rigby—do you need me that much?"

Lindy tried to wiggle free, but Connor held her tightly between his body and the door. She felt the whole length of him flatten against her body, his hips pressed into hers, his chest crushing her breasts, stealing the breath from her lungs, pinning her against the door. She looked up at him and her lips quivered. When Lindy answered, her voice was a bare whisper. "I do need you . . . but—"

Before Lindy could say another word, Connor slid his arm behind her legs and lifted her into his arms. He closed her mouth with his and demanded the warm return of her kiss. Lindy fell limp in his arms and didn't care if he had said he didn't want to love again; the passion behind his kiss told more than his words. Connor wanted to live again; he was just afraid to say it. He thought he could protect himself by denying love, by running away from anyone he thought he might care about. Connor had a huge heart that hadn't stopped beating just because he'd lost his family. He cared about her and Luke more than he knew and she was going to show him, she was going to open up his eyes again.

Connor lowered her to the bedding and lay next to her, shedding kisses over her forehead and down the slope of her nose until his mouth claimed hers again. They kissed un-hurried, bridling a surge of passion that lay ready to burst from its molten core; they savored the warm flow that coursed through their veins as a howling wind whipped around the barn and yellow lamplight flickered between their shadows. Lindy warmed with the heat Connor's touch drew as his hands smoothed over her breasts. She felt the heated touch of his fingers slip inside her blouse and gasped from the sudden rush of pleasure roused by his gentle fon-dling. She whispered his name as she felt her will dissolve under the spell that Connor's hands weaved around her. Then the magic was broken by a crash of thunder, an end-less pounding that shook them from their web of passion.

"Lin! Connor! Are you in there?" Luke called hoarsely from outside the barn.

"Hell, that boy has timing," Connor swore, getting to his feet. This time, he didn't offer an apology for his language.

Hastily buttoning her blouse and combing the straw pieces from her hair, Lindy breathed a sigh of relief. How had she let it happen? Another moment and Connor would have discovered her charade. He would have known that she had never been with a man before. She had been following his lead and the instinct she had felt coming from inside her, but she wasn't sure just how convincing she could have been. Lindy smoothed her hands over her skirt and waited for Connor to open the door.

Connor glanced back at her with a look that was less than happy, and waited for her to say something.

"It's good Luke found us or we would have...done something we would have regretted." Connor stared at her silently as she rambled. "I don't blame you. We both for-got ourselves. It was the storm. This wouldn't have hap-pened otherwise. It's best we just forget the whole thing."

"Forget? Mrs. Rigby, I couldn't look at you without thinking of holding you in my arms. I'll remember this day long after I've left Broken Gate. But I wonder—"

Lindy felt her heart begin to beat a rapid rhythm.

"I wonder if you'll remember lying in my arms the day your husband arrives."

Chapter Nine

Except for the inconvenience of having to find more than one hundred scattered ewes, it was almost as though it had never rained. The earth was dry again, and the sun shone with the same old intensity as before.

From atop their horses, Lindy and Luke guided a line of sheep under the crude sign Lawrence Falen had erected before his passing. The words *Broken Gate* had been painted on the bottom of an old wagon bed and nailed between two whittled tree trunks. There was wide-open space on either side of the entrance, yet it didn't seem proper to ride around the sign, so everyone who approached Broken Gate from the west came under the sun-bleached words. Lindy wished her father were alive to see her drive the white stream of sheep under the sign he had made.

Connor leaned against one of the gray tree trunks, counting Falen sheep the old way—by dropping a bean into a mason jar for each one that walked by him. But more often than not, his eyes trained on Lindy rather than on the sheep, and each time Lindy heard the dull plink of another bean in the jar, she was reminded of Connor's presence.

Thinking of him under the hot sun made Lindy swelter even more. She felt the tension between them and knew that if they found themselves alone again, the thread of restraint they maintained would break and she would have to face the dilemma of telling Connor that she had never been married. Lindy had never thought such a well-meaning lie could become so troublesome. Now she was going to have to find ways to avoid Connor. During the day that would be easy enough, but the night—there was her biggest worry. Luke still insisted on sleeping outside with Buddy and the band, thus leaving his room to Connor. When Connor had suggested alternating nights, Luke, considering Connor their guest, had politely refused.

With a faint heart, Lindy glanced down at Connor from under the wide brim of her hat. Just as she had sensed, Connor was staring up at her, and he was not in the least bit startled that she had caught him.

"That's seventy-five frijoles," Connor said. His eyes were cool pools of blue, tempting Lindy's calm exterior.

Lindy heard another bean plink to the bottom of the mason jar. "That means we're ten short," she said flatly, trying to keep all hint of emotion out of her voice.

Connor set the jar on the ground. "Come down off your horse. Luke and I'll search for the rest since they're probably the ones that wandered the farthest."

"I'm surely capable of find—"

Connor reached up and surrounded Lindy's waist with his hands, pulling her down from her horse. "I know. You're very capable, but Luke and I will go."

After Lindy's feet touched the ground, Connor's hands lingered on her waist. A rash of goose bumps spread over her body with startling dispatch, her cheeks flared warmly and her legs wobbled beneath her skirt. She silently cursed the ease with which Connor could ambush her attempt to steady her emotions. Lindy dared to look into his eyes. Was it mischievous intent that put the sparkle there or just the slant of sunlight?

"There's a present for you back at the house."

It seemed to Lindy that Connor was getting bolder by the hour and she was getting weaker by the minute. Feeling herself pulled down into his gray-blue eyes, she doubted that he would offer to trade places with Luke any time soon. In only a few hours, she would have to face Connor alone in the house. Out of habit, Lindy looked over to Luke. He relaxed on his horse, smiling as if he understood and approved of what was happening between her and Connor.

"Do you know anything of this present?" Lindy asked Luke.

Luke shrugged and his grin widened, leading her to suspect his involvement despite his denial.

Connor swung himself up on Lindy's horse and smiled down at her. "I know you're exploding with curiosity, so go see for yourself."

Lindy watched Connor and Luke until they were a distance away, and then turned to the house. She did wonder what Connor had left her.

Lindy's walk quickened as she approached the front porch. By the time she had reached the steps, she nearly flew into the house. As Connor had promised, there on the table was a small tissue-wrapped package. She brought the squarish package up to her nose and smelled its sweet lavender scent. "How'd you know, Connor O'Malley?" she asked aloud. At that moment in her life, he was an absolute angel wearing a Stetson for a halo.

Lindy held the cake of soap in her hands a long time before deciding to use it, and then she promised herself only to bathe with it on special occasions. Grimly, she admitted to herself that there wouldn't be that many opportunities to treat herself at Broken Gate, unless she considered finding all her sheep a special occasion.

Lindy held the soap against her cheek; it was as smooth and fragrant as a flower petal. Well, just having a cake of scented soap was special, and feeling hot and grimy, she decided to celebrate while Connor and Luke searched for the strays.

Lindy dragged the washtub to the secluded bathing spot and set it in the thicket of chaparral. She partially filled it with water from the rain barrel and hung her best towel, which was nothing more than a torn gunnysack, over some branches. She stripped away her riding skirt, vest and blouse; her boots and stockings followed, but her fingers stopped short of unlacing her cotton camisole. Even though Luke and Connor would not be returning for a long while yet, Lindy decided to remain in her undergarments.

After rinsing the day's dust from her clothes, Lindy draped them over the shrubs, confident they would be dry by the time she finished her bath. She unbound her hair, releasing long waves of gold that rippled over her shoulders and back. With the new cake of soap in her hand, Lindy splashed in the bath with the exuberance of a bird. Soon creamy suds covered her skin and the scent of French lavender sweetened the air. Closing her eyes, she rubbed her hair with soap until her fingers could slide through the slippery strands. Soft bubbles dripped over her temples. Lindy's senses filled with the smell and feel of the rich soap, her thoughts drifted away from Broken Gate and the harsh countryside to a field lush with green grass and flowers.

Steeped in her imagination, Lindy did not hear the soft steps that approached her. She did not sense another presence until she felt a hand that was not her own thread through her hair. Soap dripped down and around her eyes, guaranteeing to sting and blind her if she opened them.

"Who's there?" she asked, knowing it was not Luke, and praying it was not Jeb who combed his fingers up the nape of her neck. Lindy felt prickles of fear race down her arms while she waited for an answer.

"Let's see how good you are at guessing," a smooth masculine voice answered before she felt warm lips press against the side of her neck.

"Mr. O'Malley! I should have guessed." Lindy immediately splashed her face with water. When she opened her eyes, she glared at Connor's smile, and sputtered, "You're supposed to be helping Luke." Lindy suspected she had been tricked, and became indignant. "How dare you?"

"Somehow, I didn't think you would mind," Connor returned, subtly reminding Lindy of the time she had held him captive in his bath.

Lindy was forced to swallow a little of her pride, but still . . . She narrowed her eyes on Connor, particularly noticing his rolled-up sleeves. "Is this why you gave me the soap?"

Connor squatted at the side of the washtub, his arms folded over its rim, and his blistered hands dangling in the water. He leaned forward and smelled her hair. "I gave it to you because I can't resist the smell of lavender on a woman. Sneaking a peek at you bathing came as a second thought."

"What Hester must have thought when you purchased it."

"She did ask me why I was smiling at a cake of soap."

"Good heavens!"

Lindy suddenly felt completely naked to his gaze, and thanked her good sense for not discarding her undergarments.

Connor made her feel even more self-conscious when his gaze wandered from the soapy strands of hair to her shoulders, to her elbows, and then over the white camisole plastered to her chest. Pink skin pressed against the translucent material that outlined all of her curves and fine points, leaving little for Connor to imagine. Connor's lazy smile flustered Lindy further, but she was bound to treat his presence with as much decorum as she could gather, given the circumstances. Keeping her chin up, Lindy continued with her bath. Grasping the cake of soap in one hand, she smoothed it up the length of one arm and her neck, unaware of how she tormented Connor until she happened to look into his eyes. They flickered with blue flames that reminded her of sunlight trapped in a raindrop. Startled by the desire locked behind Connor's blue eyes, Lindy dropped the cake of soap into the tub. She scrambled to find it, but Connor's hand quickly dipped into the water and retrieved the soap from between her legs, his hand slipping over her bare leg.

"It'll melt away if you leave it in the water too long," Connor explained.

Lindy looked at the soap in his hand.

"We need to talk."

"Talk?" Lindy worried about Connor's smile. "About what? Has anything happened to my jumbucks?"

His smile unfailing, Connor vigorously rubbed the soap in his hands. After working up a lather, and ignoring Lindy's frown, he gathered up her hair and worked the suds through it while he lectured. Lindy was too shocked by his boldness to say very much, so she quietly listened. "Your sheep are all accounted for. It's you I'm worried about. I could very well have been someone else—someone with more in mind than washing your hair. You're a tin can on a fence post out here—a clear shot for anyone who passes through."

"You sound like Sheriff Hayes," Lindy said with a pout. "Besides, I brought my rifle."

Lindy looked around and saw that she had left her Henry near the crop of chaparral—too far away for her to retrieve quickly in case she had needed it.

"I can see it protecting that thorny shrub," Connor said dryly, and then added with a touch of amusement, "unless, of course, you intended to drown your assailant."

Lindy knew Connor was right. She had neglected to set the rifle within reach, but she wasn't about to admit her carelessness. "I'm quite safe here, Mr. O'Malley."

Connor ignored Lindy's tart remark while working her hair into a lather. Soon she began to relax as his fingers massaged her scalp. She leaned her chin on her knees and closed her eyes while Connor shampooed her hair. His touch was wonderful.

"Your father wasn't safe. I don't believe it was Indians who killed him, because they usually don't stray far from the bison. Sheriff Hayes is a man to listen to, but I see his words are falling on deaf ears where you're concerned."

Lindy turned her thoughts to Connor's suspicions. "If it wasn't Indians, what do you think happened to my father?"

"It's conjecture at this point, but there are a lot of folks who hate and fear woollies bad enough to resort to murder."

"You think my father was murdered?"

"Anything's possible out here, so you're going to make *me* a promise just as I made you one—under similar circumstances," Connor added.

Even though a thin barrier of cotton lay between Lindy's skin and Connor's hand, she could feel his warm touch slowly slide down her back and then close around her waist. He breathed against her neck, sending shivers over her skin, taking away her tight control and replacing it with an urge to turn in his arms and wrap herself around him.

"Promise me you'll hire some trustworthy men to help you."

Lindy almost sat straight up in protest, then remembered how revealing her wet clothing was. "I don't need any more help. And besides," she added tersely, "I can't afford to pay anyone."

"Yes, you can." Connor dared to disagree. Lindy stared at him, and laughed rather than argue. "I know you have an account in the bank," he said.

Lindy forgot her modesty and turned to face him. "How do you know that?" She wiped the dripping soap from her forehead.

Connor's eyes crinkled with his grin. "Luke told me your father had sent you money, and combined with the nest egg you brought with you from Australia—"

"That little—how dare you pry like that!" Lindy shouted, reaching out for the gunnysack hanging behind him.

Connor caught her arm. "Don't be angry with Luke. He didn't think of it as a secret, and I wasn't digging for secrets. If I had been, there's no telling what I might have come up with."

"Go away," Lindy demanded, pressing her lips together in a pout.

"Not until you promise to hire help."

"I'm not hiring men." Lindy folded her arms over her chest.

"You're a luscious sight, Mrs. Rigby," Connor commented. His eyes appreciatively scanned every inch of her, lingering in places that made Lindy blush. "Now, you have to admit," he continued, wiping the soap from her face with his neckerchief, "after yesterday's storm, you can't do it all alone. Even if you won't admit it, in your heart you know it's true. There's a whole lot more sheep to shear. That's why you connived so to get me to stay—only I'm not here forever, darlin'."

"You're right. You're not here forever. You can get on your horse right now. And I'll even help you saddle up." She stepped out of the tub, and grabbed the gunnysack from where it hung.

Connor wrapped his arms around Lindy and pulled her wet, soft body against his. "Not until I hear your promise. Swear you'll hire help or I promise—" Connor leaned forward, his face so close to Lindy's that she felt the rough texture of his cheek brush against hers. "You'd better hurry, darlin', before I remember we're alone."

Lindy knew Connor had her in a corner with no way out but to give in to his ridiculous demand. She finally answered through clenched teeth. "All right."

"What was that, darlin'? I couldn't hear through all your hissing." Connor tortured her by slowly trailing his warm lips down the length of her neck.

Lindy let out a whimper of frustration. "Very well. I swear I'll hire help. Now go away."

"Are you sure you don't need help drying off?" Connor teased, but then had to duck quickly as the gunnysack flew over his head.

Lindy wasn't sure she could ever forgive Connor for digging up information about her as he had, and then using it so he could leave her with an unworried conscience. He was wrong about one thing: she wasn't a wealthy woman. What money she had squirreled away was all she had, and certainly not nearly enough to entice anyone to work for her. But she had promised, and just as Connor had kept his word, so would she.

Lindy wasn't in a very pleasant mood through dinner, but the only one her abrupt manner seemed to affect was Luke, who made an earlier than usual exit. That wasn't what Lindy had planned on. Now she was left alone in stiff silence with Connor. Well, if he had any sense, he would keep his distance.

It wasn't long before Connor left the house and settled on the porch. Instead of feeling relieved, Lindy was disappointed that Connor had left without his usual "Pleasant dreams, darlin'."

Lindy listened to his steps and knew he had stopped to lean against the post. She stole a glance outside, and in the blackness that surrounded him, she saw a match flare into amber light and glow against his face while he lazily lit a cheroot. With a shake of his wrist, Connor extinguished the flame, and brought back the darkness. But Lindy knew he was there by the faint smell of tobacco that drifted into the house, and by the speck of orange light that glowed at the tip of his cheroot. Connor seemed to be contemplating the stars, or perhaps he was taking a long, last look at the sky over Broken Gate. She removed her apron and hung it over a chair. Let him go, she thought, let him run from his ghosts.

Lindy slid into bed with her father's last words. She stared at the yellow paper as though she could read the words. What did they say? Were her memories of what Matt had read to her clouded by the passage of time? Had she failed to hear the words between the lines?

Connor had tried to relax, he had tried not to think of Lindy while he counted the stars and searched for constellations, but it had been impossible when he heard her every move. He had known when she left the kitchen by the way the lamplight had moved across the farmyard; he had known when she bathed at the washbasin by the sound of water splashing on her face and neck, and he had known when she undressed and slipped into her bed by the soft rustle of linen. No amount of stargazing had been able to chase her from his thoughts. Connor knew he would have left Broken Gate sooner had it not been for his growing feelings for Lindy, but she was married and he reminded himself of that daily.

He despised himself for coveting another man's wife, but there was only so much he could say to convince himself that it wouldn't be right when he saw the same longing in Lindy's eyes. She had arranged every possible way to keep him at Broken Gate. If she had a speck of love for her husband he would have known it. But she only avoided conversation about the man. Lately, even Luke had made no mention of Bill Rigby. The mysterious man might never be coming to Broken Gate. How long had Lindy said she had been in Texas—six months? By the end of each day, Connor had felt his desire swell and his self-control weaken. His opinion was that Lindy's husband was undeserving of the woman he seemed to have abandoned.

In a way, Connor was relieved that Lindy had someone to take care of her, even if her husband was absent for the moment. Since she was presently alone, he felt obligated to arrange for some protection until her husband arrived. The storm had made him realize that Lindy was not helpless, indeed she was full of determination, but that wasn't enough to survive on out in the wilderness. A woman needed more than grit and determination—she needed good, dependable men. It had taken using some of Lindy's own tactics to convince her of that. But why didn't he feel better about leaving, now that she had promised to hire some stockmen?

His heart beat back the answer and it frightened him. He had loved Christa. He had sworn he'd never love another woman like that again. Could he love his wife's memory and Lindy too? Was he ready to take up his life again and risk heartache? His struggle with the answer was almost pointless, considering Lindy had already promised her life to another.

When the soft, yellow light from Lindy's bedroom window faded over the farmyard, Connor knew she had turned down the wick of her lamp. He waited a long while after that, listening to the occasional jingle of a bell from a restless ewe, the woeful howl of a coyote and the sounds of the horses as they settled themselves in the corral. When his cheroot had burned down to a stub, Connor flicked it to the ground. Sure now that Lindy was fast asleep, he stepped inside.

Without consciously intending to do so, Connor paused in the doorway of Lindy's bedroom. He found her slender form curled in the sleeping position of a child, and was drawn closer by a force he seemed to have no control over. She looked so soft and innocent lying there—so vulnerable, so unaware of the danger she tempted daily, so in need of a protector. She hardly seemed like the same driven woman he had seen on more than a few occasions, but more like an insecure child. Her arms were wrapped around her pillow, her hair flowed over one shoulder, and her cotton nightgown settled around her waist and hips, temptingly outlining her feminine form. Connor lightly traced her puckered lips with his eyes. As though feeling his gaze, Lindy turned in her sleep, twisting her nightgown around her legs. She kicked her feet free before settling again.

It was the first time Connor had really noticed Lindy's feet, and he was surprised they were so small and white. Each toe was perfect, and each arch curved back to smooth, pink heels. He was startled by a sudden urge to hold one of the delicately formed feet and run his hand over the curve of her arch, around her heel and around her ankle to the back of her knee. Lindy moved again, and her nightgown moved past her ankles. She seemed restless. Not wanting to be caught gazing down at her while she slept, Connor fled her room, painfully sorry he had ever entered it.

After Connor returned to Luke's room, he found it impossible to fall asleep. He heard Lindy's every move, even the small sounds she made in her sleep. He was tempted to throw a pillow over his head. Finally, after a few hours of sleepless agony, he pulled on his boots and grabbed the serape from his bed. He was halfway across the farmyard, with intentions of sleeping in the barn, when Lindy's scream called him back. Connor sailed into the house and was at her bedside holding her in his arms in a matter of seconds.

Lindy trembled in Connor's embrace. He gently brushed his hand over her forehead and said softly, "What is it, darlin'?"

Lindy clamped her arms around Connor's neck. "Stay," she whispered.

"I will. I will, darlin'," Connor consoled, stroking the back of her hair. "You had that dream again. Do you want to tell me about it?" he asked.

Lindy rested her cheek against Connor's. How she wished it was only a harmless nightmare, and how she wished she could confide in Connor the heavy burden of guilt she carried. She held him tighter as she remembered her dream and saw Hank scratching away the dirt that covered him. Lindy's heart thumped against Connor's chest.

"Will you tell me what's frightening you?" Connor asked.

Lindy shook her head. She couldn't tell him about Hank. What would he think of her then? Even if he didn't blame her, he would want her to go to the sheriff, Hank's uncle. There was no way of telling Connor without involving Sheriff Hayes and Jeb, so she clung desperately to her secret, though it scratched and clawed to be released from her conscience.

"Maybe the dreams would stop if you talked about them."

Lindy loosened her grip around Connor's neck and pleaded, "Don't leave me tonight."

Connor smiled into her eyes and pulled her closer. "I won't, darlin'. As long as you need me, I won't leave."

For the first time in her life, Lindy admitted to needing someone other than herself, and it was a frightening feeling. She had always been self-reliant, emotionally strong and confident. Now she felt herself weaken in Connor's arms and embraced the contentment she found there. It had taken the specter of Hank Cobb to finally destroy the fragile thread of control she had managed to grasp whenever Connor was near. Ironically Hank had thrown her into the arms of the man who could be her salvation. But with all of Connor's tender, whispered words, she still feared he would eventually leave her. Then loomed the plaguing nightmares that she would soon have to explain.

Lindy was so ravaged with misgivings, she hardly noticed that Connor had slipped farther onto the bed. She was still tangled in thought when he caught her chin between his thumb and forefinger and turned her face to his. With one brief look into his eyes, Lindy felt her whole body go limp. Shortly she remembered the other sticky matter—that of her fictitious husband, Bill Rigby, and her stomach plummeted. Moving away from Connor, she blurted the first diversion that came to mind. "Would you like a cuppa?"

"Maybe later," Connor said, moving closer. His gaze drifted to Lindy's lips. Lindy recognized the same blue flames that had flared in his eyes the day of the storm, and sensed what was happening. She turned away and made a vain attempt to confess one of her sins. "Mr. O'Malley—"

"Tea is not what I want right now," Connor interrupted, stopping her heart with the deep, almost desperate tone of his voice. He cupped her cheeks in his hands and searched her eyes with his. "I want you. I want you now."

Lindy could feel the warmth and texture of Connor's hands on her face; she could smell the sweet aroma of tobacco still clinging to his fingers, and could even hear his labored breath above the throbbing of her heartbeat. She had to gather enough courage to tell Connor that she was not what he thought her to be. Even with her limited experience, if she was assessing the situation correctly, Connor could have only one thing in mind, and it was not an unmarried maiden he would be expecting.

"Mr. O'Malley, I've . . . Bill doesn't . . ." Lindy stumbled over her confession when she looked at Connor's face. It was so much more difficult to undo her story than it had been to invent it, especially when Connor's eyes left hers and focused on her lips. She inhaled deeply and began again. "Bill is not . . . Oh, Lord, I need a cuppa," Lindy ultimately announced, rushing into the kitchen.

Connor lifted himself off the bed and came to the kitchen doorway.

Lindy sensed that he stood behind her and knew that his eyes watched her stumble about in the shadows as she tried to make a fire under the kettle. Although she had expected him to follow her, her breath caught when she heard him call her name. When she did not answer, Connor made it clear that he was not to be deterred this time. "Neither you nor I want a cup of tea right now."

Lindy's hand trembled as she tried to deny the emotion that began to churn inside her. "Quite the contrary. There's never been a time when I've wanted one more," she answered truthfully, expecting her legs to give way at any moment.

Connor walked up behind her, wrapped his arms tightly around her waist and rested his cheek against her neck. "I think we both want each other right now. You're a grown woman with needs, Lindy, not an innocent child saving herself for her intended."

Lindy couldn't get a word past the lump that suddenly lodged in her throat. Connor was right about one thing: she did want him. And she knew he wanted her. But he would not be getting the experienced woman he expected.

Chapter Ten

Connor peeled Lindy's fingers from the handle of the kettle, took her hand and led her back to her room, back to where her bed waited so ominously. He spun her around playfully and pulled her up against his chest. She heard the breath in her lungs rush out in a soft gasp before Connor covered her lips with his.

"Connor—" The protest was muffled by Connor's persistent kiss until she put aside her last-minute confession and relaxed in his arms.

She found it easy to surrender to Connor. His gentle caresses had soothed away the tension in her muscles, and his kisses had made her incapable of thinking of anything but how much she wanted him. When Connor sat on the edge of the bed and pulled her between his knees, Lindy felt as though she moved in a dream where only she and he existed. There was no Hank Cobb and no fictitious husband, and there was the faint hope that if she followed Connor's lead, he would not suspect she had never been married.

"I've forgotten how luxurious a real bed is," Connor said, pulling her closer. "This may spoil me."

"I didn't think Luke's bed was so uncomfortable," Lindy said, hardly aware at what point Connor had unbound her hair and pulled out the ribbons of her nightgown.

"Only because you weren't in it." Connor raked his fingers through long waves of tawny hair. "Have you any idea how you've tortured me? To hear your breathing every night, your every restless turn, to remember the warmth of your body pressed against mine and to know you were so close but beyond my reach because of a husband who doesn't care enough to love and protect his wife? Whoever this man is, he doesn't deserve you."

With that, Connor lay back and pulled Lindy on top of him, cherishing her with kisses along her neck and shoulder. His hand grazed her thigh, pushing her nightgown along, exposing the bare skin underneath to the cool night air. Feeling a sudden urge to flee, Lindy tried to concentrate only on Connor's kiss while his hand freely roamed the length of her legs and the round curve of her hips and backside in the same gentle, mesmerizing manner that she had seen him use with Buddy. Connor made her forget everything except how wonderful she felt in his arms. Pure pleasure quickly conquered Lindy's initial fear until all that was left was an intense desire that begged to be satisfied.

Tucking one hand beneath her buttocks and one behind her neck, Connor rolled Lindy over and pinned her under him in one deft movement. Not only their lips met, but every part of their bodies touched in a single, lingering kiss.

"It's warmer in here than ten feet from the sun," Connor said, sliding off Lindy, and swiftly freeing the buttons of his shirt.

Through waves of smoldering heat, Lindy watched the garment part to reveal the broad expanse of Connor's chest and the strong arms that had held her. She watched his fingers urgently work the buckle of his belt and the buttons on his trousers. Lindy's gaze followed Connor's clothes to the floor. Naked, he was even more powerful looking than she had imagined, and perfect in every way except for the thin scar running down his torso.

Her face heated and her heart began to beat frantically at the certainty of what Connor's intentions were. She trembled, knowing that if men were anything like rams, Connor would soon know how innocent she was. Maybe not, she hoped, pulling the sheet up to her chin, and thinking to postpone the inevitable with conversation. She reached out and ran her finger lightly down the thin scar that crossed Connor's torso. Connor's skin rippled in the wake of her touch.

Connor answered her unspoken question. "A Confederate saber nicked me. The war was over, only he didn't know it or want to believe it," he explained between kisses. "It happened a long time ago, and like scars, memories fade." And proving he was not to be distracted by recalling any more memories, Connor startled Lindy by suddenly tossing the sheet aside. "Don't tell me you're cold in this heat," he said, slipping the nightgown off her shoulders. Through the shadows, Connor's eyes admired the pale glow of her skin, and his hands smoothed over the mounds of her breasts.

Afraid she would shake apart from anticipation, Lindy threw her arms around him and pulled his face down to hers. "Kiss me, Mr. O'Malley."

"Connor. And it will be my pleasure, darlin'."

At once, Connor's lips claimed hers, and the rest of her nightgown was pushed aside. With a subtle movement, Connor's knee wedged between Lindy's legs, nudging them apart. She felt his hand slide down her stomach, and then pause just beneath it, his fingers slipping to where she would never have imagined. His intimate touch surprised her, but soon the maddening stroking between her legs excited her beyond caring.

"Ah, darlin'," Connor rasped, "it's been a long time for both of us."

Lindy gulped down the dread lodged in her throat. "Longer than you know. Connor, I do want you but—" she began weakly.

"Shh. Come to me, darlin'. I can't wait any longer for you." Connor slid his hands beneath Lindy's buttocks and pushed his arousal against her. Closing her eyes and bracing her hands against Connor's shoulders, she waited for him to enter her.

"You've truly been neglected by that husband of yours. I promise I'll take you as slow as I can, sweetheart."

Connor hesitated and looked down at her, bewildered. "I'd swear this was your first time, but that couldn't be possible." He paused and studied her face. "Could it be possible?" To his astonishment, Lindy nodded. "You can't possibly be... Are you telling me you've never consummated your marriage?"

"I tried to tell you, but..." Connor dropped his forehead on Lindy's shoulder and groaned. "I don't blame you for being upset with me," Lindy whispered. "You can stop now if you'd like."

"There wouldn't be a chance of that now, darlin'," Connor said in a voice even more incredulous than before.

"Oh." After some silent deliberation Lindy added, "I'm not so sure I'm going to like this. I mean...suppose it doesn't work."

Connor lightly kissed her forehead. "Don't worry, it'll work and I promise you, you'll like it. You'll hurt at first, but that'll pass. There isn't any turning back now, darlin'."

Connor was truthful. It did hurt. But once he filled her with his flesh, the pain diminished, then melted in waves of inexplicable pleasure as he moved inside her. Lindy joined his rhythm, moving as he moved, stroking, pulsing, meshing together as one—never feeling closer in body and soul to anyone in her life than she did with Connor during that time. But it was all too quickly over. They reached the pinnacle of pleasure together, their energies spent and their long, tortured desire quickly satisfied. Lindy and Connor collapsed in each other's arms.

When Connor's conscience returned, he rolled off Lindy. "Now I've taken a man's wife before he's even had a chance to, himself. You have some explaining to do."

"Connor I . . . I am sorry. I—"

Connor leaned over and placed a finger over her lips. "Wait till I get back. I don't want to miss a word of your explanation as to how you're married and still a virgin. I need that cuppa now, and it won't be tea," he said as he strolled out of the room, giving Lindy some time to collect her thoughts.

Lindy found it difficult to think of much of anything while she watched Connor walk away in his sleek nudity. She was amazed at how the muscles in his buttocks and legs moved under his skin, and how the ends of his hair curled at his neck. He reminded her of the mountain lion she and Luke had seen when they first arrived in Texas and how it had moved with the same graceful strength.

When Connor returned, he was holding a tin cup. He came to Lindy's bed and sat next to her, bracing his back against the headboard. "Begin," he said. It was definitely an order.

Lindy smelled the sweet aroma of whiskey on Connor's breath. As her father had once predicted, she had finally driven a man to drink. "Father always said, 'never drink alone.'" Before the frown faded from Connor's face, Lindy pulled the top sheet off the bed, wrapped it around herself and was gone and back again with a china teacup full of whiskey. After a choking gulp of the drink, she began. "Promise you won't do your block?"

Connor leaned his head back against the headboard. "Why do I feel like I've just been to the gates of heaven only to be turned around and sent to hell?"

"You won't shout at me?"

Connor took another gulp of whiskey and looked directly at her. "I should have brought the bottle in, shouldn't I?"

Lindy looked into Connor's soft blue eyes and cried. All her tears of guilt, frustration and hidden insecurities spilled down her cheeks. It had been wrong to lie to Connor and invite him to her bed. She would not blame him, for she was as much a party to what had happened as he was, but now she couldn't help but think it had all been a mistake. "Oh, Connor," she sobbed.

After setting his empty cup on the small table next to the bed, Connor put his arm around Lindy's shoulders. "I promise I won't shout at you. Here." He tipped Lindy's cup to her lips. "Take another drink, slowly this time."

Unaccustomed to whiskey, Lindy felt a warm, soothing feeling spread over her. Before she could drink too much, Connor put the cup aside. Lindy leaned against his shoulder and prayed nothing she had to say would make him think less of her. Avoiding his eyes, she began her confession. "I don't have a husband. I never did." Lindy felt Connor's muscles tense against her side, but continued just the same. "I only wanted people to think I was married. Sheriff Hayes would have had me off this land in a flash, and every man in Dry Bed—"

Connor grabbed her shoulders and made her face him. "You mean you've never been—and you're not— You've put me through hell for weeks, thinking I was tempting a married woman. And then worse—to make me believe I had stolen your innocence."

Lindy shook herself out of Connor's hold. "You promised you wouldn't shout. I was only trying to protect myself."

"I'm not shouting at you."

"You are! Don't come the raw pawn with me, Connor O'Malley. I'm not the only one with secrets."

"Secrets? You mean there are more?" Connor grabbed his trousers and put one leg in.

Holding the sheet tightly around herself, Lindy watched him until he was half-dressed.

As he buckled his belt, he said, "Get some sleep. We're riding into town at the crack of dawn."

In all her life Lindy had never been known to sleep past sunup. But there she was in her bed, with the sun shining in through her window, the sheet pulled almost over her head and her arm dangling over the side of the bed. Through the fog in her head, she heard Luke calling her.

"Lin? Lin," Luke called again, this time shaking her.

Lindy turned over and looked at Luke through bleary eyes. "Oh, Luke," she moaned, shielding her eyes from the much-too-bright morning.

Luke knelt and looked into Lindy's eyes. "Lin, what's wrong? Your eyes are all red."

"My head hurts...my body hurts...my stomach feels like it did when we sailed here. I think I'm dying with fever."

"I'll get Connor."

"No," Lindy said weakly, but Luke had slipped from her grasp and disappeared before she could call him back.

Connor could not find her like this. She struggled to get out of bed, but her head felt like a lead weight, and her legs like long pieces of rope. She was teetering on the edge of the bed, holding her heavy, throbbing head in her hands when Connor and Luke entered her room. Lindy glanced at them both. Luke's face was blanched with worry and Connor...well, Connor looked as he had the night before—purely annoyed.

"You see," Luke said, fretfully, "we have to get the doctor."

"I've seen this affliction before. It's fairly common among men," Connor finally said with reassuring authority. "And not life threatening. It comes upon one suddenly,

and lasts about a day. Your sister doesn't need a doctor.''
Connor took the uncorked whiskey bottle from the small
table by Lindy's bed. "A strong cup of coffee is what she
needs—then I promise you, she'll be her old self by nightfall. In Dry Bed, if she likes, she can stop in and see the
doctor.''

Lindy looked at Connor obliquely and thought she saw a
grin faintly touch his lips. Luke looked considerably relieved at Connor's prognosis. He left Connor with her and
returned shortly with the ordered cup of coffee.

The smell of the brew set Lindy's stomach off even more,
prompting her to announce, "I can't travel." She fell back
on the bed and pulled the sheet over her head. "You two go
without me,'' she said from under the sheet.

"Maybe she should rest today," Luke said, worry once
more creeping into his voice.

"It's better she get up and about," Connor offered.

Lindy tossed the sheet from her face, glared at Connor
and said firmly, "*She* is not going.''

Just as firmly, Connor replied, "Yes, she is. Luke, get the
wagon and horses ready.''

Luke hesitated. "Should I saddle Queenie?''

"Queenie will be a smoother ride than the wagon, if your
sister thinks she can stay in the saddle. If not, she can ride
with me.''

When they were alone, Connor tore away the sheet that
Lindy hid under. "Get up," he said, grabbing her under her
arms and propping her up like a rag doll.

"Go away, Connor. I'm not riding to Dry Bed.''

Answering her with only a sharp look, Connor left Lindy
balanced on the edge of the bed, and walked over to the
washbasin. He poured a generous amount of water into the
bowl and wrung out a washcloth. Returning to Lindy, he
attempted to bring some color back into her face.

"You look a fright," he said. Compassion softened his
voice.

"Luke's right. I need the doctor."

"All he'd do is laugh and holler at you for wasting his time."

Lindy was confused and then angry at Connor's cruel comment when it was obvious that she was suffering. "How could you be so daggy?"

"There isn't anything the doc can do for your state of inebriation."

"Inebriation?"

"You're drunk, darlin'. And all you can do is wait for what you drank last night to wear off. In the meantime, the day will go as usual. You're going to Dry Bed with us to hire some hands since they'll be working for you."

Lindy still held her head in her hands. "You mean I'm pie-eyed?"

"You certainly are feeling the effects of it," Connor said with sympathy, lifting her chin and dabbing the wet cloth over her forehead and cheeks. "What made you do such a thing?" Without waiting for her reply, Connor added, "One thing's for sure, from now on, you'll be more careful about how much whiskey you drink."

"Does Luke know?"

"No. But he doesn't think you're dying anymore," Connor said.

Lindy grimaced. "I thought I was gonna kark, myself."

"I'm sure you did." Connor laughed. "Where's your comb?"

"My hairbrush is over there." Lindy pointed to the corner of the room where she had thrown it the night before.

Connor returned to her with the hairbrush in his hand. He sat next to her and began to brush out the tangles in her hair, starting at the ends and carefully working his way up. As terrible as she felt, Lindy began to soften to Connor's gentle touch as he patiently unknotted her hair. "When will the pounding stop?"

"Not for a while. There, you look better already," he said. Putting the brush in Lindy's hand, he left her side to gather up her clothes.

"I don't see why we can't go tomorrow."

"Because you have a promise to keep." Connor tossed a riding skirt and blouse on the bed. "Now, get dressed."

When Connor was out of sight, Lindy collapsed onto the bed, only to hear his warning come from the next room. "If you're not ready in ten minutes, I'll dress you myself."

Not wanting to test his threat, Lindy was dressed in less than ten minutes. She took her saddled horse from Luke, who seemed to be amazed that she was standing on her two feet.

"Connor was right. You look better already, Lin."

"I'll be apples."

"That's what Connor said."

"Did he," she said, glaring over to Connor, who was seated on his horse. She gripped the reins in her hands and settled her feet in the stirrups. A soft groan, barely audible, gave testimony to her suffering.

Connor sidled up to her and winked. "If the apple feels ready to fall from the tree, you can ride with me."

Lindy was unsmiling. "Thank you for your concern, but if I don't feel up to it, I'll ride in the buckboard with Luke."

"Very well, but I'll keep close anyway, just in case—"

"I'm not going to fall off my horse."

Connor leaned over to her and whispered humorously, "It looks to me more like you might slide off."

Lindy's heels nudged her horse's sides. Queenie trotted ahead of Connor and Luke. Lindy's head felt as if it were going to topple off her shoulders, so she eased back to a walk, allowing Connor to catch up to her.

"I'm sorry I teased you," he apologized, but a grin curved his lips.

"You should have warned me about whiskey."

"How was I to know you intended to finish the bottle after I left? Maybe I should have stayed."

Lindy flushed red at the reminder of what they had shared. "I don't want Luke to know about what happened last night."

"The boy's growing up, and he's not blind. If he hasn't already, he'll be looking at women in a different light himself. And if you don't want Luke to know about last night, then that's all the more reason for me to be getting on," Connor said in a level tone.

It was as if what he had done with her last night didn't matter. He was going to leave and that was that. Lindy felt betrayed, hurt and suddenly sick. She slid off her horse and headed for the nearest bush she could hide behind.

Connor let her keep a shred of dignity by giving her her privacy and not referring to the incident with anything more than a genuinely concerned look. She was thankful Luke was too far behind them to notice.

After a mile or two of riding in silence, Connor asked, "Are you feeling better?"

Lindy nodded and said softly, "I've become fond of you, Connor."

The mustache above Connor's lip twitched. His blue eyes regarded Lindy and then stared straight ahead, focusing on a puffy white cloud hanging just above the horizon. "I'm fond of you, too." Then unexpectedly he asked, "You know how to use that pearl-handled pistol you like to sleep with?"

As if Lindy's stomach hadn't been touchy enough, that really made it flip-flop. "How do you—"

"It fell out of the blanket you hide it in."

Lindy remembered the day Connor had taken cover in her room, and the thud she and Luke had heard. She had forgotten about Hank's gun. "Oh. I just don't want to be up a gum tree, that's all."

Connor shoved back his Stetson so he could look directly at Lindy. "You have the damnedest expressions I've ever heard, and at times when communication is critical. I'm beginning to think you're doing it deliberately."

"There you go, yer gonna do yer block," Lindy replied in an exaggerated accent.

"You're obviously feeling better. Now, has someone threatened you? One of Claxton's men?"

Lindy chilled at how close Connor had guessed, and then bristled with anger that he had the nerve to pretend concern when he was going to leave her anyway.

"You're going to shoot through one day. Why does our safety even matter to you?"

"Because I'm fond of you, and I want to know that you and Luke will be safe after I'm gone."

Lindy nearly screamed. Their understanding of the word *fond* obviously differed. Connor was certainly fond of her, fond of Luke and fond of the dog. Lindy's riding gloves stretched over her knuckles. "Well I'm so bloody happy you're *fond* of me, luv, but don't bother yourself." This time Lindy gave her horse its lead and didn't stop until Connor was far behind her. And she meant to keep a good distance between them, even if Connor might decide to try to close it.

After her temper settled, Lindy had to admit to herself that it was better that Connor leave them. He was beginning to ask questions, and her answers would only lead to more questions. Before long, Connor would begin to put the pieces together, and she would be explaining Hank's death. Lindy imagined his reaction. Connor O'Malley had been Captain O'Malley, an officer of the government, someone who had enforced laws. She didn't think it would sit well with anyone that she had killed a man, least of all with a man whose wife and child had been murdered. At the very least he'd make her tell her story to Sheriff Hayes. Luke had been foolish to keep the gun; all it could do was point out Hank's killer. Connor had to leave. The sooner she found some stockmen, the safer her secret would be.

Lindy didn't have a clue as to how to go about hiring men, and she didn't want to leave it up to Connor. As she rode into town, she had the sinking feeling that she would have to rely on him to find men for her. Looking down the main street, she considered where she would most likely meet prospective stockmen. The locations were not heartening. Minerva's Saloon was the most obvious, and certainly out of the question. Quinn's Mercantile was a possibility. Hester might have some recommendations, but at the cost of turning Lindy into gossip material. That left the blacksmith, the best-looking option so far. Queenie needed shoes anyway, and that would give her a good excuse for standing about with an eye open for men who looked as if they needed work.

Toby looked up at Lindy through the legs of the big bay he was shoeing. "Nice seein' you, Mrs. Rigby. Can I help you today?"

"Queenie needs shoes."

"You're lucky. I'm just about done with this one. You can leave Queenie if you like."

"That's all right. I don't mind waiting. Isn't that Sheriff Hayes's horse?"

"Right you are. You've got an eye for horses, Mrs. Rigby, and they're a lot safer to breed out here than those woolly-backs of yours, if you don't mind my buttin' into your business. I sure would hate to hear of any harm comin' to you or your fine brother. Your father was a good man. I ain't faultin' him for his dreams, but that don't mean you have to follow in his footsteps. They're dangerous foot-steps to follow. And that's all I'm gonna say on the mat-ter."

Lindy sighed. Was there anyone who wasn't going to of-fer her their good advice? "Toby, I'm surprised to hear a lecture from you. I expect I'll hear one from the sheriff if I see him, but . . . Well, never mind. Thank you for your con-cern, just the same."

Toby wiped his hands on his sooty apron. "No trouble. It's free. Soon's I get Crackerjack outta here, I can get started on Queenie."

While Lindy waited for Toby to put the sheriff's horse in the back corral, she loosened Queenie's cinch strap and wondered what Toby had meant by "dangerous footsteps." She was about to pull the saddle off when she saw two men over the top of her horse.

"Now I know she ain't the smithy," the tall, sandy haired man said. Then, glaring at his darker-complected friend, he snapped, "You left yer manners back in Mexico? Take off yer dang hat." After that rebuke, he walked around to Lindy and took the saddle from h_r hands. "Let me help you with that. Name's..." Balancing the saddle on his thigh, he paused, as if he had forgotten his own name, then added with a peculiar tone of satisfaction, "Darby. Darby Willis."

"Thank you, Darby. It's nice to meet you and..." Lindy looked past him to the squat Mexican who nervously twisted his hat in his hands. His dark eyes seemed to smile, and a thin, black mustache tickled past his jawline. His gun belt hugged a rotund stomach. He wore black pants and a too-tight, once-white shirt that looked as though it could have belonged to a highbred Spaniard. He was a contrast to Darby, whose clothes were so baggy, it looked like two of him could fit inside them.

Darby balanced Queenie's saddle on the rail. "He's... well...heck! His name's so hard to say it don't matter."

Lindy frowned. For a man who seemed so polite, it certainly was perplexing why he didn't introduce his friend properly.

Finally Darby said, "We just call him Mex for short."

"How do you do, Mex." Lindy smiled at the grinning Mexican. "I'm Mrs. Rigby. Toby should be back any minute."

"I hope so," Darby said with almost a desperate touch to his voice. "We're kind of in a hurry, and my horse threw a shoe not one minute ago and—"

"Then you wouldn't be staying in town?" Lindy interrupted.

"No, ma'am. We're ridin' straight through. We're tryin' to catch up to a wagon train we missed in Laredo." The way Darby's amber eyes drooped at the outside corners beseeched sympathy. "My wife's dyin'. I'm tryin' to get to her before—excuse me, ma'am." Darby pulled the neckerchief from his skinny neck, and although Lindy hadn't noticed any tears, he wiped his eyes. Then Darby shook out the neckerchief with much ceremony and blew his nose.

Lindy glanced at Mex, who looked sadder than Buddy when there were no table scraps. "I'm sorry. If there's anything I can do—"

"There is," Darby answered quickly. "Since we're in a hurry, you wouldn't mind waiting—"

"Of course not! You go right ahead."

"Thank you. Because of your kindness I may get to my wife in time to see her . . . die."

"Oh, dear heavens!"

Darby blew his nose hard just when Toby looked out on the three of them. "I thought there was a goose honkin' out here! All right, Mrs. Rigby, you can bring in Queenie."

"I'll wait. This poor man is in a hurry to get to his sick wife."

Toby looked at Darby in the same suspicious way he regarded all strangers. "If you say so, Mrs. Rigby."

Clearly pleased, Darby and Mex followed Toby with their swaybacked mare. Lindy waited outside with Queenie until they were finished.

Before he led away his shod horse, Darby blessed Lindy, and Mex nodded his appreciation. When Darby and Mex were finally gone, Toby said, "They were the most fidgety fellows I've ever seen. You'd think one of *them* threw a shoe.''

Lindy's hope to find some prospective stockmen getting their horses shod was less than a success. Other than Darby and Mex, she had seen no one. The men must all be in the saloon, she thought downheartedly. Unless she wanted to brave Minerva's place herself, she'd have to find Connor. Well, after all, it was Connor's idea to hire help—not hers.

Leaving Queenie with Toby, Lindy began her search for Connor and Luke. First, she saw the buckboard, then she saw Connor and Luke leaning against it engaged in what looked like a serious conversation. Connor noticed Lindy, but didn't move to meet her. He just watched her approach with eyes so heated Lindy could feel the fire in them.

Luke was first to express concern. ''Lin! Where were you?''

''Getting Queenie some new shoes.''

''Well, Connor was—'' For some reason, when Luke's eyes met Connor's, he stopped talking, leaving Lindy to wonder about what he had not finished. *What* was Connor? Angry? Worried? And he didn't want Luke to tell her! She began to steam over the secret they were sharing. Luke had never kept anything from her before.

Since the rest of what Luke had to say was just as interesting, Lindy promised herself that she would ask him exactly what he meant to say when Connor wasn't around to silence him. ''Lin, Connor lost a twenty-dollar gold piece trying to hire a couple of men as stockmen.'' Luke's voice was filled with as much awe as Lindy felt at discovering that Connor even had that much money to lose. But the most impressive part of the story was yet to come. ''Then he won it all back and then some.''

Lindy glanced at Connor to confirm that what Luke had said was really true. Connor smiled back at her. The skin crinkled around his eyes, giving him a most mischievous look. ''Well, I'm glad you didn't lose your shirt on my account," she said, only to be mortified by Connor's whispered reply.

"I'd lose my shirt to you anytime, darlin'."

Lindy sucked in her breath, and resisted the urge to fan the heat from her face. "Did you hire any men?"

"No. No one would work with sheep. Not even to get their money back."

"You indebted them to you? That's blackmail."

Just as smartly, Connor said, "Persuasion. It didn't work, anyway. Claxton's reputation is a strong grip to break. No one's going to volunteer to make an enemy of him."

Lindy felt her blood boil. How dare one man prevent her from hiring help if she wanted to? "I'm going to hire help," she said with determination.

"I don't know how you're going to convince anyone to work for you. If *I* couldn't—"

"Just because *you* failed doesn't mean *I* will." Lindy marched off.

"Where's your sister going?"

"I don't know, but when she gets her back up like that, there's gonna be no stopping her until she gets her way."

Chapter Eleven

Dean and Boone huddled across the street from Dry Bed's only bank, an unimpressive building crowned with a plain false front. Despite its unobtrusive appearance, the word *Bank* painted on the front window made Dean's knees knock under his baggy pants. Boone was just as nervous, but managed to keep his bones from rattling by bolstering his nerve with overconfidence. A few feet down from Dean and Boone, the third member of the gang, a Mexican by the name of Armaldo, calmly waited.

"Look at him," Dean complained to Boone. "Rollin' tobacco, and not spillin' any."

Boone's eyes darted to where Armaldo relaxed in the shade of his sombrero. "Well, maybe he's experienced."

Dean doubted Armaldo was experienced in anything but stealing chickens, and maybe, in his younger years, rustling cattle. But as annoying as the Mexican's calm was, Dean felt confident knowing Armaldo would be waiting for them with the horses. If anything, Armaldo was loyal. Dean glanced back again at the Mexican as he and Boone crossed the street.

From the men's appearance, no one would have picked them out as bank robbers. Dean, in his large patched pants, rolled at the bottoms and shirred at his waist by a rope belt, was taller than most men in Dry Bed. His gun belt was on its last notch and still too big to properly span his pencil-thin frame. He had to stop and adjust it every time he took a few steps.

Boone was not as tall as Dean, but twice as wide, with oversize feet he tended to trip over when he walked. He did better in the saddle, especially if he was riding away from someone.

Before stepping up on the boardwalk, both men paused and pulled their neckerchiefs over their noses.

"If only that woman—" Dean worried aloud.

Boone tripped on the boardwalk. "What woman?" he asked, once he had recovered from almost falling on his face.

"The one gettin' her horse shod," Dean replied, his voice muffled by the neckerchief.

Boone yanked the neckerchief down around Dean's neck. "You was talkin' to someone? I thought I told you not to even look at anyone."

Dean's mouth twitched slightly. "I tried not to look, but she was awful pretty."

"Pretty will get us hung. I suppose you introduced yourself proper too."

"Whatdaya think, I'm a fool?" Dean didn't let Boone relax for long. "I told her my name was Darby and Maldo, Mex."

"That's real smart of you, Dean. I guess she got a real good look at your handsome faces, too."

Dean sulked. "What was I supposed to do? It wasn't my fault that dang horse threw a shoe, and it ain't my idea to go robbin' no banks," he reminded Boone for the tenth time that day.

Boone repeated his answer for the tenth time. "I'm sick of eatin' Maldo's jackrabbit stew. And that's not the least of it. We're down to one and a half horses, and my toes are comin' out the tops of my boots." He held up a large foot to show Dean, wiggling his toe through the hole in his boot.

Dean looked down at Boone's worn boot. The heels were nearly gone and the soles paper thin. "I told you they weren't your size before you took 'em off that carcass we found in Mexico."

"Hell, Dean, you know how long ago that was? I've walked more miles in these boots in the last two days than that prospector done in his whole life. Soon there's gonna be no point in wearin' 'em."

"Hangin' ain't worth a new pair of boots."

"Well at least I'll be dressed fine for the occasion."

"You'll be dressed fine all right," Dean argued. "All those people crowded around watchin' us swing will be sayin' to themselves, 'Look at Boone Watts, don't he look natty in those new boots.'"

"Shut up, Dean. I've run out of ideas to keep from starvin'. Now before I run short of nerve, let's get in there. I'm sleepin' on a soft bed tonight—with company, and it ain't gonna be you."

"Well, I sure as hell hope not," Dean parried, adjusting his neckerchief.

Dean and Boone walked the few feet down the boardwalk to the bank, just in time to watch Horton Howser lock the door. Boone yanked down his neckerchief and Dean's just before the banker saw them.

"Be back in a minute, gentlemen," Howser promised.

"Where's he goin'?" Boone asked.

"Now what do we do?" Dean whispered.

"We wait until he gets back. He said he'll only be a minute."

"But he's seen us."

"Then we'll have to shoot him," Boone growled.

"Shoot him? What are you talkin' about?"

"What else are we gonna do? Invite him for dinner?"

"That may not be a bad idea. Maldo's jackrabbit stew will kill anyone. I always was suspicious of what that Mexican puts in his stew."

"I'm so hungry now, thinkin' of Maldo's cookin' is makin' my stomach growl."

Dean concluded, "When a man's near starvation, I guess he'll eat anythin' and do anythin'. I'd sooner be raidin' a henhouse. You think there's any farms near here?"

"What about that woman you saw? Where do you think she came from?"

"Not from around here. She talked kinda funny."

Boone sighed. "What's that banker doin' anyway?"

The blistering heat and the dust that caked in the crevices of her damp skin all added to the annoyance Lindy felt, so when she saw that Horton Howser had locked the bank to hand-deliver Hester's change, her patience was taxed even more. As if it weren't bad enough that Claxton stood in her way, or that Connor and Luke were sharing secrets and doubting her, now she had to wait in the sweltering sun for the bank to reopen just so she could withdraw enough money to entice someone to work for her.

While Lindy paced at the door, Dean and Boone waited some yards away, their hats pulled down over their eyes. Lindy pulled out a handkerchief and wiped the beads of perspiration from her forehead just as Horton came in view.

"Mrs. Rigby," he exclaimed. "Hester and I were just talking about you."

"I can just imagine," Lindy said through clenched teeth.

Horton jiggled the key in the lock, and then shoved the door open. "She noticed your brother and that friend of yours, a Mr.—"

"O'Malley."

"Yes, O'Malley. He's staying with you?"

"Didn't Hester tell you?" Lindy asked, following behind the banker.

Horton Howser turned to look at her. From the faint expression on his face Lindy knew the whiskered banker had already heard an earful from Hester. "Mr. Howser, you know not to believe everything Hester says."

"That's true," he said, chuckling.

"However, Mr. O'Malley is staying with me as a stockman. His duties are to help with the stock, and have never gone beyond that—in case you were wondering. Since he'll be leaving soon, I suppose Dry Bed's sticky beaks will have to find something else to gossip about."

The banker's face blanched as white as his whiskers, satisfying Lindy enough to calm her temper and set an amused smile on her lips. Once Horton recovered, he assumed a more serious and distant tone. "What can I do for you, Mrs. Rigby?"

"I'd like to withdraw all of my money."

"*All* of it?" The banker's voice squeaked and his spectacles slipped down the slope of his nose. Lindy smiled and nodded. "Very well," he said, then mumbled to himself, "I'm doubtful a married woman who would let a stranger live with her knows what she's doing."

As Horton Howser bent over the squat black safe in the back corner, Dean and Boone walked into the bank. Lindy naturally turned around at the sound of footsteps, and was shocked to see two men with their faces half-covered by neckerchiefs. Even more surprising was that one of the men was strikingly familiar. They had yet to draw their guns, but their intention was certainly clear to Lindy—they had come to rob the bank.

When Dean saw her scrutinize him, his eyes bulged with dread. Boone looked over to Dean and then to Lindy. They exchanged whispers, making it obvious to her that her presence had put a snag in their plans.

Lindy realized she was in a very bad position—between two bank robbers with guns strapped to their waists and Horton Howser. If any shots were fired, she was apt to be in the way. Afraid to move lest one of the men draw on her,

Lindy stayed frozen to the spot, straining to hear their whispered plans.

"Now what?" Dean's voice rasped through his neckerchief.

"I don't know. Let me think a minute."

"I don't have to think that long. Let's get out of here before she screams," Dean said, grabbing Boone's arm.

Boone shook Dean off and looked at Lindy. "Lady, don't make a sound. That's good, stay quiet. Nice, lady. Now just move over there."

Lindy stepped aside, wondering all the while when they were going to draw their guns.

"Mrs. Rigby, you sure you don't want to reconsider?" Horton called from behind the counter.

"Ah, yes, Mr. Howser, I'm sure."

"Anyone out there with you?"

"You have two...other customers," Lindy said hesitantly.

"I'll be a minute," the banker said in an irritated voice.

With a shaky hand, Boone fumbled for his gun. To Lindy's disbelief, it fell from his hand and landed on the floor with a thud. All eyes converged on the weapon lying between Boone's feet. The bank robbers' eyes lifted to Lindy.

"What's going on out there?" Howser asked.

Dean and Boone blanched.

"I...I dropped my purse," Lindy explained, watching curiously as the two men exhaled in relief.

Boone collected his senses, scooped up his gun and hid it behind his back. Dean was so rattled, his baggy pants quivered like leaves. Sweat popped out on his forehead and poured down his face. He thoughtlessly tore his neckerchief from his face to wipe his forehead, never realizing that he had revealed his identity. At once Lindy knew where she had seen him. He was the man getting his horse shod, the man with the dying wife.

Seeing Dean unmasked, Boone holstered his gun, dropped his neckerchief around his neck and whispered to his partner, "The way our luck's been runnin', I should have known it would all go sour."

Lindy no longer felt either man would or could actually shoot someone unless their guns accidentally fired. When they began to back out of the small room, she knew that whatever had driven them to thinking of robbing a bank suddenly no longer mattered to them as much as their lives. The two were certainly not outlaws. What outlaw would drop his gun while drawing it or remove his mask to wipe his forehead? Heavens, they probably couldn't even defend themselves.

Just as the men backed to the door, Horton Howser appeared with Lindy's money. "What you got in that purse of yours? It sure made a racket. I'll be with you gentlemen in a minute. I hope you didn't come to make a withdrawal," he said, stopping their retreat.

"No. No we didn't," Dean said too quickly.

Howser threw Lindy an accusatory glance. "Good. I can use some depositors."

"We didn't come to make no deposit neither," Dean said, laughing until Boone shoved him.

Howser looked over the top of his spectacles. "Well, if you didn't come to make a deposit or a withdrawal, what did you come for?"

The men were at a loss, each looking to the other for some explanation that would extricate them from their situation.

"You didn't come here to rob the bank, did you?" Horton joked, never realizing the accuracy of his words.

"Hell, no. Do we look like bank robbers?" Boone asked.

"That's the funniest thing I ever heard," Dean added, chuckling nervously.

Howser handed Lindy her money. "Well, then, what can I do for you men?"

"Ah . . . ah, we . . ." Boone stuttered, grasping for an answer. "You tell him, Dean."

"We . . ." Dean's voice squeaked.

"Why, Mr. Howser, this man was just looking for me," Lindy exclaimed. "And what a surprise to see you here, too. I thought Toby was still shoeing your horse. This must be the friend you told me about." She extended her hand to Boone, who took it hesitantly. "G'day, I'm Mrs. Rigby."

"Nice to meet you."

"And you're . . ."

"Boone. And you've already met Dean," Boone added.

"Dean," Lindy repeated. "I could have sworn you said your name was . . . I suppose I was mistaken." She leaned closer and whispered to Dean, "Sick wife? I would never have imagined you for a bushranger."

"A what?"

"An outlaw," she explained.

"We're not," Dean whispered back.

"I have a solution for both of you." Lindy kept her voice low so the banker couldn't hear her. "You're desperate, and I'm desperate. We can help each other and no one will hang."

"Hang!"

"That's what they do to men like you."

"Now, lady—" Boone began to object.

"I need two stockmen. If you agree to work for me, I'll pay you well. And I won't breathe a word to Mr. Howser or the sheriff about exactly what kind of withdrawal you had in mind."

"And if we don't?" Boone challenged for the sake of hearing her reply.

"Then I'll see that you both hang."

"You know those men, Mrs. Rigby?" Horton asked. He was beginning to grow edgy from all the whispering.

Lindy turned and flashed the banker an assuring smile. "Yes, Mr. Howser. They're my stockmen. The skinny one is Dean, and the one with the brown eyes and dimples is Boone.''

Dean and Boone were shocked speechless at the turn of events. They had come to rob a bank, and instead, they had been signed on as ranch hands in a matter of seconds.

Lindy counted out her money and handed a small stack of bills to Dean. ''Now, get yourselves outfitted in decent clothes. Boone, it looks like you need a new pair of boots. When you're ready, I'll meet you in front of the mercantile.''

Lindy opened the door and then remembered the Mexican. ''Wasn't there another man with you?''

Dean replied quickly. ''Armaldo's a good cook.''

''If you like frijoles and jackrabbit,'' Boone added.

''Good. See that he's taken care of, as well.''

When Lindy left the bank, she nearly skipped down the street with glee. She had three stockmen even Claxton couldn't take away from her, and she had found them herself.

Riding Queenie, Lindy returned to Connor and Luke. Connor watched her dismount and hitch her horse.

''Are you going to tell us why you're grinning from ear to ear, or do we guess?'' Connor asked.

''You can guess, if you like,'' she sang. ''But I'd rather like to see your expressions when you see for yourselves.'' Lindy watched the door of Quinn's Mercantile, turning every now and then to smile at Connor's cynical face.

''Is your surprise in there?'' Connor asked.

''Possibly,'' she replied coyly.

Lindy's smile suddenly faded when Clay Claxton and Sheriff Hayes stepped out of the mercantile.

''I gather they're not who you were expecting,'' Connor whispered in her ear.

''No, they're not. But perhaps it's just as well that Claxton is here.'' Lindy watched the two men approach them.

The sheriff was first to greet Lindy. "Haven't seen you in some time, Mrs. Rigby," he said. "Good to see you, too, Luke."

Claxton briefly acknowledged Lindy and then said to Connor, "Care for another card game before you leave, so I can win back some of my money?"

Lindy had to stop herself from staring at Connor when she learned that he had been playing cards with Claxton's own men. Was he insane to try and win men away from Claxton? True, it would have been ironic to see his cowboys tending her jumbucks, but she didn't want Connor getting shot for her.

Lindy heard Connor laugh, as if it were some grand game of his. "No, Clay. I think I'll just keep the money, as a reminder of how badly you and your men play."

Sheriff Hayes cleared his throat. "Nothin' like a good game of cards to bring men together. Long as it's peaceful, it's a fine way to forget the heat." Hayes looked back to the mercantile. "You expectin' someone, Mrs. Rigby?"

Lindy waved her arm in the air, hailing Boone, Dean and Maldo as they stepped out of the mercantile. "Yes, as a matter of fact, I am."

Every head turned in the same direction. With all the attention focused on them, the three men looked afraid to take another step. Lindy hoped she was the only one who noticed how Boone's and Dean's faces paled when they saw the sheriff and Claxton regard them so intently. Afraid they would freeze to the boardwalk, Lindy dashed over to the men, grabbed their arms and pulled them along. Armaldo followed, leading a horse and a mule.

"Gentlemen, I'd like you to meet three of Broken Gate's stockmen—Dean, Boone and Armaldo."

Lindy wished she could have saved the look on Claxton's face. And from Luke's smile, she suspected he felt the same. The sheriff finally found his tongue. "Nice meetin' you men." After studying their faces, he said to Dean, "You look awfully familiar.

All eyes converged on Dean. His Adam's apple bobbed up and down his skinny neck.

Lindy came to his rescue. "Now Sheriff, everyone in Texas looks familiar to you."

"Well, that's not entirely true, Mrs. Rigby. I never thought I'd seen you before," the sheriff bantered dryly.

Lindy ignored him and addressed her stockmen. "One of you can ride in the wagon."

"That'll be Maldo. He et his horse," said Dean.

Connor leaned over to Lindy and whispered, "You handpicked these men?"

"At least I found men," Lindy retorted briskly.

Claxton, who had been silent up to this point, rested his foot on the wagon to prevent it from leaving before he had his say. He looked at the strangers directly before he spoke. "I'm Clay Claxton." He shook each man's hand, and gave them each a cigar, making sure their eyes had not missed the sparkle of his gold ring. "When you men get tired of dipping sheep and being nagged by a woman, you just come see me."

All the joy that Lindy had felt was washed away in one angry wave, until she reminded herself that her men thought she could send them to jail if they left. It hadn't occurred to them yet that all they had done was *plan* to rob a bank, and Lindy had no evidence of even that. No matter how Claxton tempted them, at least for a while, they thought she held their freedom in her hand.

Lindy mounted her horse and looked down into Claxton's steely eyes. He was the man who had invited her to lunch and then served her her own lamb on a platter; he had sent his men to scatter her band, and now he was offering to buy out her help before they even saw Broken Gate. There were a hundred things she wanted to say to Claxton, none of them nice. If she hadn't thought a tart remark would give him the satisfaction of knowing that he had goaded her, she would have given him an earful of language she had learned from her brother Matt. Instead, in a dignified manner, she said, "G'day, Mr. Claxton."

"Always a pleasure to see you, Mrs. Rigby," Claxton returned politely.

Lindy walked her horse away from the wagon before turning to Claxton. "Get your bloody foot off that wheel before we all have the pleasure of seeing your leg broke." Barely giving Claxton time to react, she smacked the rumps of Luke's team. They tore away, leaving Claxton speechless and the sheriff sporting a wide grin.

Connor rode up to Lindy, smiling. "There for a minute, I thought you were going to disappoint me."

At first, Lindy didn't see what Connor found so amusing. "And how would I have disappointed you?"

"By checking your temper and letting Claxton get the last word. You left the man looking for his tongue." Connor chuckled.

"He was speechless, wasn't he?" Lindy smiled, and they laughed together.

The ride back to Broken Gate went well until Connor began to inquire about how Lindy had found her stockmen.

"Just like that, they agreed to work for you?"

"Yes. Why do you find that so hard to believe?"

Connor looked at Lindy directly. "Because you're trying to hide under your hat, and I know you better than to accept such a simple answer. You must have tricked them with one of your expressions. I know. You told them they'd be overseeing some new kind of longhorn from Australia called a jumbuck."

Lindy raised her chin indignantly. "They know about the sheep. I was very honest with them."

Connor still wasn't convinced. "Do they know how popular sheep are in these parts?"

"I was trying to hire men, not discourage them."

"Well, if they don't know what they're going to be up against, then you've hired three fools. Unless somehow, what you have to offer is less dangerous to them than Claxton and his men." Connor studied Lindy's face, though it was hidden in the shadow of her hat.

Lindy felt her face heat under Connor's questioning. "Are you looking for a blue, Connor O'Malley?"

"There you go again—attempting to confuse the opponent with your verbal tactics. I guess I'll have to ask the three men myself to get a straight answer."

Lindy didn't want Connor to do that. At least not before she learned more about their backgrounds herself. "I don't know why you're making such a to-do over them. I would have thought you'd be happy to know you're free to leave." When Connor didn't respond, Lindy tried to read the expression on his face, but found little hint of emotion. He just stared straight ahead, his eyes reflecting the bright blue sky. "Dean, Boone and Armaldo can help me now. They'll need some training, but between Luke and me, we'll manage."

"You never did say where you found them," Connor persisted.

Lindy sighed. So they'd gone round-robin. It was as if Connor was determined to find some fault with what she had done. "All right, all right! You have your mind set on it, don't you?"

"I just have a feeling this is one of your most interesting tales."

"Then you won't be disappointed. But I warn you, it will give you a very bad impression, and possibly cloud your opinion of men who are quite decent. They were going to bail up the bank."

"Bail up. Bail up," Connor repeated to himself, squinting thoughtfully. "As in hold up?" He looked at her incredulously. "They were holding up the bank?"

"I suppose that's what you'd say."

"These quite decent men, as you call them, were going to rob the bank? While you were there, I imagine."

"It just so happened that way. But they're not really bushrangers. Look at them. The last good meal Armaldo had was his horse. Desperation led them to it. They weren't bailing up the bank just for riches. In fact, I don't believe they were very experienced at it."

"I suppose Australians are more tolerant of thieves and murderers," Connor said flatly, but had made his point all too painfully, and accidentally reminded her of her own sorry deed.

"Knowing where I've come from, that was a cruel thing to say, Connor."

"I didn't mean you'd steal or kill anyone. I'm sorry if I hurt your feelings. But hiring a trio of bank robbers? What were you thinking?"

"I was thinking of keeping my word and there wasn't a line of men waiting to get hired on!"

The rest of the ride back was suffered in silence, a heavy brooding silence. After a while, Lindy wished Connor would say anything to cut the thick air between them. An argument would have at least kept her thoughts away from what she had done to Hank. Her guilt over killing Hank had created terror inside her; it blinded her ability to see that Connor cared for her safety and that he worried over her choice of men. She kept remembering how he had said that he doubted *she'd* ever kill anyone. How wrong he was. Instead of understanding, all the terrible soul-crushing emotions—indignation, anger and fear—descended upon her. Her blood pounded at her temples, causing one tremendous headache by the time they reached Broken Gate.

As soon as she unsaddled her horse and saw to its feed, Lindy excused herself for the night and retreated to her room. She hated to leave Luke with the responsibility of showing the men around, but he seemed only too happy to take charge. As for Connor she hoped he was packing his saddlebags.

By the faint light coming through her window, Lindy knew it was dawn. She stretched her arms over her head, and remembered Connor. He was her first thought, before Luke, and before her new stockmen. She hoped he was gone so she wouldn't have to face him again only to continue the discussion of thieves and murderers. After all the experiences they had shared, some sweet and some bitter, she regretted that there could be no future for her with Connor. She smiled when she thought of him and warmed at remembering his arms around her. She was dreamy-eyed with images of Connor spinning around in her head when a loud gunshot made her jump.

"Lord in heaven!" Lindy gasped, scrambling out of bed. Her first instinct was to look out the window. What she saw made her heart stop: Connor had a pistol in his hand and was target-shooting at a row of empty bottles lined along the corral fence. She hoped he was fighting boredom with his own pistol, but feared the worst as she opened the bureau drawer where she had hastily hid Hank's Colt. Her heart sank to her stomach when she saw that it was gone. It was too much to hope that Luke had it. Lindy glanced out the window again as Connor's arm rose. He fired another shot, sending up a fountain of sparkling, shattered glass.

After the dread disappeared, anger settled in. How dare Connor enter her room while she was asleep and go through her things? Snatching her yellow blouse and brown skirt off the pegs on the wall, Lindy dressed as quickly as she could. She was in quite an aggravated state when she marched up behind him.

"You're awake," Connor said pleasantly, looking down at her half-buttoned blouse.

Lindy followed his eyes and grasped at her gaping blouse. She turned her back to his smile and finished buttoning while she berated him for the way he had woken her. "Who wouldn't be with shooting going on outside their window? I thought we were under attack." She then got to what really had her upset. Turning around to face him squarely, she asked, "What were you doing in my room?"

Connor held up Hank's pistol. "Looking for this. I didn't want to wake you. But now that you're awake, we might as well have some fun. Luke and the men you hired are out tending your flock, so—" Lindy's eyes were still regarding the gun in his hand; the sight of it raised a sick feeling in her stomach. "What's wrong? You look as if you've seen a ghost. If you don't know how to shoot the thing, I'll show you. You ought to know, especially since you took it to mind to hire three bank robbers."

"I do fine with my rifle."

"Never having seen you shoot, I wouldn't know that. Besides, you can't keep a rifle under your pillow." Connor smiled, but failed to coax Lindy into a better mood.

"I can keep it under my bed."

Irritation began to creep into Connor's voice. "Well, why in blazes do you have the thing, if you can't shoot with it?"

"I didn't say I can't shoot with it."

"Then what are you afraid of?"

At that moment, Lindy wished Luke were there so she could strangle him. Connor was going to persist with questions until she showed him that she could shoot the thing. She eyed the gun fearfully. If it were any other gun but Hank's... Her stomach began to squeeze.

"Come on. The thing's lighter than that Henry of yours, and much better at close range." Connor handed her the pearl-handled gun, but Lindy didn't see it—she saw Hank's bloodstained body.

"I can't. I can't touch it," she cried and ran away from the gun.

"Lindy," Connor shouted, and wondered to himself, "what in the devil's gotten into her?"

He examined the pistol, then looked in the direction Lindy had run.

Lindy found refuge in a patch of shade behind the springhouse. She sat on the damp earth and wrapped her arms around her knees. Overwhelmed by a resurgence of guilt and by love for a man whom she had to send away, Lindy struggled with her frustration. She remembered well what her father had so often told her, "Life is hard and it isn't fair, but that doesn't mean a Falen will quit on it."

Now, just when she was beginning to see her goals realized, it seemed that life couldn't have been more difficult or more unfair. Broken Gate had been the most important goal in her life...until Connor. Her life had been a clear path before Connor stepped onto her porch. She wasn't sure when it had happened, but now she admitted she loved him, and it was terribly painful to let him go. Eyeing the henhouse, she could almost hear Hank laughing from his grave. In death, Hank had become more of a menace than he had been in life. He was slowly destroying her, and she didn't know how to stop him.

That afternoon, Lindy's gloom was lightened by showing Armaldo the kitchen. After the Mexican had shot the head off a rabbit and stampeded the band, Luke had decided to send him back to the house with their dinner. It had been unanimously agreed upon that Armaldo was a far better cook than a shepherd.

Armaldo seemed to understand everything Lindy told him, his response being limited to *sí, señora* and a lot of smiles and nods. His black eyes shone like polished stones and his long, thin mustache curved with his smile when Lindy showed him the contents of her pantry. She had never considered it well stocked, but the Mexican marveled over the staples she always kept on hand.

"If there is anything you need," Lindy told him, eyeing the beheaded rabbit dangling from his hand, "ask me and I'll see what I can do."

Armaldo nodded and settled himself on the porch with his knife and the rabbit. Lindy watched him with reservation as he sharpened the blade, pausing occasionally to grin at her with horselike teeth. His face was nutty brown, marred with lighter-colored scars from too many close encounters with an unfriendly knife. Even when he smiled, Lindy couldn't say that Armaldo looked harmless. He looked like a bandit, a retired one perhaps, but nevertheless, a tough, old bandit. She left him just as he began to gut and skin the animal. It was not something Lindy wanted done on her front porch, but since he had already begun, she would let it go unchallenged this one time.

Whatever Armaldo did with the rabbit, delicious smells soon drifted from the house. Lindy heard the Mexican cooking and singing. It made her smile to think he liked being at Broken Gate. Since Armaldo was the cook, Lindy let him have the honor of whacking the angle iron.

The sun had settled into a rosy color over the mesquite flats. The late hour and hungry stomachs sent the men back to the house. Boone was the first to comment on the smell that teased them along. "You think that could be Maldo's rabbit stew?"

"If it is, I don't know how one skinny rabbit is going to fill our stomachs. I hope he got a few more."

"Maybe he threw in a few of them chickens or a stray woollie."

Luke immediately set the men straight. "The sheep are *not* for free-taking and Lin doesn't part with her chooks unless it's a special occasion."

Boone laughed. "Hell, we're special."

"Not special enough," Luke said, smiling at Connor who rode sullenly alongside him.

Boone was slightly disgruntled by Luke's remark, after having spent a whole day in the saddle watching sheep and imagining them prepared in a variety of ways as his hunger had grown. "Well, since Maldo doesn't have anything else to do but find food for us to eat, I'll expect we should see a feast every night. I just hope it ain't jackrabbit."

"I'm so hungry, I don't care what it is," said Dean.

Lindy stopped Dean and Boone on the porch step, and pointed to the barrel where Connor and Luke were already washing up. "We don't sit down to eat with dirty faces."

Dean and Boone were too dumbfounded to object.

Already used to Lindy's aversion to dirt at the dinner table, or anywhere else in her house, Connor held his smile in check when he looked up at their shocked faces. "Close your mouths, boys, before your tongues dry out in this heat." He walked past Boone, tossing him the cake of soap. "Just wait'll she gets a look at your clothes. There'll be no holding on to those pants on washday."

At first hesitant to wash, Boone realized there would be no supper unless he complied, so grumbling some, he took his place over the barrel. "Here," he said, plopping the soap in Dean's hands, "don't forget to wash behind your ears."

"Think of the bright side, Boone. Maldo's probably done the same."

"Well, that woman's not my mother, and let her try to wash my pants."

"You'd best do as she says if you like your neck."

"We didn't rob any bank, Dean. They're not gonna hang anyone for thinkin' about it."

"How do you know that?" Dean lathered up quickly, rinsed and hurried inside. "That don't smell like any rabbit stew I ever et."

Washing up was only the first surprise for Dean and Boone. Right after they picked up their plates and had their hands on the food set before them, they were stopped by an "ahem" from Lindy. Then Armaldo crossed himself. Dean and Boone had witnessed many a gesture from the Mexican, but they had never seen anything that could be called religious. Now that she had their attention, Lindy began to say grace.

"Thank you, dear Lord, for the meal set upon this table and for sending Armaldo to cook for us. Without his talent and Your blessing we would not be sharing such a feast." Dean and Boone exchanged astonished looks. "And," Lindy continued, "thank You for blessing us with such good men as Dean and Boone." This time it was Connor who raised an eyebrow at Lindy. "Amen," she said brightly.

Chapter Twelve

With the scant bit of light from the house and a full moon, Lindy worked the jack pump, slowly filling a bucket with wash water. From the corner of her eye, she watched Connor.

After Luke and the men had ridden out to the band, Connor sat on the porch step under the first evening star and struck a match. Cupping the small flame in his hand, he lit a cheroot. He stretched his legs out in front of him and crossed his ankles. Leaning his head back against a post, he watched Lindy, only he did not attempt to hide his lazy perusal of her while she filled the bucket.

Earlier, she had caught him eyeing Dean and Boone with undisguised distrust, and had thought that he might even decide to ride off and stay with Luke. But then Armaldo had bedded down in the barn, and she knew Connor would want to stay close to the horses. One thing was certain: Connor did not intend to leave Broken Gate that night.

With both hands, Lindy lifted the bucket and walked back to the house. When she stepped onto the porch, Connor reached out and grabbed her ankle.

"Sit awhile with me."

Lindy felt her heart stop when Connor's voice smoothed into the evening silence. She looked down at him. He stared straight ahead, but kept his hand on her ankle while he blew wisps of smoke into the air. She watched the threads of smoke thin and then disappear like ghosts into the dark. Her pulse began to beat despite all her efforts to stay calm.

When Connor's hand slipped away, he gave her a choice—she could leave or sit with him. The decision wasn't difficult; she stayed. Connor was leaving tomorrow. For all he had done for her, all the caring he tried not to show, she owed him at least a heartfelt thank-you and some pleasant conversation.

"Luke and I appreciate how you've helped us. If it hadn't been for you, I would have never hired help. It's going to work out just apples with the new men," Lindy said optimistically.

"If they don't steal you blind first," Connor replied, dampening her bright mood with his pessimism.

Lindy watched Connor puff once on the cheroot pressed between his lips. While the smoke drifted away from them, she thought of guiding the conversation to a safer subject, but then she remembered her father and how he had been unjustly exiled, and knew that she could not let Connor do the same to men who she believed had been victims themselves. "You can't say that. You have no proof they're dishonest men. They were hungry men, that's all." Lindy stood up. "I'll not sit here and listen to you accuse men of thievery without a shred of proof. You don't know what happened in the bank. If you had been there you would have seen how they never could have done what they planned." Connor reached up, grabbed Lindy's hand and pulled her back down. "I thought we were going to have a nice conversation before you left Broken Gate," she huffed, after landing hard on her backside.

"I'm not leaving," Connor announced as much to his disbelief as to Lindy's.

"You're not leaving?" Lindy choked. As much as part of her wanted Connor to stay, she was afraid. He had asked too many questions that had reached uncomfortably close to

Hank's murder. He had already had Hank's gun in his hands and he was getting close to suspecting Jeb of something. Even if it was only the cattle-versus-sheep issue, she didn't want Connor talking with Jeb. Jeb would surely say something about Hank, and then the questions would start again, and before she knew it, the sheriff would know that she had shot his nephew.

"Why aren't you leaving?" Lindy asked, trying to keep the tremble of fear from her voice. "It's all you've talked about doing. Now you're free to go."

"I can't leave you knowing the men you hired came straight from robbing a bank."

"They didn't rob a bank. They were only thinking about it."

"They had planned it, and if it hadn't been for your interference, they would have. You don't know what else they could have done—or have thought of doing. Other than Armaldo, you don't even know where they came from. How could you be so trusting of those three? I remember *my* first greeting was with your Henry." Connor looked to the barn as if he expected Armaldo to burst out with the horses.

Lindy stood up again and nearly growled with frustration. "Connor O'Malley, you are leaving in the morning. This is my station. I'm in charge."

Connor's brow rose at her declaration. Before she could leave, he stood and blocked her way with the wide expanse of his body. "You made me foreman. That means I'm in charge of the men."

"I'm firing you. I want you off my land by daybreak."

They were very close—close enough to feel each other's breath, to feel the heat from their bodies, and to see the flames of passion in each other's eyes. Lindy was the first to break her gaze from Connor and to turn away from him, afraid he would see how hard it was for her to send him away. She had to maintain a strong front, even though her sadness formed a lump in her throat.

Just as she was to make her retreat, Connor stopped her with his arms. He wrapped them around her waist and pulled her stiff body against his. "I don't plan on staying here forever, but I can't leave knowing you've invited possibly dangerous men to live with you. By inviting these men at my suggestion, you've made me responsible for your safety."

Lindy struggled against Connor, pulling at his hands and prying his arms from her. Once she was free she pushed him away. "You don't have to feel responsible. You should know by now that I can take care of myself."

Connor's chuckle was bittersweet. "Oh, that I know well enough, Lindy Falen, or should I say, Mrs. Rigby? You are a very independent lady." Connor's voice turned harsh. "All you need is a make-believe husband."

"I don't need anyone, Connor—not even you."

Connor grabbed a fistful of hair and kissed her long and hard. Lindy struggled at first, but then gave in to the demand of his kiss. When he slowly eased his hold, he was smiling. "Do you still want to fire me?"

Lindy could not force herself from his arms; she could not deny she wanted him. Her frustration welled inside her and threatened to overflow in a stream of tears. Damn him for holding her, for suddenly caring about her when it was all sure to come to an end if he ever found out about Hank. If only Hank hadn't been the sheriff's nephew, if only Connor weren't so bloody honest. She couldn't chance having to confess the murder to Sheriff Hayes, and she knew Connor would insist upon it.

"Perhaps I should be more wary of you than of my stockmen," Lindy said sadly. She went in the house and closed the door between them.

"There's got to be some reward for putting myself through this hell, and saving your neck must be it. You're a danger to yourself, Lindy Falen," Connor growled back.

After his wife died, Connor had wanted never again to feel the pain of losing someone he cared about. To protect himself from that, he wanted no part in Lindy's life. But she had been persistent in keeping him there, in making him feel responsible for her. Hadn't she done well enough for herself before he came along? he asked himself. She was feisty, independent and . . . and beautiful.

Connor had had hopeful thoughts of wooing Lindy on the porch and spending the night in her soft bed, but as it happened, he found himself tossing fitfully on Luke's lumpy mattress. For some insane notion, he had thought Lindy would be happy to hear he had decided to stay on a little while longer.

He had not anticipated how difficult it would be to leave. Then, when he had made his decision to stay, his sensibilities had been crushed when she ordered him to leave Broken Gate. He couldn't understand it. Luke hadn't reacted that way—Luke had been glad to hear he had decided to stay. Was there something Lindy didn't want him to discover about the men she had hired? That was the only reason Connor could think of why Lindy had done an about-face. It just didn't make sense otherwise. If he hadn't grown so fond of her, he'd just as soon mind his own business and get some sleep. But instead, he was thrashing around in Luke's bed thinking of how much he wanted to be with Lindy. How he ached to hold her against his chest; to feel her soft bosom and the quick beat of her heart, which didn't deny that she wanted him as much as he wanted her; to run his hand down the length of her back and marvel once again at the silky feel of her skin. He wanted to feel her fingers curl in his hair and the light play of her hands over his chest. God, how he ached to crush her body against his and bury himself in her.

Connor threw his legs over the side of the bed and stood, the male part of him alive with strong desire from his self-torture. He pulled on his boots and hurried past Lindy's bedroom without daring to pause or glance inside. But that didn't stop the sweet smell of lavender from teasing his senses or the vision of her from appearing in his mind, her hair spread over her pillow in long, rippling waves, her rosy mouth puckered in sleep like a cherub's, her cheeks glowing from the day's sun and the curve of her hip under her thin nightgown.

Connor ran outside as if demons chased him. He stopped in front of the water barrel, staring into the moon's reflection on the water's surface. He yanked off his boots and without ceremony, tossed them aside, shed his long underwear and jumped into the cold water. A long sigh of relief escaped him as he crouched down in the barrel. He cupped his hands and splashed sobering water on his face, sank down and drenched his head while curious horses gathered at the corral fence to watch the crazy man bathe. When Connor heard his mare's greeting, shrill in the quiet night, and saw the perked-up ears and large eyes of its companions watching him, he laughed, and for a moment he envied their uncomplicated lives.

Connor leaned back against the rim and gazed up at the moon that hung over Broken Gate. He felt strangely content, aware that Lindy had made him want a life for himself and that he wouldn't mind so much settling down there if she asked him. But it seemed that he had served his purpose, that she had used him to start her ranch and now saw him as a threat to her independence. Her independence! The foolish woman's sense of independence was going to get her killed. She didn't have a clue what men like Claxton were capable of.

Connor climbed out of the barrel and let the water drip from his body. Water evaporated from his skin, cooling the passions that heated his desire before he slung his underwear over his shoulder, picked up his boots and tiptoed past Lindy's room to his bed.

* * *

Finding sleep elusive, Lindy heard the splash when Connor jumped into the barrel. At first, not knowing what to think, she started at the sound. In a quiet voice, she had called Connor, and when he didn't answer her, she slipped out of her bed. In her bare feet she quietly padded over to the window and pulled aside the curtain. Her eyes widened at the sight of Connor in the barrel, gazing up at the moon, his hands clasped behind his head. "What in the devil is he doing?" she wondered aloud. Was he that hot he had to resort to cooling himself in the barrel?

Lindy's amazement at Connor's unusual behavior kept her at the window. He certainly seemed to be enjoying himself, relaxed as he was. It was almost unfair that she should be kept awake with thoughts of him when he was splashing about in the moonlight with such blatant lack of inhibitions. Feeling herself getting hot, Lindy moved away from the window. What business was it of hers what gave Connor his pleasure? But bathing in a barrel! Good heavens!

Barely back in her bed, the sound of trickling water teased her, drawing her again to the window. Lindy's eyes roved over Connor's glistening, naked form as he stood in the pale wash of moonlight. Her heart nearly leapt from her chest and her own body broke out in a sweat, she was so affected by this wonderful sight of tight muscles, broad shoulders, long muscled legs and every other interesting part of him. She gulped and breathed a weak, "Oh, my," before scurrying back to bed and burying her face in her pillow. It was going to be a trial getting to sleep now.

Before sleep finally covered her with its blanket of dreams, Lindy's final thought was of Hank, sleeping eternally in her henhouse. Hank, who even more so in death, made her life a misery through the guilt that clouded her thinking, making her suspicious of even those who loved her.

Almost as soon as Connor had fallen into a deep sleep, he was awakened by a racket in the farmyard. It took him a few seconds to orient himself before he realized what the noise was—chickens squawking an alarm. Someone was stealing chickens. Connor jumped out of bed and pulled on his boots. Paying no mind that he was only partially dressed in long, red underwear, he grabbed his rifle, ran out of the bedroom and collided with Lindy. Lindy was also unmindful of her evening attire—a thin nightgown, bare feet and her Henry.

"I'll go see," Connor said, heading for the door.

Lindy gasped, "No!" She squeezed herself between Connor and the door. "They're my chooks. I'll go."

"Lindy, get out of the way. It's dark out there. I said I'll see to them."

Lindy didn't budge. Animals were in the henhouse. Hank was in the henhouse. Dread nearly strangled the breath from her. "It's likely coyotes. I've handled them before."

"You don't know that," Connor argued. "It could be any one of the three men you hired running off in the middle of the night with a few hens."

Lindy had one hand on the door and her other hand clenched around her rifle. Connor leaned against the door, preventing her from leaving the house. She was too upset to notice that she was at eye level with Connor's bare shoulders until she put her hand against his arm in a vain effort to push him away. She noticed then. The realization that she was standing so close to his half-nakedness, the same nakedness she had ogled hours before, made her falter in her attempt to budge Connor's solid stance. Then frustration turned into an angry temper, and she leaned all of her weight into him. But still she was unable to budge the mountain of a man. "Get out of my way, Connor O'Malley, before all my chooks are carried off."

"You expect me to stay in here while you fight off whatever is harassing your hens?"

"Yes. I can take care of my own problems."

Connor's male indignation flared. "As I said, darlin',
you're not going out there in the dark, waving your rifle in
your nightgown and bare feet. Not while I'm here. God only
knows what's out there."

"God certainly does know what's out there," Lindy said
faintly, surrendering to his greater strength. She moved
aside. "There's no use fighting you when you're so bloody
determined to be responsible," she snapped.

Lindy's sarcasm was not lost on Connor. Before pulling
the door open, he took a long, exasperated look at her. "I
had a hard time getting to sleep for thinking about how you
look in that nightgown. Make sure it's still on when I get
back, because I want the pleasure of removing it."

Lindy was too startled to say anything and too afraid of
what Connor might find in the henhouse to ponder long the
meaning of what he had said. All she could think of was that
the time she had dreaded most had come—animals had finally sniffed out Hank's body and had come to dig it up.
Now Connor was going to find him. She'd have to tell Connor something. How was she going to explain why a man
was buried in her henhouse? She was in such a state of
worry, she didn't hear the three shots from Armaldo's pistol.

Ten minutes later, after a pack of coyotes had carried off
three hens and a bantam rooster, Connor softly closed the
door behind him. He heard quiet sobs from a corner of the
room, but because of the dark, he couldn't find where they
were coming from. He lit a lamp, throwing a soft amber
light over the room and found Lindy sitting on the floor
with her rifle across her lap. She looked up at him with ex-
pectant, teary eyes.

Connor knelt in front of her and pushed aside a strand of
hair that had fallen over her eyes. Lindy searched his blue-
gray eyes and saw pity in them. She knew he had found the
grave and had come to her with the terrible news. She braced

herself against her knees. There was nothing to do now but answer his questions honestly.

Connor sighed. "I'm sorry, darlin'. He's dead."

"Of course he is." Lindy sobbed, just picturing the sight that had greeted Connor. "I'm sorry you had to find him like that."

Connor rubbed her back. "The poor fellow. I wouldn't have wanted to meet my end that way."

Lindy moaned, and admitted in a teary voice, "It was my fault."

"We can get another one."

Lindy raised her head.

Connor continued his soothing rub. "We'll get a real fighter this time."

"Who are you talking about?" Lindy finally asked.

"Why, your bantam rooster."

"You mean that's all you found?"

"No, not at all."

"What else?" Lindy held her breath.

"Three hens."

She could breathe again. Only three chooks and her rooster—not Hank. But her rooster. "My rooster! Three chooks!" she wailed when the terrible news finally sunk in.

"While you were stubbornly asserting your independence, four coyotes were having their pick of the henhouse. If you hadn't insisted on running out in your nightgown, maybe you'd at least have your rooster," Connor said defensively.

"If you had let *me* take care of it, I'd still have all of my chooks," Lindy parried back, now fully recovered from the trauma of imagining Connor discovering Hank's body.

"And Armaldo would have had an eyeful."

Lindy smiled smugly. "You see? Neither one of us had to go out there. Armaldo would have taken care of the coyotes."

"Well, he may be able to kill jackrabbits but he sure can't hit coyotes. He fired off three shots in the dark and not one hit its mark. I'm surprised he didn't hit me." Connor ran his hand through his hair and said to himself, "What a night this has been." When his eyes rested on Lindy, a sly grin eased over his lips. "From here on it can only get better."

Immediately Lindy was reminded of what Connor had said earlier, and that reminded her of their state of dress—she in only her nightgown and Connor in his tight, long underwear. She was acutely aware that he was only clothed from the waist down.

Sitting on the floor next to Lindy, Connor slapped his hand on her thigh. By now Lindy was so tense, she jumped. Through the cotton of her nightgown she could feel Connor's heavy hand warm her leg.

"Lindy, darlin', would you mind pulling off my boots?"

Lindy didn't see the harm in it. In fact, after what she had been expecting, it was a relief to fill such an easy request. She walked down to his feet on her knees, grabbed the first boot in two hands and pulled. When both boots were off, Lindy planned on making a quick retreat to her room, but before she could stand, Connor leaned forward, caught her in his arms and pulled her up to him.

"Connor, do you think this is proper? You are my foreman." Lindy hoped that reminder might make Connor realize that there could be nothing serious between them.

"You fired me, remember?"

"We can't do this," Lindy said while Connor's kisses advanced along her neck.

Connor concentrated his kisses around Lindy's ear, sending shivers to her toes, and making it extremely difficult for her to think of a convincing argument against what he was so subtly proposing.

Lindy wiggled from his hold and stood up. "You're leaving in the morning."

"We'll talk about that in the morning."

Lindy ran from Connor and retreated to her room, hoping that he would not follow her. "You are leaving in the morning," she said finally from her bed.

Connor got up from the floor and picked up the lamp.

Lindy saw the soft light come into her room and knew Connor was there. Her heart thumped almost in time to his footsteps as he crossed the floor to her bureau. She heard the lamp placed firmly on the wood. Even with her back to Connor she knew from the soft rustle of clothing that he was removing his clothes. She knew he meant to have her and there was nothing she could say to change his mind. Now she could no longer hide behind the protection of a fake husband or beg her innocence. She could plead to his sense of honor and perhaps convince him to leave her be, but she knew she didn't want that. She did want Connor. She wanted to lie in his arms again, to feel the heat of his body against hers and to once again feel him fill her with his flesh.

Lindy felt Connor's body slide next to hers, and knew he was naked. His face nuzzled the back of her neck; he kissed and nibbled his way along the gentle slope of her shoulder.

"I'm not going to spend the rest of this night lying wide awake and thinking about having you. I've already put myself through that hell. I'm going to have you, darlin'. More than once, and it won't be against your will." Without hearing a word of objection, Connor wrapped his arm around her, smoothed his hand over her breasts, gently rubbing until their peaks hardened against his hand.

Lindy turned in his arms and faced him. "I don't want to lie awake thinking of you either, Connor," she confessed.

As Connor had promised, he lifted Lindy's nightgown above her hips, past her shoulders and over her head. Tossing it aside, he mounted her, impatient to bury himself in her. With a hunger just as demanding, Lindy pulled Connor's face down to hers. Their mouths touched in hungry desire. With little encouragement, Lindy opened to him and embraced each plunge of his arousal with the love and passion that spilled from her heart. Between ragged breaths, Connor kissed her damp forehead and whispered loving words. Undulating waves of pleasure washed over them and then receded, leaving them drowsy as if they had indulged in sweet wine.

Lindy relaxed in Connor's arms and rested her head against his chest. She felt a sense of comfort and safety that she wished could last for all her days.

"I've grown awfully fond of you, darlin'," Connor whispered against her neck. He twisted a tendril of her hair around his finger. "Too fond to want to let go of you just yet."

"I'm terribly fond of you too, luv," she said and turned her face to his.

Lindy felt the love flowing from Connor into her and knew his words had come nowhere close to what was really in his heart. It was easy for him to show he loved her, but so difficult to say the words. As much as she wanted to hear those words, she told herself it was better that he didn't say them. If Connor truly loved her and wanted to marry her, it would only mean she'd have to tell him about Hank, and that she could never do. Connor would despise her if he knew a man had met his maker at her hands.

Chapter Thirteen

Lindy slipped out of bed just as the sun cast a faint light over the distant mesquite flats. A blue mist still clung to the air, softening the harsh lines of the outbuildings and trees into ghostly apparitions. The morning was silent; sunrise had not been preceded by the usual squawky heralding from her rooster. Careful not to wake Connor, Lindy quickly bathed with the water from the barrel under the jack pump.

Armaldo appeared from the mist singing a cheery greeting. *"Buenos días, señora,"* he said, nodding his head and grinning with his big, yellow horse teeth.

"G'day, Armaldo," Lindy called in greeting as she brushed the tangles out of her hair.

Without another word, the Mexican passed her and went into the house. In another minute Lindy heard her cast-iron pan slam onto the stove. She thought it would ease Connor's worry some to wake up and see Armaldo making breakfast.

With her egg basket on her arm, Lindy walked to the henhouse, knowing her bantam rooster would not be strutting his bright plumage in front of her hens and that she'd find their number depleted. After such a fright, she didn't expect her hens would be laying many eggs. But this time fetching eggs wasn't the main reason she went out to the henhouse—it was to visit Hank's grave.

Evidence of the coyote attack the night before was scattered everywhere. Amid the white and brown feathers, Lindy found a long, green plume. She crouched and picked it up. It curled gracefully around her finger. Holding on to the feather, she stepped into the henhouse in prayerful silence as though she were entering a crypt, and stared at the ground under which Hank rested. It was undisturbed. The coyotes had run in and out, and had not been interested in anything other than her hens. Lindy was upset at the loss, but greatly relieved that she didn't have to worry anymore about animals digging up Hank.

Blinking away the phantom images of Hank that seemed to appear in every dark corner of the squat building, Lindy began to fill her basket with what eggs she could find. She gingerly stepped around Hank's plot as best she could. Before she was through, she felt a familiar chill come over the interior of the henhouse. This time she did not run out of the coop but stood stiff with her back against the wall, ready to face the fear that gripped her in its unrelenting hold.

"I can't give you back your sorry life, but I promise to bury you right if you leave me be. Let me live my life, Hank Cobb!" her hoarse whisper demanded. Then suddenly startled by the high squawk of a hen, Lindy ran from the dim interior of the henhouse into the arms of bright morning sunshine. Her heart pounded in her chest, her eyes closed against the sight of her henhouse and the restless spirit it housed. She prayed that if she gave Hank a dignified burial, then his ghost might finally be put to rest.

Returning to the house, Lindy saw Connor bent over the water barrel. He was bathing as she had, splashing water over his face and then over his shoulders, arms and chest. The sight of him standing there with the sunlight glistening on his wet skin and golden water drops clinging to the ends of his shaggy hair and mustache made her want him all the more. She was reminded of him bathing in the night and couldn't decide how she liked him best, with the sun sparkling off his skin or with the play of silver moonlight in his hair. When he straightened and smiled at her, she bit her lip. Where was she going to find the strength to turn him away when she was fraught with longing for him?

"I see you're returning from the scene of the crime," Connor said lightly.

Lindy nearly started at his comment. Her voice faltering, she said, "I missed my rooster crowing this morning. I think I'm going to ride out to see how the men are doing."

Connor caught Lindy's arm as she tried to rush past him. "Don't I deserve a better good-morning than that?"

"You can't stay in the house anymore," she said faintly.

"You mean to tell me foremen don't sleep with their bosses? I thought that was part of the job," Connor rejoined.

"Connor, don't. You said yourself you didn't intend on staying here forever."

"If it's what you want, I'll bunk with Armaldo."

"It's what I want," Lindy said, avoiding Connor's eyes.

"But what do we tell Armaldo? He already thinks we're married."

"You can tell him we've had an argument if you like. That wouldn't be too far from the truth."

After enduring a silent breakfast with Connor, Lindy saddled her horse and rode out to the band.

She found Luke and the men sitting around a little fire. Steam still drifted up from the spout of the coffeepot. Buddy lay on the ground, his nose pointing in the direction of the peacefully grazing sheep.

Since they drove the band from Dry Bed, it had become a habit of Luke's to take coffee in the morning instead of tea. He seemed to grow more like a man every day. The Texas air and sunshine sprouted youth like wildflowers. Lindy had to admit her young brother was showing signs of change, and since she did not see him as often as before, those subtle differences were that much more apparent.

Luke's face looked wise beyond his years, his hands and arms already muscular from work. His shoulders were widening, promising future strength. He had grown taller, too, but had not yet developed the bulk of muscles on his frame that Connor had.

When he saw Lindy, Luke pushed his sandy hair from his eyes and greeted her with a wide smile that cut a dimple in his left cheek. "Lin!"

Dean and Boone stood. Dean removed his hat respectfully. Boone watched Lindy from under dark lashes.

"I see you've taken to having coffee with the men," Lindy said cheerfully to Luke as she dismounted. "I've brought all of you some bread. Armaldo made it."

"Some coffee, Lin?" Luke asked, smiling as he refilled his cup. When his teasing didn't stir a smile from her, he asked, "Is everything all right?"

"Last night coyotes ran off with three chooks and the rooster before Connor and Armaldo could scare them off." Lindy scanned the band.

Reading her mind, Luke said, "They're all there."

"The coyotes might come back, so—"

"Well, I hope not," Boone exclaimed loudly, turning everyone's head in his direction. "It would be a dern shame not to ever see another chicken for supper. I've had enough jackrabbit to last me two lifetimes. Soon I'm gonna grow long ears and a cottontail."

"Whatdaya mean, soon?" Dean jested. "You already got the ears."

"Why you—" Boone threw himself at Dean and the two landed solidly on the ground. Rolling around together, they came perilously close to landing on the hot coals of the campfire.

"Boone! Dean!" Lindy gasped, watching them for only a moment before she grasped their shirt collars and tried to pull them apart. "Stop, before you—ah!" She took the jab of an elbow in her eye and fell back hard on the ground.

"Lin," Luke said, coming to his sister's rescue. Grabbing her hand, he helped her to her feet.

"Agh! Hell, that God dern..." Dean howled as his backside nearly smothered the fire. He rolled out of the coals, but now was so incensed, he hardly realized he was on fire.

"Oh, my God! Dean's smoking," Lindy exclaimed. She ran for the nearest blanket, snatched it off the ground and landed on top of Dean's smoldering posterior, beating him frantically.

Boone scrambled out from under Dean and sprang to his feet. For a few shocked moments, Boone and Luke watched Lindy and Dean rolling around on the ground together.

The sound of thundering hooves pounding over the ground in a hasty advance turned Boone's and Luke's heads. Connor swung down from his horse and yanked Lindy and Dean apart. "What the hell is going on?" he demanded, holding them both apart by their arms.

"I don't know, all of a sudden she attacked me," Dean said in bewilderment.

"*She* attacked *you?*" Connor asked.

"Your butt was on fire, you mozzie," Lindy said.

Dean reached back to feel his scorched pants.

While Dean inspected his breeches, Connor pulled Lindy aside, still fighting the turmoil inside him. He had been trying to summon the memory of his dead wife during his ride to the camp, and could only envision a faceless image, a faint shadow of what she had been. She had let him go, she had found her peace and had given him back his life. Perhaps, he had mused, in a ghost's way, she had led him to Lindy and his own earthly happiness, enabling him to finally release her. Happiness on earth was not everlasting; he knew it could be lost more quickly than gained. Seeing Lindy thrashing about on the ground with another man, thinking her in danger, realizing he could lose her, too, had lit a dangerous fuse inside him. Poor Dean, shaking at the end of his hand, had seen the murderous light in his eyes. Connor feared the man would not want to come within three feet of Lindy or himself again.

"I thought you were being attacked," Connor explained in a quiet and controlled voice.

Lindy shook her arm free from his tight hold. "I was only breaking up a fight between the men."

Losing his control, Connor shouted, "Women don't do such things! Look at you. Your hair's a mess and you've got a shiner." Suddenly disgusted with her, he scooped up his horse's reins and swung up into his saddle. He looked down at her, not knowing which he wanted to do most, wrap her in his arms and kiss her full lips or lift her skirt and spank some sense into her. "You are an exasperation. It's beyond my understanding why any man would want to saddle himself with you," Connor said in parting.

While she tried to make sense out of his words, Lindy watched Connor skirt around the white edge of grazing sheep. With Boone behind him, Dean cautiously approached her, his hat scrunched in his hands. "I'm sorry for the trouble, ma'am. Boone and I meant nothin' by it. We weren't really fightin', just havin' some fun. Sorry about the black eye," he added sheepishly and left to join Boone.

Lindy's fingers gingerly touched the tender skin around her eye and said to Luke, "Do you think I put Connor in a dither?"

Luke laughed. "I don't think it sits well with him to be told what to do by a woman."

"How do you know that?"

"From things he's said." So as not to look at his sister, Luke began to kick apart the campfire.

"For instance?"

"Well, you know how men talk."

"No, I don't. What'd he say?"

Luke's face flushed red to his ears. "He just has his own opinions on women. And I'm not telling you what they are, so don't think to ask me," Luke added quickly and rode away, leaving Lindy baffled at their conversation, and curious enough to ride off after Connor.

"Connor," Lindy called once she was close enough for him to hear her.

Connor turned and looked back at her. He reined his horse, waited for her to pull up next to him and welcomed her with a greeting she didn't expect—he actually smiled pleasantly. Lindy decided to oblige him with a tight smile.

"What have you been telling Luke about women?"

Not expecting her question, Connor laughed. "That was just talk between men."

"My brother's not a man yet."

"Now that's the root of the problem between you and Luke. You're coddling him like he was a boy when he isn't. But it's just natural for you—bein' a woman. A confused woman at that; not sure if you should be wearin' a skirt or pants."

Lindy felt her cheeks burn. "As long as I'm running Broken Gate, I'll be wearing the strides and if that doesn't suit you, then you can just ... just go soak your head in the barrel." She spurred her horse, leaving Connor with something to think about.

In spite of her indignation, Lindy began to think that maybe Connor was right. Maybe that was why he was so set from the beginning to leave Broken Gate. She'd certainly tested his temper the night before by insisting she take care of the coyotes herself. Of necessity, she did everything herself, for her independent nature came as natural as breathing.

By the end of the day, Lindy had herself thinking that Connor resented her and she began to feel some animosity toward all the men around her. They had each other to talk to, to confide in, whereas she had to rely on herself. Boone was even giving Luke lessons on women. That really irked her. Suddenly Lindy realized what she needed: she needed another woman to talk to; however, finding a woman to confide in wasn't going to be an easy task. She couldn't take her questions to Hester or to the preacher's wife. Tilly hardly ever said a word, and Lindy couldn't trust anyone who would roast one of her lambs anyway. Minerva could certainly answer all her questions, but heavens, she could never bring herself to walk into a bawdy place.

When Lindy returned to the house, she was greeted by Armaldo. He hurried out to her on flat feet that caused him to wobble from side to side. He grabbed the reins as she dismounted.

She liked Armaldo. Already he was loyal to her. He didn't speak much, but he was always smiling and eager to help. He seemed to think of what had to be done before she even had a chance to make the suggestion.

"Where's Connor?" Lindy asked.

"He went to town," Armaldo said, looking as if the world was coming to an end.

"What's wrong? Did he say why?"

"He didn't go for cornmeal," the Mexican flatly replied and took her horse.

"He didn't leave word for me?" Armaldo didn't seem to notice the tremor in her voice.

"No cornmeal," he repeated, leading her horse away.

Lindy waited a long time for Connor. She ate alone, sat on the porch alone and watched the sun set and the moon rise alone. Bull bats swung low and coyotes chanted nightfall. She wondered if the coyotes would come back. It was reassuring to see Armaldo leaning against the barn with a rifle across his lap. If he couldn't shoot them, at least he'd scare them away if they were inclined to raid her henhouse again.

Far over the flat ground Lindy could see the small flickering speck of Luke's campfire and wished for some company. From far off, she could hear "Beautiful Dreamer" warble from Dean's harmonica, and that made her feel even more lonesome. Throwing her head back, she counted the stars as they popped out of the dark. Lindy soon fell asleep waiting for Connor, and would have slept on the porch all night if Armaldo hadn't awakened her.

"*Señora*, go inside to your bed," Armaldo urged, gently shaking her shoulders.

"Has Connor returned?"

Armaldo shook his head and helped her to her feet. "You go inside."

Some hours later, Lindy was awakened by the loud crowing of a rooster. At first, she thought she was dreaming. Then, realizing she was wide awake and that she definitely did hear a rooster, she quickly dressed and rushed out to the farmyard. Perched on an upturned pail, a fine bantam, his bright colors gleaming in the dawn's light, was singing his heart out. He was a beautiful sight to see, though the hens themselves seemed to ignore him as they went about their business of scratching the ground. His long tail feathers of dark green and rust curled gracefully at the ends and shivered slightly at the more enthusiastic moments of his morning aria. After an exuberant flapping of his wings, he hopped down to the ground and strutted around his new domain.

Checking the corral, Lindy spotted Connor's horse. Her gaze shifted to the barn where Armaldo snoozed against its side, his chin resting on his chest and his wide hat pulled down over his face. Apparently he had spent the night on guard, for he still had his rifle lying across his lap. Lindy hurried to the barn, her heart beating fiercely as she thought of finding Connor inside.

Lindy found Connor on the floor of the barn, his legs stretched out in front of him, his head resting on his saddle, and smelling suspiciously of whiskey. She looked down at him and frowned. As though Connor sensed someone was staring at him, he opened his eyes. At that moment, the rooster let off another chorus of reveille. Connor's face tightened in pain as he lifted himself up on his elbow.

"You look a fright," Lindy said in a disgusted voice.

"I feel worse than that. It's a good thing Jester is a smart horse and knows the way back here." Connor looked up at Lindy and scowled. "You're not the only one who has a right to get . . . what do you call it?"

"Pie-eyed." She flushed at the reminder of her own bout with whiskey. "But I've learned my lesson. It seems men never do."

Changing the subject, Connor asked, "See your rooster?"

Lindy softened a bit. "I heard him first."

"I hope you like him. He nearly pecked my eyes out trying to get him into a sack just to get him here."

"Is that why it took you all night?" Lindy asked as she walked out of the barn.

Connor raised a brow at her tone and struggled to his feet. "You wanted me to leave."

"Where'd you get him?" Lindy asked.

"It's a long story of gambling, drinking and fighting. I don't think you'd approve, and since you seem vexed at me already, let's just say I was drawn to its brilliant plumage and feisty attitude." Connor ended his explanation with a private chuckle and a sly wink that made her blush.

Despite herself, Lindy smiled at the rooster. "He is beautiful—and cocky."

Connor walked over to Armaldo and nudged the Mexican's leg with his toe. "Come on, Maldo, I'll be starved in another hour or two."

"No cornmeal," Armaldo mumbled, setting accusing eyes on Connor.

"All right, I forgot the cornmeal."

Lindy looked back at Connor. He had been gone all night. Not for a minute did she think he'd spent all that time getting a rooster. She worried that a different kind of bird had caught his eye while he was in town.

"I'm going into town," she said.

"What for?" Connor asked.

"Cornmeal."

Luke seemed set on irritating Lindy by asking her the same question three times in three different ways. His current question was the most direct. "Why are we going into town?"

"Because we need cornmeal. I promised Armaldo."

"We just got flour. Can't he use flour?"

"The way Armaldo cooks, we need more than flour."

"I'd think you wouldn't want to be seen with that shiner," Luke reminded her.

Lindy clenched her teeth. This was not going to be an easy day. Since she announced the outing, Luke had balked, leaving no excuse unexplored as to why they shouldn't go. He suggested that she take Armaldo instead, since he was the one set on cornmeal. Lindy was sure Luke just wanted to stay with Connor, Dean and Boone, exchanging "men talk," as he had come to call their conversations. In the past weeks he had become so close with the men she was beginning to feel like an outsider. It would do her and Luke good to be together again, as it had been before.

"Connor would say you're as cranky as a rusty jack pump," Luke grumbled.

"Don't go picking up sayings or habits from the men, Luke Falen. I just don't like being nagged at."

"Boone says you're in love with Connor—that's why you're so ornery."

Lindy was so flustered by Luke's casual recounting of Boone's observation that she didn't notice that she had stopped in front of the saloon instead of the general store two buildings down. Before Luke could point out her error, she dismounted, still rambling on as she tethered her horse. "Boone should keep his eyes on the stock. If I needed a busybody, I would have hired Hester Quinn, and it's no business of yours what goes on between a man and a woman, either. I'm beginning to wonder if anyone's been watching the band!"

"Lin—" Luke began, trying to stop her from walking into the saloon.

"I don't want to hear any more about it. Just forget what Boone said, because it isn't true. If I was in love, you wouldn't need Boone to tell you. If I was in love, really in love, you would know it."

"But, Lin—"

"You're doing too much talking with the men. I'm not sure it was a good idea to—" Lindy stopped short just inside the saloon doors. All of a sudden, the smell of whiskey, tobacco and cloying perfume brought her to attention. Instead of resting her eyes on the familiar sight of shelves stocked with canned goods, bolts of gingham and barrels of dry goods, Lindy peeked through a veil of smoke at gaming tables, a long bar and two buxom women scantily dressed, hanging on the arms of a burly man, their mounds of quivering flesh spilling forth from their loosely laced bodices. "Oh, my heavens!" Lindy gasped.

Thinking quickly, Luke pulled Lindy out of the saloon, around the corner of the building and into the alley where she could recover from her shock in private.

"I tried to tell you," Luke pronounced with smug satisfaction.

Lindy leaned against the side of the building and inhaled deeply. "And to think I once sent you in there all alone." Her curiosity suddenly stirred, she turned to Luke. "You've been in there. What does Minerva look like?"

Luke's eyes bulged. "How would I know what she looked like? You told me not to look around."

"I didn't actually think you wouldn't. Have you seen her? I won't scold you if you tell me."

Luke answered cautiously, "I saw one lady. The one who was with Connor. Maybe that was Minerva, because she asked me what I wanted."

Lindy's brow rose in sly interest. "What did she look like?"

"Ah, Lin, Connor wouldn't..." Luke groaned and rolled his eyes heavenward. Suddenly he paled. Sucking in his breath, he grabbed Lindy's hand. "Let's go before we find ourselves in trouble."

"What's the matter with you? What did you see?" Lindy asked, then looked up to check what had turned Luke white as flour. The drab alley was canopied with silk dresses in shades of scarlet, emerald green and electric blue; stockings and black lace corsets, garters and stiff petticoats, stretched on a line between the saloon and barber shop, all waved teasingly in a seductive breeze. "Oh, my, look at that," Lindy exclaimed, clapping her hand over Luke's eyes. "It must be washday."

Luke tore her hand away. "Come on, Lin. I've seen laundry before."

"Not any laundry like that. Look at those colors and those..." She felt her face turn the color of scarlet silk.

In a suspiciously uninterested tone, Luke said, "Let's go, Lin. Wasn't it cornmeal we came for?" He walked away from his sister, stopped and waited for her to join him.

But Lindy didn't follow Luke. She was too busy thinking about what Connor had said about roosters. "It was a rooster Connor came for. Now I know what he meant by fancy plumage," she grumbled with mounting jealousy. "Oh!" Lindy yelled as she was unexpectedly doused by a deluge of cold wash water that left her dripping wet. Her hair fell around her face in heavy strands, her clothes stuck to her skin and water trickled onto her half boots. She looked down at her drenched self, stunned at how completely soaked she was. Glancing up at the window from which the clothesline originated, Lindy saw an equally shocked woman, balancing a small washtub on the window ledge. The woman leaned over the sill, her breasts nearly spilling from her chemise.

"What are you doing down there, anyway?" she asked, answering Lindy's accusing glare.

"You should look before dumping your wash water."

Luke tugged on his sister's sleeve. "Come on, Lin, let's shoot through here before—"

"I can't go anywhere like this," Lindy gasped. "Look at me—I'm soaked through to my skin."

"She's right, honey," the woman called down to them. A sweet smile bloomed like a spring tulip on her painted lips. "Come upstairs and you can hang your things on our line to dry."

While Lindy considered the woman's suggestion, Luke voiced his objection to her offer. "Lin, you can't be seriously considering going up there. I don't trust her. Let's go."

"Luke, the woman feels badly. I can't refuse her when she's just trying to make up for what she did. It won't take long for my clothes to dry once they're hung out in the sun."

"Lin, you can't. If anyone should... You just want to see what's up there," Luke accused, hardly disguising his shock.

"I do not!"

"Well? Are you comin' up or not?" the woman asked impatiently.

Ignoring Luke's moaning and groaning, Lindy climbed the back stairs, holding on to a rickety railing for support. She heard Luke's heavy breathing and footsteps coming up behind her. She looked at him over her shoulder. "I'll be fine."

"I'm not letting you go in there by yourself."

Lindy found the woman waiting for her in a small, dark hallway along with another eccentric-looking female. Every feminine part of them was an exaggeration. Their hair was not ordinary in color; one had blue-black hair and the other brilliant red. Their skin was as pale as Lindy had ever seen, like the underbelly of a lizard, and the paleness of it made their rouged cheeks and lips seem that much more vibrant. Their eyes were dark hollows, their smell so sweet that she sneezed.

"Poor thing's catchin' a chill already," the red-haired woman said. "I'm Minerva and this is Pleshette. I understand you've already met."

Lindy recognized the dark-haired woman as the one who had dumped wash water on her. "Yes, we have. I'm Lindy and this is my brother, Luke." Lindy's nose tickled and she felt another sneeze coming on.

Minerva handed her a lace hankie. "You'd best get out of those wet things." The woman's sharp brown eyes roved over Lindy. "I've seen you before."

"I come in to town for supplies. I have a—"

"Sheep," Minerva exclaimed, clapping her hands together and laughing. "You're the one who drove those woollies under Clay's nose. Well, come here and peel off those clothes and tell me all about your ranch."

"Perhaps this isn't a good idea. Luke—"

Minerva took Lindy by the hand and pulled her along. "Pleshette will keep a close eye on him. Won't you, dear?"

"I sure will," Pleshette promised. Her suggestive smile infused Luke's cheeks with color.

"Luke, you just wait out here in the hall," Lindy ordered as Minerva dragged her away from him. "Luke's just a ... he shouldn't be up here."

"Neither should you if you prize your reputation," Minerva said with a laugh.

Curiosity getting the best of her, Lindy ventured into Minerva's room. Compared to her own room at Broken Gate it was an opulent palace; an oasis in a dry, dusty place; a foreign country in the middle of town. Lindy could never have imagined such wealth in ribbons, satin, velvet, beads, ruffles, glittering red glass and mirrors all in one place. Since the wardrobe was still open, and Minerva sparsely attired,

Lindy assumed she had been caught in the middle of dressing. Lindy's attention faltered on the ruffled skirts that hung out of the overstuffed wardrobe and the round hatboxes that were stacked in towers alongside it.

Turning to the wardrobe, Minerva said, "Gifts. Mostly from Clay. Now, let's see what we can put on you." She turned and swept a ruminating gaze over Lindy's slight form. "Take off those clothes. You're drippin' on the floor."

At Minerva's direct order, Lindy inhaled deeply and began to unbutton her blouse. She dropped her outer clothes in a wet pile at her feet and pulled off her boots and wet stockings. She opted to stay in her damp undergarments rather than put on anything that had come from Claxton, until Minerva scowled at her.

"Don't be such a modest twit. You can't stay in those, either. You'll get the fever." Minerva tossed her a silk wrapper.

Lindy tied the luxurious silk around her, secretly delighting in the sensuous feel of the whisper-soft fabric caressing her bare skin every time she took a breath. A discerning smile curved Minerva's ruby lips as she gathered up Lindy's wet clothes. "I'll hang these out for you. Then we'll see what we can do about your face."

After Minerva left, Lindy peeked a look at herself in a mirror. For the first time she saw what Connor had fretted over—a dark blue shadow curved under her eye.

"Who hit you?" Minerva asked, closing the door behind her. "I don't allow men to hit my girls, you know."

"No one hit me—at least not like you think. It was an accident. I was breaking up a fight between my stockmen. Well, they weren't really fighting, but—"

"You? You were gettin' yourself between two men? You're just a wisp of a thing." The madam laughed heartily. "Sit down here. You can tell me everything while I fix your eye. I always like to hear about men," she added with a wink.

Girl talk. It was precisely what she had yearned for, to commiserate with someone of her own sex, just as Luke could do with the men.

Lindy looked suspiciously at the jar Minerva held in the palm of her hand. How could she commiserate with someone so different? "What are you up to?"

"Just goin' to try and hide your black eye. Now if you don't like the results, you can rinse it all off before you leave."

"I shouldn't have come up here," Lindy admitted nervously. She rose from the dressing table chair only to be shoved back down by Minerva's firm hand.

"You can't very well walk around town lookin' like you do, either," Minerva reminded her sharply.

"Yes, but . . . I should get back to Luke."

Minerva pushed her down again. "Relax. My, you're tight as a wire. Your brother will be just fine. Now tell me about these men of yours."

It couldn't hurt, and she couldn't sit there like a clam while Minerva fussed over her face, so in a nervous flow of chatter, Lindy told the madam all about Dean and Boone, careful to leave out the bank part, and acquainted her with Connor, without quite realizing how much she exposed her heart. By the time Lindy concluded telling her the trials of trying to establish her station, Minerva had finished fussing over Lindy's face and hair.

She gave Lindy a hand mirror and exclaimed with delight, "I'd say if that man isn't in love with you, he will be once he sets his eyes on you again."

Lindy laughed at that. "He's just fond of me." She looked into the mirror and gasped at her reflection. With her mysterious pots of cream and rice powder, Minerva had masterfully hidden the bruise under Lindy's eye, darkened her lashes, brought subtle color to her cheeks and brightened her lips. Her damp hair had been tossed and piled into an artful array of waves and ribbons atop her head. "Oh, my heavens, I can't leave here looking like this."

"Why not?" Minerva asked in a hurt voice. "You look absolutely ravishing. Just don't leave through my saloon, you're liable to be pounced upon." She laughed. "When your Connor sees you, he'll be tempted to ravish you at first glance."

Lindy wiped the color off her lips with the back of her hand. "He isn't going to do such a thing—he's leaving soon."

"Why?"

"I've told him to go." Lindy's stomach began to feel queasy.

Minerva steadied her. "Something else troubling you? Are you ill?"

"No. I'm fine. It's just..."

Lindy searched Minerva's face. Her stomach churned with the burden of guilt that had grown too heavy to carry for much longer. She had to tell someone soon, she was on the edge of crying out to the first person she thought she could trust with her secret. Despite their differences, Lindy felt Minerva was a kindred spirit; someone who had dark secrets of her own; a woman who wouldn't judge her.

Sensing Lindy's inner struggle, Minerva said, "Some things are better left unsaid, unless it's somethin' eatin' at your insides like a worm. Secrets like that destroy all the goodness in a person, leavin' nothin' but a shell of what you were. I don't think it's me you need to bare your soul to. Maybe that Connor fella. Maybe you're sendin' him away because of that secret, and it's my thought that's a damn foolish thing to do."

Minerva's gaze drifted far away, momentarily drawing Lindy's thoughts from her own problems, making her wonder what kind of secret Minerva sheltered. Almost wistfully Minerva said, "This is a hard country to survive in.

Sometimes people have to do hard things." Lindy wiped her face with her hands.

"Now don't go smudgin' all my hard work. A lone woman doesn't have energy to spare for tears." Minerva reached down into her bosom and retrieved a handkerchief. She dabbed at Lindy's cheeks, repairing the damage to her handiwork. "There, that's better," she concluded with a satisfied smile. "Now, what are you doin' in town, away from your ranch, anyway?"

"Cornmeal. My cook needs cornmeal."

"You best be leavin' here, then. And quick, before someone sees you. You have enough to worry yourself with without soiling your reputation as a lady. I'll get your clothes—they should be dry as parchment by now."

Lindy quickly dressed and was ready to return Minerva's hair ribbons when the madam shook her head, tossing red curls around her shoulders. "You keep the ribbons, and any time you need someone to talk to, you just come see Minerva."

"I can see myself out," Lindy said, not wanting to further impose on the woman's kindness.

"You make sure no one sees you goin' down those stairs," Minerva warned. "A person might come to the wrong conclusion."

Without windows for light and with the lamps not yet lit, Lindy found herself alone and disoriented in the dark hallway. The air was stagnant, reeking of unpleasant odors that she did not want to ponder. Even during the day, drunken male voices could be heard drifting up the staircase from the saloon below.

Lindy recognized Sheriff Hayes's deep timbre as he wiled away the hour playing poker with Clay Claxton. She was drawn to the edge of the inside staircase by their voices. Peering around the wall, she saw the sheriff and Claxton and some of Claxton's men through the top of a dusty chandelier. Cards were fanned out in their hands, money was spread over Claxton's green gaming table, cigar smoke ringed around their heads like a giant, gray halo. From her vantage point, it was too tempting an opportunity to eavesdrop on their conversation.

"Are you going to do something, or am I?" Claxton asked, throwing down his hand.

"You know I've tried, Clay," the sheriff said. He scrutinized his cards. "But she hasn't done anything to break the law."

At the mention of "she" Lindy leaned forward to catch more of their conversation. Since Claxton was talking, she rightly assumed he was discussing her.

One of the gamblers, whose back was to Lindy, grumbled in a spine-chilling, familiar voice, "How do you know? You ain't been out there lately, and you ain't found Hank yet."

A cowpuncher in a floppy brown hat that looked as if it had been stampeded over and then crushed onto his head answered Jeb. "That's 'cause he's been here takin' our money every afternoon. Besides, by now your brother's probably in San Antone, gambling in fancier places than this one and not giving you a second thought."

"That would be just like Hank." One of the men laughed.

"Maybe I'll pay Mrs. Rigby a visit just to keep you boys quiet," Hayes said evenly, scraping the money he had won into a pile in front of him.

In the same expressionless tone, Claxton said, "I wish you would, Hayes, before one of us finds it necessary to visit her ourselves." Then, looking up from his hand, he said more emphatically, "I've given her enough time to fail on her own, and what has she done? There's bloody sheep all over and men to watch them. If I hadn't listened to your advice, she would already know that her father's ambition to raise sheep next to cattle was utterly ridiculous. Look where such foolishness put him."

Hayes looked over his hand at Claxton, who suddenly blustered defensively, "Odds are, coming from Australia, Lawrence Falen was a man of questionable character."

Lindy slid back, flattening herself against the wall. Her heart began a drumroll. Claxton was trying to convince the sheriff that she and Luke were fugitives. If either man knew about Hank, she'd hang for sure.

Her eyes flashed in panic as she looked around for the door she had come in. She was ready to run back to Minerva when she spied Luke squeezing himself out of Pleshette's room. She grabbed his hand and jerked him around.

"Lin!" he gasped.

Finding the back door, Lindy flung it open. A rush of daylight blinded her. She ran down the steps with Luke in tow. It wasn't until they were across the street that she slowed her pace. She straightened her hat on her head. Giving Luke a sideward glance, she said, "Tuck in your shirt or someone's going to think—" She peered more closely at Luke's face and wiped her finger across a stain of lip paint smudged on his cheek. "Luke!"

Chapter Fourteen

Still shocked that Luke had consorted with a bawdy woman, and a woman much older than him at that, Lindy shot her brother another look of disbelief. Throughout the ride back to Broken Gate, Luke had refused to answer her questions about exactly what he was doing in Pleshette's room. The telltale blush on his cheeks told her enough. She should have recognized the signs leading up to the change. Luke could not have resisted Pleshette's experienced advances if he had wanted to. She knew her little brother was gone forever. In his boots walked a young man. Struggling to accept that fact, Lindy pushed Maldo's stew around her plate.

"If ever I've seen two more sorry faces, they're right across from me," Connor said.

Lindy avoided his discriminating gaze by turning her attention to Armaldo, who was still scraping the burned remains of their supper from the frying pan. "I'm sorry we were so late."

"*I'm* not hungry," Armaldo said, looking over his shoulder at Connor.

Connor caught Lindy's attention, his intense eyes prompting an explanation from her. "I didn't expect to be so long. You know how Hester can talk."

"If you were a man, I would guess you had spent some time at Minerva's place." Connor's sharp eyes studied Lindy's face. Luke choked and laughed at the same time, throwing himself into a fit of hiccups.

Lindy twittered, and was relieved that the idea was so ludicrous that Connor had only referred to it jokingly. Luke gobbled his food as though he were famished. He excused himself and left the table as soon as he had eaten. Armaldo followed Luke's happy whistle out of the house, leaving Lindy alone with Connor.

Lindy felt the tension in the room thicken as soon as she and Connor were alone. She thought of all Minerva had told her. Hank's death was eating her alive, coming between her and everything good she wanted in life. Connor was waiting for her to say something. Now was the time.

"Connor, if you hate me for today, I wouldn't blame you. I would never have hurt anyone intentionally, but—" Her words sank to her stomach when Connor wrapped his arms around her and kissed her forehead.

"Never mind, that was one you owed me. I deserved to feel the same worry I put you through when I stayed out all night. At least you had the common sense to take Luke with you."

When his lips touched hers, Connor gave Lindy a reason to avoid telling him about Hank. She forgot everything except for how wonderful it was to be in his arms again.

Connor's wide hands moved over Lindy's hips and circled her waist. He pulled her against him in a tight hug that thrilled and comforted her at the same time. Their bodies molded together without a breath of space between them. They each warmed the other, mindful that their closeness was beginning to heat their desire and pump their blood until their hearts raced together. Their thoughts clouded with passion, so that mind as well as body didn't care that they had agreed not to want each other.

"Do I have to sleep with Maldo tonight?" Connor asked through his kiss.

"No. I've missed you in my bed, luv."

"I've missed you, too, darlin'."

Connor's fingers worked Lindy's blouse out of the waistband of her skirt. Lindy loosened the buttons and let it slide off her shoulders into a soft puddle at her feet. When her fingers reached for the ties on her chemise, Connor stopped her.

"Must you do everything yourself? I'd like the pleasure of undressing you."

Lindy rested her hand over his and boldly replied, "Only if I may be permitted to do the same."

"I can't think of anything I'd like more."

As soon as the ties on Lindy's chemise were free, Connor's hands slid up her back, taking the garment with them. Once the air grazed her skin, her breasts tightened to peaked mounds and thrust against Connor's chest. Connor tossed the chemise aside, letting his eyes rest on the bare flesh in front of him. As though she was as delicate as a china doll, Connor shed light kisses down her shoulder, over her collarbones and down the rise of each breast. His hands cupped them in a gentle caress while his tongue licked and his mouth suckled her nipples, sending a rolling wave of titillating pleasure through her.

"I am fond of you, Lindy, darlin'."

Lindy pushed Connor's face away from her and looked down at him. "How fond?"

Connor smiled. "Very fond."

"Are you fond of Luke? Are you fond of Buddy?"

"It goes without saying I . . . Now what's wrong?"

"Well, you can be fond of a lot of things. I'm fond of biscuits with my tea. You and Luke are fond of coffee in the morning. Dean is fond of his harmonica and the coyotes are fond of my chooks."

Connor quieted her fretting by placing his lips on hers in a short kiss.

"Do you love me, Connor?" There was a painful silence.

"I don't know if I love you the way you want me to. I—"

Lindy turned her face from Connor's. "I'm not being fair. You don't know half there is to know about me. How could I ask you to love me?"

"Maybe we should talk, then."

"No," Lindy said quickly, pulling him close to her. "Later. There's always time later," she promised.

Lindy unbuttoned Connor's shirt and pushed it off his shoulders, gliding her hands over the flat broadness of his back. She felt his muscles tense under her hands and his kiss grow feverish as her touch rounded to his chest. Slowly breaking their kiss, she trailed her mouth down the coarse curve of his chin and throat, to his chest, over the mounds of muscles and down the center of his abdomen.

Connor sucked in his breath. His stomach fluttered with the touch of her lips. He pulled her mouth up to his and while they kissed deeply, she felt her skirt slide past her knees and drop to her feet. "I must look a sight in my bloomers and boots," Lindy said with a giggle.

"Then I shall have to take care of that without haste, and in more private quarters."

Lindy imagined what their shadows looked like from the outside. "I hope no one—"

"Armaldo falls asleep as soon as his head hits the ground, and everyone else is far away," Connor assured her as he carried her to her bed.

He tossed Lindy's boots into a corner with his own, and then settled on the bed with her. Their lips met in a lingering kiss that slowly fueled their desire to sudden impatience. Connor's hands slid down Lindy's sides, pushing away the remainder of her undergarments until she was completely naked. When her shaky fingers failed to unfasten his belt buckle, she confessed, "I've never undressed a man before."

"I assumed so," Connor said, swiftly undoing his belt.

Lindy felt the hardness of him released and a sudden rush of warm desire gripped her. When Connor slid on top of her, she felt every part of him rub against her skin until they were aligned and neatly fitted to each other. When he gazed down at her with his Yankee-blue eyes, she knew he was telling her he loved her. It was enough. She couldn't bear to hear the words and then someday hear them taken away.

Connor's cheek brushed against hers. The light abrasion was followed by the smooth and tender caress of his lips as he moved a kiss over her cheek, finally claiming her mouth fully with his. His hands wrapped under her, pressing her to him and him to her. They had become one. It was a bonding Lindy wanted to last beyond the brief moment into forever. Connor's warmth spread into her like penetrating fingers. She felt his love touch her deeply, slowly at first, then with an increasing fervor that swept her along in its swift, pulsing current.

The consummation of what they felt and could not say left Lindy and Connor drained of all energy. Connor rolled off her, pulling her up to his side. Their breathing was heavy and their skin glistening and damp. A breeze cooled their bare bodies while they rested in each other's arms. It was unsaid, but understood, that Connor would not be returning to the barn for as long as he stayed at Broken Gate.

Lindy knew she couldn't have slept for very long, but when she opened her eyes, she felt wide awake and unable to go back to sleep. She slid away from Connor, careful not to disturb him, and dressed. When she pulled open the top bureau drawer, a yellowed slip of paper caught her eye. Her father's last letter. She remembered the last time she had held it in her hand, seeking comfort from the scribbled words. Looking over to Connor, she suddenly felt alone and empty. There was more to life than she had thought, only she didn't know how to get it. Lindy closed the drawer. She heard the bed linen rustle and knew Connor had stirred.

"Lin? What are you doing up?" Connor raised up on his elbow.

Lindy turned and smiled at him. "We can't all sleep our lives away," she said cheerily. "I thought I'd ride out and surprise the men with some sourdough biscuits."

"Oh."

Lindy heard the disappointment in Connor's voice. "Why don't you join us?"

Connor feigned a yawn. "I was hoping to get a little more sleep. Why don't you join me?"

"Because I'm not tired."

"Then we don't have to sleep."

"You're as cocky as that new bantam rooster, Connor O'Malley. I have work to do today, even if you don't."

By the time Connor raised himself from bed, Lindy had made coffee and wrapped the dozen sourdough biscuits in a cloth. She tied the warm parcel to her saddle horn and nudged her horse into a gentle lope. When she reached the men, they had just rolled out of their bedrolls.

Boone looked disagreeable, and recalling that he wasn't at his best early in the day, Lindy didn't attempt to talk to him directly. Through breakfast, she chatted with Dean and Luke, aware that the silent Boone was grimly listening to every word. It wasn't until she touched upon the subject of castrating the lambs that Boone opened his mouth.

"Holy Hannah, ma'am, you certainly can spoil a man's breakfast," he said, tossing his coffee into the fire.

Lindy stared at him, and then looked at Dean. Their faces were flushed with embarrassment. After looking to Luke for some help, and getting none, Lindy set down her cup. "They're lambs, not men, for pity's sake. Luke and I can't take care of them all ourselves."

"Well, I ain't takin' any part in it," Boone snapped.

Dean remained silent even when Lindy looked at him. "How can you expect to be shepherds if—"

"Ma'am, it was never my idea in the first place to be a shepherd. It was yours." Boone slammed his hat on his head and glared at Dean. "And maybe it was Dean's idea, but it weren't never mine."

Lindy stood up, faced Boone and balled her hands on her hips. "If you're not going to pull your own weight, then—"

"Lin," Luke said, placing himself between his sister and Boone, "we can manage. There aren't that many of them." Luke's eyes begged her to be more tolerant of Boone's aversion to castrating the lambs. "Besides, we need someone to watch the ewes."

Lindy grudgingly agreed, but remained miffed at Boone's stubbornness.

Lindy stayed with the band through the morning. When she spotted Dean riding the bank of a dried-up streambed, she rode over to him.

Dean smiled when he saw her. The first thing he addressed after greeting her was Boone's outburst. "Ma'am, you can't blame Boone. He ain't lazy. This just ain't for him. The only animal he knows or wants to know is the one under his saddle. He's searchin' for the good life and in his eyes this ain't it."

"I'm sorry he isn't happy here. He can leave when he wants. So can you, Dean. I'd never turn you in to the sheriff, you know."

"I know that." Dean's eyes swept over the expanse of land. "Ma'am, I'm happy here. You're the first person who's ever given me a chance." Dean paused to run his hand over his mare's neck. "But Boone ain't never gonna be happy watchin' over sheep. I'm surprised he ain't already run off on you."

* * *

Connor reread the tattered letter before saddling his horse. His eyes swept over it as he fit the pieces of the puzzle together. He had found it hidden in the drawer with the pearl-handled Colt. Secrets Lindy guarded, no doubt the same secrets that haunted her sleep.

Her father had known it would be his last letter to his family. In it he wrote of the hardships he had encountered, his doubts and regrets, his sadness that he had failed his family. He wrote of a cattleman, Clay Claxton, who had tried to buy his land, and when he had refused, had had him beaten until he was near dead.

Connor read the last paragraph again.

I watched the vultures mill around me until I lost consciousness, dizzy from the constant circling above me. When I opened my eyes, it was night. I managed to drag myself into the house, safe from the vultures, but not safe from Claxton and his men. There is nothing the Englishman will stop at to prevent what he calls woollies from grazing a hundred miles from his cattle. I fear he will make good on his threat to kill me. There is one hope, but it is not yet safe for all of you to come here. As soon as I can, I will send for you.

Lovingly, your father.

Connor folded the paper along its worn creases and pondered Lawrence Falen's last words to his family. Lindy had been warned of Clay Claxton before she arrived, but was still determined to lock horns with him. After her father's letter, how could she have believed that Indians had killed him? And why hadn't she gone to the sheriff with the incriminating letter? It was her own damn independence, Connor swore to himself, and it was bound to plant her beside her father.

Instead of putting the letter back where he had found it, Connor tucked it into his shirt pocket. Before the day was over, he was going to talk to Lindy about it. If he stood a chance of getting caught in Claxton's line of fire, he sure as hell wanted to make it clear to Lindy that there would be no more secrets between them.

The first thing Connor did was to ride out and look for Lindy. He found Luke, sensing something was amiss by the grim set of his mouth. "What is it, Luke? Where's Lindy?" he questioned in panic.

"We're missing about ten jumbucks. Lin's off looking with Dean and Boone. I expect that rebel ewe has led them off again. If Lin doesn't decide to cook up that dumb animal for supper, Boone swears he'll shoot it himself. He spent half yesterday in the saddle looking for it, only for the ewe to decide to go on another midnight walk, and take a following with it to boot."

Connor joined the search, putting off his confrontation with Lindy for a better time.

Lindy followed the dry streambed in case any of the missing sheep had stumbled into it. Her throat was beginning to be parched, making her regret taking off without a canteen. Her white cotton shirt stuck to her damp skin. Unfastening the top buttons, she pulled her blouse out of her skirt to catch a little bit of cool air. A plaintive bleating came faintly beyond the bank of the streambed that marked the boundary between her land and Claxton's. She listened again. The sound was definitely sheep and not cow. Claxton would have a fit, she thought, as she eased her horse down the bank, crossing the bed to Claxton's land.

Lindy found the ewe and its lamb a hundred feet inside the boundary. The animals looked so forlorn, she had to laugh. "That'll teach you to follow that daggy ewe. You're lucky someone else hasn't found you first or you'd be—"

"Supper?"

Lindy swung around and faced Jeb.

"I told Clay it would only be a matter of time before we found your woollies grazing on his land," Jeb said with smug satisfaction at catching her off guard. Lindy automatically moved her hand to her rifle, but froze at Jeb's quick warning. "I ain't opposed to killin' a woman who gives me reason, and I'd say you've already given me more 'n I need."

Lindy had no choice but to sit still while Jeb slipped her rifle from her saddle scabbard. "I'm not grazing sheep on Claxton's land. These two wandered, and I—"

"Same thing," Jeb said. Without emotion or warning, before Lindy could object, he shot the ewe, nearly causing Lindy to jump out of her saddle. He aimed again at the lamb beside its mother. This time Jeb moved slowly, prolonging Lindy's agony, taunting her with a twisted smile.

"You're a coward, Jeb," Lindy said. "You really want to shoot me, but can't, so you're killing my animals instead. Helpless animals and helpless women. That was Hank's style, too, only he found I wasn't so helpless."

Jeb slowly turned the pistol around and pointed it at her. "*Was* Hank's style? I hope he had you first. Get off that horse."

Lindy slowly dismounted, keeping her eyes on Jeb, frantically trying to think of an escape, when she detected a slight movement in the brush behind Jeb. Another ewe? Even if it distracted Jeb, what could she do? Her situation certainly looked bleak, until her eye caught a piece of red bandanna. Connor!

"Come on! Get around over here away from that horse." Jeb motioned with his gun. "Closer."

Lindy moved just out of arm's reach. She saw Jeb's eyes wander down the front of her blouse.

"Unbutton the rest." When she didn't move out of sheer dread, Jeb said, "I can shoot them off, and still keep you alive enough to enjoy you."

While Lindy slowly opened the rest of her blouse, she fought to keep her eyes from the clump of chaparral where Connor crouched. Her eyes rested on Jeb's gun. If Connor made his presence known now, Jeb could kill one of them.

"If you intend to have me, then you'll have to put that gun down."

Lindy's suggestion was rewarded with cruel laughter. "And make the same mistake as my brother?"

"You took my rifle."

Jeb seemed to think about it, and then smiled. "Not until I'm sure you don't have a knife hidden under your skirt. Take that off, too. I want you down to your skin."

Under the gun, Lindy slowly peeled off her blouse and skirt, and was standing nearly naked when an anxious Jeb finally set his pistol down on a rock. As his measured steps brought him closer to her, she slowly backed away, taking him farther from the horses and his gun. Jeb's pistol was out of his reach when Connor decided to make his presence known with the deadly sound of a cocked gun.

"Don't take another step, Jeb."

Jeb froze. "I'm not armed," he said, slowly moving his hands away from his hips.

"Raise 'em."

Jeb reached his arms up over his head.

"Higher." Connor took Jeb's gun. "I've a mind to shoot you where you stand. You breathe too heavy and I will."

As soon as Jeb put his hands up, Lindy hurried into her blouse and skirt and retrieved her rife. She mounted her horse but wasn't ready to leave Jeb yet. It wasn't enough of a punishment to take his gun and let him ride back to Claxton after killing the ewe and humiliating her. While Connor still had his gun drawn on Jeb, she ordered, "Take your clothes off."

Connor looked at her with the same startled expression as Jeb, then smiled. "You heard the lady."

After a sour-faced Jeb was buck naked, Connor ordered him to mount and return to Claxton.

If Lindy hadn't been so humiliated, she would have laughed at the sight Jeb made riding away in nothing but his bare skin. But all she could think about was that Connor had been watching most of what had happened, waiting for the best moment to come out from behind his cover. She felt her cheeks burn from reviewing the whole incident.

"Did you have to wait till I was down to my bloomers?" she said.

Without a word, Connor walked past her and picked up the orphaned lamb. He put it in front of his saddle and pulled himself up behind it, cradling it in his lap. "You're lucky to still have your skin, never mind your bloomers. I don't want you stepping one foot on Claxton's land again," he said.

"I had to, the—"

"You didn't have to. That's what you have stockmen for. You knew the danger."

"I didn't know that Jeb would be nearby. How was I to know that?"

"Claxton's looking for you to make a wrong move. Don't be surprised if the sheriff pays you a visit tomorrow."

"For embarrassing Jeb?"

"For trespassing."

"Jeb killed one of my ewes."

"Jeb would have done more to you, and with Claxton's blessing." Connor took the letter out of his shirt pocket. "I've been looking for you to discuss this. Now's as good a time as any I can think of."

Lindy's eyes widened with horror.

"This is a letter from your father."

"I know that."

"What did he say in it?"

Lindy walled up her defenses with angry words. "It's none of your business. You were snooping."

"If you don't heed your own father's warnings then there isn't any way I can talk sense into your head. Maybe your next foreman can." Connor handed her the letter, and rode on ahead of her.

Lindy looked down at the paper and swallowed a lot of pride before trotting after Connor. "Connor, wait."

Connor held fast to the squirming lamb. "I'm listening."

"I have no idea what's in this letter. I can't read. Neither can Luke. Mother tried to teach me but it was a chore just getting me to sit still for lessons. Matt read to us, but he died before my father's last letter arrived. After that, I wanted a better place for us. The first place I thought of was Broken Gate. I know now that my father hadn't told us the truth. Maybe he was ashamed of leaving us to chase his rainbow. He was a dreamer who always gave us hope for something better."

"Your father warned you not to come in his last letter."

Lindy handed Connor the letter. "Will you read it to me?"

On their way back to the band, Connor read her father's last words. "This letter would point out Claxton as your father's killer. I doubt he did the handiwork himself, but it would have been like him to send someone like Jeb to do it. I think you should go to the sheriff. You want to tell me what you know about Jeb, and why he seems to hate you so? Lin, when Jeb comes after me, I sure as hell want to know why. Don't you think I have that right?"

Lindy tried to hide under her hat as best she could. Her lips were stiff and unyielding. She couldn't tell Connor now, not until she got hold of her swelling emotions.

Connor looked over to her, trying to get a glimpse of her face. "Are you crying?" Still no answer came forth. He sighed. "All right. I suppose it wasn't fair to ask you that right after... I know it's not easy being a woman, especially out here and alone, but—"

"You have absolutely no idea what it's like, so don't give me your bloody pity. It would do you men good to wear a skirt for a day! Then you can tell me what it's like to be a woman." Leaving an astonished Connor holding a bleating lamb in his lap, Lindy loped away.

The orphan lamb turned its dark, trusting eyes up to Connor. "Now stop calling me 'ma.' I'm not your ma, but it is nice to feel loved and trusted by someone, even if it is only a lamb." Connor's eyes followed the little cloud of dust Lindy had become. "What are we going to do about that woman? Just like your mother, she's going to get herself killed." Then with a visceral determination he vowed, "Hell, not if I can help it."

Connor handed the orphan down to Luke. After he told him a censored version of what had happened on Claxton's land, Luke looked at the lamb in his arms. "It's a shame this one will die, too."

"What do you mean, die?"

"Another ewe won't take it as its own without some fancy trickery on our part. That would mean tying the skin of another ewe's dead lamb onto this one."

"Do that then."

"Can't. We don't have a dead lamb."

"Well, maybe you do. Have Dean and Boone check around."

Luke shook his head. "We've been all over looking for those stray sheep. There isn't a dead lamb in the band."

Connor remained persistent. "Is there anything else that can be done?"

"Lin may have some condensed milk."

Connor gathered the lamb in his arms and headed for the house.

Lindy watched Connor spoon-feed the orphan, spilling more milk on the floor and his pants than he got into the lamb. The more her looks expressed the futility of what he was trying to do, the more he was determined to feed the lamb.

"Connor, even if you manage to save it, it won't be able to return to the band. The others won't accept it, and she won't think she's a jumbuck."

"You'd let her die?" Connor asked, dripping another spoonful down the lamb's throat.

"No. We can put a skin of another—"

"Luke said there weren't any dead lambs."

"Oh," Lindy sat back in the chair opposite Connor and watched him. Soon the lamb's hunger was satisfied enough for the animal to fall asleep in Connor's lap. Lindy smiled, suddenly warming with love for Connor. "You are a sight."

"You see? Anything is possible."

"There's something else, Connor. That lamb is going to be awfully confused."

"What do you mean?"

"She's going to think you're her mother. When she's one hundred thirty pounds she'll be following you around with love in her eyes."

"As long as you're right behind her, I see no problem in that," Connor said lightly.

Lindy looked at Connor and felt her heart tug with longing. He must have seen it in her eyes, for his mouth turned at the corners. Her own mouth curved into a smile.

"Have you any idea how endearing you look with that lamb curled fast asleep in your lap?" she asked, sidling over to him.

Connor looked down at the lamb and stroked its head with a finger. "I'd much prefer you in my lap, but—"

Lindy stretched up on her knees and kissed his cheek. "You're a very special man, Mr. O'Malley." Her mouth moved down his cheek. She pressed soft kisses over his unshaven face until her lips touched his waiting mouth. "I'm sorry about this afternoon."

"I've forgotten about it already."

Lindy felt Connor's hungry desire in the passion of his kiss and was at once stirred to wanting him. She wrapped her arms around his neck and felt his hands circle her waist.

"Darlin'," Connor said through his kiss, "why won't you go to the sheriff with your father's letter?"

Connor's question snuffed out the flame that had kindled between them. Lindy backed away, but his hand remained firm at her waist.

"He wouldn't believe any of it."

"Why not?"

"Because…because…" Lindy sighed deeply. "I should have told you a long time ago. My father was sent to Australia as a thief. He wasn't really. All he was was a poor man in love. My mother's parents, with their daughter's best interest in mind, tried to destroy their love. Using their wealth and influence in the courts, they had my father branded as a thief. He fled and took my mother with him. I'm afraid Claxton could use his influence to further tarnish the Falen name."

"You thought I'd think ill of you for your father's past? Lin, it doesn't matter to me what your background is. You should have told me this sooner. At least I would have understood why you were so ready to defend the outlaws you hired."

"They're not outlaws," she countered stiffly.

"You have to admit, they don't look like preachers or farmers."

"Exactly. Looks don't tell everything there is to know about a person. Claxton looks and sounds like a fine upstanding citizen—brocade waistcoat, gold pocket watch, polished boots, the queen's English. That's why the sheriff will believe whatever he says before he believes me. I'm from Australia, remember, the land of thieves and murderers. Sheriff Hayes already thinks I'm trouble."

Lindy was thankful Connor didn't argue, for she couldn't tell him the whole reason why she couldn't show Sheriff

Hayes her father's last words. She could not risk another visit from the sheriff when his nephew rested in her henhouse.

Connor remained thoughtfully silent, stroking her hair. The long, gentle brushing of his hand had a mesmerizing effect on her. She soon relaxed against his side. Her eyes drifted down to the lamb in his lap. "You'd best get some sleep while you can. You'll soon find out how often little lambs want to be fed."

"You mean it's not asleep for the night?"

Lindy laughed. "Heaven's no!" She stood at Connor's side and patted his shoulder. "Don't worry—they grow quickly. There's more canned milk on that shelf over there," she said, retiring to her room.

When Lindy opened her eyes again, it was dark. She heard a clattering in the house and knew it must be what had awakened her. Connor's voice came softly into her room. He was talking to someone. As she came fully awake, she remembered the lamb. Grabbing her robe, she padded out to Connor. The room was dimly lit in the yellow glow of lamplight. Connor looked up to her with bleary eyes. He was spooning milk into the lamb's eager mouth.

"I haven't had a wink of sleep," he complained through a bashful smile.

Lindy gathered the squirming lamb in her arms. "I warned you. Go to bed. I'm wide awake now."

Connor's brow arched devilishly. "You joining me?"

"If this little lamb lets me." She laughed lightly as she watched Connor drag himself into her room. The next sound she heard was her bed giving way to Connor's full weight.

Chapter Fifteen

Connor would be furious, but Lindy was not about to let Jeb or Claxton bully her. There were going to be times when her sheep would wander onto Claxton's land. Still, she couldn't see any reason why the two of them couldn't live in peace. A little understanding and working out the differences before they began had seemed like a good idea at the time. But now that she looked down at Claxton's sprawling ranch, let her eyes wander over his remuda and the men who looked like guards of a fortress rather than cowboys, Lindy began to have second thoughts. And so did Dean, who had insisted on going with her.

"Ma'am, it ain't too late to turn back. No one's discovered us yet."

"No, I've thought it through. We've come too far to turn back."

Dean sighed to himself. "Let's go, then."

Dean and Lindy crouched low and returned to their picketed horses. When they looked up it was into two rifle barrels.

"Well, who do we have here? Cattle rustlers, I'd say."

Lindy straightened slowly. She recognized the man who held her at gunpoint to be one of Jeb's friends, Frank Lloyd.

"You know we're not cattle rustlers."

"What are you doing sneaking around in the bushes fer then?"

"I've come to talk to Mr. Claxton."

Lindy and Dean were escorted to the house, wondering if they'd see their guns and horses again. They were put in a sparsely furnished room where Frank kept a gun on them until his boss could be summoned.

It had been a long time waiting. Lindy wondered if Claxton had had to make himself presentable for guests or if he had been on the range. It soon occurred to her that he might have gone to town, and that she would have made the trip for nothing but a good tongue-lashing from Connor.

Dean nervously chewed the inside of his cheek and crossed and uncrossed his ankles. He sat up ramrod straight, slouched down and then repeated the whole set of motions again until Lindy thought her own nerves were going to snap just from watching him.

"I don't like not having my iron," Dean whispered to explain his fidgeting.

"He'll be here soon," Lindy assured him.

Finally Claxton entered the room, and as Lindy had expected, he was dressed impeccably, no dust dulling his shiny black boots or his clothes. He casually puffed on a cigar, sending a cloud of smoke over their heads.

"Well, well, well," he muttered to himself as he looked over Lindy. He gave Dean hardly any notice. "To what do I owe this pleasure?"

"I think you know why I'm here."

"How would I know that? But I am curious to find out." He held his hand out to her.

Lindy reluctantly placed her hand in his and followed him into his study. "My man—" she began to say before he closed the door behind him.

"I don't discuss business in front of my men. You shouldn't either."

"I don't hold anything from them if it involves the station."

"Ah, yes, your station. I was afraid that's why you came. I was hoping it was purely a social call."

She gave a short laugh at the ridiculousness of the idea. Claxton turned to the polished sideboard and she heard the clink of crystal decanters as he chose his drink. Her eyes swept about the opulent room, over the walls covered with bookshelves, the windows draped in rich fabric that hid the working ranch outside. When she tapped her foot with impatience, the floor was soft under her toes, not from dirt, but from a thick Oriental carpet. The chairs were stuffed and comfortable. Claxton had spared no expense in creating an illusion of gentility in Texas.

Claxton poured whiskey into two cut-glass tumblers, and extended one to Lindy. When she hesitated he said, "You must drink to our meeting. I apologize. I should have asked you if you preferred sherry or brandy. I'm hurt to the quick to have to talk business with a beautiful woman when I'd much rather be embracing her. Something Connor O'Malley must have the pleasure of often." Claxton winked knowingly and took a gulp of his drink.

Lindy hated that he had made her blush. "Mr. Claxton, I didn't come here to be insulted." She stared hatefully at him while he poured himself another drink. "Mr. Claxton—"

"Please call me Clay. I know you've refused to before, but I'm insisting. All my business acquaintances call me Clay."

"Clay," Lindy began, almost choking on the personal touch it put on their meeting. "Yesterday one of my ewes and her lamb strayed onto your land."

"I know all about the incident," Claxton said, smiling.

Of course Jeb would have told him. However, she doubted if he had approached his boss naked as a jay. No, she supposed Jeb would have omitted that part of the story.

"Then you know I tried to bring them back to my side of the streambed, and Jeb shot the ewe before I could do that."

"He did just as he had been told."

"I have no doubt of that, but was it necessary?"

"It's the law of the range."

"*Your* range. I thought we could come to a friendly agreement, because I'm not going away." Lindy continued, trying to keep her temper in check, "If I see your cows on my land, I promise not to have my men shoot them, and if any of my—"

Claxton laughed. "You'll have to come up with something better than that," he said, reaching out and pulling a strand of Lindy's hair through his fingers. The back of his hand ran over her cheek and down her neck, making it all too clear to her what she would have to do to strike a bargain with him. Claxton relaxed in a chair opposite her, waiting for the answer that would satisfy him.

"What if I were a man? What kind of promise would you want from me?"

Claxton chuckled. "You'd be dead alongside your sheep."

"You killed my father and made it seem like Indians, didn't you?"

The smile faded from Claxton's face. Lindy immediately regretted her rash words. Claxton could very well keep her and Dean as prisoners, and that was the very least he could do. But she had said it, and wasn't about to back down.

Claxton's black eyes flicked over her. "Where did you hear something like that?"

"Just now from your own lips. My father was planning to raise sheep next to your ranch, and when you failed to discourage him, you had him killed. Only you didn't figure his daughter would show up with the sheep. Now that you're dealing with a woman, you're in a quandary as to what to do."

Claxton took another gulp of whiskey. "As you say, I am in a quandary. The sheriff would be suspicious if anything fatal happened to you, but that doesn't mean it can't. I assure you, my neck wouldn't be the one in the noose."

Lindy shrank back against the door and turned the latch. She looked at Claxton, who confirmed what she had already discovered.

"It's locked. However, I don't intend to keep you here forever. It won't take that long to come to an agreement."

"You can't mean to keep me here?"

"Oh, I do."

"What about my stockman?"

"He'll have to stay, too. But I'm sorry, his accommodations will not be as comfortable as yours. We can continue our talk at dinner. Zack will show you to the guest room."

Claxton unlocked the door, and standing outside it was the man Lindy assumed was Zack, her guard. Zack was not one of Claxton's brawniest or tallest men, but he was young and lean, his face softened with a week's growth of blond whiskers, his smile clearly indicating he was enjoying his responsibility. Lindy guessed that he couldn't be more than seventeen or eighteen. Without a choice, Lindy walked on ahead of Zack's gun.

"You don't need to point that at me. I'm not going to jump you," Lindy said, with biting sarcasm. Zack chuckled. Lindy wasn't sure if it was her accent that set him off or the ridiculous idea that she could actually overcome him. Feeling the barrel of his gun nudge her back, she stepped into a room and heard Zack lock the door behind her. Sitting on the edge of a bed, she held her head in her hands. "What am I to do now?"

Dean prepared to wait out the night locked in the shed. He swatted at flies and thought that it would have been a whole lot safer and easier robbing banks and trains than being a shepherd. What Lindy had suggested had seemed easy at the time, but then, anything she said was agreeable to him. He couldn't help but admire her spunk. She knew exactly what she wanted out of life and no one was going to stand in her way, not even Claxton. It was too bad for them that Claxton felt the same way.

Dean thanked his stars that he had had the foresight to tell Boone Lindy's idea, and hoped, as he sat in the close dark quarters of the shed, that Boone had the sense to tell Connor where they had gone. Lindy had sworn him to secrecy, and he'd hated breaking his word to her, but figured the only way she'd find out was if they needed someone to rescue them. She couldn't get too mad at him for saving her neck.

Dean watched the sky darken through a slit of a window that was hardly big enough for a man's hand. He guessed he had been sitting and pacing the dirt floor for nearly four hours before a dull thud sounded outside the shed.

The next thing Dean knew, the door to his jail squeaked open. "Connor!" His hoarse whisper was barely audible. "Am I glad to see you!"

"Where's Lindy?" Connor asked.

"In the house somewhere."

"We don't have a lot of time to look for her. We'd best get going before the two I clobbered wake up," he said as Dean tightened his gun belt.

Lindy had tried to open the window, but it wouldn't budge. Zack had heard her pounding at it, and had looked in on her just in time to catch her trying to get it open. From his grin, she knew the window had been permanently sealed. The only way out would have been to break it. That thought occurred to her, but Zack informed her that the shattering glass would alert him for sure, and he'd be on her tail before she had one hand out the window. It seemed he almost wanted her to try it, so other than occasionally looking out the window, she had left it alone. She worried about Dean.

Claxton could kill him for cattle rustling if it suited him. She had worked up a good steam of anger when Zack opened the door again.

"Clay wants to see you. Now," he said, grinning.

Lindy brushed past him, immediately got her bearings and, to Zack's surprise, headed for the front door, banking that he wouldn't shoot her in the back.

"Hey," Zack called. "Lady... whoa!" he shouted, now running after her.

Lindy flew through the front door into the cover of night, not knowing what her next move would be, but sure she wouldn't make anything easy for Claxton and his men.

"What are you saying, Zack? That the woman just walked out the front door?" Claxton was furious.

"She ran out."

"Why didn't you stop her?"

"You said not to hurt her. Besides, she can't get far."

"She damn well better not," Claxton said. "I don't enjoy being made a fool of." Claxton twisted the gold ring around his finger, then said, "She'll go for the horses first and that's how we'll nab her. Keep the remuda well guarded. Leave two saddled horses hitched close by. Make sure they're in sight of the men but don't make our intentions obvious. She won't go for the horses if it looks too easy."

"We'll get her," Zack promised, starting for the door. He was determined, himself, not to be made a fool of. When news of Jeb's humiliation at her hands had reached Zack's ears, he had had a good chuckle. Now it seemed he was on the receiving end, and if he didn't catch the woman himself, he'd have a lot to live down.

Lindy was making enemies fast in Claxton's camp as she managed to slip through the darkest shadows to avoid them. It seemed to the men that she had disappeared with the stealth of an Indian.

Lindy hadn't been able to find where Claxton had taken Dean, and it worried her that she might not find him. Playing hide-and-seek was easy enough, but Lindy knew her time would run out with the first light of dawn. Even if she had managed to find Dean and get far enough away from the house, Claxton's men would soon find them on foot. She needed a horse, but it seemed every man on the ranch was stationed by them. She had spotted two from her hiding place when their riders came in and had hitched them to a rail. They were far enough way from the guarded remuda for her to sneak up to, but she knew the men would be alerted as soon as she mounted. Then she would have to outride them. It seemed to be her only chance.

Lindy kept to the shadows, inching her way closer to the horses, when an unidentifiable sound alerted her. She ducked between two water barrels and listened. Hearing nothing more, she forced her stiff legs to move. She was closing the distance between herself and the horses when a hand clamped over her mouth and an arm wrapped around her middle, dragging her behind an outbuilding. Lindy was pulled back into the shadows and flattened against the side of the building. Her eyes widened. It was Connor! When he was sure she had recognized him, he slowly slid his hand from her mouth.

"Connor," Lindy whispered with what breath she could gather. "Thank God it's you."

"What do you think you're doing coming out here?" Connor asked angrily.

Taking affront, Lindy matched his ire. "Get off of me, Connor."

"Not until I get a promise out of you. For once you're going to do as I say without an argument. Agreed?"

Lindy looked at him suspiciously and conceded with a nod of her head.

"I want your word you'll do as I say until we get back to Broken Gate. *If* we get back," he added.

"You have my word."

"No matter what."

"Yes."

"Good." Connor smiled with satisfaction. "Those horses you were going after were put there just for you. Claxton set a trap for you. Dean's safe for now. He and Boone are waiting with our horses. Now would be a good time to go get them." He shoved men's trousers and a dark-colored flannel shirt in her hands. "Put these on."

Without a word, Lindy slipped out of her riding skirt and into the clothes Connor had given her. She tucked in the shirttails and pulled the belt around her waist as tightly as she could. Connor pulled up her hair and tucked it under a large-brimmed Stetson.

"My hat," Lindy protested, not wanting to part with her father's hat.

"It stays," Connor said firmly. "Now you almost look like one of us." Connor was satisfied that in the dark, she would look like a man. He stuffed her clothes under his arm. "Go straight to where the men are waiting for you. No matter what. Understand?"

Lindy's eyes looked to where he pointed. She agreed to stay on a straight path until Dean found her. Then they would leave together. They would not wait for him. With luck they would see each other back at Broken Gate.

"Connor." Lindy's voice faltered. Her hand touched his arm. "Be careful. If anything happens to you—"

A fleeting shadow of worry passed over Connor's face. "I'll be fine. You just let Dean and Boone get you safely out of here. Get goin'," he said, "and keep low."

Three shots fired into the air brought most of Claxton's men running. They all expected to find the woman in the hands of one of their own, so were only a little surprised to see her lying on the ground. Their stomachs filled with dread when they remembered that Claxton had specifically or-

dered that she not be hurt. Before any of them could ex-
amine her closer, they heard Claxton coming up behind
them, swearing up a storm.

"I thought I said no shots. Where is she?"

Claxton elbowed his way through the men. He looked
down at the body. A muffled moan came from under Lindy's hat. Claxton squatted down to remove it from her face
and nearly fell backward in shock. "What the hell? Zack!
You imbecile."

A silent moment was replaced by laughter as Zack struggled up on his elbow. He winced at the pain in his head
where Connor had hit him with his gun butt. When Zack
regained his senses enough to notice that he had been
dressed in Lindy's clothes, his face turned scarlet. Knowing
that this was something that would ride him to his grave, he
began to tear off the blouse, swearing as he shredded it to
pieces. "I'll kill that woman," he swore amid the hoots and
chuckles of the other men.

Claxton watched Zack shimmy out of Lindy's riding
skirt, trip on it in his haste and fall to his knees. "Not until
I say you can," Claxton warned, and then looked to the rest
of the men. "Have any of you cowboys given it a thought
that the woman is using this moment to get away?"

Their faces became stone serious.

"She's made fools out of all of you," Claxton declared,
throwing down his cigar. "Someone get my horse."

Lindy had to stifle a scream when Dean touched her
shoulder. His hushed voice sounded in her ear. "The horses
are over there."

Lindy followed him through the chaparral and prickly
pear. Boone and three horses waited in the shadows. Never
had she thought the sight of a horse could be so wonderful.
Boone helped her mount behind Dean.

"I'll be waitin' here for Connor," he assured her as if hearing the worry in her mind. "You make sure Maldo has something for us to eat when we get back."

Lindy grasped Boone's hand. "I'll be sure he prepares one of my fattest chooks."

Boone's eyes melted over her. "That'll be nice, ma'am."

"You and Connor hurry," Lindy said, swallowing the lump in her throat.

Lindy felt the adrenaline pulse through her veins as Dean's horse fairly flew over the ground, raising a cloud of dust behind them. The wind whipped Zack's Stetson off her head, tossing her hair behind her in their wild flight from Claxton and his men. Her arms tightened around Dean's waist, her fingernails digging into his sides as she fought to keep her seat. Knowing that Connor had planned to give her and Dean extra time to get away, Lindy worried that he had compromised his and Boone's safety. If Connor or Boone were killed for her sake, she could never forgive herself.

Over the pounding noise of their retreat, Lindy heard gunfire snap behind them. Dean pushed blindly into the black night. Without the aid of moonlight, any ditch could mean a sudden tumble for horse and rider. Putting all her trust in Dean and his horse, she prayed that they were way ahead of Claxton and his men, and that Connor and Boone would find their way safely back to Broken Gate. As if in answer, lightning flashed and a low rumble of thunder sounded.

By the time they reached Broken Gate, it seemed as if they had been riding for half the night. Armaldo and Luke, their rifles in hand, ran out to meet them.

"Lin!" Luke called. "Thank God you're safe."

"Connor hot as a pepper you visit Claxton," Armaldo announced.

Lindy's chest heaved with each breath she took.

"Where's Boone and Connor?" Luke asked.

"They're right behind us," Dean said optimistically.

"So would be Señor Claxton, and I will be waiting for him," announced Armaldo, raising his rifle and patting the bandolier that crossed his chest. He turned sharp eyes on Lindy. "You won't do any good out here. You better go inside and feed that lamb."

Lindy suddenly realized the full consequences of her foolish meeting with Claxton. Never had she thought it could evolve into a gun battle between the two ranches, endangering the lives of all who were dear to her. She stared into the black distance. More lightning illuminated the sky to silver gray. Mesquite and chaparral suddenly appeared and disappeared with each subsequent flash of light.

In a vain attempt to ease her worry, Dean made light of the approaching storm. "Just what we need, a good soaking rain to cool down tempers."

After dressing Zack in Lindy's clothes, Connor had been doing a fairly good job of leading Claxton's men away from Dean and Lindy until his horse stumbled into the dry streambed, throwing Connor to the ground. The bay struggled to its feet, but Connor failed to recover as quickly. Downed by the excruciating pain of a dislocated right shoulder, Connor put caution in every movement. Awkwardly he pulled his pistol out of its holster with his left hand, and with his back propped against the bank of the streambed, he waited for Claxton.

Now that he had literally dropped out of sight, Connor worried about Boone. Miles back, in an effort to confuse Claxton, he and Boone had separated amid the hail of bullets singing at their backs. He hoped Boone had been luckier than he and had made it to Broken Gate unscathed. With any luck, the black night, coupled with lightning and thunder that almost guaranteed a stampede, had turned Claxton and his men around. One thing was certain; mother hen that she was, Lindy would be frantic if any of them were missing for long. He hoped to God someone would tie her to a chair.

Wind whipped across dry ground, stirring up grit and gathering tumbleweeds in its path, rolling them down into the gully. The breeze cooled the fever that came over Connor, chilling him until his teeth chattered. More lightning flashed, thunder rolled, announcing the downpour to come. Sure that salvation would come only from his own hands, Connor attempted to climb out of the streambed, but the ripping pain in his shoulder impeded his success. Weak from his efforts, he collapsed against the bank. Large drops of rain began to pelt the ground, intensifying the smell of the earth with each assault.

The rain picked up its rhythm. It changed from an irregular pattern to a steady onslaught of striking drops, running in rivulets down the once dry banks and pouring off the brim of Connor's Stetson, soaking him to his skin. Dust became damp, then slick, then turned to mud. Failing to gain a secure foothold in the slippery sides of the bank, Connor knew it would be nearly impossible for him to climb out of the streambed by himself unless he could find a spot that was less steep.

Water rushed over his boots, reminding him that the streambed was filling quickly as the sky opened and poured down everything it had. As he felt his way downstream, Connor searched for a way out, aware of the rising tide of water now cold against his shins.

Thoughts of Lindy numbed his pain. He couldn't understand what had possessed her to think she could ride into Claxton's camp without stirring up the whole hornet's nest. Was it a test to see how far his patience could stretch? Or did she have some sort of death wish? Truly the saying "barefoot and pregnant" began to sound appealing. He imagined it was the only way to keep her home. The thought of Lindy caring for his children replaced the chill that had seeped into his bones with a warm longing. Images of her with a babe in her arms and two clinging to her skirt as she waited on the porch for him urged him on and gave him the strength to pull himself out of the streambed.

Beneath his gasping breath and the din of the storm, Connor thought he heard a human sound. For a second, a flash of lightning outlined a horse and rider, and at the same time, made him visible to whoever was near.

"Connor, are you there?" a voice called.

"Luke," Connor answered. He winced with pain when he moved.

His slicker flapping against his legs, Luke slid down from his horse and grabbed Connor's arm. Connor responded to Luke's help with a mighty howl. "I think I've dislocated my shoulder."

"All right, then, you grab on to me."

Gradually they conquered the slippery distance to Luke's horse. With Luke balancing him from behind and after a barrage of colorful language, Connor was ready to ride. Once Luke swung up behind him, he asked, "Did Lindy—"

"She made it back with Dean. When your horse came in we knew you were in trouble."

"What about Boone?"

"I don't know. He could be lost in this storm." Luke steadied Connor when he slumped forward. "Can you hold on?"

Connor clenched his jaw against the stabbing pain.

Lindy jumped when the door slammed open, spilling the cup of tea in her hand. Thoroughly drenched, Boone stepped into the house.

"Thank God!" Lindy said. She hurried to his side.

A puddle quickly formed at Boone's feet. Droplets dripped off his hat and ran down his face. "No one was goin' to keep me from a chicken dinner. Where's Connor?"

"He hasn't returned yet."

"I thought I saw his horse."

Lindy quickly turned away from Boone's face when she saw the dread in his eyes. Holding back her tears and mustering up a strong facade, she added, "Luke's gone off after him. He'll find him."

"I'd best wait outside. I'll let you know when they ride up."

Lindy nodded. "I'll make some coffee. You'll need something to warm you up."

"Thank you, ma'am," Boone said, backing out the door.

The coffee was thicker than mud by the time Lindy heard the welcome sound of a single horse. She nearly ran over the men in her haste to reach Luke. A startled cry caught in her throat when she saw Connor slumped over Luke's horse. The rain, still heavy, washed over her as her trembling hands lifted his head.

"Has he been shot?"

Luke pulled Connor from his horse. "He's apples, Lin— just thrown from his horse."

"But why is he unconscious?"

"You gonna let us near him or you plannin' on standin' out here in a downpour tryin' to figure out why?" Dean grumbled. He hoisted Connor over his shoulder, carried him into the house and laid him on the table.

"His shoulder is bad, but that's all," Armaldo said after his eyes and hands swept over Connor's limbs.

Lindy hung over Connor, holding his cold hand in hers. "This is all my fault. Oh, Connor."

"You sit down," Armaldo ordered.

Lindy yielded to the authority in Armaldo's voice and moved out of the way. Dean, Luke and Armaldo stood around Connor. Steeped in worry, and succumbing to tears, Lindy was vaguely aware that Armaldo and Dean had taken charge of Connor's injury. Her head snapped up at an agonizing sound.

"There, it's done," Armaldo said simply, casting her a smile as he picked up his rifle and stationed himself once again on the porch.

"Maldo put Connor's shoulder back," Luke said in awe.

"He'll live, ma'am," Dean announced.

Lindy moved to Connor's side, gazing down at his pale face, and feeling dreadfully culpable for the whole mess. She wiped her eyes with the corner of her apron and declared to all of them, "I'm sorry. I've just learned a terrible lesson and nearly at the expense of all of your lives."

Luke perked his head up and pressed for more. "What's that, Lin?"

Lindy gulped down her pride. "You don't have to enjoy my humility so much, Luke Falen. It's true, I don't know everything. Some things are better left to—"

"To men?" Luke said eagerly, flashing his sister a dimpled smile.

"No, you goose, to those more knowledgeable."

The corners of Luke's mouth drooped.

"What in heaven's name did you expect me to say?"

"No one changes in a night," Dean pondered aloud as he poured himself a cup of coffee. "I don't expect Claxton will be ridin' over here in the morning, a changed man either." He took a sip and grimaced, then looked down into the cup, seeming to contemplate whether or not to drink any more.

"Is something wrong, Dean?" Lindy asked innocently.

"No, ma'am. I think I'll just be gettin' where I'm needed," he said, setting down his cup.

"Me, too, Lin," Luke said. "Thanks to this storm, the band's been scattered from here to kingdom come. Buddy's worried the pads on his paws thin while we were looking for each other, rightly thinking we should have been looking for sheep."

Connor stirred. A deep moan rumbled from his throat. "This table's killin' my back," he complained, struggling to sit up. Swinging his feet to the floor, he stretched his lower back, then ran his hand cautiously over his shoulder.

"Armaldo and Dean shoved your shoulder back," Luke explained.

Lindy's eyes briefly met Connor's. "I'll get you some dry clothes."

"Best you get warmed up," Dean said with a wink, as he and Luke slipped out the door, leaving Connor and Lindy alone.

After an awkward moment of silence, Lindy said, "You had me worried."

Connor ran a hand through his disheveled hair. "*I* had *you* worried? Weren't you the one rescued from Claxton's camp? What were you thinking of—not even telling Luke where you were going," he rebuked sharply.

Lindy shrank from his tone. "Luke would have told you, and after learning what was in Father's letter, I had to go. I knew you would stop me. I didn't even want to tell Dean."

"Telling Dean proved to be wise. You might have very well ended up like your father." Connor pinned her with his eyes. "You didn't tell Claxton about the letter, did you?"

Lindy paused. When she contemplated the floor and bit her bottom lip to still its quivering, Connor's voice sounded like thunder.

"You told him!"

"I didn't exactly tell him, but he knows my suspicions well enough."

Grabbing his shoulder, Connor swore under his breath. "Now Claxton has one more reason to want you out of Texas." Crushing his Stetson on his head, he said, "Before we give him another, I'm going to help Luke and Dean gather up your sheep."

"Connor, you can't...your shoulder...you need dry clothes." Lindy drew her body close to his and pleaded, "There'll be plenty to do in the morning. Please rest for the night."

Connor asked, "You're not worried about your sheep?"

"The men will manage."

"I suppose Claxton is doing the same," Connor stated. Then he caught her intense look. "Now what are you thinking?"

"Connor," Lindy said, her eyes bright with an idea, "if the storm has scattered all the livestock, then there could be longhorns all over my land."

"And sheep on Claxton's land."

"If we find some of Claxton's unbranded cows..."

"I don't like the glint in your eye or the direction your thoughts are taking. You're thinking about penning Claxton's cattle, aren't you?"

"I didn't say that."

"I know you well, Lindy Falen, perhaps better than you know yourself. Haven't you had trouble enough?"

"I couldn't ask for any more than I have already, so why not? If his men get the chance, they'll shoot my jumbucks quick enough. So why not round up his trespassing cows and brand them as our own? We can put them in the stock pen temporarily."

Connor shook his head. "I've no doubt we'll find more than a few dead sheep, but are you sure you want to declare war?"

"Claxton's already made this a war, beginning with my father's murder. I'm only fighting for what's mine."

"Penning up Claxton's cows is going to bring all his wrath down on Broken Gate and you."

"If they're not branded, then they're not his, are they?"

"You know he won't look at it quite the same way. He's going to brand you a cattle rustler."

Her decision was made. "Dean and Boone will round up the mavericks tomorrow." Standing on her tiptoes, Lindy pecked Connor's cool face with kisses, softening the stern lines of disapproval etched in his forehead. "We can talk more on this in the morning. Right now I don't know if there'll be any cows on my land."

Connor's arms dropped to her sides. His hands encased her waist in a possessive hold, and he buried his face in her hair and inhaled her scent.

"I'm keeping you from your rest," Lindy said weakly, feeling his hands move up her back and his warm breath against her neck.

"Do you have a restful place in mind, darlin'?"

Lindy's smile was full of wicked promise. "In a soft and deep feather bed." Her fingers worked at the wet leather that spanned his waist. "But first, you'll have to shed these drenched clothes."

Lindy's brows drew together and her lips puckered when Connor appeared to consider her suggestion. Kissing the top of her head, he said, "I think, for this once, you're right."

Chapter Sixteen

The following afternoon, Lindy counted twenty head of cattle enclosed in the stock pen. They were enough to satisfy her revenge for Claxton's threats against her and her men. She felt satisfied that she had shown the cattleman that he could not bully her and get away with it, but she could sense Connor felt differently. His quiet mood did not match her elation. He leaned on the fence, grimly watching Dean and Boone.

The men had been quick to stoke up a fire for the branding irons. The irons rested in the hot coals while the bawling stragglers milled around their enclosure. Crushing the last of his cheroot under his boot, Boone lifted a red-hot brand from the fire. The air waved around him in ripples of heat.

"What do you think, ma'am? Shall we make these mavericks ours?" Boone asked with a devilish smile.

Connor touched Lindy's arm. "Before you answer that question think about the repercussions. By now Claxton knows how short he is. The first place he's going to look for his stragglers is here."

Lindy crossed her arms over her chest. "I know that. And I also know how many of my own stock are missing."

Their attention was drawn to Luke, who rode up to them in a cloud of dust. His horse paced in a circle while he breathlessly told them his news.

"I've found them—thirty in all, at the bottom of a ravine. The ones I looked close at had their necks broke."

Connor offered a logical explanation. "Frightened by the storm, blinded by the rain—they could have caused their own death."

Lindy flattened her hands on her hips. "Why are you siding with Claxton? He had a hand in that and everyone here knows it."

"I'm not taking sides. That's precisely the argument Claxton will make. Most don't think sheep are the brightest of animals. Claxton already has the public on his side." Connor stepped closer to Lindy and put his hands on her shoulders. In a low voice meant only for her he said, "You can't win this one. You'll come out of it looking like the outlaw."

"I'm not an outlaw, I'm just fighting for what's mine. If you don't want to be a part in this then you can leave now."

Lindy became uncomfortably aware that all eyes were staring at them. Connor grabbed her hand and dragged her to the house.

"Ma'am?" Dean's voice trailed after them, "Do you want us to—"

"No," Lindy snapped, stepping quickly to keep up with Connor. Once over the threshold, her angry words pelted Connor. "What are you doing? You're spoiling everything."

"You don't need anyone except yourself, do you, Lindy Falen? You've put up a fence and won't let anyone climb over it."

"I don't know what you're talking about."

Connor turned his back to her so she couldn't see his face. "Forget about Claxton and his damn cows. You're playing right into his hands and he'll crush you, darlin', sure as sunrise.''

Lindy wrapped her arms around Connor's waist and rested her cheek against his warm back. ''I know you're right, but—''

Connor peeled her hands away and turned around in her arms. His eyes moved over her face, lingering on her lips. His mouth touched hers with sweet longing.

''Don't brand the cattle,'' Connor said between the kisses he strung down her neck. ''Will you trust me on this?''

Lindy nodded and brought her lips to his. Connor's hips pressed into her with the demand of his desire. A lusty warmth burned between them, melting them together. ''Can I brand half the cattle?''

Connor planted a tender kiss on her forehead. ''No. There are other ways to catch Claxton without making yourself a rustler.''

Lindy sighed. ''Cow hunts are not against the law.''

''Those cows are Claxton's and you know it.''

''They're wild, unbranded strays. He killed my jumbucks,'' she reminded him.

''I'm sure, but you can't prove that. Must we argue about this now?'' Connor said impatiently. He crushed her next words with a forceful kiss, effectively discouraging any more talk about Claxton's cows.

Lindy sighed with contentment. She turned her face up to Connor's and relished the tender kisses he placed over her face.

''The men must be wondering what's taking us so long,'' she said, smoothing her hand over Connor's chest.

''I'm sure they've already guessed what—''

''You don't mean they would think that we're . . . they wouldn't . . .'' Fretfully Lindy combed her fingers through her hair. ''We were coming to a decision as to what to do with the cattle is all.''

Connor chuckled and pulled her up against him, placing a hearty kiss upon her lips. "I'm sure they'll just think that we were working out that problem."

Lindy pushed him away. "Luke will be getting suspicious."

"You're only thinking of that possibility now?"

Feeling an overwhelming dizziness sweep over her, Lindy clutched Connor's arm. What she must have looked like was reflected in the concern that suddenly masked his face.

"Are you all right?"

"Yes. Of course I'm all right," she said, smiling to disguise the turmoil her stomach was in.

"You're as pale as a ghost. Maybe you should rest. It's been a hard night and day for all of us. I'll tell the men you're not feeling well, so you can rest."

"No. I'm fine. Really," Lindy said with more conviction as she felt the wave of nausea subside.

"I think you should rest before you really do get sick."

A looming dust cloud drew Lindy's attention to the window. A group of five or six riders approached Broken Gate. "Connor?"

"Yes, darlin'?"

"Could a person get hung for cattle rustling?"

"It's a little late to worry about that when you have twenty longhorns penned in like chickens. The sooner we get them off your range the better."

"I think it might be too late for that."

Connor looked over her shoulder. "Claxton," he announced without surprise. "If I were you, I'd tuck that pistol of yours in your skirt."

Before Lindy could stop him, Connor found Hank's Colt in the little bureau and handed it to her.

"No. I can't," Lindy said, looking down at the gun.

"At least let Luke have it, then." Connor looked at her inquisitively. "There's something about this gun's past that makes you afraid, isn't there?"

Lindy tried unsuccessfully to keep the guilt from strangling the strength in her voice. "I'm not afraid of it."

"Then take it for protection."

Lindy had no choice but to take the gun. Unhappily, she wrapped her hand around its cold handle and hid it within the folds of her skirt, all the while conscious that Connor was measuring her reaction.

"Shall we greet your visitors?" Connor asked grimly.

Lindy followed Connor out of the house just in time to see Claxton, Frank, Jeb, Zack and the sheriff rein in their horses. Claxton and the sheriff dismounted. The others remained seated on their mounts, their hands close to their guns. Claxton smiled pleasantly, a contrast to the fury Lindy knew had to be whirling like a dervish inside him. The other men didn't hide their emotions as well. Zack and Jeb looked down at her with murderous eyes, a snarl curling their lips, waiting for Claxton to unleash them. Frank sat poised smugly in his saddle, ready to strike on command with fatal accuracy. Grimly regarding them all, Lindy had no doubt Claxton was the one who held their desire for revenge in check. She found the sheriff's unreadable expression to be the most unsettling of all.

Lindy watched in dread silence as Claxton's eyes moved from the penned longhorns to the branding irons still heating in the smoldering fire. A very satisfied smile crossed his lips.

"Well, sheriff," he said, puffing out his chest. "Do you need any more evidence than this? Now the woman's stealing my cattle. It isn't enough that she let those animals feed on my land like fat little maggots."

"That's not completely true, sheriff," Connor said in Lindy's defense. "Some sheep have strayed over the boundaries the same as these mavericks have done."

"You don't think we're all dolts, do you, Connor?" Claxton said, laughing and stepping closer to Lindy.

Lindy felt faint when Claxton looked down at the hand she hid at her side. He leaned close enough for only her to hear his whispered words. "You're not that foolish, are you, Mrs. Rigby?" He turned his gaze to his men, then walked over to the branding irons. He pulled one out of the coals and held the glowing Broken Gate brand up for the sheriff to see. "Mrs. Rigby, you weren't thinking of marking my cattle with your own brand, were you?"

The sheriff waited for her reply. Lindy thought quickly for an answer. "I don't raise cattle, Mr. Claxton. I don't have any interest in them except to keep them away from my jumbucks and off my land. These beasts were found grazing on my land. I've merely had them penned for you. If you look closely, Sheriff, you'll notice that none of them have been branded."

"Mrs. Rigby," the sheriff said, glancing at the long iron rod Claxton held, "How do you explain what all this looks like?"

Connor stepped forward and addressed the sheriff. "It looks like Mrs. Rigby has done a good deed for Mr. Claxton by gathering up his strays. Now he can take his men and his longhorns out of here so we can get back to branding our own livestock."

Claxton's men couldn't help but snicker. "You don't believe that, do you, Clay?" Jeb asked.

"It's not what *I* believe. Sheriff?"

Sheriff Hayes sighed heavily. "Mrs. Rigby, I have to warn you that this kind of thing is going to get you into hot water. I'd hate to put a pretty thing like you in my jail, but you are becoming a nuisance. You can't go around roundin' up your neighbors' cows without givin' them the wrong impression. I'm going to let this fly as your ignorance of our ways, but be forewarned..." Hayes's hard eyes clearly warned that he was serious. "Next time I won't be so understanding—and it won't matter that you're a woman."

Lindy's eyes found Claxton's. "I promise, Sheriff, that I'll be more careful from now on."

The sheriff mounted his horse and said to Claxton, "From now on try and keep your cows on your own range."

In angry silence Claxton pulled himself up on his shiny black horse. It wasn't until the sheriff had left that he looked down upon Lindy. All of their hateful eyes were upon her: Jeb, who blamed her for his brother's fate and the embarrassment she had caused him; Zack, for escaping him; Frank, who itched to join in any revenge against her; and Claxton, for being the woman who could destroy him. Lindy's sweaty hand fearfully tightened around the gun still hidden in the folds of her skirt. Connor stepped beside her.

"One day you won't be so lucky, my lady," Claxton said in a smooth, well-bred manner. "As of today I'm taking away all the restraint my men have been told to hold on to. There's quite a few who have issues they'd love to settle with you."

"They'll have to settle with me first," Connor warned.

Lindy found herself leaning on Connor for support as another wave of nausea and dizziness overcame her. She felt as though her bones had turned soft and wished the men would stop throwing threats and ride away before she embarrassed herself by swooning. Then the worst happened. The two-and-a-half-pound Colt slipped from her hand and dropped to her feet. The thud it made drew everyone's attention. Even Lindy found herself staring at it.

Without thinking, she looked up to Jeb. His eyes were the same sharp color as the polished blade of Armaldo's knife, his lips twisted into a snarl, frightening her with his unspoken promise of revenge. Lindy felt terribly ill. While she trembled under Jeb's frosty glare, beads of cold sweat collected on her brow. Her stomach knotted and threatened to retch at any moment.

It was then that a quick-thinking Luke opened the corral gate, and with a loud whoop sent the skittish longhorns stampeding out of the enclosure. It was instant chaos: cows bawled, startled horses squealed, barrels and troughs were overturned, the men shouted over it all. The dust the animals stirred was blinding. Before she was trampled, Connor scooped Lindy off her feet and ran for the house. Claxton and his men had no choice but to drive the stampeding longhorns back to their own range.

Before the dust settled, Lindy heard Boone's loud yahoo cut through the yellow haze. "If that doesn't call for a celebration I don't know what does. Dean, go get your fiddle," he exclaimed.

Lindy's spirit brightened at the prospect of any distraction that would keep her from worrying about Jeb, but just as suddenly her smile faded. "The gun. I dropped it over—"

Luke handed her the dust-covered Colt. Lindy was very aware of Connor watching her and saw the interest in his eyes. She explained, "It was my father's and I'd hate to lose it." Connor's silence and doubtful look were less than comforting, so she quickly returned to the subject of a celebration.

"I think Boone's suggestion is a wonderful idea." Lindy avoided Connor's scrutiny and looked at Dean and Boone. "What do you think of a dance?"

Boone smiled and said smoothly, "If I get the first dance, Dean and I will have the wagon yard ready in less than an hour. That is, if it's all right with Connor."

When Lindy glanced over to Connor she looked into faraway eyes. "Connor?"

He returned her smile and said, "We may have to draw straws for the first dance."

It was close to nightfall when Lindy walked out to the barn. She wore a yellow cotton dress with all the petticoats she owned underneath and her mother's lace shawl wrapped around her shoulders. Her hair was pulled away from her face and tied loosely with Minerva's ribbons. The extra attention she had given her appearance gained smiles from the men when they saw her.

Dean, Boone and Luke stood by a small campfire in the wagon yard. The barn loomed darkly behind them. Whatever could be used as a bench had been dragged out to the fire. Lanterns were hung along the fence posts. Armaldo sat on an upended barrel. Dean held a fiddle in his hand, his harmonica in his shirt pocket. Lindy nervously scanned the wagon yard for Connor, but he was nowhere in sight. Perhaps he had changed his mind about joining them. Disappointment dampened her mood.

Upon seeing Lindy, Dean ceremoniously tucked the fiddle under his chin and began playing a jumpy tune, sure to set anyone's legs to dancing. Boone walked over to her in his uncertain way, and held his hands out to her. She had certainly been blessed with a good group of men. No matter their supposed backgrounds, they were a faithful lot.

She put her hands in Boone's. "It's my pleasure to dance with such a handsome man as you, Boone Watts."

Boone reddened from ear to ear at her compliment. Luke clapped his hands, and Armaldo tapped his toe in time to the music while Boone awkwardly skipped around the wagon yard with Lindy in his arms. Boone was far from light on his feet, or on Lindy's, for that matter. He tripped over his own feet and once almost became fatally tangled in her skirt.

Anxious to join in the fun, Luke cut in, rescuing his sister from the stockman before her feet and ankles were bruised purple. Luke and Lindy spun around the wagon yard to quick fiddle music, clapping and foot stomping. They fast became exhausted from all the laughing and dancing.

Luke waltzed Lindy in front of Armaldo. When it seemed that all the coaxing in the world was not going to move the

Mexican off the barrel he sat on, Lindy grabbed his hand, but Armaldo dug his heels into the dirt.

"If Maldo doesn't want to dance, then I think I'll just take his place." Armaldo breathed a sigh of relief when Connor stepped out of the shadows and into the amber glow of the fire. In the dim light, his eyes became the color of blue slate. An exciting chill ran up Lindy's spine when he grabbed her hand and swung her up against his chest.

Gazing down into her eyes, he said in a husky voice, "You look beautiful."

"I thought you'd changed your mind about dancing."

"It's been a long time. I almost lost my nerve. My wife . . . liked to dance."

"You still miss her."

"I've let her go, or she's let me go—I'm not sure which happened first, but I do know my life is in my hands again." As he spoke, Connor took Lindy's hand.

Succumbing to the mood set by Lindy and Connor, Dean put down his fiddle and slipped his harmonica out of his shirt pocket. Placing the instrument to his lips, he breathed into it, gently bringing forth the notes of "Beautiful Dreamer."

Lindy rested one hand on Connor's shoulder and the other in his hand. He placed a hand on her waist, and as if they danced in the grandest ballroom, ceremoniously whirled her over the hardened earth. The musician played on, and the stars glittered overhead like candles in a chandelier.

Connor danced Lindy to a private corner of the wagon yard. She leaned against the corral fence, gazing at the stars and listening to the melancholy notes warbling from Dean's harmonica. Connor's hand caressed her cheek. Sliding his fingers under her chin, he turned her face up to his. A lantern, hung from a fence post, bathed his face in soft yellow light and set his hair on fire with streaks of orange and gold.

"You're quite a woman, Lindy Falen. Your father would be proud."

Lindy was so burdened by the guilt she harbored that she could not graciously accept Connor's admiration without feeling even more loathsome. The truth could not be denied any longer. After what she had brought upon them all, Lindy couldn't help her honest response. Indeed, she yearned for the relief her confession would bring, and had accepted the risk that once Connor heard she had murdered a man, he would despise her and leave with the first blush of dawn. After drawing in a deep breath, she replied sadly, "No, he wouldn't. I haven't done anything to make him or anyone else proud. I've disgraced my family name." Feeling a hot tear tumble down her cheek, she turned her back to him.

"You don't mean that. Look at all you've accomplished. You have your station. I'm sure it's all your father dreamed of."

The cries she had tried to hold inside turned to soft sobs. "Oh, hell," Connor mumbled and pulled off his bandanna and shook it out. Turning her into his arms, he dabbed her eyes. "If it's your reputation you're worried over—"

"My reputation! You *would* think of that. That's not even the worst of it," she said, taking his bandanna and blowing her nose in it.

"It's not? Then what . . ." His eyes swept over the length of her and lit with understanding. "Lin, you're not . . . you would tell me if you were with child?"

"What!"

"Now that I think of it, when my wife was—"

"Connor! I certainly am not."

"How do you know that you're not? You haven't been feeling well."

"I would think I'd be the one who'd best know, don't you? I have enough to worry about without being . . . Why are you staring at me like that?"

"Tomorrow we're going to see the doc."

"Connor, I was making a confession, but it wasn't that! I was trying to tell you that I . . . I killed a man," she said in a quick rush of breath.

"Did you say you killed a man?"

"I'm afraid it's so," Lindy said in the barest whisper.

"Who? Why?" Connor pressed, disbelief echoing with each word.

"It doesn't matter. You can leave me now. I'm sure you want to."

"Lin—"

An explosion and a sudden flare of light brightened the wagon yard as the barn burst into flames.

"The barn's ablaze!" Lindy gasped. Hearing the high-pitched squeals of a horse, she cried, "Jester's in the barn."

"Give me your shawl." Connor drenched her shawl in the trough, wrapped it around his head and ran into the burning structure.

"Connor!" Lindy cried above the roar and crackle of the fire.

"Get in the house," he yelled as he vanished into the barn.

Her men and Luke had disappeared into the black shadows, leaving her alone to watch bright flames dance against the night sky, growing larger, feeding voraciously on the dry wood. Flaming boards peeled away from the building's frame and fell in broken and scorched pieces to the ground. The fire roared in her ears, silencing her cries for Connor to hurry. In minutes there would be nothing left of the barn. Lindy had never felt so helpless as she did then.

Then, unexpectedly, an arm wrapped around her throat and something hard and cold touched the back of her neck. A loud click exploded in her ear.

"Jeb," she said before she even heard his voice.

"You knew I'd come back," he said.

"You set the fire."

Jeb laughed. "I had help."

"Of course a bitser like yourself wouldn't be brave enough to come alone. Even here wild dogs run in packs."

"You're awfully brave considering your situation. You must expect your friend to come out of that barn. Don't count on it. Even if he does, Frank or Zack will pick him off. You won't get away this time," Jeb vowed as he pushed her back toward the house.

The hem of Lindy's skirt caught on her heel. It did not completely throw her off balance, but it was enough to cause her to stumble. Banking that Jeb wouldn't kill her yet, she fell to the ground, hoping to trip him in the process, but Jeb was too surefooted. He quickly reached down and grabbed her arm, pulling her up against his foul-smelling body. Jeb must have seen the hate in her eyes when he looked at her.

"You'd like the chance to kill me, wouldn't you?" he asked.

Lindy remained coldly silent, thinking only of how she could escape him.

"You would, wouldn't you?" Jeb pressed. "Don't even think about it, 'cause you ain't gonna get the chance."

Jeb dragged her to the house. The whole inside was aglow with orange light. Harsh shadows danced like devils over the walls. Her room was hot and smoky. Beads of sweat began to pop over her body. Broken Gate, her paradise, had become hell on earth. Jeb threw her onto her bed and glared down at her with red eyes.

The sound of gunshots gave Lindy some hope, but Jeb was quick to destroy it. "That's Zack . . . or Frank."

"Or Connor," Lindy said.

Jeb viciously grabbed the china doll from her bed and threw it against the wall. Lindy flinched when she heard its head shatter but didn't turn to look. Jeb caught her chin in his hand. "I could do that to you just as easy. What happened to my brother?"

When Lindy didn't answer him, Jeb yanked her up from the bed, pulled her over to the wall and pushed her head against it. "What happened to Hank?"

The sound of close gunfire filled Lindy's heart with hope. Still holding her by the hair, Jeb pulled her with him to the window.

"You can't fight my men and still hold me," Lindy pointed out to him. Jeb swung her around and pinned her between him and the window.

"You just watch me and pray Connor's bullet don't kill you first," he said, smashing the barrel of his gun through the window and shifting her in front of him like a shield.

Lindy had no intention of watching Jeb pick off any of the men dear to her. Just as he took aim, she sank her teeth into his arm. Jeb's reflexes threw her aside, but his hand caught her skirt before she could get completely out of reach. She swung her foot up to kick him, but in an instant he released her skirt to deflect the heel of her boot with his arm. Free of his hold, Lindy ran out of the house. She heard Jeb coming up behind her and a voice shouting his name. It was Connor. Connor was somewhere. Connor was alive!

When Jeb's gun exploded behind her, Lindy realized that he really meant to kill her. Another shot fired and buzzed by her ear before she skidded behind a wagon. Her chest heaved with each breath.

Connor was out there, her men, too, and Luke. Luke. She prayed he'd be all right. There wasn't any time for weakness. She had to do something. If only she had a gun. She glanced back at the house. Hank's gun. It was in her room. The distance from the wagon to the house now seemed like miles. Swallowing her fear, Lindy stepped out from behind the wagon.

Jeb was waiting for her. He had found Hank's gun in her room. He stood between her and the house, and aimed the pearl-handled Colt at her heart. How ironic to be killed with Hank's own gun. Lindy closed her eyes. She didn't want

Jeb's face to be the last thing she saw on earth. But instead of hearing the expected explosion of gunfire, Lindy heard the click of an empty chamber. Connor must have emptied the chamber the day he used the pistol for target practice.

Jeb quickly spanned the few feet between them. "Lucky for you my brother's gun's empty."

"Jeb, Hank's dead. Do you want to end up like him? I can convince Connor to let you go. Hank fooled you, Jeb. He didn't want you to know he was coming out here. He—"

"Shut up!" Jeb's voice snapped like gunfire.

"Let her go, Jeb."

"Connor," Lindy called out, then was silenced by Jeb's wide hand cupped over her mouth.

Jeb pulled Lindy in front of him, ensuring his own safety while he backed into the shadows.

"Jeb," Connor called again, "Drop the gun and let her go."

Jeb dragged Lindy into the nearest cover, the henhouse, and tossed her on her knees. The dank and musty coop immediately stirred images of Hank's burial. Hank lay no more than two feet beneath them. Jeb's shoulder leaned against the narrow opening of the henhouse. He spun the cylinder of his pistol, feeding the empty chamber with cartridges he pulled from his pocket. When the gun was fully loaded, he smiled at Lindy's astonished face.

"I wish Hank was here to see this."

Lindy stared at the ground in front of her knees and then lifted her eyes up to Jeb. "He's here, Jeb."

This time Jeb looked surprised. "What are you talkin' about?"

"This is where I buried him. Right here."

Jeb's eyes lowered to the dirt floor and back to Lindy's face. "In a henhouse?"

Lindy nodded.

"You buried my brother here?" The roosting hens clucked at the volume of Jeb's voice. Jeb swatted and swore at the squawking bird that flew in his face.

"My gun stopped Hank from killing my brother. I'm sorry for it, but I don't regret that Hank never got his chance to carry out what he intended."

At first, Jeb didn't say anything, he just stared at the earth as if he could see through it. The unnatural silence frightened Lindy. She expected Jeb to threaten her, hit her—anything but his frightening silence. She backed into the corner of the henhouse and watched as Jeb frantically began to claw at the earth.

"Hank," he said as if he expected his brother to call up from his grave. "I told you not to. You wouldn't listen."

Lindy was sure Jeb's fragile hold on sanity had snapped. The loaded gun lay on the ground behind him while he dug into Hank's grave. "What did you tell him?" Lindy asked Jeb as she backed away from him. A shadow passed the opening to the henhouse. She saw it briefly and heard the faintest sound. Her heart pounded like a runaway horse. She prayed it was Connor.

"I told him it was too soon."

"Who, Jeb? Hank?"

"Claxton. I told him it was too soon. Hank wouldn't listen. He always wanted to be better than me. He was going to show Claxton."

"Claxton?" Lindy wondered. "What was too soon?"

Jeb scraped away more dirt. When he wiped his face with the back of his hand, Lindy noticed he was crying. "Jeb, I'm sorry. I didn't want to kill Hank."

"I told him," Jeb repeated. "I told Claxton it was too soon after we killed the old man."

Lindy felt as though her breath had been choked off.

"We should have waited longer before killing you, too." Jeb stared at her with crazed eyes. For a lucid moment he remembered who had killed his brother and reached back for his gun. In that moment, Connor sailed through the opening, his full weight landing on Jeb, flattening him to the ground. Lindy heard a dull thud, then saw Jeb's body go limp and his face fall into the hole he had dug.

Connor gathered Lindy in his arms. "It's all right, Lin, it's safe now. Frank and Zack ran back to Claxton. As soon as I get Jeb out of here, I'll be back."

"Luke. Where's Luke?"

"Luke's fine. Everyone's safe, Lin. There's nothing to worry about."

Lindy closed her eyes. If only she could believe that there was nothing to worry about.

Chapter Seventeen

"Can't I say anything to convince you to stay?" Lindy pleaded.

"I appreciate what you've done for me, ma'am, but being a shepherd ain't for me," Boone admitted before pulling up into his saddle.

"What will you do?"

"Don't worry. I'm not planning on robbing any banks if that's what you're thinking. It's too dangerous. I might just end up on another sheep ranch," he teased, smiling down at her with warm, brown eyes. "Or like him." Boone nodded toward Jeb, who was slumped over his horse, his hands tied to his saddle horn. Connor kept a watchful eye on Jeb and a tight rein on his horse while Boone made his goodbyes. "After Connor and I give that rascal to the sheriff," Boone continued, "I'm on my way to San Antone."

"Take care of yourself, Boone. I'll miss you. And before you even think of doing anything close to robbing a bank, you get back here."

"I'll do that, ma'am."

As Lindy watched Boone and Connor ride off, sadness touched her heart. What if Connor didn't come back? A scant few words had been said between them since her confession and the fire. If his somberness was a clue to how he felt, she could guess he had already decided not to have anything more to do with her. And if he hadn't come to that conclusion, she was sure he would once Jeb told the sheriff about Hank. Jeb would remind Hayes of the time they had searched her property, of her lies and how she had cold-heartedly murdered his brother. Connor would hear all the rest of the sorry tale from Jeb.

Hayes was sure to ride out to Broken Gate, looking for Hank's corpse. The thought of finally admitting her crime to the sheriff, pointing out Hank's grave and imagining his response, turned her stomach. Time would tell if Hayes was a man able to overcome the blood tie between him and his nephews.

Armaldo, Lindy's self-appointed guard, glanced at her nervously. His hand reached out to steady her when she felt herself sway.

"I think I should lie down," Lindy said, and retired to her room.

She tried to rest, but every time she drifted off to sleep Connor's lamb woke her. And every time she glanced at the lamb she was reminded of Connor. She hadn't even had the chance to thank him for saving her life or to apologize for involving him in her troubles.

"A lamb in the house," she said, picking up the lamb and carrying it to the kitchen. "Father should see this. Connor's made a pet of you. Now what do we do? You don't even know what you are, do you?"

The next morning, the smell of Armaldo's breakfast sent Lindy flying out of the house. The Mexican left the pan of eggs and frijoles he had been stirring and chased after her, stopping short at the sight of a dust cloud on the horizon.

Lindy saw it, too.

"Riders," Armaldo said.

Before Lindy could guess at who it was, the Mexican said, "Señor O'Malley." He looked at Lindy and his brow furrowed. "Are you still sick?"

"It's Sheriff Hayes. If I didn't feel sick before, I certainly do now." No doubt, Jeb had told him about Hank. Her time of atonement had come.

"There are more," Armaldo announced.

Lindy watched the riders as they drew closer. Hayes most likely had brought his deputy, who, by now, had returned from San Antonio.

"Is there something wrong?" Armaldo asked.

"I may as well tell you what Dry Bed is surely buzzing over. I killed Jeb's brother and buried him in the henhouse." She measured Armaldo's expression, which was first one of surprise, then his droopy mustache twitched with the budding of a full grin.

"In the coop? You are an ingenious lady, *señora*," Armaldo's eyes gleamed with new respect.

"*Señorita*. And I'll likely hang for it."

Proudly preparing to defend her, Armaldo raised his rifle. Lindy quickly pushed the barrel down with her hand. "Thank you, but I'm in plenty enough trouble without the death of a sheriff and his deputy on my hands."

"They will not hang you. You come to Mexico with me."

Lindy felt her stomach roll. "They will. Hank was Sheriff Hayes's kin."

Her life flashed by. Poor Luke would grow up without her, perhaps even blaming himself for her hanging, and Connor would never know how much she loved him. There was not much point in confessing her love for him now when she was going to hang for murder. How she wished she had told Connor how much she loved him before it had all come to this.

"The doc?" Lindy wondered aloud when she recognized Doc Barker riding between Connor and the sheriff. Then she remembered her conversation with Connor two nights before. He wanted to be sure she wasn't carrying his child. That was the only reason Connor was coming back to her.

When Lindy saw the grim expression on the sheriff's face, and the dour look of his deputy, she had to grasp Armaldo's arm to keep from collapsing. What if she *was* with child? Would the sheriff delay her hanging until after her child was born? Was that the reason Connor had returned—to protect the life of his child?

Lindy's grip slipped from Armaldo's sleeve. Her world revolved, spinning in tight circles, drawing her into the black vortex. Voices faded into a great rush of sound, and as soon as she realized she was going to swoon, she felt herself fall onto something soft. She would learn later that Armaldo had caught her, carried her to her room and guarded it, allowing only Connor and the doctor to slip by him.

When Lindy opened her eyes, her surroundings slowly came into focus. She was lying on her bed staring at the back of a black-suited gentleman. As if sensing that she was awake, he turned away from the doorway and looked back at her.

"Well, now I can see the bright color of your eyes," Doc Barker said as he looked at her closely.

Lindy's mind took a little longer to clear. When it did, she remembered the fire, the sheriff and Jeb, and that she had confessed murder to Connor. She also remembered that Connor had brought the doctor from Dry Bed and felt a sudden rush of heat warm her cheeks.

"Your color's good, too, but that's expected for someone in your condition," Doc Barker commented with a pleased smile.

"My condition?"

"It amazes me how many women can tell if their horse is going to foal, but fail to suspect that anything's amiss when it comes to themselves. Shall I tell the father the good news or—"

"You mean I'm...oh, my heavens." Lindy felt a wave of panic roll up from her stomach. Of course Connor would have told the doc his suspicions, and the whole town thought she was a married woman! Hester would be ear deep in gossip. This new complication, too startling to bear, was enough to make her fall back into her pillow. "You haven't said anything to Connor?"

"I was just about to. Shall I call him in?"

"No," Lindy almost shouted, then more softly she said, "Not yet. I need a few minutes to...to comb my hair. Is the sheriff out there too?"

"He's been waiting to see you, but I told him he'd have to wait a little longer." His brows knit with concern when he looked at Lindy. "Now I want you to rest and see me when you're in town."

"I will," Lindy said faintly, wondering if the sheriff would trust her to stay at Broken Gate or keep her in jail until her child was born. "Dr. Barker," she called, "tell Connor I'm feeling fine. Just so he doesn't worry while I'm getting myself together."

"I'll do that, ma'am."

Lindy waited until she heard the doctor ride away before stepping out of her room.

Armaldo stood next to her door like a sentry. The rifle in his hand, along with his pledged loyalty, made her worry. "Armaldo, we're short-handed with Boone gone. I know you're more of a cook than a shepherd, but I need you to help Dean now."

With only a look of argument, Armaldo honored her request.

As Lindy expected, the sheriff waited for her on the porch with his deputy, Connor and Luke. She took a deep breath. There was no more delaying it. All four sets of eyes converged on her at once. "Luke, luv, I need to talk to the sheriff alone." From his expression she thought he was going to protest and was thankful when he finally shoved his hands in his pockets and walked away to join Armaldo and Dean.

Connor began to leave with Luke. "Connor, I need you to hear this too."

As if it had happened yesterday, Lindy told the sheriff everything. She recounted Jeb and Hank's harassment, their threats and finally the day Hank attacked Luke. As she spoke she measured Sheriff Hayes's reaction—what there was of it. There was no hint of either condemnation or approval revealed in his expression when she admitted to killing his nephew. When she came to the end of her soul-bearing, he simply asked, "Can I see your father's letter?"

For the first time, Lindy dared to look at Connor. His face was serious as he appeared to be considering everything she had said. "Yes, of course. I'll be a minute."

She returned with the worn piece of paper and anxiously watched the sheriff read it.

Hayes finally drew a long breath and spoke. "With this, what happened here the other night, and Jeb's confession, there's no doubt Claxton was behind your father's killing and that he ordered his men to do whatever they could to scare you off your land. And we know what his final plan was."

"Jeb's confession?" Lindy asked.

The sheriff puffed out his chest and sighed. "At first he tried denying it but then thought that having a sheriff for an uncle was a guarantee he'd be set free. He admitted Claxton paid him and Hank to kill your father and make it seem like Indians had done it. Then when you showed up, the two boys were commissioned once again. Only Hank decided to take matters into his own hands. Now when Hank disappeared..." Hayes looked over to the henhouse. "I'm gonna miss them boys at the poker table."

"I'm so sorry. I—"

"No, I'm sorry for the trouble my own kin gave you." Hayes's voice became faint, his eyes distant. "My sister tried but...they were always difficult boys." He cleared his throat and asked, "Where was I?"

"When Hank disappeared," Connor said.

"When Hank disappeared," the sheriff continued, "Claxton figured it would be wiser to tread carefully, even though Jeb thought differently since he now had a personal interest in you. Eventually Claxton figured you weren't goin' anywhere. According to Jeb," the sheriff said, smiling, "you were an embarrassment to Claxton and made him as jumpy as spit on a griddle.

"Now if you had taken my advice from the start and moved in with Widow Lawtey, none of this would have happened. I still don't think a woman belongs out here alone, but why would you listen to me?" The sheriff tucked her father's letter into his shirt pocket. "If you don't have anything else to tell me, I've got a number of names on my dance card and Claxton's one of them."

"You mean I'm not going to hang?"

Hayes smiled faintly. "Not for protecting yourself. What kind of sheriff do you think I am? I hope I have a better reputation than that."

"But Hank was your nephew. I thought—"

"Now don't go implying I'm corrupt."

Lindy found it hard to believe that she would be vindicated so easily and that real justice was being delivered by Hayes's hands. His own nephew, Jeb, was in jail facing a trial for the murder of her father, and for his part, the same fate awaited Claxton. And Hank—Hank was still buried in her henhouse. As hateful as he had been, he was still the sheriff's nephew. "You'll be wanting Hank's body," she said, glancing over to the squat building.

"I suppose he'll be buried back behind the church next to Cleave Sutter. Sutter was hanged for stealin' horses four years ago." Hayes chuckled. "Clay's horses, if memory serves me right."

After the sheriff and his deputy rode off to round up Claxton, Lindy and Connor stood alone on the porch, each uncertain of what to say, and afraid to be the first to break the thick silence that had fallen around them. So much had happened in one night to put distance between them. She was no longer sure of how Connor felt toward her, and was afraid to hear that he was going to leave. With all her heart she wanted him to stay, but not out of guilt or obligation. Lately, she had not given him much reason for loving her. She would not beg Connor to stay. It had to be his own decision and not swayed by Doc Barker's news, so she held her last secret with a trembling heart.

Connor commented on the safest subject he could think of. "It's a hot one."

"Dry as a chip."

"The doc said there's nothing wrong with you, just fatigue," Connor said.

"Too much excitement, I suppose," Lindy replied, avoiding his eyes.

"Nothing rest can't cure," Connor stated stiffly.

Connor had made it easier for Lindy to wonder if Doc Barker knew what he was talking about. At the moment, the prospect of a baby was easy for her to doubt. It was rational to blame the dizziness and the fatigue on all the stress she had been under. Her chooks hadn't laid eggs for a week after the coyotes had raided the henhouse. She was sure that as soon as her life got back to normal her body would return to its normal functions. Connor was right, her condition was nothing a little rest wouldn't cure.

Now that they had covered the subjects of the weather and her health, Lindy worried what the next topic would be. Her nerves were frayed just wondering how Connor felt about her now that he knew of her dark side. Sure that he had already made his decision to leave, she said, "I suppose you don't have to worry about me anymore. Especially since you've found out I can take care of myself." She looked out over the mesquite flats, afraid to see what lay in Connor's eyes.

"I knew that from the first day I saw you. You should have told me about Hank sooner. It would have explained why you spooked every time you saw his pistol and turned white as a sheet every time Jeb came around. Yes, I figured that much out. Did you really think I would have turned you in to the sheriff?"

Lindy wouldn't face Connor until he tipped her face up to his and forced her to look into his blue eyes.

"Did you?"

"I didn't know what you'd think if you knew what I'd done. But I was sure you would have made me go to the sheriff, if only to ease my conscience. I couldn't have admitted to killing his kin. I thought it better—safer—not to tell anyone."

"So you lived with the nightmares and the fear of being discovered?"

"I didn't have a choice. Hank never let me go. I thought the memory would fade, but instead it grew into this terrible monster that threatened to destroy all I loved." Lindy searched Connor's face for a sign that he understood. She looked for compassion but saw only a hardness in the set of his jaw and his ice-blue eyes. She pulled away from him, putting a cold distance between them. "He's buried and done with now. It's time we both get our lives back on the road."

That was as close as Lindy could get to telling Connor goodbye without falling apart and begging him to stay. She held Doc Barker's secret inside her, waiting for Connor to show her he loved her, but he merely took his hat off the hitching post and placed it squarely on his head. He put the tip of his boot in the stirrup and swung himself onto his mare's back. He looked down at her from under the shadow of his hat and said, "You still don't need anyone, do you?" At that, he turned his horse around. No other words were needed—they each had chosen their own road to follow.

Lindy couldn't watch Connor ride away without the floodgates parting and spilling tears all over her face, so she retreated into the house. With her back pressed to the door, she surrendered to a hot flow of tears. Why couldn't she beg him to stay? He hadn't galloped away. He had given her the chance to call him back and she hadn't. What had stopped her? Was she so afraid to admit that she loved him and needed him? Lindy wiped her wet cheeks with her apron.

"I'll manage without him," she said out loud. "I'll make myself a cuppa and then everything will be grand, just as before. It'll be me and Luke and…and…we'll all be fine," she concluded firmly.

Connor's lamb gazed up at her with its dark eyes and bleated. Every time she looked at the lamb, she was going to think of Connor and she was going to regret letting him ride out of her life, but it wasn't fair to hold him there any longer. She began to convince herself that he had never wanted to stay.

She set the kettle on the stove and waited until steam poured from its spout. Making tea was an unsuccessful attempt at occupying her hands and mind. Her thoughts kept drifting back to Connor. Staring into her teacup, she remembered when she first served him tea, how awkwardly he held the delicate cup, how he politely drank the hateful brew while listening to her chatter, and how she had later tried to please him with her dreadful attempts at brewing coffee.

A plaintive sound interrupted her misery. The high notes of the music seemed to stretch like taffy, warbling and thinning to barely a whisper until the next flow of notes reached out to her. She could almost feel Dean's lips slowly pull the music from his harmonica. It was the same tune she and Connor had danced to.

The sound continued, coaxing her to the porch, then to the wagon yard. It seemed to be coming from behind the black mound of charred wood that had once been her barn.

At the sight of it, she felt a heavy melancholy weight her body. The smoky smell of the air turned her stomach.

Lindy looked to the black pile of smoldering ashes and wondered if Claxton had watched his men's handiwork sprawled in the sky. How unaware she had been, as she had danced to Dean's music, so securely wrapped in Connor's arms.

She had always liked hearing Dean play, but now it only made her more melancholy. Picking up her skirt, she crossed the wagon yard to the burned barn. The music was coming from the other side. Rounding the side of the mound, crunching warm ashes under her feet, Lindy was careful to keep the hem of her skirt off the ground and to watch where she stepped. The music was clear now as Dean gently coaxed a melody from the tiny metal box.

"Dean, where did you get a new harmonica? And what are you doing?" When Lindy looked closer, and saw Connor standing behind Dean, half-hidden by a structure of charred beams, she thought she might be dreaming. She had seen Connor ride off, and in such a state of anger and disappointment that she would never have expected him to return. But he was there, silhouetted against the rubble, his horse's reins held loosely in his hand.

Connor stepped out from behind Dean and said, "It was Hester's last harmonica. I rode out to give it to Dean."

Lindy bit her bottom lip to keep it from trembling and struggled to keep her legs under her. "It was nice of you to bring Dean a new harmonica."

"I thought he'd be needin' it for the celebration."

"A celebration?" she asked.

"After the new barn's built, of course."

"Of course," she said hesitantly. "Then you'll be staying until it's done?"

"And the bunkhouse for the men—that is, if you still need me."

Lindy's heart began to flutter. An uncontrollable smile broke into gleeful laughter as she flung herself into his arms. "Oh, luv, I do need you, more than you know, and not for building barns and bunkhouses—for building dreams. Not one of my dreams could ever come true without you."

Connor brushed his hand over her hair and looked down into her eyes. "I hadn't gone farther than the men's camp before realizing that I found what I'd been looking for right here. Dean insisted on drawing you out with his music. Armaldo threatened a shotgun wedding if I headed in any other direction than Broken Gate, and Luke agreed to help him tie you up if necessary."

"Those bushrangers."

"It was all unnecessary. Nothing could have kept me from riding back to you. I want to build a life with you. You've given me the strength and desire to want to start again. I want a home and a family, and I want it all with you."

"Connor—" Lindy looked behind him. Dean had disappeared like the notes of his music. "You don't think I'm a terrible person?"

"Why would I think that?"

"Because I killed a man and...well, Luke thinks I'm bossy and should be wearing strides instead of a skirt. He said no man in his right mind would ever want me as his wife if I didn't start acting more like a woman."

A smile teased Connor's lips. "Luke said that?"

"*You* even said I was too independent for my own good."

"You're all the woman I'd ever want," Connor professed as he slid his arms down to her waist and pulled her up against the hard length of his body. He lowered his mouth to hers. His kiss was sweet and lingering; parting her lips, he delved inside the warm, wet recesses of her mouth. Lindy's insecurities crumbled as she felt the promise of Connor's love with each heartbeat. She felt a spark of desire and the familiar surge of heat flare between her legs. Connor pressed his cheek against hers. Its coarseness reminded her that he hadn't shaved. She held his face between her hands and saw the love in his tired eyes.

"How blind I was not to see love when it was staring me in the face," she confessed. "I was so sure of everything I wanted that I almost forgot the most important thing of all—your love. When I thought you had finally left me for good, I realized that nothing else was important to me."

"Nothing will ever come between us."

A bleating sound rose from their feet. Connor and Lindy looked down at the lamb nuzzling between their legs.

"Nothing but a hundred-and-thirty-pound ewe," Lindy said, projecting the size of Connor's lamb as a full-grown ewe. They both laughed at the lamb's complaining. "Ever since you left to ride Jeb into town, she's been following me around with a lost look on her face. I could hardly walk without her getting under my feet."

"Get used to it. One day they'll be babes at your feet."

Lindy felt such a glow from the inside out that she was sure that at that moment the high color in her cheeks matched the sunset. She was suddenly hopeful that the flower of life bloomed inside her. "Connor, I've made some bad choices but for good reasons. I never told you about killing Hank because I thought you would hate me or make me confess to Sheriff Hayes, and I made up a husband so people wouldn't think I was alone."

Connor's expression became guarded. "Is there another secret you've yet to tell me?"

"Sort of. Doc Barker—"

Connor's voice was alarmed. "He said you were fine, just tired."

Lindy hurried to calm the worry in Connor's voice. "I am fine. The fatigue and the dizzy spells, and the state my stomach has been in lately can all be due to the excitement but, the doctor thinks that maybe there might be a baby—"

"Maybe?"

"Most likely...no...very likely," she admitted with a smile.

Connor gathered her up in his arms. "Lin, I'm terribly fond of you and..." He combed his fingers into her hair and lowered his mouth to hers. "And," he murmured against her lips, "in love with you."

"Ah luv, how I've dreamed of hearing those words."

"It's not a dream, darlin'. You have me forever locked in your heart."

* * * * *

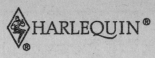

THE WEDDING GAMBLE
Muriel Jensen

Eternity, Massachusetts, was America's wedding
town. Paul Bertrand knew this better than
anyone—he never should have gotten soused at
his friend's rowdy bachelor party. Next morning
when he woke up, he found he'd somehow
managed to say "I do"—to the woman he'd
once jilted! And Christina Bowman had helped
launch so many honeymoons, she knew just
what to do on theirs!

THE WEDDING GAMBLE, available in
September from American Romance, is the
fourth book in Harlequin's new cross-line series,
WEDDINGS, INC.

Be sure to look for the fifth book,
THE VENGEFUL GROOM, by Sara Wood
(Harlequin Presents #1692), coming in October.

LOOK TO THE PAST FOR
FUTURE FUN AND EXCITEMENT!

The past the Harlequin Historical way, that is. 1994 is going to be a banner year for us, so here's a preview of what to expect:

* The continuation of our bigger book program, with titles such as *Across Time* by Nina Beaumont, *Defy the Eagle* by Lynn Bartlett and *Unicorn Bride* by Claire Delacroix.

* A 1994 March Madness promotion featuring four titles by promising new authors Gayle Wilson, Cheryl St. John, Madris Dupree and Emily French.

* Brand-new in-line series: DESTINY'S WOMEN by Merline Lovelace and HIGHLANDER by Ruth Langan; and new chapters in old favorites, such as the SPARHAWK saga by Miranda Jarrett and the WARRIOR series by Margaret Moore.

* *Promised Brides*, an exciting brand-new anthology with stories by Mary Jo Putney, Kristin James and Julie Tetel.

* Our perennial favorite, the Christmas anthology, this year featuring Patricia Gardner Evans, Kathleen Eagle, Elaine Barbieri and Margaret Moore.

Watch for these programs and titles wherever Harlequin Historicals are sold.

HARLEQUIN HISTORICALS…
A TOUCH OF MAGIC!

HHPROM094

DESTINY'S WOMEN
Trilogy

The DESTINY'S WOMEN TRILOGY by Merline Lovelace is sexy, historical romance at its best! The plots thicken and the temperatures rise with each page of her books. A fresh new voice in historical romance, Merline has already begun to lure readers with her exciting, bold storytelling. In ALENA, #220, May 1994, Roman Britain explodes with passion. In SWEET SONG OF LOVE, #230, July 1994, love blossoms amid the rich pageantry of the Middle Ages.

Now, in September, look for SIREN'S CALL, #236, the final book in the DESTINY'S WOMEN TRILOGY. Set in Ancient Greece, passion and betrayal collide when a dashing Athenian sea captain finds his life turned upside down by the stubborn Spartan woman he carries off.

Available wherever Harlequin books are sold.

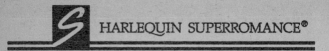

This September, discover the fun of falling in love with...

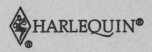

love and laughter

Harlequin is pleased to bring you this exciting new collection of three original short stories by bestselling authors!

ELISE TITLE
BARBARA BRETTON
LASS SMALL

LOVE AND LAUGHTER—sexy, romantic, fun stories guaranteed to tickle your funny bone and fuel your fantasies!

Available in September wherever
Harlequin books are sold.

HARLEQUIN®

HARLEQUIN®

Don't miss these Harlequin favorites by some of our most distinguished authors!
And now you can receive a discount by ordering two or more titles!

HT #25525	THE PERFECT HUSBAND by Kristine Rolofson	$2.99	☐
HT #25554	LOVERS' SECRETS by Glenda Sanders	$2.99	☐
HP #11577	THE STONE PRINCESS by Robyn Donald	$2.99	☐
HP #11554	SECRET ADMIRER by Susan Napier	$2.99	☐
HR #03277	THE LADY AND THE TOMCAT by Bethany Campbell	$2.99	☐
HR #03283	FOREIGN AFFAIR by Eva Rutland	$2.99	☐
HS #70529	KEEPING CHRISTMAS by Marisa Carroll	$3.39	☐
HS #70578	THE LAST BUCCANEER by Lynn Erickson	$3.50	☐
HI #22256	THRICE FAMILIAR by Caroline Burnes	$2.99	☐
HI #22238	PRESUMED GUILTY by Tess Gerritsen	$2.99	☐
HAR #16496	OH, YOU BEAUTIFUL DOLL by Judith Arnold	$3.50	☐
HAR #16510	WED AGAIN by Elda Minger	$3.50	☐
HH #28719	RACHEL by Lynda Trent	$3.99	☐
HH #28795	PIECES OF SKY by Marianne Willman	$3.99	☐

Harlequin Promotional Titles

#97122	LINGERING SHADOWS by Penny Jordan	$5.99	☐
	(limited quantities available on certain titles)		

	AMOUNT	$
DEDUCT:	**10% DISCOUNT FOR 2+ BOOKS**	$
	POSTAGE & HANDLING	$
	($1.00 for one book, 50¢ for each additional)	
	APPLICABLE TAXES*	$ _____
	TOTAL PAYABLE	$ _____
	(check or money order—please do not send cash)	

To order, complete this form and send it, along with a check or money order for the total above, payable to Harlequin Books, to: **In the U.S.:** 3010 Walden Avenue, P.O. Box 9047, Buffalo, NY 14269-9047; **In Canada:** P.O. Box 613, Fort Erie, Ontario, L2A 5X3.

Name: _____

Address: _____ City: _____

State/Prov.: _____ Zip/Postal Code: _____

*New York residents remit applicable sales taxes.
 Canadian residents remit applicable GST and provincial taxes..

HBACK-JS